PRAISE FOR
KATHLEEN O'NEAL GEAR AND W. MICHAEL GEAR

People of the Silence
"An exciting, skillfully crafted, and fast-paced story that also serves as an engrossing look at ancient culture. . . . The authors lavish . . . passion and rich detail on this fine addition to their fascinating series."
—*Publishers Weekly*

People of the Lightning
"This epic historical romance is a fascinating, well-told tale of ancient superstition and culture, set in Florida approximately 8,000 years ago, amid a hauntingly eerie, mystical, and primeval landscape. . . . [An] absorbing portrait of ancient life."
—*Booklist*

People of the Lakes
"An adventure saga imbued with a wealth of historical detail . . . centers around a totemic mask with great evil power."
—*Publishers Weekly*

People of the Sea
"A rousing tale of deadly pursuits and spiritual journeys. . . . Free of the dusty earnestness that so often clogs the movement of other fictional efforts by conscientious anthropologists like the Gears."
—*Kirkus Reviews*

People of the River
"A novel that is a breathtaking adventure story with uncanny parallels to our own time . . . so well researched and evocative one can almost smell the drying pine needles, and feel the heat and choking dust raised by the stampeding of thousands of warriors."
—*Rapport*

People of the Earth
"A great adventure tale, throbbing with life and death. . . . The most convincing reconstruction of prehistory I have read."
—*Morgan Llywelyn*

www.Gear-Gear.com
Forthcoming*

PEOPLE
of the MIST

KATHLEEN O'NEAL GEAR
AND W. MICHAEL GEAR

TOR®

A TOM DOHERTY ASSOCIATES BOOK
NEW YORK

PEOPLE OF THE MIST

Copyright © 1997 by Kathleen O'Neal Gear and W. Michael Gear

All rights reserved.

Maps and interior illustrations by Ellisa Mitchell

A Tor Book
Published by Tom Doherty Associates, LLC
175 Fifth Avenue
New York, NY 10010

www.tor-forge.com

Tor® is a registered trademark of Tom Doherty Associates, LLC.

ISBN 978-0-7653-6753-2
Library of Congress Catalog Number: 97-14682

First Edition: November 1997
First Mass Market Edition: November 1998
Second Mass Market Edition: January 2011

Printed in the United States of America

0 9 8 7 6 5 4 3 2 1

To Lucia StClair Robson and Brian Daley
Friends, through the dark and, we hope, into the Light
to come.

B.C.

13,000	10,000	6,000	3,000	1,500

PEOPLE *of the* WOLF
Alaska & Canadian
Northwest

PEOPLE *of the* EARTH
Northern Plains & Basins

PEOPLE *of the* NIGHTLAND
Ontario & New York &
Pennsylvania

PEOPLE *of*
the OWL
Lower
Mississippi
Valley

PEOPLE *of the* SEA
Pacific Coast & Arizona

PEOPLE *of the* RAVEN
Pacific Northwest &
British Columbia

PEOPLE *of the* LIGHTNING
Florida

PEOPLE *of the* FIRE
Central Rockies &
Great Plains

A.D.

0	200	1,000	1,100	1,300	1,400

PEOPLE *of the* LAKES
East-Central Woodlands
& Great Lakes

PEOPLE *of the*
WEEPING EYE
Mississippi Valley
& Tennessee

PEOPLE *of the* MASKS
Ontario & Upstate New York

PEOPLE *of the*
THUNDER
Alabama & Mississippi

PEOPLE *of the* RIVER
Mississippi Valley

PEOPLE *of the*
LONGHOUSE
New York
& New England

PEOPLE *of the* SILENCE
Southwest Anasazi

PEOPLE *of the* MOON
Northwest New Mexico
& Southwest Colorado

PEOPLE *of the* MIST
Chesapeake Bay

North

Anasci Temple

Susquehannock

White Snake Rising Town

Black Warrior River

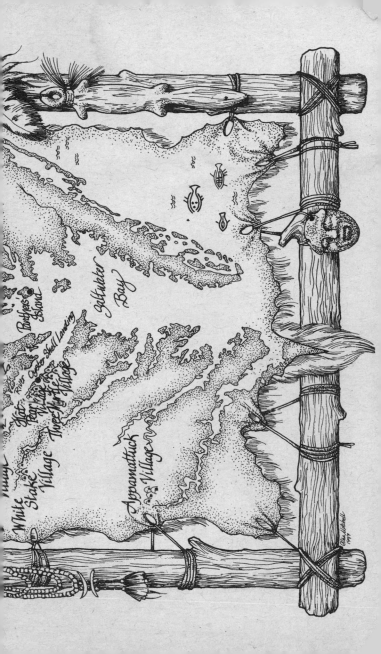

Acknowledgments

People of the Mist and the other books in the prehistory series would not have been possible without the thoughtful encouragement of Tom Doherty, Linda Quinton, and the rest of the Tor/Forge staff. They have stood behind the project during the years, and to them we owe the deepest gratitude.

Harriet McDougal, our longtime editor, deserves special recognition for her constant encouragement and understanding. When we can't see the forest for the trees, she is our chainsaw. Thanks, Harriet, we know how lucky we are to have you.

Lucia StClair Robson, author of *Mary's Land*, offered us her house as a base of operations during our research on the Chesapeake area. Lucia, thanks for everything, including your warm hospitality—and most especially for the Rollerblade experience. Thanks, too, to Ray Williamson and Carol Carnett for the valuable discussions on archaeoastronomy.

As always, Harold and Sylvia Fenn, Rob Howard, and the rest of the special people at H. B. Fenn deserve the warm thanks we send them.

Foreword

For the prehistoric occupants of the American mid-Atlantic coast, the Chesapeake Bay was a paradise. The rich estuary's environment and temperate climate provided everything the people needed for survival. Yearly migrations of waterfowl and anadromous fish provided a wealth of seasonal food resources. The forest provided nut harvests, and a habitat for turkey, deer, bear, raccoons, and other animals. From the marshes, the people collected cordgrass, wild rice, muskrats, arrow arum root for tuckahoe bread, and other foods. On shallow mudflats, they caught crabs, dug clams, and harvested oysters. Deposits of silty loam soil grew corn, beans, squash, tobacco, and sunflowers, among other agricultural staples. In such a land of plenty, only the miracle of applied English obstinacy and ethnocentrism could have led to starvation in the Jamestown colony in 1608.

Today, the Chesapeake is still noted for the wealth of its resources, its natural beauty, the yearly migration of waterfowl, oysters, crabs, agriculture, and, oddly enough, when one travels a short distance up the Potomac, politics.

Not much has changed since the days of the Late Woodland period. Then, as today, the chiefs demanded, and were paid, tribute.

People of the Mist is set during the period archaeologists call Late Woodland II; the date is around 1300 A.D. This was a period of cultural change for the Algonquian peoples of the coastal plain east of the fall line. At least three separate archaeological complexes are present during this transition to larger villages and incipient chieftainships. For the purposes of the novel we have identified three ethnic associations: the Upriver villages (Montgomery complex); the Conoy (Potomac Creek complex); the Independent villages and the Mamanatowick's villages (Rappahannock complex). Interested readers are referred to Stephen B. Potter's *Commoners, Tribute, and Chiefs: The Development of Algonquian Culture in the Potomac Valley* for an in-depth account of the archaeological evidence.

Culturally, these people shared many subsistence patterns, relying on fishing, collecting and gathering, hunting, and agriculture. Archaeologists separate them by their pottery styles, burial practices, and house shapes. All three groups traded inland for tool stone, copper, and luxury items. These goods traveled east-west along the Potomac watershed, as well as north-south up the Chesapeake to the Susquehanna River, and down the piedmont to the Carolinas. To defeat the vicious clouds of mosquitoes, they greased their bodies; and, while later Europeans would complain about their smoky houses, the blue haze allowed them to sleep in peace.

Historically and ethnographically, we know that these Algonquians, unlike their northern kin, were matrilineal—tracing descent and inheritance through the mother. Women owned the houses, fields, and children, and, as is common among such peoples, women enjoyed considerable latitude in their sexual relationships. The division of labor and responsibility was well defined between genders. Most notably, men hunted, fished, attended to construction, and made war, while women employed themselves in agriculture, food preparation, child rearing, and clan administration.

From the archaeological record, we know that villages

were expanding at this time, and palisades were being erected. People do not build fortifications for fun; it is hard, time-consuming work. At the same time, many longhouses were still located outside the palisades, indicating that while warfare was endemic, it wasn't overwhelming. We have attempted to reflect these oscillating intervillage relationships.

Within two hundred years, Europeans would arrive in the Chesapeake Bay and change the lives of the Native peoples forever. The Rappahannock complex would evolve into the Powhatan chieftainship of John Smith and Pocahontas fame: the Conoy would interact with Lord Calvert's Catholic settlement in Maryland. Within the next one hundred years, ninety percent of the native population would be dead and the cultures decimated. Today we have only the biased writings of the first European colonists, and the very fragile archaeological record, to allow us to glimpse what life was like on the Chesapeake before the first European ship sailed into that most remarkable of estuaries.

We can only imagine what The Panther would say if he could see it today.

Introduction

Adam Jones sat uncomfortably in the lawyer's office, wondering why a Washington, D.C., law firm—especially one as renowned as Koult, Wesson & Brown—couldn't afford to keep *this* month's editions of *Time*, *Newsweek*, and *U.S. News and World Report* on the sleek mahogany waiting-room tables. Around him, exotic potted plants, oak paneling, and expensive carpet let him know that he wasn't just in any law office, but a powerful one.

From the fortresslike desk guarding the glass doors came the continual cadence of muted beeping, and the soft whisper of the receptionist's musical voice: "Koult, Wesson and Brown. How may I help you?" A pause. "Just one moment and I'll connect you."

Now, what kind of job would that be? Adam wondered. Just sitting there all day long, answering the phone over and over and over. But then, she sat in an elegant, climate-controlled office, dealt with people who smiled pleasantly whether they meant it or not, and need not worry about finding the place stripped bare some morning when she came to work.

In contrast, Adam's cramped office was a six-by-eight cubicle that included two four-drawer file cabinets and shelves that sagged under the weight of books, reports, and irregular stacks of paper, that lined each of his four walls. His desk—when he could find it under the forms, requisitions, and other clutter of administration—was a battered oak veteran of numerous surplus sales. Light came from a single overhead fluorescent. When the old black Bakelite rotary phone on his desk rang, it jangled with the enthusiasm of a Times Square New Year's Eve.

And, as he'd found out last Monday, his office could be stripped right down to the toed nails in the floor-boards. The week before, he'd been off to the annual meetings of the Society for American Archaeology in Atlanta, leaving the museum running on reduced hours with volunteer staff. Not much happened in April, not like summer when the tourists came through.

But the shock of walking up to his little museum, opening the door, and seeing the empty display cases, the litter on the floor . . .

"Mr. Jones?"

Adam glanced up to see a well-dressed man crossing the carpet. Tall, athletic-looking, he wore an immaculate dark gray suit with white cuffs showing. The royal blue tie seemed to flash on his white button-down shirt. Behind him, the glass door to Koult, Wesson & Brown's inner sanctum was gliding silently closed.

"Yes." Jones stood, offering his hand.

"I'm Jesse McCoy." The lawyer's shake was firm. His eyes, expression, looks—everything about him was just plain smooth. A no-nonsense professional. "I've reserved a conference room for us. If you'll just follow me." As they passed through the door to the firm's inner sanctum, McCoy asked, "Something to drink? Coffee, perhaps?"

"Coffee would be fine. Thank you."

"Cream and sugar?"

"Black, please." Adam was glancing in at opulent offices brimming with computers, walls of impressive-looking books, mahogany tables and stuffed chairs worthy of the White House. Those were the outside offices, the ones with windows. On the inside row, younger people tapped at word processors, stood over whining and hissing photocopy machines, and huddled over files of paper.

The conference room was small, wood-paneled, containing a round wood-veneer table stocked with a yellow legal pad, three pens, and a half-full coffee cup emblazoned with "To the World's Greatest Dad!" Three comfortable-looking chairs were spaced equidistant from each other, their chrome frames gleaming in contrast to the gray upholstery. As Adam seated himself, McCoy paused at the door and spoke to a young man wearing a white shirt and tie: "One coffee, Tom. Black, please." The door clicked shut.

"Coffee will be here in a moment." McCoy seated himself to Adam's right behind the yellow pad, and sipped from the "Greatest Dad" cup. "I have to admit, I don't think we've ever had an archaeologist come in for a consultation before." McCoy lifted an eyebrow. "I always wanted to be an archaeologist. Took a class as an undergraduate."

"A lot of people do." Adam shifted, realizing the chair looked a great deal more comfortable than it felt. At that moment, young Tom entered, setting a porcelain cup on the table to Adam's right. He gave them a plastic and professional smile, then left with studied efficiency.

McCoy scanned his yellow pad. "According to our phone conversation, a Native American tribe called the Piankatanks . . . am I saying that right?"

"Yeah, Piankatanks. Piankatank was a town that Powhatan destroyed in 1608. The men and boys were killed and the women and girls taken off for slaves."

McCoy lifted an eyebrow. "I'm not following this. This town was destroyed in 1608 by Powhatan? I've heard of him."

"Father of Pocahantas."

"Right, John Smith and all. I liked the Disney movie."

Adam winced. "That's part of the whole problem. People get their history from Disney . . . and it's all so rosy, charming, and sanitary that history has become nothing more than a Technicolor dream. That's what leads to things like my museum!"

McCoy shifted uneasily. "Why don't you start at the beginning."

Adam sipped his coffee. Good stuff, some sort of French roast. "Three or four months ago I started getting letters. Desktop-publishing sorts of things. Nice little Plains Indian logo with buffalo and geometric designs. The text stated something to the effect that under the law the Piankatank Nation required the return of their cultural heritage. Would we please send them a complete inventory of our collections."

"You still have the letters?"

"Yes, I have to keep all correspondence." Adam frowned into his coffee. "I thought it was a joke. The Piankatank? I'm an archaeologist specializing in the area and I still had to look them up. Then I really thought it was a joke. Archaeologists do this sort of thing to each other all the time, especially with the NAGPRA scare these days."

"NAGPRA? That's . . ." McCoy was scribbling notes on his yellow pad.

"Native American Graves Protection and Repatriation Act. That's what this is all about. Congress, in its infinite wisdom, tried to fix a problem—and created a disaster. In essence, the law states that human remains and cultural goods obtained in archaeological excavations must be returned to the Native American people."

"And that's a problem?"

"Which people? Who? Look, I just lost a museum full of Native American artifacts to a group who claim they are descended from a village destroyed by Powhatan's warriors in 1608. They went to Judge Al Kruse, waved

NAGPRA in his face, and got a court order releasing their 'cultural heritage.' " Adam took a deep breath to relax. "They took all the Algonquian collections, and the Iroquoian and Monacan material as well."

"Monacan?"

"They're a Siouan group that lived east of the fall line."

"I thought the Sioux were in the Dakotas."

"They are. These people spoke a related language." Adam toyed with his coffee cup. "So you see, the Piankatank, whoever they are, have taken everything. That's the problem with NAGPRA. Anyone with a Native American identity can grab anything they want. Congress mandated that we give the cultural remains back to the Native people, and left it at that. It's a good idea written into a lousy law."

"So, you don't think the Piankatank are really Indian?"

Adam spread his arms. "Can you define Indian? We no longer categorize people by blood. I know people, registered on tribal rolls, as white as you or me. I've seen them *live* their Native American beliefs. If they go on vision quests, use the sweat lodge once a week, dance the traditional dances, are they Indian?"

"I'd say so." McCoy rolled his pen thoughtfully. "The government recognizes the tribes, don't they?"

"It's not that easy. The U.S. government doesn't officially recognize the Piquot, Pamunky, or Piscataway. Among many others. But they're Indian, aren't they?"

"Did you have bones in your collections? Actual human remains?"

"Some. Mostly bits of human bone from an ossuary in Maryland. But those remains wouldn't have been the ancestors to the Piankatank. Remember, I mentioned the Iroquoian material? We had two skulls, supposedly Susquehannocks killed in northern Pennsylvania during a raid by the Conoy Confederacy in the sixteen-thirties. The Conoy sold them to the Powhatans, who then sold them to a white plantation owner in the early seventeen-hundreds. We've had them for years.'' Adam glared at his coffee cup, his jaw set.

''That really seems to bother you.''

''Yeah. Think about it. *If* the Piankatank really are Piankatank Indians, they're Algonquin, right? Now, assuming they still practice their aboriginal religion—which I doubt—they're going to sing those two Iroquoian souls to Okeus.''

''Okeus?'' McCoy gave him a baffled look.

''He's the Algonquin god of chaos. But the point is, these two Susquehannocks are being sent to an afterlife full of their enemies. They should go to the Iroquoian Village of the Dead. Even if you don't believe in Native American religion, it's immoral and unjust. A violation of the spirit of the NAGPRA law. As much an affront to those Susquehannocks as conducting a German Lutheran ceremony over a Jewish holocaust victim's grave—and we're sanctioning this! It's a moral abomination!''

''I see.'' McCoy's pen scribbled quick notes on the legal pad.

''Do you? This idea of Native peoples respecting the dead only goes so far. Sure, the Algonquins revered their dead, kept the bodies of their chiefs in the temples for years so they could commune with the ghosts, but they trashed the corpses of their enemies, cut off scalps and took trophy heads. When they punished their criminals for things like murder, or incest, they broke the culprit's legs and threw him screaming into a bonfire. In the case of the Susquehannocks and Powhatans, these people *hated* each other. If you could ask those two Susquehannocks, the last thing they would have wanted would have been to be 'repatriated' to Algonquins.''

''Then you completely oppose NAGPRA?''

"No, not at all. If we have human burials in our collections that can be documented as belonging to an ethnic affiliation, a member of the tribe, then they should be returned to their proper descendants. That is moral and just, and archaeology can be part of the solution, but without that proven affiliation, I'd say it is more unjust to hand over Native American skeletal material to be reburied by the descendants of that person's hated enemies than it is to leave it on a museum shelf."

"Perhaps." McCoy leaned back and sighed. "I didn't realize it was such a mess."

"There's more." Adam tossed off the last of his coffee. "As an archaeologist, according to the law, I have to contact the nearest Native American group prior to excavating a burial from an archaeological site. But, if I'm working at a historic plantation, excavating slave quarters, I don't need to contact any African-Americans. If I'm working at a military post in the West, I don't have to get approval from the nearest small town."

"In other words, you're saying the law is racist."

"Isn't it? NAGPRA gives Native Americans legal precedence over other racial types. Any Native American group can claim artifacts from a museum, but the State of Virginia, or Maryland—recognized by the American government as political entities—can't lay claim to collections in the American Museum of Natural History. What would happen if the State of Ohio asked to have Ulysses S. Grant's bones returned to Ohio?"

"They'd be whistling in the wind." McCoy tapped his pen on the tabletop. He seemed to be staring at nothing, expression blank.

"Further, this law violates the separation of church and state. It gives precedence and legal recognition to a Native religion. A Catholic can't reclaim a burial from a museum on religious grounds. Can a Jew?"

"No." McCoy studied his notes pensively. "Let's get

back to your specific problem. Did your museum hold legal title to these artifacts? I mean, did you *own* them?''

''Most of the artifacts were the property of the museum. Yes, we legally owned them, mostly through donations over the years. We also curated archaeological collections excavated by contract archaeologists working in the region. Many of the artifacts taken by the Piankatank were the property of the landowners from whose land they had been excavated. They allowed us to care for them with the provision that they be displayed to the public. So, in that sense, it's theft.''

''And who actually owns your museum? You?''

''No, it's owned by the city of Potomac Cove. We have a board of trustees that works with the city council.''

''Do they wish to file suit?''

Adam winced. ''I get the distinct impression that they'd rather just let it go.''

''Then you're thinking about a class-action suit?''

''I suppose.''

McCoy nodded as if fitting pieces together in his head. ''Right offhand, I'd say that litigating this would be like opening a can of worms. What's at question is, at its roots, a constitutional issue. A whole list of them.''

''Then, I could win?''

McCoy shrugged. ''We're talking about the law here. Mr. Jones, winning cases depends on the legal tactics used, the presentation of the facts, argumentation by the attorneys, and the persuasion of the judge. You know, don't you, that your opposition will be the entire Department of Justice? They keep their big guns just down the street, and they'll wheel them out just for you.''

''Uh-huh.'' Adam rolled the empty coffee cup between his hands. ''Did I miss something in civics class? Hasn't the government become an accomplice in theft here?''

McCoy leaned forward, one eyebrow lifted. ''Let's be

blunt about this. You, as an individual, can't get the museum's artifacts returned. That's up to your town council and board of trustees. You'll have to convince them to tackle the problem of the Piankatank. You, however, have the ability to file suit against the government in an attempt to overturn NAGPRA.''

''I see.''

''If you decide to do so, my fee is three hundred dollars an hour, plus expenses that include my research team, phone calls, paperwork, even travel expenses if they become necessary. Let's say that we win in District Court. The government doesn't like to lose—and they have you, along with about another two hundred million taxpayers, to draw upon for financial resources. The case will automatically go to appeal . . . and I can guarantee you, a case like this will be fought all the way to the Supreme Court.''

''And that means?''

''Five or six years, Adam.'' McCoy pushed back in his chair, eyes neutral. ''And I'd say about one hundred and fifty thousand in legal fees, minimum, to make it through the legal thrust-and-parry to land it in the High Court's lap. Do you have that kind of money?''

Adam slowly shook his head. ''I make twenty-two thousand a year, Mr. McCoy. I drive a fifteen-year-old Blazer with one hundred and thirty thousand on the odometer. I rent a trailer house.''

McCoy watched him, face expressionless.

''What about the ACLU? They do things like this, don't they?''

McCoy gave a dry laugh. ''My suspicion is, Mr. Jones, that they'd be on the other side. And prepare yourself for this. Right or wrong, this case will be partially tried in the media. The nightly news will be happy to show evil scientists intent on exploiting victimized Indians. Are you ready to be cast as a thief stealing their cultural heritage?''

''I'm not stealing anyone's heritage! This is about fairness, not just to the Native peoples, but to the dead as well!''

''Perhaps, but this is the dawn of the twenty-first century. Moral dimensions and ramifications mean little—unless a big chunk of money is involved. Prepare yourself. You'll be cast as a white male seeking to retain control over another people's cultural heritage.''

''A white male? My maternal grandmother was a registered Cherokee. Cherokees are matrilineal, making me technically Cherokee.''

''You have blond hair, Mr. Jones. I doubt your appearance would make much of a case, no matter who your grandmother was.''

''Didn't you agree with me about all the problems with NAGPRA?''

''Definitely. But as an attorney, I can tell you that knowing right, and proving it in a public forum or court of law, are two very different things.''

Adam sank back in the chair, a sick sensation in his gut. McCoy watched him impassively. Finally Adam shook his head. ''You know, I've spent all of my life trying to learn about the people who were here before Columbus. Everything we know about them is because of archaeologists, ethnographic sources, and Native oral traditions. We don't teach their history in our schools. Students don't read about Cahokia when they study pyramids. We know more about ancient Mexico, Egypt, and Iraq than we know about our own country.''

''I suppose.''

''Now, with a stroke of a politician's pen, that's all swept away.''

''It happens.'' McCoy shrugged. ''The Indians would tell you that it has happened for a long time.''

"All those artifacts that I dug out of the ground were made by people, Mr. McCoy. They were being carefully preserved so that future generations could see them, learn from them, as I have. It has nothing to do with controlling another person's cultural heritage, it's about disseminating it. It's part of a *human* heritage that we all share. Now those artifacts have been loaded into a truck somewhere and hauled off. To what? Reburial? Resale on the collector's market? And what of the fragile netting, the bone, and bits of copper? They'll be thrown away as junk by the people who took them, who'll never know they were more precious than gold to the prehistoric Algonquin."

"In that case—assuming your Piankatank are actually Indian—the only people they're hurting are themselves."

"No, Mr. McCoy, it's hurting all of us. Everyone loses in the end." Adam stood, an empty feeling in the pit of his stomach. "We still have a great deal to learn about ourselves, about who and what we are as humans. I think we can respect the dead for what they can teach us today, as well as respect them for who they were when they were alive."

"That's an enlightened perspective."

Adam sighed. "I don't feel enlightened, Mr. McCoy. What is happening is wrong—and I can't do anything about it by myself."

"Then you don't wish to pursue this matter legally?"

Adam spread his arms wide. "On twenty thousand a year? I could offer you my soul in exchange for your legal services. That ought to be worth something. The ancient Algonquin people would think so." At the blank look in McCoy's eyes, Adam smiled ironically, "Well, thanks for your time . . . and the coffee."

"I'm sorry I couldn't help. Good day, Mr. Jones."

McCoy rose, stepping over to open the door. In silence, they walked down the plush corridors toward the tall glass doors.

At the same moment, at a specialty store in affluent Georgetown, a young woman held the door open for her tall companion. Navajo flute music gave atmosphere to the crowded shelves filled with dream catchers and art depicting feathered Indians and buffalo. Turquoise jewelry, beaded leather bags, and painted Northwest Coast masks caught the bright light, each displayed to the best advantage. A row of buffalo skulls, bleached and white, had been painted with scenes of mounted warriors shooting arrows into galloping herds. Along one wall, behind glass, rows of brightly painted katchinas danced. Beneath them, expensive Southwestern pots were categorized by pueblo and maker.

The young woman wore her honey-brown hair long, a single turkey feather tied neatly in the silky locks at her shoulder. Her Eddie Bauer denim shirt accented the pale blue of her eyes. A beaded belt snugged tight Levi's to her hips, and Minnetonka moccasins covered her dainty feet.

The tall man, blond hair close-cropped, wore a T-shirt emblazoned with ''Ban the Washington Redskins.'' Below faded jeans, Luchese boots rapped hollowly on the tiled floor. He carried the big box with ease as they approached the counter.

The middle-aged clerk wore a dark suit, a magnificent squash-blossom necklace draping her blouse. A beaded brooch confined her silver-streaked black hair. She used a thin white finger to press horn-rimmed glasses onto a straight narrow nose.

"May I help you?" She greeted them with a practiced smile.

The tall man placed the box on the glass counter and returned her smile, but it was the young woman who spoke: "We're from the Piankatank Confederacy." She offered a card. "Our medicine man has just gone through our collection, and these artifacts no longer have importance to our people. They've been killed by the Whites, their Power broken. We were wondering if your store would be interested in acquiring them."

The clerk watched with interest as the blond man began removing pieces one at a time and laying them carefully on the counter. Items of carved shell, bone, and stone were placed in neat rows.

"Algonquin and Iroquois manufacture," the clerk stated, recognizing the workmanship. "I see museum accession numbers on some of them. Are they authentic?"

"They are." The young woman withdrew a folded paper from her pocket. "And this is an affidavit drawn up by our tribal attorney, documenting that the Piankatank tribe legally owns these items. None of these artifacts falls under the jurisdiction of the Antiquities laws. You may check with Judge Kruse's office if there are any questions."

The clerk scanned the paper, and returned her appraisal to the artifacts laid out on the counter. "We do a very good business in American Indian crafts here. Our customers include Japanese, Kuwaiti, German, as well as some of the better American buyers. Perhaps we can be of assistance."

"Yes, we know." The woman gave her a satisfied smile. "You're the best in the business. That's why we came here."

The clerk picked up a shell gorget depicting a spider. "Burial piece. Mississippian if I'm not mistaken."

The young woman shrugged. "This is only a sample.

If the price is right, we have a great deal more to offer. Even two remarkably well preserved skulls.''

The clerk nodded and smiled. ''If the affidavit is in order, I think we can do business with the Piankatank Confederacy.''

The young woman looked up at the blond man and smiled her satisfaction. ''Good. We've done our homework. We are selling authentic artifacts: museum-quality pieces, not reproductions. I think your buyers will appreciate that.''

The clerk lifted an eyebrow, appraising the young woman, then studied the artifacts with a practiced eye. ''My people will have to inspect the items, of course, but provided they agree with your claims, we can start at ten thousand for this first lot. Provided, that is, that we can have an exclusive on the rest of your collection.''

There Is a Shadow

I tell you truly, the source of life's greatest delights and glories is Death. It is our soul.

Bright and shining.

Yes, I know, you have been taught all of your life that the soul is some mysterious, hidden being, like a cloaked child secreted in a corner of your mind, but that is a lie.

Death is soul.

Anyone who is truly alive knows this. He can feel Death staring from his eyes every moment, watching, reminding him, making him cherish each breath.

Sunrises are beautiful because Death knows sunsets. Spring is glorious because Death knows winter.

Why, then, do so few of us see the murderer within?

The terrors of the world are not outside. They are his.

The dark abyss that is always about to swallow us belongs to him.

He is curious, a wanderer, walking in the emptiness, his steps silent. His cries mute. His grief unending.

We all glimpse him at one time or another, his shadow tiptoeing around inside us, and are afraid.

We know that shadows cannot exist without light.

Shadows live on light.

I tell you again, my friend, Death is our bright and shining soul.

And the soul casts a shadow.

He is always there. Dark. And terrifyingly alive.
He stares through our eyes. He moves when we move.
He touches those we love.

. . . We must be vigilant.

One

Red Knot stopped where the palisade overlapped to form a protective entrance to Flat Pearl Village. Here, defenders could remain sheltered and shoot attacking warriors restricted in the narrow space between the posts. She stared nervously out into the morning, hesitant at stepping from the palisade's security. What she was doing wasn't wrong. She told herself that over and over.

The sky had grayed with the new dawn and mist ghosted over the calm water in the inlet. To her right, the canoes down at the sandy landing were barely visible, their outlines blurred by the clinging haze. Above the canoe landing, the gardens lay fallow now, the corn and beans harvested from withered brown plants. Here and there, grass-thatched houses stood among the fields. Gentle streamers of blue smoke rose from the smoke holes in their roofs. Beyond the gardens, at the foot of the tree-covered ridge, the stubbly cornfields gave way to the thick forest.

Red Knot glanced back at Flat Pearl Village. The longhouses, the House of the Dead, and the storage buildings stood silently in the gloom, their rounded shapes reminding her of hunchbacked monsters.

Grandmother Hunting Hawk's brown-and-white dog watched her with pricked ears. Like her mistress, the animal was worn by the years, her joints swollen and painful. She hobbled a few paces and studied Red Knot with mild curiosity.

Odd, Red Knot thought. Hunting Hawk usually kept the old bitch close to her bed on cool mornings like this. Why was the dog out wandering? With so many people in the village, perhaps the animal was just on edge.

Red Knot studied the path she would have to take. Time was running out. She cocked her ear, listening. Not a sound came from the houses behind her, or from the predawn forest surrounding the village and its fields. Soon, however, the winter birds would begin to sing, and the village to stir. The honored guests would be fed before starting off.

The guests—all had come to Flat Pearl Village in *her* honor. Red Knot clamped her jaw in determination. Echoes of her grandmother's endless lectures spun through her head. Honor. Duty. Respect. They blurred into meaningless words.

I owe something to myself. I can't be what they want me to be, go where they want me to go. Memories of Copper Thunder's face haunted her. Even in relaxed moments, he looked more like a cunning witch than a man. If the thought of him even touching her brought a twist of revulsion to her stomach, how could she allow him to mount her? She might be Shell Comb's daughter, but the very thought of taking her rightful place and stepping into that tangled web sickened her.

Her village, clan, and family—she was letting them all down. Red Knot closed her eyes, imagining the gray world around her, damp, cold, and misty. *Like everything else in my life.*

She knotted her fist in the cloak that covered her shoulders, and slipped out of the palisade. Her moccasin-clad feet walked silently and swiftly, cutting across the frosted gardens. As she hurried, she could just see her breath in the half-light.

The winter-bare trees along the riverbank lay no more than two bow shots ahead. Once she reached them, she would have taken the first step toward freedom, and a brighter future.

I am a woman now. The thought stuck in her mind. And, yes, she felt different—but oddly the same. Four days past, she'd stepped out of the Women's House, the menstrual lodge, for the first time. She had been ritually washed and decked out in resplendent finery. Her face still stung from the new tattoos on her chin and cheeks.

In response to the runners who had been sent out at the onset of her cramps, guests had arrived from the surrounding villages. Speeches had been given, and gifts exchanged. Her clan had prepared a marvelous feast in her honor, the wooden dishes piled high with venison, duck, oysters, roasted corn, steaming tuckahoe, and smoked fish.

To everyone's amazement, Copper Thunder, accompanied by four canoes of warriors, had arrived on the last day of the celebration.

Red Knot had danced before him and the rest of the honored guests. Despite the presence of Copper Thunder, she had danced for young High Fox, her steps driven by desperation as his eyes gleamed for her.

As she thought of him, her heart quickened. Now, or never, she had to take this one chance at happiness. What would happen, how it would all work out, she had no idea; but others had done as she was doing. They had become legendary among her passionate people. Their stories were sung in the Weroansqua's Great House. Perhaps, one day, songs would be sung about Red Knot and High Fox, and the love that had driven them to abandon their clans.

She hurried through the trees, darting between the boles. To her right, water lapped at the sandy shore. To her left, she could see the dim haze of one of Hunting Hawk's cornfields. Once past that, she would head left, skirting the cleared land, and climb the steep ridge on the old deer trail.

"I'll be waiting at Oyster Shell Landing." High Fox's words echoed. His solemn eyes haunted her, his handsome face radiating love. *"Meet me at first light."*

No, this wasn't wrong. Not in the eyes of the gods. They only reacted in rage over lying, murder, or that most horrible of crimes, incest.

She ran, feet pattering on the damp leaf mat. Over the years all the fallen branches had been scavenged for cooking fires, so she need only worry about roots that might trip her.

She almost missed the trail, but, heart beating, she sprinted up the steep winding path, her breath beginning to labor. The white-tailed deer had originally forged this route down to the cornfields, but they ran it no longer. Her people had all but hunted them out on the narrow neck of land surrounding the village. Now, only occasional deer raided the fields, and they did so at risk of an arrow. Was it not better to have the deer in the people's belly than their corn in the deer's?

She panted up the ridge, and thanked the Spirits that they had granted this warm spell and held off the snow that would have betrayed her tracks. Her toes drove into the soft, mulched soil.

When she reached the great beech tree, its smooth bark marred by the years, she stopped to catch her breath. Six men would have to stretch fingertip to fingertip to reach around the tree's circumference. She stepped past the beech, out onto the rounded ridgetop, into the shade of the other forest giants. A robin chirped in the high canopy of bare branches, and a squirrel skittered across the fallen leaves.

Morning was coming. She had to hurry.

Red Knot took a deep breath, and started forward. She

had only to cross the ridgetop, then descend the steep path on the other side to the—

"Just as I thought," a familiar voice called from behind her. "It's all in the blood."

Red Knot spun, gasping, the worst of her fears suddenly realized, as a blanket-wrapped figure stepped from the deep morning shadows behind a walnut tree. "What are you doing here? You're supposed to be in your . . ."

The blanketed assailant moved with uncanny speed. Red Knot glimpsed the war club, heard it whistle as it sliced the air. . . .

The loud crack of breaking bone echoed across the quiet misty hills.

Two

Shell Comb, first daughter of Hunting Hawk, hesitated as she looked out from the shadowed doorway of the House of the Dead. She took a moment to steady herself.

Today she began life again. She had been cleansed, purged of the mistakes of the past and the price they'd exacted from her soul. She could start over, live as a Weroansqua's daughter should. She had proven to herself that she was worthy of the awesome responsibility of authority. Still, as she watched the clearing beyond the doorway, she nervously smoothed her hands on her deer-hide skirt.

Several people moved in the plaza, attending to various tasks. Rosebud's daughter, White Otter, carried a water jug toward the gate. Old Blue Moon urinated on the back of his house, too blind to find his way outside the palisade. Shell Comb started when she saw the Great Tayac, Copper Thunder, slip in through the opening in the palisade, glance furtively around, and stride arrogantly toward Hunting Hawk's Great House.

Shell Comb coughed and rubbed her sore windpipe.

Where has he been? And to what purpose? The Great Tayac had no allies here, and wouldn't have until properly married into the Greenstone Clan. How long had he been gone from the village? A cold shiver raced down her back. Well, if his absence meant trouble, she would know soon enough.

She needed all her wits with one cycle of her life finished, and another beginning. This time, she would be smarter, wiser. The final stitch had been sewn into a bag too long open. Why, then, did her heart leap and her muscles tremble?

She made sure no one looked in her direction, then stepped out to meet this new day. With steely control, she forced herself to walk across the plaza toward the Great House. The Guardians, upright posts carved into the likenesses of human and animal faces, watched her pass the smoking fire pit in the plaza's center. The ground here was hard-packed from the dancers the night before.

Old man Mockingbird tottered toward her, blinking in the half-light. He heard her cough, and tilted his head to squint at her. "Best tend to that, girl," he warned. "Shouldn't be out in this cold."

"Thank you, Elder." And Shell Comb hurried past.

Hunting Hawk's Great House nestled beneath the spreading branches of three mulberry trees: a sign of her status. The house had been constructed of two rows of black locust interspersed with cut red cedar saplings, their butts set into the ground. The limber tops had been bent over and lashed together to create an inverted U. Cross braces of red maple gave the framework strength, bound together with pliable yellow pine roots, and the whole house had been covered with sheets of bark. The interior was six paces wide and nearly forty in length. Woven matting divided the Great House into three separate rooms.

Shell Comb ducked through the low doorway and made her way across the mat-covered floor. Bedsteads, made of poles laced with a wicker of saplings and bark, lined the walls. Mats had been laid over the wicker, and then layers of deerhide added to form snug beds. As she passed, people rolled up their bedding and placed the matting and hides to the side to create sitting room.

No one so much as glanced at her. But surely they should have viewed her differently, or at least sensed the change in her life. Today, as never before, she had proven herself worthy to be her mother's daughter. Any question of her ability to take over this building, and control of clan business, was now behind her. In the presence of the blessed ancestors, she had atoned for her lack of judgment. Black Spike might never have been. Life had come full circle. Balance had been restored.

The Great House, like all those in the lineage holding, belonged to old Hunting Hawk. Upon her death, since she had no brother to inherit, the lineage holdings—houses, land, fishing and hunting grounds, shell beds, slaves, and property—would pass to Shell Comb.

She looked around at the wealth that would be hers. Large baskets were hung from the walls, brimming with corn, dried squash, acorns, hickory nuts, chinquapins, chestnuts, and beans. The tightly tied bundles of hemp stacked to one side waited for women to process the silky fibers into cordage or soft fabrics. Flat Pearl Village controlled rich resources, and its people rarely went hungry.

Copper Thunder sat beside the central fire, watching Shell Comb with oddly luminous eyes. She glanced at the big, round-bottomed ceramic pot that rested over the glowing coals. It held a steaming stew of corn, oysters, squash, and diced fish. As second in line to Hunting Hawk, her first concern was to insure the well-being of her family's guests.

This morning, Shell Comb would have gladly side-stepped that duty. She wanted nothing more than to be alone, to have the time to think and reflect. But as she looked around, she did not see her mother. Hunting Hawk was gone, and with such an important guest seated before her fire! Shell Comb marched forward. Facing these people, especially this powerful man, would be an ordeal, but it couldn't be helped.

She tried to keep her hand from trembling as she stirred the fire. Fatigue weighted her bones. Would it betray her? How long had it been since she'd had a full night's sleep? From the onset of Red Knot's first cramps, Shell Comb had attended to the girl, sending messengers, supervising meals, coordinating the arrival of the guests, orchestrating the dances, and struggling to behave as a Weroansqua's daughter should. Her own competence surprised her, hinting at reserves she had never known.

Responsibility—as befitted the future Weroansqua of Flat Pearl Village—bore a terrible price. Why hadn't she understood before? She glanced down at her right hand, worked the muscles, and made a tight fist. What incredible power she would wield.

Shell Comb remained a beautiful woman despite the thirty-two Comings of the Leaves she had survived, and the six children she had passed from her womb. Some said her large dark eyes could snare a man's soul and bend it to her will. The story had always amused her. She recognized her vanity, moderated it when necessary, and surrendered to it when circumstances permitted. And she had surrendered much too often. But when Ohona and Okeus had battled for the world after the Creation, they'd insured that, hadn't they?

Trace your ancestry back, and there you'll find Okeus, staring at you with that malicious smile on his face. Face it, Shell Comb, your seed sprang from his loins. No matter how many generations removed, you are still his daughter.

She loosened her feather mantle from around her shoulders and let it slide down around the curve of her hips as the fire's heat reached her. The chill was finally leaving her bones—as the sadness and confusion eventually might.

Of her six children the third had died at birth; five, two girls and three boys, had lived to be named. Her oldest son, White Bone, had drowned in his sixteenth summer when he was caught on open water by a terrible storm. His canoe had been found beached on the Western Shore, but his body had never been recovered. Her third son, Grebe, had been killed in his fifth year by lightning: his seared body had lain under a splintered black oak. The scar could still be seen, spiraling down the tree's bark.

Fever had taken her eldest daughter barely a year after her birth. She had never been lucky with children. But then, as Hunting Hawk could confirm—provided she ever dared to—that trait ran all through the lineage. *Do I dare to try and have another?*

At times, she wondered if perhaps some evil had slithered inside her, impregnating her with a dark spirit that blighted the fruit of her loins. Where else had the insatiable craving come from? Why had she thrown caution to the winds so many times? Why had the wrong seed taken hold so often?

She shivered at the thought, aware of that same desire stirring as she studied Copper Thunder.

The Great Tayac crouched across the fire from her, arms clasped around his drawn-up knees. No one would call him a handsome man. His nose was too large for his face; the jaw made a person think of a snapping turtle's. Forked eye tattoos surrounded his eyes, and a black band followed his jawline across his mouth. Older tattoos had faded and blended with his dye-stained skin. He wore his hair in a roach, both sides of his scalp shaved. But when he looked at Shell Comb, that penetrating stare sent a shiver through her. Secrets hid behind those stygian eyes, along with fleeting glimpses of his quick intelligence. He'd kill at the slightest pretext, and when he struck, it would be like a timber rattler: lightning fast, ruthless, and equally cold-blooded.

We promised Red Knot to this serpent? What have we gotten ourselves into? Her harried soul frayed further.

Copper Thunder wore a brown bearskin over his left shoulder, leaving his right breast bare. A large conch gorget, suspended from a choker, hung at the hollow of his throat. The polished white shell was etched with the effigy of a great spider. Below it hung a necklace of copper-tube beads, a wealth of them. They gleamed in the firelight. The colorful flaps of his breechclout hung down front and back. A decorated deerhide sash crisscrossed his belly; the shells sewn to it sparkled in the firelight. He'd laid a folded blanket beside him. From the dampness on his leggings and moccasins, he'd been far out beyond the palisade.

He turned his gaze to the flames that leapt around the burning wood. Behind him, ten warriors sat cross-legged on mats. They'd already rolled their sleeping robes and stored them near the longhouse door in preparation for leaving. They talked in low tones, and laughed as they discussed yesterday's feast and last night's Newly Made Woman Dance.

Copper Thunder pointed to the stew. "Is it ready?" he asked in his heavy accent.

She struggled to sound calm. "A while yet, Great Tayac. We added a jar of smoke-dried fish. Allow it to soften. I wouldn't have you carrying tales of poor food away from here.''

His smile didn't reach his hard eyes. "You may rest assured, Shell Comb, I will leave here completely satisfied.''

It *had* been a mistake to promise Red Knot to this spider. Unlike the other great chiefs, Copper Thunder had built his own chieftainship, carved it out of Water Snake's to the south, and Stone Frog's Conoy Confederacy to the north. Both Water Snake and Stone Frog hated and feared Copper Thunder, but as much as they feared him, their generations-old enmity kept them from allying and crushing the upstart between them.

As Shell Comb considered him, their eyes locked across the fire, measuring, probing. Those dark orbs seemed to ask, *Are you worthy?*

She ground her teeth. She had endured the worst, and seen it through. If she could do that, she could do anything. Her heart seemed to swell, becoming as stone-cold and calculating as his. If his soul heard, he gave no sign.

After a moment, he asked, ''Are you sorry to lose your daughter?''

She molded her face into an emotionless mask, betraying nothing. ''We all have responsibilities, Great Tayac. To our families, to our line, and clan. I have done mine. Red Knot . . . well, she has her responsibility to become your wife.''

''I didn't ask if your daughter would do her duty. I asked if you were sad to lose her.''

''Yes,'' Shell Comb croaked, throat tight. She took a breath, and forced herself to say, ''When a daughter is born, every mother knows that their time together is limited. Just as a father's time is with his son.''

''Last night. Who was that young man?''

She struggled to maintain her composure. ''Who? I don't understand.''

"That young man, the one you showed such distaste for. High Fox. Yes, that was his name."

Shell Comb busied herself with the stewpot. "Red Knot is leaving with you today, Great Tayac . . . a woman on the way to becoming your wife. She . . . she didn't just pop out of the earth as a grown woman. Until eight days ago, she was a girl. You were a boy once. Didn't you look at many girls that you knew you'd never marry?"

He nodded, watching the smoke rise toward the soot-stained bark roof. It hung in a thick haze before drifting out the rectangular smoke hole. "You didn't approve of High Fox."

"I didn't? What would make you think so?"

"Your face. The fear that I saw there. Whenever you looked at him, you appeared desperate."

"Perhaps you read me wrong. The boy was her childhood friend, nothing more." With feigned indifference, she grasped the stack of wooden plates that lay under the sleeping bench. They clattered as she pulled them toward her. As she'd hoped, his gaze had lingered on the sleek curve of her waist, and the way her full breasts hung under the fabric of her dress. Perhaps a man was just a man—even if he was a Great Tayac. The serpent stirred within her.

"The girl aside," Copper Thunder said, "what do you think of this arrangement between your clan and mine?"

Shell Comb considered her words carefully. Traps lay on all sides and she dared not make the smallest of missteps. "We welcome this match, of course. Greenstone Clan gains as much as you do, Great Tayac. Your country lies upriver, controlling the trade route to the interior. You are closer to the resources we need for tools. The hunting is better in your forested hills. Your corn crops are more reliable than ours. In return, you gain access to our shell beds, our fishing grounds, and all the wealth of our rich lands.'' She forced an artful smile. ''I doubt that my daughter, with her sense of responsibility, would allow her husband to starve to death.''

''Perhaps not, but the Mamanatowick, the High Chief, Water Snake, will be uneasy about Copper Thunder's foothold so close to his country. You may be visited by his warriors.''

''Greenstone Clan cares little about Water Snake's concerns. He, and the Weroances, the Low Chiefs who serve him, have attempted to meddle in our affairs before . . . much to their regret.'' She paused. ''Great Tayac, we considered all of these things before we agreed to the marriage. We're not the simple waders in shallow waters that you seem to think us.''

Shell Comb used a helmet crab shell to ladle his plate full of steaming stew, then called over her shoulder to several of the slave women, who came to scoop the thick stew into the wooden bowls. One by one, Copper Thunder's warriors accepted their food. Only when all the men were served did the slaves take their own fill and retreat to their side of the longhouse to eat.

Copper Thunder sipped at his stew and said, ''I don't think you—of all people—wade in shallow waters, Shell Comb. No, you go very deep . . . down where the water is dark and murky.''

Shell Comb smiled, as if hearing a compliment, and said, ''It is only when we're down there in the darkness that we know just how fleeting life is.''

Hunting Hawk ran her tongue over her toothless gums as she hobbled painfully around the bark-covered wall of the House of the Dead, heading for the entry. The dampness in the chill air masked the odor of decay, but its pungency still hung sweetly in her nostrils.

The morning remained gray, cold, and threatening. Patches of fog rolling in from the bay crept up the river, and feathered through the trees beyond Flat Pearl Village.

Hunting Hawk leaned against the weathered bark wall, and breathed deeply, trying to remember when she'd ever felt this tired—not even after the birth of her children. But childbirth, like so much of life, was a compromise. The Creator, Ohona, had made women to create life in a joyous process. The capricious Okeus had meddled, as he did in all things, assuring the pain and agony that process took. But a woman usually forgot the pain within days of delivery.

"You always liked a good joke, didn't you, Okeus?" she asked, raising her eyes to the blustery sky. Dark clouds scudded across the blue.

Well, no matter. Having passed fifty-three Comings of the Leaves, and placed three husbands in the House of the Dead, her time for sex—fun or purposeful—was long gone. Her breasts now lay flat on her chest and sagged down even with her navel. Her skin, after years of painting with puccoon root, had darkened into a red-black color and wrinkled into the texture of cedar bark. Once sharp, her eyes had lost the ability to see anything at a distance. Some said her nose looked more like a shriveled mushroom than a shriveled mushroom did.

She shook her head and rubbed a hand over her sore hip. Walking, even for a short distance, shot pains up from her ankles, knees, and hips to blur with the burning ache in the small of her back. She used a walking stick, one made of sassafras that she could lift and sniff—at least her nose still worked well enough—for the pleasant aroma.

She reached up and tugged at the gray-shot braid that hung down to her shoulder. Once upon a time her hair had been long and glossy like Red Knot's.

Red Knot. She winced sorrowfully, a dull pain in her heart. She'd always liked the girl, so young, bright-eyed, and mischievous. Being Weroansqua meant doing a great many unpleasant and distasteful things. Her first responsibility was to Greenstone Clan. She had gambled everything on the alliance with Copper Thunder—including Red Knot. Besides, she'd seen plenty of pretty children during her long years. Seen a lot of them grow into dull-eyed adults, worn down by the cares and trials of life.

Life meant pain: it hid behind every smile, every sigh at the beauty of new day, or the chortle of a baby's laughter. Okeus had seen to that just after the Creation, too.

She ducked into the House of the Dead. The perpetual fire had burned down to a bed of glowing coals. The only additional light came from the gray shafts entering through the doorway and smoke hole overhead. It took a moment for her eyes to adjust to the anteroom's darkness. This was the central building in her town, ten paces across, and forty-five long. High walls rose four times the height of a man to the rounded roof. Mat walls divided the building into three large rooms.

Hunting Hawk hobbled across the anteroom, mumbling the ritual greeting to the fire as she went, and stopped long enough to bathe her body in its cleansing heat. Along the south wall Green Serpent— Kwiokos, or High Priest—lay curled in his nest of deerhides. A large gourd rattle and several deerhide bags lay close at hand. His face was tipped up to the light, eyes closed, and his slack mouth was open. That hooked nose jutted arrogantly from patterns of wrinkles. His eyebrows might have been rabbit tails stuck to his brow, so white and fluffy were they.

Along the north wall, two other bundles of bedding were occupied by Lightning Cat and Streaked Bear. Lightning Cat was the long and lanky apprentice, always keen to please, and ready to undertake any task. Streaked

Bear, in turn, had a short stocky frame more suited to hard physical work than to the pursuit of the sacred.

Hunting Hawk considered kicking them awake, but relented. The celebration had lasted most of the night, and the priests had led the singing and dancing. Even a priest deserved rest now and then.

Her hips sent twinges up her back as she entered the long hallway with its carved images of the Guardians, wind spirits, and the spirit animals. Skilled hands using stone and shell tools had laboriously carved each bust from thick pieces of wood. Finally the images were painted with bright colors, and eyes of polished shell, or copper, had been added to allow the spirits to see.

Behind the Guardians rested stacks of tribute, offered to Hunting Hawk as was a Weroansqua's due: baskets of corn, nuts, squash, and seeds; smoked meat, fish, shellfish, and fowl; net bags filled with puccoon root, tobacco, shell beads, copper, and small sacks of antimony; piles of tanned deerhides, colorful feathers, exquisitely woven fabrics, and pots of dyes. Not all of the items were tribute. Greenstone Clan also kept their war trophies in the House of the Dead. Scalps, dried human hands, severed fingers, necklaces of human teeth, and trophy skulls—each carefully polished and painted—lined the walls. Beneath them, bows and bundles of arrows were neatly stacked next to a pile of wooden shields: materials for her warriors during times of conflict.

Hunting Hawk touched each of the Guardians with a finger as she passed. Normally the touch reassured her, but this time, her unease grew, as if the Guardians had seen into the dark labyrinth of her soul.

She stopped at the entrance to the sanctum. Another fire—also burned to coals—glowed in the central fire pit. A head-high scaffold stood out from the back wall, and upon it, in careful rows, lay the bodies of her ancestors.

Each corpse was wrapped in matting to protect the desiccated bones and skin.

In the shadows beneath sat the statue of Okeus, his shrine surrounded on three sides by corn husk matting. His long black hair had been pulled into a tight knot on his head. The expression on his carved face always perplexed Hunting Hawk. Did that curved mouth mock her, or leer at her? Okeus' chest was painted white, and heavy necklaces of copper and shell beads hung from his neck. Around his waist he wore a finely tanned deerhide girdle decorated by paintings and shell beads. The god's outstretched arms were painted in lightning bolts. The right hand propped up a beautiful war club; two stone celts had been set into the intricately carved wood. A shock of corn hung from the left hand. His thighs were stained black with white spots running down their length. Now he watched her from the gloom, white-shell eyes gleaming.

Hunting Hawk slipped her age-gnarled fingers into the pouch at her side and withdrew a handful of corn flour and mashed walnuts. This she sprinkled onto the red eyes of the coals. The meal blackened and burst to flame. As quickly as the fire flared, the offering was consumed. Hunting Hawk could sense Okeus' satisfaction.

"I have unleashed the storm. Terrible things are coming, aren't they?" she asked the squatting god. "Whose fault was this, Okeus? Was the mistake mine?"

A shiver played down her back as she stared into those shining eyes. For the briefest instant, she thought she heard laughter, and then silence.

"Don't scorn me, wicked god. I've served you well enough over the years."

She raised her eyes to the scaffold, and the mat-wrapped bundles that lay there. "Greetings, old friends," she whispered, and stared thoughtfully at the dried corpses.

"Well," she told them bluntly, "I've done it. Time will tell if it was for the clan's best, or not." She propped herself against one of the posts, the wood honey-colored with age and soot. "I've done something terrible. But necessary. I had no choice. I want you to know that. No choice at all."

She could sense the ghosts stirring, and cocked her head. Someone had once told her that in the final moments of life, a person could finally hear the ghosts talking. But nothing came to her ears.

"It's this feeling I've got. I'll be up there with you soon. We'll just have to wait and see who the next Weroansqua will be. Someone who truly knows her duty to clan and lineage. I hope she's worthy of all of you."

Flat Willow eased his muscular body between the tree trunks, each foot placed with care. As a boy, he had studied the praying mantis, each movement the mantis made as it stalked and captured its prey; now he, too, hunted like the mantis, every movement spare and precise.

He wore only a breechclout, his skin greased against the cold. A bone skewer pinned his long hair into a bun on the left side of his head. His legs were clad in leggings, moccasins on his feet. An ash-wood bow filled his left hand, and an arrow lay nocked against the bowstring in his right, ready to be drawn and released.

Of all the days he'd lived, this one would be the hardest. He needed to kill, to make him forget, to still the dull ache in his breast. As long as Red Knot had been a girl, he could stand to be close to her. But now she was a woman—and promised to a man Flat Willow despised.

So, as the others had danced, feasted, and celebrated

Red Knot's womanhood, and the arrival of Copper Thunder, Flat Willow had suffered. Then Stone Cob had accosted him, assigning him the most onerous of duties. Well, events had taken care of themselves. Even predators could make deals among themselves; and one day Stone Cob would pay—as they all would. He had learned patience and stealth from the mantis.

His life had changed last night after Red Knot's dance. And this morning he had taken matters into his own hands. What had prompted him? Betrayal? Revenge? Or the unexpected opportunity? Perhaps the reason didn't matter. What did was that he had committed himself, and acted. Afterward, stunned by what he'd done, Flat Willow had quietly drifted away, preferring the stillness of the forest and time to think about future and past.

The sullen gray morning made for perfect hunting. The leaf mat was damp and silent underfoot. Any colder and it would have rustled with frost. Drier and it would have crackled with the shifting of his weight. The stringers of mist carried by the faint breeze would confuse the deer's keen eyes at the same time they carried Flat Willow's scent away.

Two years had passed since the summer day when he'd emerged from the *Huskanaw* ceremony where the boy he had once been had been ritually "killed." He had been tested to determine his strength and endurance, and to determine how much pain he could endure without crying out. His skin had been tattooed, and finally the priest had struck him dead with a Power wand, driving the boy's soul from his body. After that he lay in a painful daze as his body was painted black like a corpse, and funeral songs were sung over him and his fellows. He'd fasted for days, and drunk sacred datura and yaupon tea. Then the priest had whipped him painfully to his feet, splashed him with water, and blown tobacco smoke over his body to purify him. The black paint of death had been washed off before he was repainted red with puccoon root and slathered with bear grease.

A man had been born where a child had once stood.

From that time forward, Flat Willow had dedicated himself to the hunt. He had sworn before Okeus' altar that he would be the finest hunter in the Greenstone Clan. Day after day he stalked through the woods, practicing his craft. He learned the ways of the deer, the bear, and the bobcat. His soul became one with the forest. To the core of his being, he'd believed that his growing fame would bring him notice, and allow him to approach Shell Comb after Red Knot was made a woman.

With the silence of smoke, he crossed an open patch and slipped into the trees, no more than a shadow in the gloom, as he followed the small heart-shaped tracks of a deer.

His eyes missed no clue. His ears caught the faintest sounds. When he found the pile of droppings, he touched them to feel the heat. He was close now, almost upon them.

He sniffed the damp air to judge the breeze. Before him, the trail split. On a hunch, he ghosted to the right, sensing that the deer would head for the oak grove and a few last acorns before bedding down for the day in the dense hawthorn and grapevine cover.

He followed the slope of the ridge, testing each step through his moccasins. Between the bare branches, he could see the fog-patched inlet shining silver down below him, then . . . the barest flick of a tail caught his attention. No more than a bow shot ahead, a doe stood at the edge of the oak grove, her head up, ears alert.

Flat Willow froze, the first thrill of the hunt tingling each nerve. Only when the doe dropped her head to pluck up an acorn did Flat Willow take one more slow step.

A second doe stepped into his sight, a fawn by her side. Flat Willow waited until her head lowered; then he slipped behind the bole of a towering red maple.

The world faded as Flat Willow's attention focused on the deer. Step by careful step, he closed the distance. He crossed the trail that led down to Oyster Shell Landing and eased into the lee of an ancient beech. Patiently, he edged his head around, seeing a young two-point buck no more than fifteen paces ahead. The buck pawed at the leaves, seeking to uncover buried beechnuts.

Flat Willow slid his left foot around the tree, and prepared for the shot. His heart strengthened as he shifted his weight and settled his right foot. Raising the bow, he pulled the arrow back to his ear, sighting down the slim shaft. One last breath filled his lungs; he centered the stone point on the deer's back to compensate for the arrow's drop.

This was the moment he lived for. *You are mine!*

The buck's head jerked up, startled, ears pricked. The animal stared up toward the ridgetop, body tense.

As Flat Willow released his deadly shaft, the deer snorted and leapt away. The arrow arced through empty space and disappeared into the leaf mat beyond.

Flat Willow exhaled explosively. The deer raced away, white tails flagging.

In their wake he heard the thumping of moccasins, the whipping of branches, and the puffing of breath.

Flat Willow made a face and straightened. What silly fool would be running through the forest on a morning like this? From habit, he plucked another arrow from the bark quiver hung over his shoulder.

Through the trees he glimpsed someone charging down the trail. The man leapt, slipped, and jumped in his headlong rush.

For an instant, Flat Willow considered hiding, then got a good look at the young man: High Fox, from Three Myrtle Village. Flat Willow rolled his eyes in disgust. Of all the people to meet today, none could have been as bad as High Fox. Red Knot's eyes had always been for him, a mere stripling; and in contrast to a fine hunter like Flat Willow, why, there was just no comparison.

Flat Willow cocked his head, surprised when High Fox saw him and tried to stop short. He had a panicked look on his face, eyes wide. The youth's right foot slipped out from under him, and he landed flat on his bottom, skidding in the leaves.

"High Fox! It's just me. Flat Willow."

High Fox gaped as he slid to a stop, glanced around as if for an escape route, and rose on trembling legs. He wiped his hands on the flap of his breechclout.

"What's the matter?" Flat Willow demanded. "Is it trouble?" He took a step up, and stopped when the ashen High Fox shook his head.

"No. N-No trouble."

"But you were running like a madman," Flat Willow declared suspiciously. "You ruined my hunt! Scared the deer."

High Fox gave him a weak smile. "Sorry. I . . . I was just in a hurry, that's all. Late. I'm late."

"Late for what? It's barely morning."

"I know. I-I stayed too late at the dance last night. That's all. I have to get back. Home, you see. I had . . . well, chores. Something for my father."

Flat Willow frowned, reading the terror in High Fox's face. "Go, then."

High Fox tensed, his muscles knotted. Taking a deep breath, he seemed to regain some of his control. The smile still looked forced. "Sorry. I guess I must have looked pretty silly."

"I've seen rabbits run faster, but not many."

High Fox's lips quivered as he descended the steep trail toward Flat Willow. "Deer, huh?"

"Some does, a fawn, and one nice little buck that was

half a heartbeat from dead when you came crashing down the trail.''

"I'm sorry. Really, I am. I know how rare they are around the village.'' The fragile smile died and High Fox's eyes widened. What caused that glazed look, as if something had scared him half out of his skin? Had Copper Thunder figured out that the boy had been nosing around Red Knot? Or was he still upset about what had happened at Three Myrtle Village yesterday morning? Flat Willow had heard bits of the story bantered about before the dance last night. Apparently, a young girl named Sun Conch had begged him to marry her, and been rebuffed, harshly, by Black Spike.

"Are you all right?''

High Fox was no more than a step away. Every muscle trembled, and his breathing was labored. "I apologize for scaring the deer. Maybe, if you scout around, you can pick them up again. I'd try that way.'' He pointed back the way Flat Willow had come.

"I just came from that way.''

"Well, you know how deer circle.'' He licked his lips. "Sorry, I—I have to go. I'll make it up to you, I promise.''

As High Fox edged wide around Flat Willow, he saw the dark red stain on High Fox's right hand. "Are you hurt?'' Flat Willow asked.

"Just a cut.'' But tears glimmered in his eyes. He fought to blink them away. "A foolish fall. My hand landed on an old stump.''

"It happens. Be more careful.''

"Yes, I will. Good hunting!'' High Fox called, and hurried off.

Good hunting? Flat Willow wondered as he watched High Fox running down the trail. He shook his head, and turned back to where he'd taken his shot. He started out to find his lost arrow, but the oddness of it all stopped him. What had High Fox been doing here? And most of all, just what had he seen to set him off like that?

Reluctantly, Flat Willow gave up on the arrow for the time being, and cut back to the trail. He followed it down far enough to see Oyster Shell Landing through the gray tracery of branches.

High Fox was pushing a slim canoe out into the water. Then he jumped lithely into the boat, seated himself, and began paddling down the inlet. If he'd cut his hand as badly as the blood would indicate, it didn't seem to hinder him.

Flat Willow dropped to a crouch. Why would High Fox have a canoe beached on this side of the neck? Why hadn't he landed at Flat Pearl Village?

"Well, High Fox, it's going to be good riddance. You stupid fool!"

High Fox, the Weroance's spoiled son, had had everything—even Red Knot. But, as of that very morning, Flat Willow had taken charge, begun the slow process of paying them all back.

You'll see, High Fox. You'll never underestimate Flat Willow again. He slapped his thigh and rose to resume the search for his lost arrow.

Three

Hunting Hawk ground her empty gums against each other. By midday, it had become apparent that Red Knot was missing. A quick search of the buildings within the palisade came up empty, as did the search of the houses in the fields just beyond. Hunting Hawk scowled at the people gathered within the palisade. Why did organizing for a search create so much milling and confusion? Even fish—mindless as they were—could come together without much effort.

The visitors from the surrounding villages stood in little clumps, talking to each other in low voices. That wary look on their faces irritated her. Curse it all, it was an embarrassment.

Copper Thunder stood to one side, his warriors in ranks behind him. She studied his face, trying to read the sardonic expression. Was that smugness, wry humor, or subtle irony?

To her right, Nine Killer's lieutenants, Stone Cob and Flying Weir, were calling out orders as Nine Killer detailed parties of warriors to search different areas. Nine Killer didn't look like a War Chief. Most of the women were taller than he, but looks could deceive. Heavy-lidded eyes and fat cheeks made him appear sleepy and lazy. Broad-lipped and wide, the man's mouth gave him a bland expression. Those bandy legs might not be fast, but they could carry him long after the swiftest of runners had played out. His too-long arms could paddle a canoe nonstop the length of the Salt Water Bay. And as Nine Killer liked to point out, there was a great deal more to war than imposing size. He'd won his name after having snuck into Mattaponi Village and single-handedly killed the Weroance and eight of his warriors, then, to the bafflement of his enemy, mysteriously vanished into the night. One didn't underestimate a man like that.

"Very well, let's go!" Nine Killer called out, and thrust his bow toward the palisade gate. "You know what to look for. She's probably just wandered off to be alone, but don't take chances. Ignore nothing suspicious."

His warriors trotted out sharply, heads held high, backs straight. As they went they clacked war clubs against their bows, the clatter in time to each prancing step.

Hunting Hawk shot a sly glance at Copper Thunder and his warriors, fully aware that the show was for their benefit. The visitors remained expressionless, some looking studiously bored, but she could see the gleam in those dark eyes. The scrappy reputation of Greenstone Clan's warriors had been fairly won. Even the Mamanatowick, Water Snake, despite all the resources of his subchiefs, avoided clashes with Greenstone Clan.

Black Spike, Weroance of Three Myrtle Village, stood on the other side of the dance ground, his arms crossed as he watched the warriors depart. His strained expression, the tension in his posture, caught Hunting Hawk's attention.

Black Spike had always been a handsome man, tall, muscular, and quick of wit and action. Three Myrtle Village lay half a day's journey east in the next large inlet. Over the years, the two villages—mostly populated by Greenstone Clan—had allied themselves for practical and political purposes. Her own daughter, Shell Comb, had lived there during the time she'd been married to Monster Bone.

Black Spike kept knotting his jaw muscles, and his hands clenched, relaxed, and clenched again. Why should he care so much about a missing girl? No doubt she'd be found sulking out in the trees, and within a week the entire thing would be forgotten.

Hunting Hawk arched a grizzled eyebrow as Black Spike gave Shell Comb a direct inspection from across the dance ground. For a long moment, their eyes held, challenging, answering, and desperate. What was that look they traded? Some private communication? But just as quickly, Shell Comb turned forcefully away.

The muscles bulged in Black Spike's taut cheeks.

Hunting Hawk's attention shifted as Copper Thunder strode purposefully toward her.

"Honorable Weroansqua," he said, "are you sure that I cannot offer my warriors to assist you?"

"It isn't necessary, Great Tayac." She gestured toward the forested ridge. "My people know the country. All the little nooks and crannies."

His dark eyes seemed to burn. "She wouldn't have . . . run off, now would she?"

Hunting Hawk stiffened. "Never!"

"But it is not unheard—"

"She knows that I'd have Nine Killer scour the ends of the earth until he found her and dragged her back. Red Knot would never disgrace her clan in such a manner."

"I see." Copper Thunder's expression betrayed nothing.

"Most likely she just went for a walk, to sort out her spirit. Consider: In the last eight days, she's gone from a girl to a woman, and tomorrow she leaves with you to become a wife. From the moment of her first cramps, she's been pestered by everyone. I'd guess she just needed a moment to herself, to think and reflect."

Copper Thunder fingered the war club hanging from his breechclout. It had been intricately carved, a pointed stone set above a sharp copper spike. "I've noticed the women in your family think and reflect a great deal. I wonder if I'm doing myself any favors by marrying into your line."

"I don't know. Are you?" Hunting Hawk gave him a bland look to cover her sudden unease. Bloody bats, he didn't suspect the depths of her complicity, did he?

He chuckled. "My men and I would really like to be of help. A sign of our new relationship."

Hunting Hawk nodded reluctantly. "Very well. Great Tayac, dispatch your men. On the slim chance that she's in some kind of trouble, it might not hurt to have some extra eyes out there."

Copper Thunder lifted his hand and snapped his fingers, and his warriors wheeled in unison, trotting out like a school of fish. Beyond the palisade, Copper Thunder's second called orders and men dispersed with cool efficiency.

"They're well trained," Hunting Hawk noted.

"Of course. A man doesn't accomplish what I have without discipline."

"And ruthlessness," she added.

"That, too, but then, living between the serpent and the stone, as you do, you can understand the value of that."

"Indeed I can." *As you will soon learn, my friend.*

Copper Thunder stood uneasily, his eyes narrowed.

Hunting Hawk caught Yellow Net's eye as her niece walked past. She could see the woman's anxiety as she shot a worried glance at Copper Thunder. Hunting Hawk smiled to reassure her. As Yellow Net took a deep breath and walked off, Hunting Hawk asked, "Something on your mind, Great Tayac?"

"Just wondering. That's all. Why me, Weroansqua? Water Snake would have been a more logical choice for an ally. His country lies immediately to your south. Despite what your daughter told me this morning, you could have obtained inland goods through him as well as me."

Hunting Hawk smiled crookedly. *Be careful, woman. He smells the trap.* "What if I told you I just had a feeling in my gut?"

"I wouldn't believe it. Tell me honestly, have you ever done anything based on a gut feeling?"

"Of course . . . and so have you. You're a sly one, Great Tayac. Always feeling out your opponent, seeking to learn more of his strengths and weaknesses."

He shrugged it off. "Among my people, one does not become Tayac, let alone Great Tayac, without studying his associates. A smart leader never sleeps."

"No, she doesn't."

He shot her a sidelong glance. "You know, don't you, that some parties would profit by abducting your grand-daughter."

"I've been trying not to think of that. But, yes, it's a possibility. And the consequences would be dire indeed."

He took a deep breath. "It would be a slap in the face to you and your clan, and to me and my people. We would have no choice but to destroy the offender."

"Whole villages would be burned, their people murdered. No one would be safe."

"Let us hope that your first thought was the right one."

Hunting Hawk clasped her hands together, as if locking them around that hope. "I'm sure the explanation will be simple."

No, despite her worries, he didn't suspect a thing.

Quick Fawn reached down for a piece of firewood, the first she'd seen since leaving the village. At twelve, she was willowy, and pretty. Her mother, Yellow Net, had combed out her long black hair until it gleamed. Her heart-shaped face and sparkling eyes were the envy of her friends. Her slim body had just begun to round, promising a woman's beauty to come.

At least a hand of time had passed since her mother had sent her out for wood. The chore of keeping the fires going was an endless one. Years of collecting around the village had forced her to travel farther up the neck of land. But, to be truthful, she had been dallying, wanting time away. Her confrontation with Red Knot after the dance the night before still bothered her. So much was happening, she needed time to think about it.

A squirrel dashed from branch to branch above her,

and perched, staring down with beady black eyes.

"Better be glad you're up there, free, my friend," she told the bushy-tailed rodent. "You don't want to be a human girl."

As if in agreement, the squirrel flicked its tail and bounded into the higher branches.

Quick Fawn climbed farther up the slope to where the old oak had fallen. The bole was huge, and until last year it had been the biggest tree in the forest above Flat Pearl Village. Then, in a storm last summer, lightning had riven it. To everyone's amazement, the heart of the great trunk had been hollow and rotten. The tree had cracked down the middle, and half had fallen, splintering the branches of its neighbors as it crashed down onto the forest floor. The other half still stood, weathered and dead, waiting for the inevitable storm that would topple it as well.

The tree's corpse provided a wealth of wood for the young collectors from Flat Pearl Village.

Quick Fawn looked at the litter covering the ground, and then up at the bare sky. When the mighty oak fell, it had opened a huge patch of forest to the light.

She laid her wood to one side and climbed agilely up the fallen section of trunk. Placing her back in the crook of one of the broken branches, she leaned her head back and stared up at the clouds.

"I don't think I want to be a woman," she told the silent sky.

Red Knot was her best friend. Together they had played, worked, and dreamed. They had laughed, flashed smiles at the boys, teased them unmercifully.

Quick Fawn thought back to that summer night, not five moons past. Canny leader that old Hunting Hawk was, she'd sent runners to the surrounding villages, announcing a celebration to mark the final weeding of the fields. Of course, the visitors had arrived early to find the people of Flat Pearl still out weeding the corn, beans, and squash. Naturally, they had pitched in, and what would have taken Flat Pearl five days took less than one.

Hunting Hawk disposed of large quantities of last winter's stores that were on the verge of molding, emptying storage baskets and pots. What better way than to fill the bellies of her friends and allies from the surrounding area?

From the corner of her eye, Quick Fawn had watched Red Knot and High Fox, side by side, weeding the rows. Corn, beans, and squash alternated in the field. Here and there, an old stump, the wood charred, thrust up like crows' beaks. Bent over, High Fox and Red Knot had talked, laughed, and shared special smiles.

At first, Quick Fawn had been included in their games, but later, after the feast, while Flat Willow had been strutting and leaping in his hunting dance, they had slipped away from the circle of dancers around the ceremonial fire in front of the House of the Dead.

So I followed. Quick Fawn rubbed her face and sighed as she stared up at the scudding clouds. In the dark trees beyond the canoe landing, she'd lost them. Only later did she finally discover them, bathed in moonlight on the sandy bank of the inlet.

High Fox had passed his Blackening and rebirth into manhood but two moons past. And Red Knot, at fourteen, hadn't had her first menses; nevertheless, their bodies were locked together. Quick Fawn watched the moonlight shining silver on their greased skin. It cast twin crescents on High Fox's buttocks and back, and shone silver on the backs of his legs as his hips moved rhythmically against hers.

Their audacity had stunned Quick Fawn. What if someone found out? A man didn't couple with a girl. Red Knot would be beaten, and every sort of abuse heaped upon her in punishment. And High Fox at the very least would be dishonored, at the worst killed out-right by Nine Killer and the Flat Pearl warriors.

Like a shadow, Quick Fawn had faded into the cover of the trees, and placed a hand to her pounding heart. She had glanced around, frightened, to reassure herself that no one else was close.

The next day, High Fox left with his father, Black Spike. Red Knot walked as if in a private mist. She had a happy, moony look.

"Do you know what you're doing?" Quick Fawn asked that afternoon. They were using heavy pestles, made from straight branches, to pound corn kernels into flour. Each beat of the pestles was accompanied by the hollow thump of wood. Together, they beat out a rhythm.

"Know what I'm doing?"

"You and High Fox!" Quick Fawn whispered. "I know about the two of you! But I'm your friend. What if someone else finds out? You could be ruining your life!"

Red Knot laughed, her supple body flexing as she thumped the heavy pestle down on the dancing corn in the mortar hollow. "No, my friend. Just the opposite. I'm saving myself. Blessed bats, Quick Fawn. We're going to be married, live the rest of our lives together. He's going to be a great chief someday, maybe even Maman-atowick. And I'll be his wife."

Quick Fawn frowned down into the powdered corn and hammered it with extra vehemence. "I suppose that Hunting Hawk and Shell Comb have agreed to this?"

"Oh, they will. I'm sure of it. Mother has always had her way with Black Spike, and Three Myrtle Village. Why would they object?"

"I think your sight has been blinded by High Fox's radiance, my friend. The Weroansqua and your mother never do things for convenience, or because someone wishes. You are the granddaughter of a chief, the daughter of a woman who will become chief. Remember that. You're not like other people.''

Those words had been prophetic. Less than a month before Red Knot became a woman, it was announced that she had been promised to Copper Thunder.

How well Quick Fawn recalled her friend's eyes that day. Shock, disbelief, and desperation all mixed together to turn that pretty face into a mask of crushed hopes.

No, I don't want to become a woman. Let me stay as I am. Free, happy, and without worries beyond my daily chores.

Everything had come to a head early that very morning. In the darkness before dawn, Quick Fawn had sneaked out to see her friend. Red Knot had spilled her plans: ''I'm running away with High Fox! We're leaving at first light from Oyster Shell Landing!''

Quick Fawn rubbed her face, an empty feeling in her gut, as she recalled her desperate pleas that Red Knot couldn't run off, couldn't betray her responsibility and duty to the clan.

And they'd argued, almost to the point of violence.

I could have stopped her. Quick Fawn closed her eyes, seeing the triumph in Red Knot's face.

What a fool her cousin was. The War Chief would hunt her down and bring her and High Fox back in disgrace. Quick Fawn sighed, and pulled her knees up until she could rest her chin on them. The forest had grown oddly quiet.

Quick Fawn frowned at the prickle of premonition. On the point of hopping down to resume her wood collecting, she caught a faint movement in the corner of her eye.

She froze when two tens of warriors filed past on the slope below her, bows strung, arrows nocked. The faintest whisper of moccasins sounded on the damp leaves. Dark eyes gleamed warily as they scanned the forest around them. Each face was painted in red and black, the colors of war and death.

She knew them by their hairstyle—the right side of the head shaved bald, a long, braided roach falling down the back from the center scalplock, and a war fetish pinned into the tightly wrapped bun on the right. These men belonged to the Mamanatowick, Water Snake.

But what were they doing here, sneaking through Flat Pearl lands?

Quick Fawn tried to swallow down a fear-choked throat. Her heart hammered hard, fit to burst her chest. Every nerve screamed at her to run, but panic had frozen her to the old oak.

One of the warriors seemed to look right at her. The world swayed as Quick Fawn's guts went runny.

And at that instant, a rabbit burst from beneath her, frightened by the closeness of the men, and streaked away, its fluffy white tail bobbing with each leap. Distracted, the warrior watched the rabbit go, his pace unbroken.

She remained there, gasping for breath after they'd passed, then slid off the fallen oak. Her wobbling legs would have failed her but for locking her knees.

"I have to warn the village!"

Quick Fawn had earned her name because she was the fastest girl in Flat Pearl. Now she lived up to her reputation, hair streaming out behind her as she streaked away, arms pumping, bare feet pattering.

Nine Killer juggled his thoughts as a magician did green walnuts. That ability had saved more than one war party from disaster. He could take up a problem, give it a moment's thought, and toss it up again as he entertained yet another thought, eventually recapturing the first in an uninterrupted flow.

Ideas raced through his head as he trotted up the ridge trail ahead of four warriors. Life in Flat Pearl Village reminded him of dancing on a spiderweb. One had to move one's feet quickly, lest they become stuck. Balance was a precarious thing at best. Even flailing around could leave one entwined for whatever spider lurked in the shadows.

Fortunately for Flat Pearl, and Greenstone Clan, Hunting Hawk had always been a nimble dancer. Her keen mind had kept the territory between Oyster Inlet and Duck Creek autonomous. That the Independent villages often accomplished their goals through manipulation, military prowess, and intimidation was of no concern to anyone: the final arbiter was survival.

But now the Independent villages lay like an uncracked nut between three stones. To the south, the Mamanatowick, Water Snake, brooded and schemed, forever seeking to extend his influence over the Independent villages, while in the north, across the Fish River, the Tayac, Stone Frog, had strengthened what had been a weak coalition of Conoy villages into a strong confederacy.

In the west, Copper Thunder was the new element. Less than ten Comings of the Leaves ago, he had arrived in the upriver villages to the west. His mother, a woman of the Pipestone Clan, had married a Trader, and followed him off to the wealthy chieftainships inland. Copper Thunder had been born there, raised on the great rivers; and he told stories of fabulous cities, and stupendous temple buildings atop man-made mountains that gleamed under the sun.

Such stories stretched Nine Killer's credulity, but so many of the Traders insisted that such marvelous chieftainships existed that a kernel of truth must lie within.

Copper Thunder had returned to his mother's people as a young man—and such a man: his face was tattooed in a peculiar fashion, as if his eyes looked out of two swallowtails. He carried a fearsome war club inset with a nasty copper blade. The spider gorget he wore was said to belong to some secret society of warriors who served the Serpent Chiefs. Others said he knew strange ways, that he spoke to alien gods, and enchanted evil spirits to his will.

All of these things might be true, for he had welded the squabbling upriver clans into a cohesive alliance for the first time in the memory of men. With them at his back, he'd managed to defeat first Stone Frog, and then Water Snake.

Both battles had been won with inferior numbers of warriors, and had inflicted great losses on the larger forces. And now the Great Tayac, as Copper Thunder styled himself, sat astride the most important trade route to the interior. Along that line flowed all the copper, chert, and rhyolite for tools, fine fabrics, dyes, and steatite for pipes and bowls.

That lonesome young man had collected an amazing amount of prestige, authority, and power. His strength seemed to be growing by the year. Many now said there was no way to stop him.

But is that true? Nine Killer listened to the shouts of his men echoing through the forest, and considered what sort of man it took to accomplish such a thing.

Copper Thunder was more than just a long-lost kinsman of the Pipestone Clan. He had some other quality, something that set him above other men. Whatever it was, it differed from the proclaimed deity of men like Water Snake, who believed himself to be part god. In all the times Nine Killer had dealt with the Mamanatowick, he'd always known instinctively that he dealt with another *man*—albeit a powerful one.

Copper Thunder was a different matter. Nine Killer need but look into those eyes and his soul shivered. People said that the Great Tayac carried a powerful amulet, a tablet engraved with the image of a creature part bird, part man, and part snake—and whispered that it made him invincible.

Nine Killer tightened his grip on his bow, reassured by the resilient wood. He'd made the weapon himself, carved it from the fire-hardened branch of a hickory tree. Of all the warriors he'd met, only five had been able to draw it to full arc. With it, Nine Killer could drive an arrow clear through an enemy warrior's oak shield and into his body—no matter what intrigues good or bad spirits might contrive.

He had been thinking about this new alliance between Hunting Hawk and Copper Thunder. As War Chief, who wouldn't? After all, he would have to bear the brunt of Water Snake and Stone Frog's rage.

Things were changing. The old, ordered ways had crumbled, largely because of the arrival of Copper Thunder. Were it not for him, and the expansion of the upriver clans, things might have stayed pretty much the same around the great Salt Water Bay. But, like Okeus after the Creation, Copper Thunder had brought chaos to the country. Those three stones were closing in on the Independent villages, grinding away with ever more determination.

Nine Killer frowned. Thinking of Okeus always made him nervous. After all, temples and shrines were erected to the dark god. He was worshiped and placated, whereas Ohona, god of Creation and order, was mostly forgotten. Okeus always made Nine Killer feel as if he were standing on a high point while lightning flashed and banged in the sky. A man never knew when he was going to be blasted.

Okeus and the Weroansqua had a great deal in common. Perhaps old Hunting Hawk had saved them again by this alliance to Copper Thunder's Pipestone Clan. The test would be to see if Hunting Hawk was truly capable of handling Copper Thunder—and Okeus only knew what would happen if . . .

A young girl came dashing down the trail, her long black hair streaming out behind. For the briefest of moments, Nine Killer thought she was Red Knot, then recognized his niece, Quick Fawn.

"Warriors!" the girl cried. "Warriors, Uncle! Almost two tens of them!" She pulled to a stop before him, bent double and gasping for breath. "By the . . . old oak. They passed . . . bows ready . . . faces painted. Coming this way!"

"Whose warriors?" Nine Killer put a gentle hand on his niece's head. "Did you recognize them?"

"The . . . the Mamanatowick's!"

Nine Killer turned to his warriors. "Water Snake's warriors are on the west side of the ridge. If this is a raid, they'll stick to the bottom of the slope, just up from the trails along the beach. Stone Cob, break left, warn the others. Flying Weir, assemble your men. Let's lay a trap for these cunning infiltrators, and see what comes of it."

At his signal, the two warriors charged off through the trees toward the other parties of searchers. The two remaining warriors quickly strung their bows, plucked arrows, and looked to him for orders.

"Stay with me, niece. We'll climb down the slope. I think I know where they'll pass." He dropped to a knee and looked the gasping Quick Fawn in the eye. "Was Red Knot with you?"

"No." Quick Fawn panted. "Is something wrong?"

"She's missing. And now you tell me the Mamanatowick's warriors are out there."

"But she should be long . . ." She tossed tangled black

locks back as she straightened, sudden worry shining in her eyes. "I . . . yes, I see, Uncle."

"One thing at a time, girl." Nine Killer gave her a reassuring smile. "We'll deal with the warriors, and then we'll find her." He patted her on the back. "Go now. Warn the village. Two tens of warriors is hardly a threat, but they could cause mischief."

Winged Blackbird hurried forward, balancing speed against silence. His line of warriors followed behind him.

He didn't particularly like this situation, sneaking down the narrow neck of land controlled by Flat Pearl Village's renowned warriors, but being War Chief to Corn Hunter, Weroance of White Stake Village, carried risk along with status. Winged Blackbird had trained all of his life for this, and now, in his second year as War Chief, he knew just how tenuous his position was.

His only hope was stealth. They had to get in fast, accomplish their task, and get out before that cunning Nine Killer figured out just how weak they were.

Only three days past, he'd been sitting before the fire in his family longhouse in White Stake Village. His wife, Sees-Through-Shell, had been relating the gossip as Winged Blackbird knotted a new fishing net from cordage. Then Corn Hunter's runner had arrived.

Winged Blackbird had taken a moment to don his best shell necklace and tie on his stuffed blackbird. He wore the bird on the shaved right side of his head, just above the ear. Then he picked up his war club and went to see the Weroance.

Corn Hunter had been surrounded by his priests, some of the clan leaders, and a stringy, tattooed fellow: a Trader by the name of Barnacle. Winged Blackbird knew of him, a shiftless sort, and not well liked. From the stories told, he must have had no less than four or five different mothers—for no other explanation could account for his various claims of clan affiliation. In all the years that Barnacle had been plying the waters of Salt Water Bay, no clan had ever claimed him, and, it was said, those who had investigated his lineage had never found anyone who knew of him or his family.

Corn Hunter wore a grim expression, brooding, his square jaw propped on a meaty palm as he stared thoughtfully at Barnacle. The Weroance had begun to gray, his body gone soft and round in the gut. Old tattoos had faded into his age-darkened skin until they were barely recognizable. Water Snake had placed Corn Hunter, his younger brother, in charge of White Stake Village nearly twenty years past. The appointment had been enforced by the Mamanatowick's warriors in the beginning, but over the years Corn Hunter had proved a solid man, if somewhat unimaginative. His duty to his older brother had consisted mostly of stabilizing the northern borders, and checking on Flat Pearl Village and the allies of Greenstone Clan.

Few failed to realize that Water Snake wished to control the territories held by the Independent villages. Over the years, he had sent several expeditions to bring Flat Pearl, Three Myrtle, and Oyster villages under his sway by intimidation or conquest. Each had been met and repulsed by Greenstone warriors and their allies. Winged Blackbird owed his appointment as War Chief to just such a raid, when his predecessor, Net Sinker, had been killed in combat with Nine Killer.

"Barnacle has brought news," Corn Hunter had told him. "Hunting Hawk, of Greenstone Clan, has promised her granddaughter to Copper Thunder. As we speak, the girl is becoming a woman. You will take warriors and go north. See if what the Trader tells us is true."

Shocked by the news, Winged Blackbird had asked, "How soon, my chief?"

"Now. Tonight. Make sure that Hunting Hawk knows that this marriage will displease the Water Snake."

"Tonight? But I'll need several days to collect my warriors. Some are hunting, others are fishing. It—"

"Tonight, War Chief!"

"And what am I to do? Just tell her she can't marry off her granddaughter?"

"I leave that to you. You are War Chief. You may pursue the matter as you think best, but this marriage must not take place."

Winged Blackbird had managed to pull together two tens of warriors. What he could do with such a tiny force remained to be seen. The first part of his plan was to arrive unexpectedly at Flat Pearl Village—posing as a hunting party that just happened to be in the area. A peaceful visit, that's all.

Hunting Hawk was smart. The old woman hadn't held her position and maintained her independence all these years by being a fool. She'd see the subtle threat. His greatest challenge would be the artful delivery of the message so as not to threaten overtly, but to imply dire consequences should the marriage proceed.

"We are getting close," he told his warriors. "Be alert."

Not a stick of fallen wood lay on the forest floor, and some of the stumps had been chopped down with stone axes. Beneath the nut trees, the soil lay beaten down by the collectors of hickory, pinaquin, and walnuts.

So far, so good. With luck, he and his warriors could just walk up to the palisade and call out a greeting. A little more luck, and Hunting Hawk would receive him politely, and provide a feast. He'd be hurrying south by nightfall, his message delivered.

Just as he decided he might have a glimmering of a

chance, a man stepped out from behind a thick tree trunk to block his way.

Winged Blackbird held up his hand, bringing his warriors to a halt. His heart skipped as he recognized that short figure, the bandy legs, and muscular arms. The famous ash-wood bow was strung, and Nine Killer had an arrow nocked.

"Greetings, War Chief," Nine Killer called out. "What are you doing skulking around in Flat Pearl country?" He cocked his head skeptically. "Not a raid, I hope?"

Winged Blackbird gestured the "hold" command to his nervous warriors. Nine Killer couldn't be alone out here, could he? Anticipation raced in Blackbird's veins. If he could take Nine Killer's head home to White Stake, they would sing honors in his name for moons. He'd prepared for this, ready to kill any lone villagers before they could raise the alarm—but Nine Killer, that would be some trophy!

"A raid, great Nine Killer? No, we are a small hunting party. Since we were just south of your lands, we thought perhaps we would come and visit. A gesture of our goodwill to let you know that we were in the area, and not the cause of alarm."

Nine Killer gave him a brazen smile. "I'm glad to hear that, noble Winged Blackbird . . . but I'm puzzled. Why didn't you come down the main trail?"

"It was out of our way," Winged Blackbird lied, and gave the subtle signal for his men to fan out.

If Nine Killer understood the shifting of warriors, he gave no sign. Rather, he seemed very sure of himself. A sickening premonition grew in Blackbird's gut.

"Out of your way? On this narrow neck of land?" Nine Killer drew his arrow back. "That's far enough, Winged Blackbird. If your warriors take another step, I'll drive this arrow through your heart and into that tree behind you.''

''A man alone shouldn't make threats, War Chief.''

''Make a move, War Chief, and you'll be the first to die.''

Someone hissed from behind Winged Blackbird, and he caught movement out of the corner of his eye. Flat Pearl's warriors stepped out from behind the trees, each with a strung bow, surrounding his small party.

His mouth went dry. If this went wrong, his party would be caught in a crossfire, wiped out to the last man.

''Nine Killer, I come in peace, wishing nothing more than to speak with Hunting Hawk.'' He lowered the butt of his bow to the ground, smiling in what he hoped wasn't visible bravado. ''Had I come for war, do you think I'd have brought but two tens of warriors with me?''

''If you came in peace, would you come with your faces painted for war, strung bows, and arrows ready to be released?'' Nine Killer slowly shook his head. ''What am I to do with you?''

''Allow me safe passage to speak to the Weroansqua. I will deliver my message, and be gone.''

More and more warriors slipped from the forest, joining Nine Killer's forces. A bad situation was getting worse. Winged Blackbird bit his lip and shrugged at Nine Killer's continued silence. ''It is up to you, War Chief. If you wish a battle, you will probably win. In your position, I would be considering just that. But, I urge you, think this through. If you start this, are you ready for the consequences? These are perilous times. The Mamanatowick might react with rage at the murder of one of his messengers. Is an easy victory today worth the kind of war you will have to fight tomorrow?''

''Yes . . . and no,'' Nine Killer replied as he allowed his bowstring to slacken just the slightest. He seemed to be mulling the notion in his head. "I think you had better give me your message. Before the gods, I will deliver it to the Weroansqua word for word."

"And why do you not wish me to tell Hunting Hawk in person?"

Nine Killer gave him a deadly grin. "Because Copper Thunder is in Flat Pearl Village. I suspect I can control my warriors, and their passions. I'm not sure I can control him, or his—nor that I would want to try."

The nervous chill intensified. "Then this marriage is a finished thing?"

"If I were gambling, I wouldn't bet against it, War Chief. That's your message, isn't it? To tell Hunting Hawk not to allow this alliance with Copper Thunder? You must have just heard that Red Knot had begun her bleeding. That's why you only have two tens of warriors. Corn Hunter panicked, sent you before you could prepare a larger party."

Curse him! What does he do, read minds? "My Weroance does not panic! We did not want to threaten Flat Pearl, only to give, as you would say, friendly advice."

Nine Killer drew his bow back fully again. "The advice is given—now go. Take your warriors, and don't let the sun set while your feet are still on Flat Pearl ground. I give you your life, War Chief. *Don't* make me regret it."

Nine Killer jerked a nod and the warriors behind Winged Blackbird melted away.

"There is your way out, War Chief. Leave now."

Winged Blackbird backed up, aware of a bead of sweat that trickled down his temple and over his painted cheek. They might have come quickly, but now they left at a run.

"Close, wasn't it?" Blood Berry asked, running easily at Winged Blackbird's side.

"Very."

"What will you tell the Weroance when we return?"

"Just what happened—and that we delivered his message."

"And then?"

"That will be up to the Weroance, and the Mamanatowick. But look about you carefully, Blood Berry. I don't think this is the last we've seen of Flat Pearl territory."

"Then, Nine Killer might indeed live to regret letting us go?"

"To use his words, if you were a gambler, you'd best not bet against it."

The last thing Nine Killer needed was to have Copper Thunder trotting down the trail at the head of his warriors, but here he came, arrogant as a rutting bull elk. The Great Tayac looked fearsome, the cloud-filtered light giving his gruesome tattoos a threatening appearance. Maybe that was why the far-off Serpent Chiefs liked to wear that forked-eye design. It made them appear less than human. The copper spike in the Great Tayac's war club looked bloody in the dappled shadows cast by the trees.

"What news, War Chief?" Copper Thunder asked, slowing to a walk. His warriors glanced around curiously at the men who stood vigilantly on each side of them.

Nine Killer scuffed the leaf mat with his toe. "Oh, a great deal of news."

"You have found the girl?"

"She is a woman, Great Tayac. Red Knot. And, no, we haven't found her."

Copper Thunder lifted his heavy war club. "Then why are you standing here? It would seem that if a search is being conducted, your men should be spread out. Searching.''

"I'm waiting to make sure that my scouts don't report that Winged Blackbird has doubled back."

"Winged Blackbird?" Copper Thunder's lips pressed into a hard line. "I don't like riddles, War Chief."

"No? Great Tayac, I've just intercepted a war party from White Stake Village. These warriors were under the command of Winged Blackbird. He works for the Weroance, Corn Hunter, of White Stake Village. Corn Hunter is Water Snake's brother. It seems that Winged Blackbird was sent with a message for Hunting Hawk. The Mamanatowick doesn't want you marrying Red Knot. I'm to deliver that message to Hunting Hawk."

The faintest of smiles bent Copper Thunder's lips. "That fast, eh?"

"You and Hunting Hawk have shaken the hornets' nest, and the insects are buzzing."

"This was a large party?"

"Two tens. Yellow Net's daughter was out gathering wood and saw them skulking along the bottom of the ridge." He pointed downhill with his bow. "I caught him just yonder."

"And you let him go?" Copper Thunder's face darkened as if a mighty rage were brewing.

Nine Killer planted his bow firmly before him. "I did."

"In the name of the gods, *why*?"

"I am not *your* War Chief." Nine Killer peered into those dark, dangerous eyes. He might have looked into a black abyss, the sort that sucked the soul right out of a man's body. "I serve Greenstone Clan, and Flat Pearl Village. Not you."

A deep guffaw boomed up from the Great Tayac's belly. With that he smacked Nine Killer on the shoulder. The blow would have rocked a lesser man on his heels.

"You're a worthy one, War Chief. I hope Hunting Hawk knows your value."

"She does." Nine Killer noticed that Copper Thunder's warriors had relaxed. Some even smiled.

Copper Thunder gave him a knowing grin. "We understand each other, you and I. Yes, I think we do. Now, tell me, warrior to warrior, why let the enemy go?"

"I know him. Winged Blackbird is better demoralized than dead. He'll report back to Corn Hunter that the message was delivered, and they'll both be shaken. Corn Hunter did this thing on his own—rushed it—and sent his warriors unprepared against us. He will hesitate before informing the Mamanatowick of his action. Whereas an ambushed messenger can stir a rage for revenge that can fire men's souls into action regardless of consequences."

Copper Thunder stared down the ridge toward where the encounter had occurred. "Such a shame to just let them go."

"Perhaps, but the important thing is what they take with them. None of those twenty will want to come back. If someone orders them to, they will return with half-empty hearts."

A malicious gleam entered Copper Thunder's dark eyes. "Yes, well, let's get on about finding my wife, shall we?"

The Great Tayac strode away, directing his warriors to fan out in a search pattern.

Nine Killer took a deep breath. How curious that Copper Thunder talked about killing with a great deal more passion than he talked about Red Knot.

I need to find Red Knot, put her in Copper Thunder's canoe, and have this over with!

He lifted his bow and gestured his warriors forward. "Come along. Let's find Red Knot."

Four

Flat Willow stood slowly, his gut twisting as he smacked the damp leaves from his hands. Around him the midday forest was oddly quiet. In the distance, he could hear men's voices, but for once the implications didn't settle into his mind. The only thing more hideous than murder was incest.

He leaned against the smooth trunk of the great beech tree. Death wasn't new to him—he'd dealt enough of it to animals, and even to men, during the last war with the Water Snake's warriors.

"Why did you climb up here again?" he asked himself absently.

Because she was the center of my dreams. He closed his eyes and took a deep breath, knowing he shouldn't have come back to the ridgetop. Better to have continued stalking the deer. He opened his eyes, fixing the scene in his soul: She lay sprawled on her face, one arm thrown out, her right leg bent at the knee. The left leg was straight. Her long black hair was piled over her head in a tangle. Leaves had been hurriedly tossed over the corpse with some pulled away around her head, as if by a hasty hand.

The left side of her skull had been crushed, and the wound had bled profusely. Smudges on her skin showed where High Fox's fingers had rested on her cheek.

"Why, Red Knot?" he asked. "Why did this have to

happen to us? I had it fixed, you see. It was the only way I could have you.''

The thoughts wouldn't quite come together. He forced himself to see her murder as an unattached hunter would: perplexing. An enemy warrior would have taken her captive for a slave. A vengeance killer would have left her out in the open to be found by her relatives: insult to repay injury. Nothing had been cut from her body for a trophy: no scalp taken, no fingers or ears cut off.

Bending down, he carefully lifted her deerskin apron from her rounded buttocks. Like most women, she'd plucked her pubic hair, and her vulva was exposed by the lifted right leg. He touched the dribble of moisture with a fingertip and sniffed it.

Urine, and not the slightest tang of semen; proof a man hadn't been inside her. As to the urine, her bladder had relaxed in death. He'd seen enough of that from the deer he'd killed.

He dropped her apron and squinted at her right hand. It clutched something he hadn't noticed before. He lifted her stiff arm from the leaves and pried a bunched necklace from the stiffening fingers. A stone shark's tooth, carefully drilled, hung from a leather cord. To either side were four drilled pearls, and to either side of those, a series of polished shell beads.

Odd, he couldn't remember the necklace. Where did it come from? Did Red Knot ever wear a necklace like this one? Did anyone in the Flat Pearl Village?

High Fox! Flat Willow smiled in satisfaction.

With care, he replaced the necklace, then collected leaves and spread them over the bloody girl's corpse, letting them sift down naturally. Then he did the same where Red Knot had been dragged, leaving just enough sign that an experienced tracker could work out the trail.

He glanced down the slope at the tracks the girl had made climbing. From the depth and the imprint even the blind could see that she'd come up this way from the inlet below, skirted the giant beech, and started across the ridge.

Walking to one side, he followed her probable path across the flat ridgetop. Here and there, the leaves were depressed, as they would have been by moccasined feet.

There, midway across the ridge, the leaves were disturbed. He studied the bloody leaves thoughtfully, and walked to one side to collect more leaves. These he carefully strewed over the coagulated blood, hiding it from view.

Circling again, he considered the mashed leaves at the base of the walnut just off the trail. Carefully plucking them aside, he found the faint smudge in the leaf mat that might have been a moccasin print. This, he left uncovered for easy discovery. The bark had several small scars on it where it had been picked at with a thumbnail. Flat Willow picked at it some more.

A pace from the tree he found a chewed twig of sassafras branch. He lifted it to his nostrils, sniffing the faint tang. Search as he might, he could see nothing else out of place. The walnut, witness to it all, could offer no more clues.

Flat Willow crossed the ridgetop, and stared down the trail that led to Oyster Shell Landing. High Fox's toe prints marked the earth. He'd climbed up the trail, and made wilder scrapes as he'd charged back down in headlong flight.

Flat Willow chuckled to himself, grinning, and shook his head. *By Okeus, High Fox, you haven't the sense of a rock.*

Fingering his bow, he turned again, staring at the blanket of leaves that covered the ridge. No one had a keener eye than he. The story read plainly enough. Red Knot had come climbing up from the west, and High Fox from the east. They had met—and he'd killed her before turning to flee.

"See anything?" a voice called from down the ridge. "No," came a more distant cry. Then, "Red Knot!"

Do I want to be the one to find her body? Or should I just walk away? Where is my best interest?

Flat Willow smiled grimly and cupped his hands around his mouth. "Up here! Come quickly! I've found Red Knot—and she's been *murdered*!"

Hunting Hawk waited at the opening of the palisade, watching the warriors bring Red Knot down the forested trail. Her arms and legs had been lashed unceremoniously to a meat pole. Her head was hanging, her hair dragging the ground, the long black locks matted with blood and dust. Her mouth slack, eyes half-open, she stared dryly at the empty sky. Whispering people clustered in a knot behind Hunting Hawk, unwilling to press too close.

Only Shell Comb stood beside her, a gray pallor in her attractive face. She had gone rigid, as if a snake had coiled its smooth length around her flesh. Her hands were clenched into tight fists, the muscles of her jaw bunched. Something indescribable burned behind her eyes: a desperate shining that radiated pain and horror outward from the soul. She teetered, every muscle rigid, as if her balance was suspect, and she hovered on the verge of collapse.

Well, at least Shell Comb looked as a Weroansqua should during such a time of trial. Hunting Hawk lifted her chin, forcing her gaze to the procession winding through the stubble and stumps of the fields. The grisly burden swung with each step.

Nine Killer led the way, a thunderous darkness in his

expression. Oh yes, Hunting Hawk knew that look well—
and it boded no good for Flat Pearl Village.

What does he know? What does he suspect?

Behind Nine Killer, the warriors marched, fingering
strung bows. To a man they glanced uneasily back at the
forest. In the rear walked Copper Thunder, with his warriors in a tight cluster. They spoke in low tones. Nothing
in their manners reassured her.

*This is going to be complicated, like an onion, layers
upon layers.* She pondered Quick Fawn's frightened report of White Stake warriors skulking in the woods. Who
knew what mischief they might have committed had the
warriors not been out beating the bush? Each new element uncovered on this grim morning flared like a spark
near thatch.

She shifted, refusing to wince at the pain in her hips
and lower back. Standing always hurt these days.

It wouldn't be long now before she was laid up in the
House of the Dead. They'd slice her withered belly open,
extract her intestines and organs. With great care Green
Serpent would skin her carcass and tan her wrinkled skin.
Her bare corpse would lie there, drying and decompos-
ing, until Green Serpent directed Lightning Cat and
Streaked Bear to pluck the last of the slack brown meat
from her bones. After that, they would stretch her tanned
skin over her dried skeleton, stuff her with grass, and
sew the hide together.

Amid great ceremony, she would be laid up with the
rest of her ancestors, venerated and worshiped, her spirit
providing leadership and protection for the village, guid-
ance and inspiration for Shell Comb and other successors.

*And when my ghost meets the others, what will they
say? How will they deal with me?* Her lips twitched uncomfortably. What could a pack of ghosts do to hurt another of their kind? If they decided to punish her, what
remedy could they inflict?

You're a silly old woman. The things you've done had to be done. Flat Pearl remained independent, a leader among the Fish River villages. Greenstone Clan was respected the length and breadth of Salt Water Bay. No matter what crimes she'd committed, those results spoke for themselves.

She glanced at Shell Comb, noting the woman's steely determination: she stood by force of will, her face like a mask, as her daughter's body was borne toward her.

Perhaps Shell Comb had finally come to understand the responsibility of becoming Weroansqua. For once, she acted like a leader, stoic, a model for her people. Only by knowing Shell Comb as she did did Hunting Hawk sense the underlying brittleness. But then, that which was brittle didn't mar or dent. It snapped. With time, however, provided it didn't break catastrophically, it might temper into a tough resilience.

There is hope, after all. Hunting Hawk almost sighed with relief—would have, but for the solemnity of the occasion.

Nine Killer crossed the beaten dirt to stand before her, face expressionless, as if carved from wood.

"What happened out there?"

Nine Killer drew a deep breath, filling his broad chest. He held it for a moment to still his inner turmoil. "A busy morning, Weroansqua. We began our search for Red Knot. As we worked up the neck, young Quick Fawn came running to tell us that enemy warriors were approaching. I quietly recalled my men, and laid a trap—into which Winged Blackbird obligingly walked. Finding himself somewhat at a disadvantage, he told me he was on a peaceful mission, bearing a message to you from his Weroance."

"And that was?"

"The Weroance of White Stake Village wished to delicately express his displeasure at the idea of our marrying

Red Knot to the Great Tayac. In short, Weroansqua, Corn Hunter must have heard that Red Knot had become a woman. He panicked, and sent Winged Blackbird to try and talk you out of it."

Hunting Hawk glanced sidelong at Shell Comb to gauge her reaction. Her daughter's eyes glinted. Good—she was thinking, using her head for something besides grief.

"I see." She gestured to where two warriors still supported the pole with Red Knot's body. "And this?"

"The White Stake killed her, didn't they?" Shell Comb called out stridently. "They murdered my daughter to keep her from marrying the Great Tayac!" She stepped forward, a fist raised. "For this, they shall pay dearly!"

Hunting Hawk bit off a growl. Well, it was too much to expect her impetuous daughter to change completely. She asked, "Before we get too carried away, and charge off to war, would you finish your report, War Chief?"

Nine Killer glanced uneasily at Shell Comb, and said, "After turning Winged Blackbird away, I sent several scouts to follow him, insuring he didn't double back. After that, I resumed my search for Red Knot. It was then that young Flat Willow called out. It was he who found the body."

"Flat Willow?" Hunting Hawk searched out the youth hanging back among the others.

Flat Willow hesitantly stepped forward, and glanced around uncomfortably. He shifted from foot to foot, then bowed his head, looking cowed.

"You found her, Flat Willow?"

"Yes, Weroansqua. I was hunting. I'd have never gone up on the ridgetop, but for High Fox. He made me miss my shot . . . lost my arrow . . . and the deer ran . . . and . . ."

"High Fox!" Black Spike cried, stepping out from the

crowd. "Are you talking about *my* son!"

Flat Willow flashed the Three Myrtle Weroance a side-long look. "As you say . . . your son."

Black Spike started forward, and was barely restrained by a kinsman's hand.

"Easy, Black Spike," Hunting Hawk said. "We'll get to the bottom of this. No accusations have been made." She stepped forward, placing a hand on Flat Willow's shoulder. "Slow down, boy. Take your time. Relax now, and tell it slowly."

Hunting Hawk watched the young man lick his lips and lock his legs; worried eyes met her stare. With deliberate concentration, he told of his morning hunt, of the spooked deer, and High Fox charging down the trail. He related High Fox's odd words. Then he told how he had finally given up finding his lost arrow, and backtracked High Fox to the ridgetop.

"But I don't think High Fox killed her!" Flat Willow shot a measuring look at Black Spike. "He wouldn't! He *loved* her!"

A gasp came from the crowd. Shell Comb had fire dancing in her eyes. Black Spike broke free of the restraining hand and took a step forward, shoulders bunched, veins standing out on his arms. "What are you saying, hunter?"

Copper Thunder stood with his muscular arms crossed, a neutral expression on his face, but those crafty black eyes betrayed the thoughts racing within his skull.

"It was the White Stake raiders!" Shell Comb stepped to place herself between Flat Willow and Black Spike. "The lying vermin stopped the marriage, all right. They killed her—and then sought to appear here and misdirect us! We *can't* let this pass! The sooner we strike, the better. Before they prepare!"

Copper Thunder's eyebrow rose in the faintest surprise.

Hunting Hawk hitched around on her walking stick. "And your thoughts on this, Great Tayac?"

Copper Thunder gave Shell Comb a flat stare and said, "For the moment, I'll reserve my judgment. We've seen at least two sides to this trouble. I wonder how many more will turn up now that the anthill has been kicked."

Black Spike stepped forward, a fist clenched. "And what of my son?"

"We don't know yet." Hunting Hawk studied his strained face. He looked terrified, and angry.

Turning back to Red Knot's swaying body, Hunting Hawk asked, "How did she die?"

"A blow to the head, Weroansqua." Nine Killer bent down to pull the blood-clotted hair back from the side of the girl's head. "She was struck here, the blow powerful enough to crush the skull. If you feel, the bone broke inward, into her brain. She must have died instantly."

"Was anything found near her?"

Nine Killer held up a necklace from which dangled a shark's tooth, pearls, and shell beads. "This, Weroansqua. Flat Willow says he found it in her right hand."

Black Spike made a strangled sound, and turned rapidly away, calling out, "I've had enough of this! My people and I are leaving!" Eyes glittering, he pointed at Hunting Hawk. "If you wish more of me, or my people, Weroansqua, you come with your warriors to get it!"

Hunting Hawk watched him stalk away, gesturing angrily at the rest of his people, and a sick sensation deadened her heart. Three Myrtle had been her staunchest ally over the years. Granted, High Fox was Black Spike's son, but how could a simple shark's tooth drive such a wedge between them?

She took a step, ready to hobble after him, but Shell Comb's hand caught her by the shoulder. "Let him go, Mother. This is a shock, that's all. Let him settle down, and we'll send him a message clearing his son."

Hunting Hawk shot an inquisitive look at her daughter. "Will we? If you ask me, young High Fox is the most likely culprit here."

Shell Comb lifted her chin. "Is he? When the forest is crawling with White Stake warriors? Come, Mother, let's be realistic. Who has the most to gain here? Water Snake, that's who. Look at what he's done! With one murder he's stopped a marriage and alliance between us and the Pipestone Clan. He's strained a friendship that goes back generations between us and Three Myrtle— our clan brothers! If this isn't a master stroke, what is?"

"And you think we should go to war with White Stake over it?"

"Yes!" Shell Comb stepped up to Copper Thunder, searching his eyes. "And what of you, Great Tayac? This is a slap to your face, as well as ours. Corn Hunter has killed your wife! Done it with impunity! Are you willing to just stand there and take it, or will you join us in bringing this beast to his knees?"

Copper Thunder seemed nonplussed. "For the moment, I will bide my time, wait and see. If it appears that this petty Weroance did indeed kill my Red Knot, then I shall act. But in my own good time, and in a way he, and his Mamanatowick, will regret in this life and the next."

Hunting Hawk fingered her chin. The Three Myrtle villagers who were leaving shoved their canoes out into the water and piled in. In shocked silence they set their paddles and stroked away, the Vs of their wakes spreading behind them.

Something is not right here. She felt as if she were looking at a broken pot, and half the pieces were missing.

"Nine Killer," she called, "do you think the White Stake warriors did this to us?"

"No, Weroansqua!" But just as soon as he said it, he cast a wary glance at Shell Comb, looking for all the world as if he'd like nothing more than to retract that statement. Lamely, he added, ''At least, it doesn't seem likely. Winged Blackbird's war party could have caught her, killed her, and left no trace. Skilled as they are. But it doesn't feel right.''

Hunting Hawk motioned the two uneasy warriors holding Red Knot's body. ''Take my granddaughter to the House of the Dead. Tell . . . tell Green Serpent to smoke her, but to do nothing more until I tell him to.''

''Yes, Weroansqua,'' Flying Weir said reverently, and he and Squirrel trotted off with their swaying burden.

''Mother!'' Shell Comb wheeled, fire in her eyes. ''Are we going to—''

''Enough!'' She made a chopping with her hand. ''We will do nothing until I have considered all sides to this thing! Unlike you, girl, I must think before I act! A policy I expect you to begin to emulate. That, or Okeus help us, you'll be a slave washing Water Snake's pots within a week of my death!''

Turning from her horrified people, she waddled painfully for her Great House. She had to sit, to think, to try and see the correct path through this madness. Otherwise, it would destroy them all.

Five

High above the winter forest, two black dots wheeled through the lavender rays of dusk. Sun Conch tucked her bright feather cape around her drawn-up knees, and tipped her chin to watch them. They must be eagles down from the north. They spiraled, their lazy flights the only movement in the gleaming bowl of the sky.

As Night Woman gathered the world in her arms, the cold deepened. Sun Conch shivered. The woodpile sat to her right, on the north side of the fire, and just beyond it stood the doorway to her mother's house. As she reached for more wood, her eyes strayed to the entry. The grass-thatched longhouse flickered orange in the jumping light of the flames. Whispers seeped around the curtain—her mother's voice low and forlorn, her aunt's angry.

"Panther take her!" Aunt Threadleaf's old voice hissed. "She's shamed us! Her punishment must be severe!"

Sun Conch placed the branch in the fire and watched the sparks crackle and dance as they climbed into the evening sky. The Panther, a powerful witch, lived by himself on an island in the bay. Curses spoken in his name were said to fly like arrows to his ears, and cause him to cast spells upon the person cursed. That's why people only uttered them in the most dire situations.

Sun Conch stared sightlessly at the flames, and wondered what to do. High Fox had promised to run off with Red Knot. What did it matter now that Sun Conch had thrown herself at him, that she had pleaded for him to marry her?

"We should outcast her for a time. Let her think on—"

"No, no," her mother said. "I don't think we need to be so harsh."

"Then a good beating is definitely in order. She can't go on like this. I will not tolerate this defiance of clan, family, and tradition!"

A cold pain, like an icicle, pierced Sun Conch's heart. She gazed out across the plaza. The shaggy houses of Three Myrtle Village stood silent, blue curls of smoke rising from the smoke holes in their roofs. A palisade, an oval wall of upright posts twice the height of a man, surrounded the village. Within it, nothing moved. Nothing breathed. Even the eagles had vanished from the night sky, leaving her more alone than she had ever been in her four and ten Comings of the Leaves.

While most of the village had gone to attend the Newly Made Woman ceremony at Flat Pearl Village, Sun Conch and her family had been ordered to remain here. Black Spike had been disgusted by Sun Conch's behavior. He'd declared before the entire village that his son, High Fox, had done nothing to encourage "such an embarrassing incident." All the while, High Fox had stood at his father's side with his head bowed, and his whole anguished heart in his dark eyes.

She had hurt for him. And for herself. How could she have done that? Just blurted out her feelings in the middle of a plaza filled with people?

"You know why." She mouthed the words so no one would hear.

He'd told her the night before that he would not allow his precious Red Knot to marry the old man her Greenstone Clan had promised her to. He'd said he was going to run away with her, run all the way to the Father Water if necessary, and never return.

Desperation had wrenched Sun Conch. She'd had to tell him, no matter the cost.

Her aunt's hoarse whispers grew more insistent, and tears blurred Sun Conch's eyes. She pulled a stick from the woodpile and prodded the fire. Blue flames flickered through the orange, like the fluttering of bluebird wings. Stalwartly, she kept her tears at bay. She would not cry. Not ever again. The only time tears did any good was when someone was there to comfort them.

"Did you know of this?" Aunt Threadleaf asked.

"That she had taken to the Weroance's son? Such arrogance! How could she think that she, a plain-faced potter's daughter, could marry into that family?"

Sun Conch shoved her stick into the fire and watched it burn.

Her feelings for High Fox had started to change two Comings of the Leaves ago, after his Blackening. High Fox had been reborn a man, and his steps had turned lighter, his smile more teasing. He had looked at Sun Conch strangely, his eyes suddenly luminous, and she had heard his unspoken words as if he'd shouted them. He could not speak for her until she had become a woman—but his eyes had promised that he would.

Then, at last summer's solstice celebration, his attention had shifted to the beautiful Red Knot, granddaughter of the Weroansqua, Hunting Hawk, of Flat Pearl Village. Red Knot's status had matched his own. Though not yet a woman, Red Knot had taunted High Fox like one, running her hands over High Fox's muscular arms, smiling up at him as if he knew more than First Woman herself. Sun Conch had hated her for it, but she'd done nothing. Perhaps if she had . . . maybe he . . . maybe . . .

She clenched handfuls of her feather cape. "You are a fool," she said, barely audible. "He loved her. Not you. He never loved you."

The wind shifted, bathing her face with the fragrance of cedar smoke; it spun before her soft brown eyes and, in the eddies, she saw High Fox's face, as it had been two days ago, the shining light gone, replaced by a soul-deep ache. She had seen that look before, the day his beloved dog had limped into the village after being attacked by a bear, and High Fox had had to brain him with his war club.

Her mother's voice pleaded, "Do you not recall your first love, Threadleaf? The terrible pain and longing? I do. I—"

"You did not humiliate your clan! You waited until you stepped out of the menstrual hut for the first time before making your love for Windsong known. And then, you told me, and I told the clan. We went to speak for you! You knew your place, your duties. Sun Conch knows nothing."

Aunt Threadleaf pushed back the door curtain and glared out at her. She had a fat, deeply wrinkled face with white-filmed eyes that had always struck fear into Sun Conch's heart. Red images of birds painted her deer-hide cape.

"Come closer, girl," Threadleaf demanded.

Sun Conch obediently rose, and went to kneel less than two hands away. "I am here, Aunt." Her normally deep voice came out shrill.

"Did you couple with him?"

Sun Conch's lips parted in shock. For a moment she could only stare at Threadleaf in mute disbelief, then she sputtered, "Wh-what? I am not yet a woman! Do you think I would—"

From inside the house, her mother said, "Threadleaf, for the sake of the Spirits! She is a child and High Fox knows it. Do you think he wishes to die? He would never risk—"

Aunt Threadleaf swung around to scowl through the entry. "Do not tell me what a young man will risk when his loins are aching. I, of all people, know. I birthed eight sons."

When Threadleaf turned back, she lifted a brow and slowly, deliberately, examined Sun Conch, her filmy eyes moving from Sun Conch's fringed moccasins to her pale face. When she spoke, her voice cut like finely flaked chert. "Well, you aren't much to tempt a man, I will give you that. Now. Tell me again, niece, what happened between you and High Fox? Did he toy with your affections? Or did you chase him like a weasel in heat?"

"I-I told you!" she answered frantically. "We are friends. We have always been. I started to love him—"

The force of the blow slammed Sun Conch to the ground. She landed hard, clawing and spitting dirt. Blood filled her mouth. When she tried to sit up, her vision swam in a sickening blur.

"Threadleaf!" her mother cried. "Get out of my way! What have you done?"

Sun Conch forced herself to stand, and stumbled across the plaza toward the passage that led out of the palisade. Her legs shook. She had not eaten since the "incident," and felt hollow, her soul floating like dandelion seeds aloft on an icy breeze.

One of the village dogs saw her, and starting barking. She ran.

"*Sun Conch!*" Aunt Threadleaf shouted. "Get back here. I order you to return!"

She glanced over her shoulder at her aunt and mother standing beside the fire. They both wore knee-length deerhide capes over their frayed mantles. Her mother's expression was tortured, and that, more than anything else, tore Sun Conch's heart. She rushed ahead, her moccasins flying over the frozen soil of the plaza. The darkness had strengthened, the birds gone silent. The forest beyond the palisade stood quiet as death.

"Sun Conch?" her mother called. "Please! Come back!"

Sun Conch hurried out through the narrow passage between the overlapping courses of posts and into the open.

The towering winter-bare trees seemed to lean over her, limbs swaying back and forth, rustling and murmuring with the night wind. She took the damp, leaf-clotted trail to the inlet. The faint howls of wolves sounded in the distance, calling to each other across the rolling hills.

She forced herself to slow down. Roots and rocks thrust up in the trail. If she fell and hurt herself, she would have to call for help, and she would rather plunge a deer bone dagger into her own heart.

All her life, she had wanted nothing more than to be a warrior and to marry High Fox. She had dreamed of taking the war trail with him, of their protecting each other during the day, and twining their bodies at night. Now none of that would be. High Fox was gone, and her aunt would insure that her clan never allowed her to take up weapons.

You should go down to the inlet, steal a canoe, and leave. If it weren't for Mother...

A mournful sound worked its way up Sun Conch's throat. She clapped a hand to her mouth to stifle it. She had been born a weak child. Until two Comings of the Leaves ago, her mother had spent half of every day tending to Sun Conch's illnesses and moods, making excuses for her ineptness at games, or her inability to work hard, protecting her from the torments of the other children— and now this.

And you thought you could be a warrior? You can't even leave your mother! the voice inside her mocked.

The moon's pale gleam penetrated the branches, and silver triangles danced across the trail at Sun Conch's feet. She broke into a headlong run.

This was her fault. All of it. If she had become a woman, perhaps High Fox wouldn't have been forced to look elsewhere for companionship, or if she'd been more beautiful and exotic, like Red Knot, maybe he would have loved her instead. But, no, the forever plodding and practical Sun Conch did not know how to flirt or flaunt. For that matter, she didn't know how to do anything without thinking about it extensively first. At least not until two days ago.

And that one act might have ruined her life.

She sprinted onto the beach, stopped, and bent over to

catch her breath. The cold air smelled of frozen mud and fish. The water shone like rippled slate in the moonlight, patterned by the breeze. To her left, seven canoes rested, drawn up on shore, their painted hulls reflecting silver.

And now you've run away from Aunt Threadleaf. You know what's waiting for you when you go home, don't you? The worst beating you've ever had in your whole life. Everyone in Three Myrtle Village would hear it, and by the end of the moon, everyone in the Independent villages from Duck Creek to Oyster Inlet would have talked about it.

And you wanted to be a warrior? Sun Conch straightened. The irregular inlet stretched about ten tens of body lengths across. Trees whiskered the dark banks. Her gaze followed the moonlit waves rolling in to lap softly at the shore, and she wondered about High Fox. Had he and Red Knot escaped? Were they even now on their way to the Father Water and the legendary cities of the Serpent Chiefs? For many Comings of the Leaves Sun Conch had listened to the Traders' stories of the Father Water country. They described glorious man-made mountains, and houses the size of her entire village. She had smiled at them at first, but she'd heard so many Traders tell the same stories that she'd started to half-believe them. And they'd brought things back. Copper ornaments, and magnificent shell gorgets etched with the frightening and wondrous image of a Bird Man, his wings spread, his man's eyes staring out at her as if to melt her soul. She remembered High Fox turning one particularly intricate gorget over and over in his hands, his mouth open in awe.

"Blessed gods, I miss him. If only I had . . ."

Movement caught her eye. She whirled in time to see someone rise up from the belly of a canoe. Like a silhouette cut from windblown shadows, it wavered; then she saw a hand grab unsteadily for the hull.

"Sun Conch?" a wavering voice called. "Is that you?"

Stunned, she stood like a wooden statue. It could not be . . . She took a step toward him, and her pulse pounded in her ears. *"High Fox?"*

"Oh, thank Okeus." He scrambled from the canoe and started toward her. "Sun Conch, the dark god himself must have sent you here. I've been hiding since late afternoon, waiting for Night Woman to smother the light. I was coming to you. You were the only one I could think of. The only one I could trust."

He threw his arms around her and drew her against him in a grip that drove the air from her lungs. He had seen eight and ten Comings of the Leaves, and stood two heads taller than Sun Conch. Her face rested in the middle of his greased chest. She could smell the musty tang of his sweat, and something else, something fetid, like the stench of old blood.

She pushed back to look up at him. His perfect oval face, with its pointed nose, bore streaks of dirt. Confused, she stammered, "Wh-what are you doing here? I thought—"

"I know, but . . ." His voice went tight. "She's dead."

Sun Conch stared openmouthed. "Who? Who is?"

He dropped to his knees, grabbed Sun Conch around the waist, and buried his face in her feathered cape. The desperate choking sound he made terrified her. "Blessed Okeus," he said, "my pretty girl. My Red Knot. She's dead! Murdered."

For a long moment Sun Conch couldn't speak. Elation mixed obscenely with sadness—sadness that the young, beautiful Red Knot had been killed, and elation that High Fox had come running home to her. The emotions fused so completely they seemed one. Then High Fox looked up and she saw tears glimmering on his cheeks. She swiftly knelt in front of him. "What happened?"

"It—it started at the dance. Copper Thunder, he—he watched Red Knot like a wolf on a blood trail. I couldn't stand it, Sun Conch. I waited until I could get Red Knot alone, then I—I . . ." He fell into broken sobs, and clutched at Sun Conch's cape as though it were a rope thrown to a drowning man.

"I'm here, High Fox," she soothed. "I'm right here. Now, tell me. All of it. What did you do?"

"I convinced her to run away with me!" he cried, his eyes swimming. Words poured out, rapid, often broken. "But someone must have overheard. We . . . I—I don't know who. I saw no one, but he must have decided to stop her, and he—oh, gods." High Fox leaned forward and braced his forehead against hers. "It's my fault. I killed her, Sun Conch! I did it."

Sun Conch went white and her eyes widened in horror. "You . . . you killed her? You—"

"No!" He stared down at her and a driving fear invaded his voice. "Don't you accuse me! I didn't do it! I—I tell you, I didn't. She was dead when I found her. Just sprawled there. Blood . . her blood was everywhere." He looked down at his right hand, and shivered.

His fingers dug into Sun Conch's shoulders like eagle's talons, and Sun Conch had to grit her teeth to keep from crying out. She said, "Of course you didn't kill her. You could never do such a thing to . . . to someone you loved, High Fox. I know that. Now, let me go. You're hurting me."

As if realizing his strength for the first time, he released her and took a step back, his dark eyes huge. "Oh, Sun Conch, forgive me. I didn't mean to harm you. Never you. You are the only one I trust." He shook his clenched fists. "Help me, Sun Conch. You must help me. Please. I beg you!"

She forced a calm into her voice that she did not feel.

"I will do anything you ask me to. You know I will. But you must explain to me *exactly* what happened. I don't understand any of this."

He threw up his hands. "I don't either, I . . ." He blinked and abruptly frowned at her mouth. "You—you're bleeding. Your mouth. What—"

"It's nothing," she answered. "Forget about it."

"What happened? It looks like—"

"I fell, High Fox. I was running through the forest to get here. It was dark. It was a stupid thing."

His brows lowered as if he knew she was lying. "Did someone strike you?" Anger tinged his voice. "Who? Why? Is this part of your punishment for daring to say you loved me, for—"

"Let it go!" she ordered. "Please, High Fox. We have more important things to discuss. Do you think Greenstone Clan killed her for trying to run away with you? For ruining their alliance with the great Copper Thunder?"

"I do not know. Truly. They might have, but I told no one except Red Knot what I had planned. I—"

"You told me."

"Of course," he whispered, and a small smile turned his lips. "You are my best friend."

All the misery she'd been holding inside for two days suddenly flooded to the surface. "And you are mine, High Fox. I missed you so much, I thought I would die."

He took her hands in a crushing grip. "It's all right. Everything is going to be fine. You just need to help me think this through. I'm lost, Sun Conch. They—" His voice dropped to a whisper. "Sun Conch, they will think I did it."

"How could they, High Fox? Everyone knows you loved her."

He shook his head. "No, Sun Conch. They don't know that I loved her the way I really did. People . . . they

thought we were friends. They don't know that I . . . we
. . . Someone saw me. Running away from her dead body.
It was Flat Willow.''

A well of cold grew in Sun Conch's belly. Flat Willow
had the soul of a stalking cat. If he'd seen High Fox
running away, he would surely tell it. She pushed back
from him. ''Then you must go to your clan elders. Explain. Tell them you didn't do it. You are the Weroance's
son. They will believe you.''

He smoothed his fingers over her hand. ''My poor innocent girl. What our people think does not matter. Flat
Pearl will hunt me down. They—''

''But you didn't kill her!''

''No, but everyone saw my face that night. I looked
like a rabid dog. Blessed gods, I could not watch her
leave with that filthy old man. The thought of them together was like a swarm of biting flies in my belly. I had
to do something! But no one will understand my actions.
Don't you see? They will think I convinced her to run
away with me so that I could kill her. That if I could not
have her, I would allow no other man to.''

''Even if the people at Flat Pearl believe you guilty,
your Sun Shell Clan will not. They will protect you.''

He laughed, but the mirth quickly turned to choking
whimpers. ''Old Hunting Hawk has always hated me.
She will demand that I be turned over.''

''Your clan . . . and your father . . . will refuse.''

''Yes,'' he said. ''I know. Black Spike will refuse and
so will the Sun Shell Clan elders—it will shatter the alliance. Don't you see, Sun Conch? This murder means
war. And I—I don't know what to do. I can't think
straight.''

Moonlight streamed down, silvering his exposed skin,
and Sun Conch saw what looked like speckles of blood
on his fingers. Without realizing it, she recoiled, her heart
thundering.

High Fox seemed to know what she was thinking. He pulled his hands away. "What is it?"

"Nothing, I just . . . I—I don't feel very well. I haven't eaten in days."

His fists flexed open and closed. "I should not have come home. There is nothing for me here. I've no right to ask you for anything. Especially not after what happened two days ago. I should have stood up to my father that day in the plaza. I—"

"No, you shouldn't have!" Cheeks blazing, she said, "I do love you, High Fox, but I was wrong to say it before the people. It shamed your father to have a potter's daughter from Star Crab Clan make such a declaration about his son. You are the son of a great Weroance, whereas I—I am nothing. If you'd defended me, it would have only made things worse."

High Fox lifted his hand, and gently touched her cheek. "You may be the daughter of a potter, but you are the only true friend I've ever had. And I do love you, Sun Conch. Until I met Red Knot, I—I always thought we . . ." He took his hand away and clenched it into a hard fist. "That's what I should have told my father. That you were not to blame. I was."

Hope leapt in her veins. She laid a hand, feverish and urgent, on his arm. "We could run away, High Fox. You and I. This instant! I would go with you to the Serpent Chiefs. Please. Take me away with you!"

Tears glistened in his eyes. "My poor sweet girl. Do you think I can forget how young you are? Your clansmen would kill me, Sun Conch, and have every right to."

"Not if we leave! I—I can be your wife, High Fox. Truly, I can. If you will only let me, I promise I—"

"Please!" He squeezed his eyes closed as if in pain, and stepped backward, away from her. In the moonlight he resembled a tortured warrior. "I can't make another mistake on top of the one I've just made. Somehow, I've got to prove that I didn't do this thing.''

A gust of cold wind swept across the water and fluttered long strands of her black hair before Sun Conch's eyes. She did not have the strength to brush them away. As long as she remained a child, he would not touch her. The cold truth left her feeling sick and empty.

To hide the tremor in her hands, she tucked them beneath her arms. ''You are right, of—of course. You can't have our village against you at the same time that Flat Pearl is accusing you of murder. One enemy is enough.'' She managed to draw a breath into her lungs, and held it for a time. As she slowly let it out, she asked, ''But how can we prove that you didn't murder her?''

''We can't. Why would anyone listen to us? My father is the most powerful man in his country. He will not care what we say. Even if I were guilty, I don't think he would turn me over to Flat Pearl. It would make him appear weak in front of Hunting Hawk, and that old woman would certainly use it against him. Think, Sun Conch. I am barely a man, and one soon to be accused of murder, and you are but a child. Who would listen to us?''

Sun Conch paused uncertainly. She turned the problem before her, considering different sides, possibilities she'd never thought of before. Faces flitted through her thoughts. She rejected all but one. The only man alive who truly terrified her. ''Who would listen to us?'' she repeated absently. ''No one, perhaps. But I think I know someone they will listen to.''

''Who?''

She waved his questions away. ''We need to sit down and talk. I must know every detail of last night. Do you understand me? Everything! The expressions on people's faces, things that were said. Even if you do not think something important, I want to hear about it. High Fox, if we are to save your life, I must be able to describe your trip to and from Flat Pearl Village as if I had been there with you. I know you are weary. So am I. Are you able to do this?''

He looked at her in silence for a long time, then sat down on the moonlit sand, and through a tired exhalation said, "Tell me where to start.''

"From the moment you left the palisade with your father. What happened after that?''

High Fox scooped up a handful of damp sand, and began molding it into different shapes. "Father went a little mad. I've never seen him as red-faced and emotional as he was that day. He slammed his war club into every tree we passed, cursed me and my mother, promised to 'take care of me' when his responsibilities to the Weroansqua were over. I swear, Sun Conch, I feared to show him my back.

"When we arrived at Flat Pearl, our people split up and Father ordered me to walk at his heels in silence. I was not even allowed to speak to people I knew. Then, at the dance that night . . . blessed gods . . .'' He dropped the ball of sand and gripped handfuls of his unkempt hair. "Red Knot was so beautiful. She kept looking at me, you know, looking at me in that special alluring way, and I wondered if Copper Thunder saw, and what he might be thinking. No man misunderstands that look, especially when it's directed at another man. I thought I would explode, Sun Conch. Danger pressed in on me from all sides. My father, Hunting Hawk, Copper Thunder. Even Flat Willow stared at me with a sort of amused hatred in his eyes. I felt like a man in his first battle, desperate, afraid.''

He flung the ball of sand out into the water, and grimaced at the silver rings that bobbed outward from the splash. "Then Red Knot started dancing in front of me. Dancing for me alone . . .''

Sun Conch sat cross-legged, her feathered cape tucked beneath her, and watched the arrival of morning. The stars had faded to pale awl pricks of light, and the heavens gleamed like wet slate. She exhaled a frosty breath. The night had been cold and damp. A rim of ice crusted the shore.

High Fox lay to her left, wrapped in his blanket. His handsome face shone with the dawn. He had finished his story less than two hands of time ago, and fallen into an exhausted sleep.

As Sun Conch studied him, she twisted the softly tanned hide of her red deerhide dress into tiny peaks, then smoothed them away. He had not told her the whole truth, and she knew him well enough to be certain of it. She did not know why, but she trusted him. If he had kept some things to himself, then he must have reasons, good ones. Still, the gaps in his story left her uneasy. She kept trying to fill them in with her own imagination, which did no good at all.

Quietly, she rose to her feet, and headed down the shore toward the line of canoes. She always thought better when she was walking. Off in the distance, a huge flock of geese honked as they flew in irregular chevrons across the pink sky. Water lapped softly at the sand four hands away, and gulls rode the waves in the distance. Their feathers flashed silver whenever a wave rolled beneath them.

She shivered as she walked, for more reason than the morning air and High Fox's secrets. No one had come looking for her during the night, and in the corners of her soul she could hear her aunt's gruff voice saying, "Leave her be. A night alone in the dark and freezing cold will do our little Sun Conch some good. Perhaps it will remind her of the importance of her relatives.'' She'd heard Aunt Threadleaf say such things about other wayward girls, and Sun Conch could imagine her mother's torn expression.

She kicked at a piece of driftwood.

Usually the shore bustled with people, fishing, hunting birds, collecting wood. Today there was no one. She felt oddly as if time had frozen. As if only she and High Fox still lived, and breathed. Tracks lined the shore. She identified a deer, several birds, and a raccoon, but saw none of them. Her moccasins pressed into the icy mud of a world gone still and silent.

When she reached the canoes, she could make out folded fishing nets, and paddles. Here and there lay shell fishhooks, and harpoons. Her uncle Sawtooth's slim dugout nestled in the middle of the group of canoes. White zigzags of lightning decorated its hull. It would be the easiest for her to control. She had ridden in it many times before, and knew its quirks. It tended to pull to the right. . . .

A cry split the morning, and Sun Conch spun around.

High Fox lay on the beach breathing in short gasps, his hands clawing at the sand. Mournful sounds came from his lips, desperate sounds, like those of an animal caught in a trap.

She folded her arms and hugged herself.

He cried out again, and bolted upright, panting.

"I'm here," Sun Conch called softly, and headed toward him. "You're safe. I've been keeping watch all night, as I said I would."

High Fox seemed to deflate. His shoulders hunched forward and he rubbed shaking hands over his face. "Blessed Spirits, I—I dreamed that my father was hunting me. That he had joined forces with old Hunting Hawk to find me." He pulled his hands away and gazed at them as though he'd never seen them before. "They cut off my hands, Sun Conch. Both of them. Hunting Hawk cut them off, then my father threw them into the ocean. Wh-what an awful dream. My blood flooded our village. My entire clan drowned in it."

Sun Conch stood awkwardly, uncertain how to respond. "You didn't kill her, High Fox. No one is going to hurt you."

He exhaled hard, said, "I pray you're right," and stared out at the shining water.

"I promise you that he will come, High Fox. I will make him. Together, we will prove your innocence."

Sun Conch turned toward her uncle's dugout canoe, and High Fox got to his feet. He stood for a moment, and seemed to be bracing himself, then walked toward her.

"Sun Conch, please, go carefully. This is a dangerous task. It may cost both our lives."

"No gain comes without an equal amount of loss." She pushed the canoe off the sand and into the water.

"Wait. One moment, please." He trotted to his own canoe, and drew out his bow, war club, and quiver, then hurried back and handed them to her.

"No, High Fox. You will need your weapons, I—"

"I will make new ones." He thrust them at her. "You always wanted to be a warrior."

Sun Conch reluctantly took them, surprised by the weight of the war club. "We must hurry, High Fox. It will be light soon. My relatives will be coming down for water and wood. And the sooner we begin this journey, the sooner it will end."

"I know. I just . . ." He shifted his weight from one foot to the other, hesitating; then, as if he'd made a decision, he stepped forward and pulled her into his arms, holding her tightly. "Sun Conch, listen to me. Just for a time, don't say anything. I think sometimes that you know me better than I know myself, and so I—I'm sure you are worried that I did not tell you everything last night." She twisted in his arms, wanting to respond, but he tightened his hold, said, "Hush, please. I want you to know that I will tell you. Not now, but soon. When I can. Will you trust me?"

"I trust you. I do not understand, but I trust you. If I am your best friend, as you say, then why can't I know?"

"I can't tell anyone, Sun Conch." He stroked her hair. "I can't even talk to my own soul about it. Not yet. Perhaps in a few days I will be brave enough. Then, I will tell you."

Sun Conch sighed and nodded. "I have to go. I have much to do today. A long way to go."

He gradually slackened his hold on her, and she stepped out of his arms and turned toward her uncle's canoe. She waded out into knee-deep icy water, and pulled the canoe off the sand. It rocked and bobbed in the incoming swells.

She stepped into the boat and rested the weapons on the gunwales.

High Fox pushed the dugout into deeper water, and gave it a hard shove. "Be cautious, Sun Conch. You know he's dangerous!" he called after her. "There is no telling how he will greet you. Keep your bow ready!"

"Look for me in two days," she said, and dipped her paddle to send the slim canoe forward. "I'll meet you at the place we agreed upon."

"Sun Conch?" High Fox shouted. "You carry my soul in your hands. Hurry back to me!"

The words *to me* lingered in her heart as she guided the dugout along the shoreline, past the fields and patches of woods, and into the main channel of Fish River. Dawn's light shimmered from the green water and painted the tree-covered shores with patches of pale blue.

"I will save him," she told the gulls that fluttered

around the canoe. "He did not kill Red Knot. I know he didn't."

A big white gull dived at her, squawking and flapping its wings. When Sun Conch looked up, she found the bird peering at her through one skeptical eye.

She took two more strokes with her paddle, and inhaled a deep breath of the salty morning air. As she paddled out beyond the wide mouth of the Fish River, The Panther's island, small and wooded, made a hazy mound on the distant horizon across the choppy waters of Salt Water Bay.

Fear tickled her belly.

She glanced up at the hovering bird: a laughing gull, called that because of the strange humanlike cackles it made as it hunted the shore. People said The Panther could change himself into any animal he wished. Dog, worm, or bird. They also said he could scare a person's soul right out of her body, but the person didn't always die. Often, the terrified soul wandered the land, whimpering and thrashing tree branches, until it turned into an evil forest spirit with hollow and lifeless eyes; the person's soulless body continued to move among the living, but could no longer speak or take care of itself.

She had seen one soulless body in her four and ten Comings of the Leaves. An old man named Brightness. He'd lost his soul the previous summer. Every day after the event, his family had set him on a grass mat outside their house and, while he'd peered openmouthed at nothing, drool had dribbled down his chin. The horror still coiled in Sun Conch's belly.

Above her, the gull let out a loud laugh, and flapped away. She paddled as if being chased by enemy warriors. The canoe shot across the bay, skimming the water like a swallow.

She'd seen four Comings of the Leaves when she'd first heard of The Panther. Old Wolf Leggings, one of the Sun Shell Clan elders, had been racing through the village with a bag of salt in her gnarled hand. As she'd scattered it around the palisade, she'd whispered darkly that "The Panther" had returned. "He's making corn husk dolls of each of us," she'd said, "and witching them." That same night a big black dog had loped around the palisade, howling Wolf Leggings' name. They'd found her the next morning, dead, her fingernails clawing at the earth, as if she'd been trying to dig a way out of her house.

A cold gust of wind lifted the hair on Sun Conch's neck. She shuddered and stopped paddling. The canoe listed sideways. Aunt Threadleaf had cursed Sun Conch using The Panther's name. Had he heard?

"Panther?" she called to the fluttering gulls. "I am coming to speak with you, but I am just a girl. I mean you no harm."

The gulls cackled and dove, their wings glistening whitely against the golden background of dawn.

She steered her canoe toward the point in the distance. Despite her resolution, her gaze kept straying to the skies. Clouds hung low over the eastern shore. Never had she paddled so far, and the muscles in her arms, chest, and shoulders began to ache. She hadn't understood the immense size of the Salt Water Bay, or the terror that lurked in those long swells that raised and lowered her canoe.

Gasping and wincing at the pain in her strained body, she paddled on. She flinched at her skin blistering on the wooden paddle handle, but the sores would heal later. As she neared the low island, wind-sculpted trees crowded the shore. Shadows leapt everywhere, ghostly and indistinct, like forest spirits vying for the best position from which to view her arrival.

"I am coming, Panther!" she said. "I'm afraid. I'm very afraid. But no one is going to stop me. Not even you."

Six

The water of the bay shone like silver in the midday sun. Ducks speckled the surface and, here and there, jumping fish left ever-widening rings that interlocked and vanished into nothingness. In the distance, the western shore resembled humped gray fuzz capped by billowing clouds.

At the edge of the water, the marsh grass gave way to pebbly mudflats. He came here at low tide in mud-soaked moccasins. In one hand he carried a digging stick, in the other a leather sack.

Over his long life, he'd had many names, but now he only knew himself by the name given him by his victims: The Panther.

Periodically, he'd stop, use his stick as a lever, and pry a clam from the mud. At other times, he'd whack a skittering crab in the shallows, and drop it into his bucket with the clams.

To his left, dormant cordgrass rose in thick unbroken ranks, a vast carpet that spread to the east before finally giving way to the distant groves of trees. To his right lay the great Salt Water Bay, its spirit mysteriously quiet today.

His only company was the birds. Herons and egrets watched from a safe distance; plovers, turnstones, and sandpipers trotted out of his path, to rush in behind after he passed. Overhead, a handful of gulls soared. The old man cracked a clam's shell with the hard butt of his stick, and tossed the treat up for the squalling gulls. As they snatched the morsel in midair, he grinned, never tired of their aerial grace.

He found the place he was looking for and sloshed out into the water, as if walking straight out into the bay. The chill ate into his calves, and then his arthritic knees as the water deepened. Around him, small fish darted and churned the surface. His reflection wavered as he walked, and periodically he glanced at his distorted image. He wore his gray hair loose, letting it tumble around his shoulders in a stringy mass. A ragged breechclout hung from his lean hips, and a faded red fabric cape lay over his left shoulder, its tattered threads hanging. Panther's skin had turned grainy with age, and had loosened from the ropy muscles on his arms, legs, and belly, but his eyes remained keen, staring out from under a weathered brow. His nose, once hawkish, had grown long and curved over a flat mouth.

He had reached the oyster bed. Under his feet, the soft muck was broken by the hard, sharp outline of the oysters. He walked and the bottom rose until he was midcalf in depth. Here he peered down, prodding with his stick. Satisfied, he bent and levered up a cluster of oysters. He inspected them, grunted, and dropped them into his sack. The next cluster came with an oyster drill attached. He used a gnarled thumb to scrape the moss from the drill's shell, decided the colors were good, and dropped it, too, into his bag.

Within minutes, he'd filled his bag, slung it over his shoulder, and trudged back through the shallows. On the shore, he retraced his way northward to the small spit of dry land with its tufted trees.

A narrow path—little more than a track through cordgrass, spatterdock, and pickerelweed—marked the trail through the marsh. He stopped at a stand of wild rice, and inspected the empty awns he'd harvested earlier.

The narrow trail led to a slight rise, dry enough that

the marsh gave way to grass, brush, and finally a copse of trees. He walked into the shadows of pine, sassafras, and then into an oak grove. There, at the highest point on the island, stood his rude house. He'd built it in a small clearing, partly overhung by the spreading branches of the mighty oaks. Home consisted of a dome-shaped framework thatched with shocks of cordgrass. To either side, one to the east, the other to the west, stood even smaller huts—shrines to the twin gods, the entrances closed off with ratty deerhide hangings.

The remains of a small fire lay smoldering in a pit before the doorway. He sighed as he lowered his sack next to a huge polished log half-sunk into the earth beside the fire.

"I'm not as spry as I used to be," he told the empty air. He winced as he rotated his arm and massaged his bony shoulder. Ducking into his house, he surveyed his scant belongings. A wooden bedstead was covered by deerhides, the majority of them shedding what little hair remained. A second firepit glared up at him from the middle of the floor like a cold black eye. Net bags were tied from the roof, bulging with dried herbs, ears of corn, nuts, cordgrass seed, and wild rice. A bow stood next to the bedstead, and across from it, a stack of arrows leaned against the wall.

Panther's eyes lit on the big, round-bottomed pot. The rim had cracked and chipped off, but its corrugated surface could be seen through the smudged soot. He picked up the pot, peered inside, and rubbed the crusty interior with a callused thumb.

Ducking outside into the slanting afternoon light, he settled his pot by the smoking ashes, located the leather bag he used for water, and headed east through the trees to a small freshwater seep less than two bow shots away. Here he lowered his bag and dipped it full before returning to his house.

One by one, he washed his clams, oysters, and crabs, placing each in the round-bottomed pot. The last of the water just covered his catch.

Growling to himself, Panther bent on crackling knees to blow the coals in the fire pit to life. When he absently inhaled the swirling ash, he went into a fit of coughing.

Choking, he rocked back on his haunches, cleared his throat, and barked a harsh laugh. "And they call me a sorcerer!"

When the fire blazed, he placed three rocks in it for a tripod, and trundled his pot onto the heat. Satisfied, he watched the flames lick around the sides. The corrugated surface served to conduct more of the fire's heat to the stew.

Wistfully, he rose, reentered his house, and inspected his net bags, selecting corn from one, acorns from another, some beechnuts, and rose hips. He added these to the stew and settled himself on the log to watch dinner cook. If only he had squash to cook. He loved freshly baked squash more than anything on earth. At the thought of it, his mouth watered.

"The only thing worse than a fool is an old fool," he muttered to himself. "No, even worse than that, a *crazy* old fool, and Panther, you're that."

He scratched under his grizzled hair. "But, if *I'm* crazy, then what does a man make of the rest of the world?

"Even crazier! If it wasn't what would I be doing here?

"Avoiding it all.

"Blood and dung! I'm here for the peace."

He paused, remembering the pain, the voices inside his head, and the day he'd packed up and left the human world. "You've always been a fool.

"No, old man. Just crazy." He chewed at his lip with stubby brown teeth. "Of course, you really know you're crazy when you catch yourself answering your own questions.''

In the years since he'd come here, he'd watched the seasons come and go ten times.

A man should have answers in that amount of time. He made a face at the fire and rubbed his dry brown hands together. But did he?

At that moment, the two crows landed in the winterbare black oak above, and stared down at him with inquisitive black eyes.

''What is it?''

One of the crows looked to the west, ruffled its feathers, and cawed.

''You don't say?''

Curious, the old man rose and followed a beaten trail to the western end of his little island. The waves had cut a beach here, and the bank dropped off steeply. At the edge of the trees, he peered out against the setting sun's glare.

A young woman was paddling a canoe across the rolling water, each stroke so perfectly timed that she seemed in no hurry.

Panther eased deeper into the late-afternoon shadows and watched the slim vessel approach. The voyager seemed hesitant now. Finally, she laid the paddle across the gunwales and let the canoe drift.

Panther's old eyes hadn't dimmed enough that he missed the indecision on that pensive face.

What? Another young fool coming for a love charm? Or does she wish me to bewitch some rival? Youngsters could be such idiots. As he had once been.

A long time ago . . .

Panther waited patiently. The slim woman licked her lips, and mustered courage. She took a deep breath, committed herself, and plunged the paddle into the water to send the canoe toward the landing.

Seven

From his hiding place, Panther took stock. The young woman had long black hair and the moony face of an owl, round, with large dark eyes, and a short beak of a nose. She wore a red and blue feathered cape. One of Water Snake's, or a woman from the unallied villages?

The canoe grated on the bank, and the young woman stepped into the water and dragged her dugout ashore. As she picked up her bow from the bottom, she strung it, and hung it over her shoulder. Then she slung a quiver over the opposite shoulder, and lifted a war club that looked too big and heavy for her slight frame and thin arms. Clutching it tightly, she started forward.

Well, if she's come to kill me, best of luck. Others have tried before. And like them, this poor young fool would be cast adrift, her corpse lying in her boat. Panther had heard that some of his victims had been found. The others, he assumed, had been swept out to sea.

Panther hid behind a tree. The young woman squared her shoulders and crept stealthily up the path.

Panther frowned. Where had he left his bow? In the house most likely. Well, no matter, he knew his little island like the back of his hand. Warily, he followed her, using the trees for cover as he paralleled her trail.

Despite the years, not all of Panther's stealth had deserted him. The nervous young woman hadn't the slightest notion that the hunter was now the hunted. Glee warmed The Panther's gut.

As sure as snow in winter, the woman made her way to the little clearing and stopped to peer at his hut, the steaming pot of stew, and the leather sacks left empty by the fire.

Shivering, she glanced around for any sign of life. The fading daylight made her even more anxious as she searched the shadows.

They're not as brave as they once were. What's happened to women these days? Panther crouched behind a tangle of huckleberry bushes and watched patiently.

She calmed herself, knotted up her courage, and called, "Elder? Are you here?"

Panther stayed put, taught by the long years of solitude that all things eventually come to their conclusion. Only the young and the foolish hurried things along.

The woman walked stiff-legged now to keep her knees from buckling. She approached the domed house awkwardly, and called out again: "Elder, I am Sun Conch, of the Star Crab Clan! A girl of Three Myrtle Village! I have come to speak to you!"

A girl. Not a woman. Very curious.

One of the crows squawked in the tree, and the girl jumped half out of her skin. She wheeled around, staring at the silent forest. "Please, Elder!"

Panther remained motionless until she started pacing, bending to study the ground for tracks.

Like a ghost, Panther slipped to the back of his house and carefully lifted a section of grass matting away. He ducked inside. At the head of his bed, he found his bow, and groped about for his arrows. To his disgust, they stood canted against the wall. Picking through them, he realized they'd warped. It took a moment to find the straightest, but a mouse had chewed most of the fletching off the shaft.

His bones cracked as he strung the bow, prayed the gut string wouldn't snap, and took three tries to draw it.

Muscles straining, he stepped to the doorway and emerged behind the frantic Sun Conch.

"Drop your war club, girl!"

Sun Conch froze, every muscle knotted. For an instant, she seemed to waver between collapsing and bolting like a terrified fawn.

"I said, drop the club."

The war club slipped from her nerveless fingers to thump hollowly on the ground.

"Turn around."

Her legs almost gave way as she turned, eyes wide. Her lips moved, but no words came.

"What? I *can't* hear you!"

"You . . . you weren't there! I just . . . just . . ."

"Yes, yes, you looked, but you didn't see. Now, did you come here to kill me?"

Sun Conch shook her head so hard it might have snapped her neck.

Panther gauged the glazed fear in her eyes, the way she shook, and gratefully released the tension on his fragile bow. Every muscle sighed with relief. "Then what do you want?"

Sun Conch gulped like a fish on the bank. "To find you, Elder."

"For what? Come on, girl, how many times do I have to ask?"

"I . . . we need your help!"

As night descended and the air grew cold, Panther hunched over the fire. Sun Conch crouched opposite him, her rabbitlike eyes taking in every movement. The first stars were burning through the haze.

Night was peaceful here, except during the times when

the great storms rolled in off the ocean. Panther's house sat just high enough that the storm surge didn't wash it away, but the little stream that drained the freshwater marsh would be brackish for days afterward.

Firelight flickered on his house, the two shrines, and the overhanging branches of the oak. Panther fished around in his turtle-shell bowl for another clam, used a wooden sliver to pry the shell open, and sucked out the meat. Since his molars had fallen out years ago, clams were just right. They could be gummed enough to be swallowed.

"Now, then"—Panther wiped his lips—"just what sort of help did you have in mind?" He raised an eyebrow. "Some foolish spell or something?"

Sun Conch winced. "No, Elder. It's my friend, High Fox. He's from Sun Shell Clan. His father is Black Spike, Weroance of Three Myrtle Village. High Fox is in trouble. Terrible trouble."

"And what might this be? He can't get a woman?"

Her round face went very pale. "N-No, Elder. They think he killed her . . . I mean, well, she wasn't really his woman, but she would have been."

Panther's expression soured. "Youngster, you're flustered. I decided not to kill you, and until you give me reason to change my mind, I won't. All right? Now, why don't you start at the beginning."

Sun Conch nodded and pulled her feathered cloak closed around her throat. "Her name was Red Knot. Of the Greenstone Clan. She was the daughter of Shell Comb, and the granddaughter of Hunting Hawk, of Flat Pearl Village."

"Yes, yes, I know of Hunting Hawk. Go on." Blessed Ohona, how many years had it been since he'd seen her? How the sun had gleamed in her sleek black hair. He could remember the warmth of her smile, the way her doe-skin dress had hugged those saucy hips. They'd been enemies then. Actually, he supposed, by definition, they still were.

"Elder, High Fox loved Red Knot. They wanted to marry. But Hunting Hawk promised Red Knot to Copper Thunder, the Great Tayac."

Panther straightened, his interest perked. "He's the upstart from somewhere over the mountains, isn't he? Pipestone Clan, I've heard." *Could it be?* But no, that was years ago, and far from here.

"Yes, he is, Elder. His power and influence have been growing. He's allied the upriver villages, defeated Water Snake and Stone Frog's warriors. Some say he's not completely human."

"Gull dung, girl. They say that about me."

"Uh, yes, I—I've heard that." Sun Conch looked as if her stomach hurt.

"You were saying?"

"I was saying that Red Knot was made a woman a few days past, and Copper Thunder came to Flat Pearl Village to claim her. But she didn't want him. Red Knot and High Fox were desperate, Elder, and High Fox made this plan. He would meet her at Oyster Shell Landing, and they would run off together."

Panther caught the tightness in her voice, and saw the pain that glistened in her eyes. "That disturbed you?"

She lifted a shoulder and shook her head. "It doesn't matter now. I—"

"You love this High Fox, too."

She sat completely still.

"Answer me!"

". . . Yes, Elder."

"All right. Go on."

Heaving a breath, she said, "Anyway, High Fox left the final dance early and paddled around the neck of land to Oyster Shell Landing. Red Knot was supposed to sneak away before dawn and meet him there. She never made it. High Fox got nervous and climbed the ridge. He found her. Dead. Her head was crushed and she'd been left there. Now they . . . I mean, everyone at Flat Pearl Village believes he did it.''

''I see.''

''But he *didn't*! I know him. He's my friend! He loved her! Why would he kill her?''

''Maybe she told him she wouldn't go with him. Men have killed for lesser reasons than the passions of a thwarted heart.''

Sun Conch's expression went hard. ''No, Elder. It isn't in him to do such a thing. I swear to you, I have known him my entire life. You must believe me.''

Panther fished out another of his clams, and sucked the body from the shell. He gulped it down and cast a curious glance at her. ''I never said I didn't believe you, I just offered another explanation. People do lots of odd things for lots of odd reasons. They've too much of Okeus in their souls, and not enough of Ohona. We're silly beasts, girl, governed by even sillier ideas.''

Sun Conch lowered her eyes, and awkwardly clasped her hands. ''He is not a beast, Elder. He is a good man.''

''So, what do you want me to do, eh? Go and speak for your friend? Tell everyone he didn't do it?''

At that, Sun Conch looked up, hope bright in her eyes. ''You must, Elder. I know everyone would listen. You are The Panther. People respect you.''

Panther laughed. ''They do, do they?''

''Yes, Elder. Of all the men on earth, you are the most . . . respected.''

''Corpse rot! I am the most feared.''

She blinked. ''They are both the same, aren't they?''

''Some lot you know. Fear and respect may be aligned like two sticks of wood, but never confuse them.'' Panther devoured an oyster from his stew. ''And how do I know this High Fox didn't kill her? Just take your word for it?''

"Yes—I-I mean, no. I . . . I don't know. I give you my pledge that he didn't. Isn't that enough? Shell Comb is trying to blame Winged Blackbird, and I've heard—"

"Who? Winged Blackbird?"

"War Chief for Corn Hunter, Weroance of White Stake Village. His warriors were there the morning Red Knot was killed. He—"

"How do you know?"

"After High Fox discovered Red Knot's body, he paddled around to a wooded section of bank, hid his canoe, and sneaked up to the village. He hid until afternoon, Elder, listening to the things people said."

Panther quirked a brow. Sun Conch did not seem to realize how this act undermined her friend's story. He said, "What happened to Net Sinker? I thought he was War Chief for White Stake Village."

"He was killed two years ago by Nine Killer." Sun Conch frowned. "How long have you been out here?"

"Since this little island was water. You'll have to tell me the things I need to know. Why were Corn Hunter's warriors at Flat Pearl?"

"The Mamanatowick wanted the marriage stopped. He's no fool. Copper Thunder allying with the Independent villages is a threat to him. Water Snake's wanted us for years. And now, with Copper Thunder's influence growing . . ." She paused, her mouth open, as if she feared to say more. "Elder, if they don't blame this on High Fox, the whole country is going to explode like a sealed boiling pot. Copper Thunder, the Water Snake, and the Independent villages will tear each other apart."

"So, let them."

"Let them?" she blurted. Disbelief lined her young face. "Elder, do you know what you're saying? Tens of tens of people will die! Old people. Little children who've done nothing wrong!''

Panther's narrow-eyed glare burned through her outrage, and she shriveled like a punctured bladder.

''Girl, for the most part, people are as mindless as a school of mullet. They blunder through life with no direction, charging this way and that, muddying up the water while the crafty heron of death plucks them up one by one. I left people, and their petty squabbles, behind me a long time ago.''

Sun Conch's eyes filled with tears. ''But, Elder—''

''Don't look at me that way, girl,'' Panther ordered. ''Just why are you so anxious to save this High Fox? Because you love him? Because you think now that Red Knot is out of the way that he will marry you and ask *you* to run away with him?''

Her jaw trembled. ''I asked him, Elder. No, I—I begged him, to run away with me. He wouldn't. He's too honorable.''

The tormented expression on her face touched a part of Panther's soul that he thought long dead and buried. ''Answer my question: Why are you so anxious to save High Fox?''

Sun Conch reached out imploringly. ''Because he *didn't* do it!''

''You have *faith* that he didn't do it.''

Sun Conch's extended hands clenched to fists. ''No, Elder! Some things a person knows, down deep in the soul. This is one.'' She stared angrily across the fire at Panther. ''He didn't kill Red Knot, Elder. I *know* he didn't.'' Her brow pinched, and she said, ''What is happening is wrong—and I can't do anything about it by myself.''

Panther gazed thoughtfully at the girl. She had finally forgotten her fear, and Panther considered that for a moment. She had come here not for glory, or personal gain, or any advantage, but for the life of her friend.

"Tell me, Sun Conch, what happens to you if High Fox is blamed for this?"

She gave Panther a confused look. "I'll be very sad, Elder. It's not right. High Fox loved Red Knot more than anything. If they catch him and kill him . . ." Sun Conch placed her hands on the sides of her head, pressing as if to stop the thoughts. "If they do that, I'll see it through his eyes, live it with him. Wondering how, and why, a man could love a woman with all of his heart—and then be condemned for her murder. How would you feel, Elder, if it happened to you?"

A pain, like a bone stiletto, pierced Panther's heart. Sickness welled in his stomach. The ache, buried for so many years, slithered out from the dark place where it hid behind his bones. *Yes, you know, don't you?*

"Elder?" Sun Conch had leaned toward him, worry on her owlish face.

Panther raised a hand, hoping it didn't tremble. "It's all right, girl. Just a twinge, that's all."

For the first time in many Comings of the Leaves, his soul had been touched. "Are you human, girl, or a wicked spirit sent to torment me?"

"What?" she asked in confusion. "Human? Elder, I don't understand."

"Nothing, nothing."

"Elder, is it so wrong to do something just because it's right?"

Panther lifted his bowl and drank the liquid down to the thin coating of sand in the bottom. This he rubbed away with his fingers. "Right? As I understand the situation, if your High Fox is exonerated, Copper Thunder, Water Snake, and everyone else are going to war. Is it better to sacrifice one man to save others? Or to save one and sacrifice countless innocent people? You're the one who worried about going to war. You tell me. What is right?''

Sun Conch stared at him. Finally, she murmured, ''I don't know, Elder. Do you?''

How many years had be been wrestling with just this question? That familiar darkness stirred his soul, slithering around inside him. How did a man know what was just when even the gods themselves did not? He couldn't help but glance suspiciously at the two shrines flanking his house.

Sun Conch followed his gaze. ''What are those, Elder?''

''Come, I'll show you. Then, perhaps, you can answer your own question.'' He rose stiffly, rounded the fire, and walked to the eastern shrine. Sun Conch followed warily and took a deep breath as Panther lifted the weathered and cracked deerhide flap.

The fire cast wavering orange light into the interior. There, seated on a squat wooden frame, sat a pale statue the size of a man. Wooden offering bowls lay before him, empty.

The figure was made of wood, molded clay, and sewn hide. It was painted in white clay, but a thick black band circled the chest, its interior dotted with white spots. Sunbursts painted its cheeks in faded red. Wavering lines extended down the arms where they rested on the knees. The legs were blue, crisscrossed by irregular lines.

A patch of hair, cut from a bear's hide, covered the top of the skull, and glinted with small sections of shell. Polished oyster-shell eyes decorated the face, and gave the god a wide-eyed nacre stare. The nose was thin, straight, and painted a faded yellow. A broad mouth, the corners turned down in sadness, had been carved into the wood.

''Seen him before?'' Panther asked.

"No." But she knelt, her eyes wide in reverence, and bowed her head lest she offend the deity.

"Not many people have, girl. It's one of the things wrong with the world. All out of balance. You look upon Ohona."

Sun Conch jerked her head up, wonder in her eyes. "Greetings, Great Lord."

"Go back to the fire, girl. A skim of stew remains. Cup up a handful and bring it over here for the bowls. Ohona is hungry."

Sun Conch hastened to comply. She ran back to the fire, scooped a cupful of dregs from the bottom of the pot, and returned. Hesitantly, she let it dribble into the bowl.

"Thank you for the world you made for us, Great One," Panther intoned the old prayer. "Bless this food to your use and shed your benevolence upon us."

To Panther's surprise, Sun Conch reached beneath her cape and drew out a small twist of tobacco, which she laid before Ohona. "Thank you, Great Lord. Bless me . . . and my friend High Fox. He is blamed for something he didn't do."

Panther let the flap drop and studied Sun Conch. "Best scoop up what's left for the other one."

The fearful glance Sun Conch gave the other hut showed that she understood who the occupant must be. She went back to the pot, scraped up what was left, and met Panther at the western shrine. Panther lifted the flap to expose Okeus to the gaudy light of the fire. Painted in black, he was the opposite of Ohona. He had a white band on his chest, dotted with black. His shell eyes glimmered in the firelight, but unlike Ohona, he was smiling as if in great glee.

Sun Conch bowed low, her forehead almost touching the dirt. Cautiously, she poured the remains into the empty bowl before Okeus. Then looked up at Panther. ''Aren't you going to ask his blessing?''

''No.''

Panther let the flap drop and walked over to his fire. He settled himself on his log and picked up the boiled oyster drill. With a splinter, he coaxed the body out of the interior; then he plucked off the horny plate and popped the animal into his mouth. As he chewed, he used the corner of his breechclout to rub the moss from the shell's exterior.

Sun Conch returned slowly, glancing back and forth between Panther and Okeus' shrine.

''Sit down, girl. You're not ready for the answer yet.'' Panther squinted at the polished shell, and belched.

Sun Conch just stood, frowning.

Panther didn't even look at her. ''Why should I become entangled with this mess your friend High Fox has gotten himself into?''

After a long silence, Sun Conch said, ''I'm sure Black Spike would pay you handsomely for defending his son.''

''I see. And what could he give me that I don't already have?''

''He's the Weroance. He is paid whatever tribute he asks from his people. You could have corn, copper, tobacco, steatite, greenstone, shell, puccoon . . . why, anything.''

''I grow or gather enough food for my needs. The same with tobacco. Copper and puccoon? Those are for showing off, proclaiming wealth and status. Who would I preen for? The seagulls? They don't care, and, frankly, neither do I. Stone for making tools? I've already built everything I need.''

She shifted uncomfortably, and the bright feathers of her cape shimmered in the firelight. ''You must want something.''

"What I want, no man can offer me." Then, on impulse, he gave Sun Conch an evil glare worthy of Okeus. "What about you?"

"I want to save—"

"No. What about you? What if I want you? Hmm? If I go and speak for this friend of yours, will you give yourself to me? Become my slave? Live here and do my bidding? Is it worth that much to you, Sun Conch? Do you believe in 'right' enough to sacrifice yourself in your friend's place? Give up your clan and family? How about your very soul?" Panther laughed at the girl's horrified expression. "Ah, I see. Well, no matter. I've actually enjoyed talking to you. Tomorrow, the weather will be calm again. Go. Tell your beloved High Fox that I wish him luck."

Like a puffer fish losing water, Sun Conch wilted to the ground. Her cape spread around her.

Panther finished polishing his shell, and stood. "I'm going to sleep now, girl. As you value your life, don't bother me. Oh, and I'd push off before sunrise. The water is quietest at that time of day."

Panther left her there, looking sad, and ducked inside his house. He laid the shell on his bed, and eased the loose thatch aside. Slipping out into the darkness, he replaced the thatch and glided into the woods. In the shadow of an old oak he slithered down under the leaves, sighed, and tried to sleep.

But the girl's words kept haunting him: *"I'll see it through his eyes, live it with him. Wondering how, and why, a man could love a woman with all of his heart— and then be condemned for her murder! How would you feel, Elder, if it happened to you?"*

Why had he been so hard on her? Because she had seen into his soul? Understood his pain, and shame?

Panther growled to himself. His thoughts chased themselves around and around.

Panther lay under the leaves until long after the morning's light had grayed the skies, giving young Sun Conch more than enough time to paddle off for the Western Shore. He listened to the birds, and studied the drifting puffs of cloud. Finally, he brushed the leaves away and forced his rickety bones to rise.

When he strolled into his house clearing, Sun Conch was kneeling before the smoking fire pit, her head bowed.

He bellowed, "What are you doing here?"

Sun Conch turned, and Panther could see courage in every line of her round face. Long black hair draped her chest. "I thought about it all night, Elder. You are right. If a thing is truly just, then a person must be willing to do whatever is necessary to assure it." She looked at him with clear eyes. "If you will speak for High Fox, I will give myself to you, for . . . for whatever you wish to do with me."

Panther experienced the oddest sensation, as if his heart had just dropped through his stomach.

Nine Killer sat in the middle room of Hunting Hawk's longhouse, the interior lit by a crackling fire that sent sparks and thin tendrils of smoke up toward the domed ceiling. Dancing yellow light cast shadows on the support poles, the hanging baskets, braids of corncobs, sacks of herbs, and the people who sat around the fire.

The crawling sense of premonition in Nine Killer's gut disturbed his digestion of the excellent corn and duck he'd just eaten. Red Knot's death had precipitated a disaster that he was just beginning to grasp. But which of the participants was tugging the fragile weaving of his life apart?

Hunting Hawk sat in her usual place on the mat behind the fire. She leaned forward, watching the leaping flames, her dark eyes pensive. Had her once-sharp mind lost its clarity of purpose? Had she misjudged the needs and interests of Flat Pearl Village?

To her left, in the place of honor, Copper Thunder sat like an oiled serpent, curiously calm at the murder of his betrothed.

Nine Killer surreptitiously studied the Great Tayac. He almost looked amused by the sudden uncertainty that plagued Greenstone Clan. Why? What was his purpose here?

To Hunting Hawk's right sat Shell Comb, her beautiful features barely hiding her distress. Her vehement insistence that Winged Blackbird and his warriors had killed Red Knot bothered Nine Killer.

He had never trusted himself when it came to Shell Comb. Her beauty always left him off balance, plagued by a desire for her which he knew was lethal. Of all the terrible deeds humans could commit, incest was the most dreaded and loathsome. Tall and willowy though Shell Comb might be, she remained his cousin. They were both Greenstone Clan, and such a mating would be incestuous in the eyes of his people. The punishment for such a crime would be immediate and agonizing death. Nine Killer's family would probably be rounded up, and burned with him, including his sister, Rosebud, her daughter, White Otter, and the rest of the children. The idea was that only burning purified the insult to the gods, and their mortal descendants. To insure that the gods were placated, those who engaged in incest were burned slowly, the flesh seared from their bones so that their screams carried to the spirit world.

Despite such dire consequences, Nine Killer never allowed himself to be alone with Shell Comb for any length of time, unsure of his resolve should she ever offer herself.

The Kwiokos, Green Serpent, sat on the right side of the fire, Lightning Cat and Streaked Bear dutifully behind him. The old priest looked tired. His eyes wandered as if the purpose of the council eluded him.

Hunting Hawk's niece, Yellow Net, sat just to his right. A prominent member of the community, Hunting Hawk had always sought Yellow Net's advice on matters concerning the village. She was the daughter of Hunting Hawk's younger sister, and an old friend of Shell Comb's. A somber expression creased Yellow Net's face.

"I have received a message from Three Myrtle Village," Hunting Hawk said wearily. "Black Spike informs us that if we want High Fox, we will find his warriors waiting for us. He claims his son is innocent."

"He is." Shell Comb gave her mother a level stare. "This is a distraction. We are losing time and advantage as Corn Hunter prepares for our retaliation."

"The young man's tracks led right to the girl's body." Hunting Hawk glared back. "Corn Hunter's warriors were found on the other side of the ridge. From where Quick Fawn saw them, and where Nine Killer intercepted them, they could not have killed her."

"They could have. If you assume they killed her as a distraction, then doubled back around the ridge to catch us unaware." Shell Comb narrowed an eye, as if daring her mother.

Hunting Hawk glanced at Nine Killer, ignoring the statement.

Nine Killer sighed, and spread his hands. "It is possible, but I don't think it happened that way."

"And why not?" Shell Comb had turned her attention on him. Curse it, a man could melt under those eyes.

Why did she have to look at him that way?

"If Winged Blackbird's warriors had killed her, wouldn't they have simply retreated, their mission accomplished? A dead Red Knot couldn't marry the Great Tayac. They would have scalped the girl, mutilated her in some way to send us a message, a warning not to ally with the upriver villages."

"Assuming they knew who she was," Copper Thunder added. "Perhaps, unaware, she walked right into the middle of them. They killed her so she could give no warning, and hurried on."

Tayac, you know better than that. Even if a war party didn't recognize her, they would have taken a trophy, something to give Corn Hunter. What game are you playing, beast?

Before Nine Killer could respond, Yellow Net shook her head. "No. Winged Blackbird knew her." Her gaze shifted to Shell Comb. "A year ago . . . you took her with you when we traded for rhyolite."

Shell Comb nodded slowly. "Yes, she played with many of the children. Even Corn Hunter's. They would have known her." She gave Nine Killer a forgiving look. "Perhaps they didn't kill her, War Chief. But I . . . it's just . . ."

"Trying to protect Three Myrtle?" Hunting Hawk asked. "Is that it? You lived there for a long time."

Shell Comb stared down at her hands. Nine Killer bit his lip, touched by her sudden vulnerability.

"I saw her ghost," Green Serpent said, a faraway look in his eyes.

"What ghost, Kwiokos?" Hunting Hawk asked sourly. "What are you talking about, old man?"

Green Serpent's mouth opened, his tongue pink in the walnut brown of his withered face. "The morning she was killed. Her ghost was in the House of the Dead.

Looking at the bodies of the ancestors. She came back to join them.''

''Her ghost?'' Copper Thunder asked, a light tone in his voice. ''Are you sure it was hers?''

Green Serpent frowned, drawing the wrinkles in his forehead together. ''I think. Well, you know, there are so many. Sometimes it's hard to tell them apart. I didn't pay much attention. They walk around all night, you know. She seemed to be in such a hurry. That's what brought her to my attention.''

''You were *asleep* when I was thère just after dawn!'' Hunting Hawk snapped. ''What's the matter with you?''

Lightning Cat winced, and glanced at Streaked Bear. A knowing glance passed between them.

Deadpan, Copper Thunder suggested, ''Perhaps we should ask her ghost who the killer is?''

''Yes,'' Green Serpent agreed. ''I shall. Next time I see her. I keep looking for the killer, but the vision wavers, and the Spirits aren't speaking clearly.''

Don't bait the old man! Nine Killer shifted, his dislike of Copper Thunder deepening. *The dung-eater is mocking us. He is like a weasel, and we are the mice. Why doesn't Hunting Hawk throw him out? Is she that afraid of him? Or doesn't she see it?*

Hunting Hawk seemed totally oblivious, staring at the fire. ''The ancestors talked to me that morning. But I couldn't hear them.''

''Mostly, they shout.'' Green Serpent nodded his head. ''You're lucky you couldn't hear them.''

''And did *you* hear them when my mother was there, noble Green Serpent?'' Shell Comb watched him with a hawkish intensity. When the priest gave her an empty look, she spread her hands wide and stated, ''No. As my mother said. You were asleep.''

''Leave him be,'' Hunting Hawk ordered. ''Clawing at ourselves isn't going to solve this thing.'' She met

Nine Killer's eyes. "What would it take to lay hands on High Fox?"

"That depends on Black Spike, Weroansqua. You know the mettle of the Three Myrtle warriors. We've fought side by side often enough. But, before you decide on this course, I would caution my Weroansqua to consider it very carefully."

"Oh, I will indeed, War Chief." She tilted her head as she studied him. "You don't want to do it, do you?"

Copper Thunder's lips quirked in amusement. Did anyone but Nine Killer see it?

"No, Weroansqua. In the first place, it will be a difficult raid. Black Spike will have his scouts out. He's prepared for us. Second, assuming we penetrate his defense, we'll pay dearly for it. And, if we do break through, there is no telling where the youth will be. He may not even be in the village. And, finally, my warriors have friends and family among the Three Myrtle warriors. Some are blood kin, others are of the same clan. If you order this, your warriors will comply, but their hearts will not be in it."

"And you, War Chief?"

"I will do as you order." He dared not look at Copper Thunder for fear that he might lose his control at whatever expression the Great Tayac might betray.

"We don't know for sure that the boy did it," Yellow Net observed in a calming voice. "He most likely did, but Shell Comb is correct, it could be someone else." Her gaze flicked toward Copper Thunder; then she said, "The stakes are particularly high here. A miscalculation could doom us all."

Nine Killer chanced a look at Copper Thunder, and found he'd fixed his gaze on Yellow Net. That amused conceit had vanished and now a flat intensity filled his lidded gaze.

No good will come of this, Nine Killer assured himself.

Eight

The slim canoe rose and fell with the swells, reminding Panther just how vulnerable these small dugouts were. Crossing the Salt Water Bay always carried the chance of disaster, even on a calm day like this. While the canoes were safe enough in the narrow inlets, and along the rivers, a sudden wind, or even a relatively modest shower, could swamp a dugout in the open water.

Hands braced on the gunwales, Panther looked over his shoulder at Sun Conch, who paddled rhythmically, resignation in the set of her young face. *Well, bat dung! The girl figures she's mine now and already dead, so why should she fear drowning? After the scare I put into her, she might even be looking forward to it.*

And to think, some people thought The Panther to be incredibly clever!

Overhead, billowing clumps of cloud alternated with the pale blue winter sky, but on the water, sunlight sparkled across the rolling surface, belying the murky depths. What possessed the sunlight to dance on the bay? It was as if sun was so completely incompatible with water that the beams bounced off it.

In the distance a flock of terns sailed low over the swells. To Panther it was a temptation of fate that they should dip so fearlessly to skim the crests.

Mysteries. Mysteries everywhere.

Panther took a deep breath, filling his lungs with the cool air. The bay's damp musk lingered in his nostrils, salty, its special tang familiar to him, if not reassuring today.

He half-turned, careful not to rock the boat. "Just where exactly are we going?"

"Flat Pearl Village," Sun Conch answered.

"No. We will go to Three Myrtle first."

"Elder, the people of Three Myrtle don't wish High Fox dead. The problem is in Flat Pearl. I will take you there."

Panther gave her a flinty squint. "Girl, we'd better get some things straight. You do not order me . . ." At that moment, the canoe lurched and bobbed. As water slapped against the hull, cold droplets spattered on Panther's skin. Despite his death grip on the gunwales, he glared down into the water. "You stop that! I'm putting Sun Conch in her place right now, but I'll deal with you later!"

Was it imagination, or did the swells lose some of their violence? Panther lifted an eyebrow, satisfied, and turned his attention back to Sun Conch. "You want me to save High Fox, don't you?"

She gave him a puzzled look. "Yes, Elder."

"Then you will take me to Three Myrtle Village. Before I deal with Hunting Hawk, I must talk to High Fox, hear his side of the—"

"High Fox isn't at Three Myrtle Village, Elder."

"Then, where is he? You said he'd fled after he found the girl's body. He didn't go home to the protection of his family?"

Sun Conch paddled methodically, each stroke driving the canoe diagonally across the waves. "No, Elder. Well, I mean, he went home, but only long enough to tell me his trouble. Then he was supposed to leave. He knew Hunting Hawk would be hunting him. He didn't think he'd be safe in Three Myrtle."

Panther tensed as the canoe bobbed precariously and slid down into the trough of a swell. Water ran over the heat-stained wood in the bottom, coursing around his feet, mocking him with his own mortality. "Think we ought to bail? It's getting deep."

Sun Conch asked mildly, "You're not afraid, are you?"

Panther screwed his face into a mask of resolution and turned to glare. "No! Now, just where is High Fox? I need to speak to him. I can't do a blood-rotted thing for him until I hear his words about what happened."

"Very well, Elder. He is hiding on a small island. I will take you to him."

"Good." But Panther's heart quaked as another swell slapped the side of the canoe, spattering him with droplets. When he looked down, the water ran over his toes. Corruption take all canoes. This was no way for a man to travel. He looked around for the bailing cup.

And, if I live long enough to see this High Fox, and if I think the boy is lying to me, by Okeus' balls, I'll wring the very soul from his body!

A chill wind blew out of the moonless night, down from the northwest, over the hilly Conoy Peninsula, and across the leaden waters of the Fish River. It moaned through the bare trees, stirred the brown leaves, and whistled around the palisade posts of Flat Pearl Village. As it came swirling across the palisade it shook the houses, and scoured bits of sand, charcoal, and shell, spattering them against Nine Killer's squinting face as he crossed the plaza to his sister Rosebud's house.

His nerves were bothering him. To relieve them, he'd been pacing the length and breadth of the village. He'd even gone to the extent of placing Stone Cob and Crab Spine—to their disgust—on guard. Now, as he ducked into the sheltered lee of Rosebud's longhouse, he drew his feather cloak tightly about his shoulders.

Not even ghosts would be out on a night like this.

He shivered: a mixture of cold and the unknown. Protected from the worst of the gusts, he leaned against Rosebud's thatched wall and listened to the wind roar through the night.

Unease had been stalking him since the day of Red Knot's death, staring at him from the wind-whipped darkness with invisible eyes. That morning, his world had started to come apart, and he felt powerless to prevent it. But where did the root of this evil lie?

Murder, in itself, was horrifying to his people. If it really was murder. He cocked an eyebrow, hearing faint laughter from inside. His niece, White Otter, probably. The girl was always bubbling and laughing, even when taking care of her siblings: Slender Bark, Little Shell, Two Birds, and Sea Rice.

If Winged Blackbird, or one of his warriors, had killed Red Knot, it wasn't murder, but war. A tactical move in the deadly game played by the Weroances and the Mamanatowick. Were that the case—and Nine Killer wished desperately that he could believe it—the response would be simple: he needed but marshal his warriors, slip his forces into White Stake territory, and extract revenge. If he escaped without significant losses, and managed to blunt Winged Blackbird's inevitable counterattack, then the equilibrium would have been maintained in the age-old manner.

But what if that was what he was supposed to believe? What if Winged Blackbird hadn't killed Red Knot?

Then my raid will sting Corn Hunter into a crazy rage. He'll lose all of his sense and throw everything he's got at us. The last time that had happened, it had taken every warrior in the Independent villages to stem the attacks.

Nine Killer rubbed the back of his neck. Three Myrtle

Village wouldn't join them, not until an apology had been made to Black Spike. The careful balance between the Independent villages had been upset, and now wobbled about like a wounded warrior struck upon the head.

Perhaps that had been the plan from the beginning. Nine Killer tucked his arms tightly under his feather cloak. Throughout his life, the Independent villages had been as constant as the tides. Petty squabbles had been solved by select delegates from the other villages, driven by the ever-present need for unity against the growing influence of the Mamanatowick.

Red Knot's murder played right into Water Snake's hand, the first great crack in the alliance that had stymied him to the north. But was he this sophisticated? How could he have orchestrated such a subtle and effective strike? He would have had to know precisely when Red Knot would be on the trail to Oyster Shell Landing, and how to kill her.

Nine Killer stiffened, a wind colder than that of the night freezing his soul. *He would have to have someone here, a traitor in Flat Pearl Village, to accomplish it.*

If . . . If Water Snake was the key to this. If, however, Copper Thunder was responsible, the murder made a great deal more sense. With his many warriors, the Great Tayac had the opportunity, as well as the means to have the girl followed and ambushed. But his marriage to Red Knot gave him access to the Independent villages. He was getting everything—and with a minimum of risk. Sort it out as he might, Nine Killer saw no advantage accruing to Copper Thunder by killing Red Knot.

Nine Killer smiled grimly into the night. Too bad he couldn't blame Copper Thunder. How pleasing it would be to break a war club across the Great Tayac's teeth!

He bent his head back to stare at the dark sky. Every now and then the wind brought him the scent of wood smoke, teasing him with images of sitting inside, warm and cheery by the fire. It had been at least a week since he'd seen his wife, White Star. Normally, he'd be inside her longhouse on a night like this. He'd be playing with his sons Rabbit, Lance, and Cricket, and swapping lies with his brother-in-law and old friend, Half Moon. Because of his friendship with Half Moon, he'd married White Star, and, over the years, they had come to love each other.

Later, when you've wrestled your way through this. And that left him with the final, and most likely, solution to the problem: Maybe, as a girl, Red Knot had promised High Fox she would marry him; but life changed when a girl became a woman—as it did when a boy went through the Blackening death during the *Huskanaw*. Perhaps Red Knot had run off that morning to tell High Fox that she was going to marry Copper Thunder. High Fox couldn't accept that, and enraged, he killed her.

That made the most sense. He had known where she would be. His tracks led to the girl's body. Flat Willow had *seen* him, talked to him. What more proof did they need?

But Nine Killer knew well that if he went to claim High Fox, Black Spike would resist. If he attacked, the alliance would split as surely as if hacked apart with a stone-bitted ax.

It was only a matter of time before honor would compel Hunting Hawk to act. He was sure of it. Her granddaughter had been murdered, and no matter the cost, such a thing could not be allowed to pass uncontested.

Nine Killer looked southward, beyond the palisade through the darkness. There, three days' hard run across ridge, forest, and stream, the Water Snake lay coiled in his lair, his head raised to this same cold wind that blew the smell of destruction to Nine Killer's keen nostrils. If war broke out between Flat Pearl and Three Myrtle, the

Independent villages would be sending their tribute to Water Snake by spring.

And I, my warriors, and the rest of Greenstone Clan will be dead. He lowered his head. His wife and sisters, and their children, would be taken as slaves, the women forced to bear other men's children, all made to work in the fields, and live little better than dogs.

"Okeus help us," he whispered. "Isn't there some way out of this?"

Two days in a canoe were more than enough for The Panther. Crossing the open water of the Salt Water Bay had terrified him. He'd spent the first night on an exposed beach, half-frozen despite the small fire that he and Sun Conch had put together. They'd camped up in the woods last night, but the fierce wind had robbed them of any warmth the trees might have furnished.

Now the slim canoe coasted through reeds, cordgrass, and cattails up to a low island. At high tide it looked like little more than a wart in the water.

Panther shook his head. Why not simply brain the girl and have this over with? But then he'd have had to paddle himself back across the bay, and, to be honest, he wasn't sure he could do it. His butt ached, his joints had swollen, and every muscle in his body had cramped.

When the canoe finally slid to a halt in the thick cordgrass, Panther gave Sun Conch a hollow-eyed stare. "We're here?"

"This is where he said he'd go, Elder."

"Give me your hand."

Sun Conch gave him a blank look, as if frightened to touch him.

"Oh, for the . . . Help me up, girl! My joints are stuck!"

Sun Conch swallowed hard, and pushed through the thick grass. "Sorry, Elder." She pulled Panther to his feet with a crackling of stiff joints. The rounded canoe rocked under his feet, and Sun Conch held him from pitching into the swampy muck.

"Here, put your arm around my shoulder, Elder."

When he did, she lifted him bodily from the canoe, and practically dragged him stumbling through the water. Panther winced as the grass sawed at his legs. Each of his steps was accompanied by the sucking squish of the mud.

Okeus take him, the girl was as strong as a boar bear! Panther's withered brown lips curled into a secret smile. Maybe he'd better not make her too mad. She might pull his head off his shoulders.

Sun Conch released Panther when they reached the scrubby grass on dry land, then stepped away and called, "High Fox? It's Sun Conch! I've brought him, as I said I would!"

Panther inspected the little island. No more than a bow shot across, it didn't even support trees, indicating that at times the storm surge covered it with salt water.

Panther remarked, "There's no fresh water that I can see. Nothing to make a fire out of except dry grass."

"I know," Sun Conch said, "that's why he's here. Who would ever come to look for him on this desolate island?"

"Probably the crows, vultures, and gulls after he dies of thirst or freezes to death."

"High Fox?" she called again. "We are here! Where are you?"

Panther glimpsed movement to one side in the thick grass, and spun in time to see a tall handsome youth rise to his feet. He carried a nocked bow in his hands, and a war club hung from his waist. His eyes had a wild look, as if his soul teetered on a thin bridge over terror. He wore an old deerhide cape around his shoulders. Bits of grass and mud clung to his cold skin. His hair was a tangled black mass. Where did the animal end, and the human begin?

"High Fox?" Sun Conch said and spread her arms. She took two steps toward him. "It's all right. This is The Panther."

"Are—are you certain?"

"Yes, of course I am! Do you think I would bring anyone else here to your hiding place?"

The young warrior wet his lips, but he did not lower his bow.

Careful, old man. He's panicked, desperate. Too frightened to think clearly. Panther knew how brightly fear could pump in the veins, and the way the lungs never seemed to fill. How the nerves tingled and tightened, and horrid specters lurked in the imagination. Judgment frayed . . . and finally snapped.

Afterward, only the consequences remained.

"I *am* The Panther," he said. "Sun Conch came to me, offered herself in order to save you. It isn't often, young warrior, that a man your age can command such loyalty and devotion from a girl. So I came, at least this far. Now I must hear your story about what happened, do you understand?"

High Fox nodded, and the tension on his bowstring eased. His eyes dulled. "I didn't kill her. I swear. Okeus, hear me, on my soul, I didn't kill her."

Panther walked up to the youth. "Come, High Fox. Let's go build a fire, and make some warm tea. Then, we will hear your tale."

Eyes locked with The Panther's, High Fox whispered, "I loved her. You must believe me."

Sun Conch clamped her jaw and looked away, and

Panther said, "I make you only one promise, High Fox. I will see that you get what you deserve. Fair enough?"

"Yes, Elder. Fair enough."

"Then come."

High Fox said, "We're a short distance from the cove where the canvasback ducks winter." He turned and pointed to an inlet on the mainland.

"Yes," Sun Conch agreed. "I know the place. No one lives there because the swamps surround it. It's a good place to camp, Elder."

"Good," Panther said. "Let's go there. We will hear High Fox's story, and decide our course of action."

Panther sighed, knowing he had to get back in the canoe and endure the ride once more, but he'd be crabbit before he spent the night on this poor excuse of an island.

Shell Comb walked down to the water's edge below Flat Pearl Village, a small pot in one hand. Night had fallen, cold and bracing. Overhead, patches of stars intermixed with black splotches where clouds blocked the night sky. Behind her in the village, the dogs barked at some perceived injustice, and she heard a shrill voice as one of the women scolded a child. The only other sound was the perpetual lapping of water against the shoreline.

She bent down and filled her pot with water. A fish splashed in the darkness.

She turned, making her way along the familiar path that led to the sweat lodge, a thatched structure built into the bank.

A low fire burned before the door, three stones already hot in the fire's center. She pulled the hanging aside and ducked through the low doorway.

No more than two paces by three across, the low-roofed hut was built by tightly thatching a sapling framework. A large stone, like a dull red eye in the darkness, lay in the pit excavated centrally in the earthen floor. To her surprise, the air billowed steam. She could just make out the figure in the rear of the sweat house, a big man.

"Come in," he said in his accented voice. "The heat is refreshing."

Shell Comb seated herself and placed her pot to one side. He bent forward, dribbling water on the dull red rock. Steam cackled and hissed, rising in a cloud to fill the small room.

She closed her eyes, allowing the penetrating heat to seep into her pores. She shouldn't have come here, but he fascinated her, something in his personality drawing her to him.

"I've needed this," Copper Thunder confided. "It cleanses more than the body, you know."

"Yes." She leaned her head back, letting the moisture bead on her skin. "It is said that steam leaches evil out of the soul." At least, she fervently hoped so.

He laughed softly. "Oh, I doubt that. There are so many cracks and crevices in the soul that evil can hide where it will. Steam it if you wish, but I've known a great many wicked men who sweat like great rivers, their souls just as black when they stop as when they start."

"And does that include you?"

"Most likely, but then, I've never believed that pot of stew the priests dish out."

"I don't know what to think of you." She could feel his measuring gaze through the darkness.

"Think what you will. Some of it, if not all, might even be true."

She weighed his words, then chose to ignore them. "Why are you still here?"

"To see what happens next."

"Are we just an entertainment?"

"I wouldn't use those words."

"Then, what words would you use?"

"I am an observer." He shifted, placing limp arms on his knees.

She imagined his muscles, slack now, his skin sleek with water. What would it be like to run her fingers down that smooth flesh? *Something is crooked in my soul. All of my life I've been fascinated by strong men. What triggers that excitement?*

Copper Thunder said, "I'm surprised at you. You exhibit great control. I had expected you to weep for Red Knot, to rend your soul with grief, and pull out whole hanks of your hair."

"Great Tayac, I am my mother's daughter. Grief is for those who have the luxury of expressing it. My people look to me for leadership. For the moment, they need to see strength."

"Do you always contain your desires so? I had heard otherwise."

She smoothed the water from her face and leaned her head back. "And what, may I ask, did you hear?"

"That you are a hot-blooded woman. One accustomed to feeding her desires."

She gave him a challenging stare, that thrill beginning deep in the pit of her stomach. "Life is short, my friend. Okeus saw to that just after the Creation. As my daughter discovered, only the foolish ever bet on another sunrise. Let's just say that I've enjoyed all I could, taken the risks . . . and paid the prices."

"And if you go to war with Three Myrtle Village?"

"I would avoid that if possible." She paused. "Are you just talking, or do you have something in mind?"

"I always have things in my mind. But, for the moment, I'm more interested in your thoughts. Assume you go to war with Three Myrtle Village, what will the outcome be?''

''A splintering of the alliance among the Independent villages. Water Snake will see his opportunity, and act. But you know all this, don't you?''

''It would seem that you are trapped.''

''We will see our way through. But what about you? What do you gain? If the alliance is broken, you've lost a counterbalance to the Mamanatowick's desire for northern expansion. If he controls the south bank of the Fish River, he can turn his energies toward you.''

''Indeed he could. On the other hand, he will need to strip warriors from all of his holdings. That would give me an opportunity to strike his frontier villages. He'll be weak, bleeding himself in the north.''

Her mind's eye could see it. Water Snake would lose men. In essence, he would be fighting a war on two fronts. ''So, you wait like a rattler by an eagle's nest. Only when the soaring hawk diverts the eagle's attention do you steal his fledgling.'' She grinned warily. ''The problem is, the hawk may waver, and the eagle might turn at the last moment.''

''There are always risks,'' he said. ''As you just told me.''

The faint light from the hot stone faded, and she could actually feel his smile in the darkness.

''But those who are smart minimize their risks, Great Tayac. Wouldn't it have been better to create a bond with Greenstone Clan, and then wear Water Snake down? That was your original plan, wasn't it?''

''Of course.'' He paused. ''So, tell me, who do you think killed Red Knot?''

She filled her lungs with the pungent steam. ''High Fox. Who else?''

''You didn't believe that at first—and you don't sound convinced, even now.''

"I don't trust Corn Hunter. Never have. It still bothers me that his warriors were out there." She ground her teeth, fists knotted. "His warriors had the opportunity, didn't they?"

"They did," he answered.

"I watched you, you know." The heat was working into her joints, draining the tension that knotted every muscle. "My daughter's death didn't seem to affect you."

He shifted in the darkness, the faint light from the hot stone faded now. "She was a girl, Shell Comb. Do not think my words unkind, but I've seen two tens more Comings of the Leaves than she had. You and I both know it was a marriage of convenience. Much like many of yours have been."

"You would prefer an older woman then?"

Silence. Then he said neutrally, "I might."

"Someone who thinks a great deal like you do?"

"It would be . . . refreshing, for once in my life."

"Your other wives haven't satisfied you?"

He chuckled. "The needs of the flesh, yes. I have provided children for their lineages." Another pause. "From the tone in your voice, I can't help but wonder what is in your head. The other women of marriageable age in your clan are taken."

She smiled then, safe within the cloak of darkness. "And, what if I found you a woman? One capable of thinking the way you do? Would you find that . . . refreshing?"

"It would depend," he said carefully. "I would have to see just what the marriage offered."

As her thoughts wrapped around the idea, she murmured, "The future is always full of surprises."

Nine

The fire crackled and spat flames under the mist of freezing rain that drifted down from the low clouds, icing the trees and leaf mat. Where the ground was exposed, footing was treacherous.

A pot of fish boiled on the flames, the aroma enough to send pangs into The Panther's stomach. Boiled fish, while no great culinary delight, was still food and fuel for a cold night.

The Panther cocked a grizzled eyebrow at the heavens and huffed his disgust in a frosty breath. The chill ate at his bones, and he couldn't seem to get close enough to the fire to stay warm.

Across from him, High Fox looked just as miserable, hollow-eyed, as if part of his soul had been stolen. Panther studied him. If he was truly innocent, that might indeed be the case. A person didn't recover from such a thing, at least never completely. Years from now, High Fox would quiver in his dreams, wrongly accused, being dragged to his execution, protesting his innocence. What more horrible nightmare was there?

To his right, Sun Conch sat hunched in her feather cape, wet hair framing her round face and large dark eyes. Water dripped from her short beak of a nose. She should at least reflect a little optimism. After all, The Panther was here to hear her friend's explanation of what happened.

"I pronounce the fish done," Panther growled. "If I

don't eat, and right now, you'll find out just how cranky I can get.''

"I thought I'd seen it in the canoe," Sun Conch said, as she reached for wooden tongs. "You mean you can get worse?"

Panther slitted an eye. "Don't press me, girl."

Sun Conch swallowed hard, murmured, "Never," and plucked the six boiled mullet from the water. She laid them out on sections of bark and handed the first two to Panther. The second helping went to High Fox, and Panther examined their faces as the young man took the bark plate from her hands. Sun Conch's eyes brimmed with love. In response, High Fox clamped his jaw and tried to smile.

Panther blew on his fish to cool them, and began picking his dinner apart. As he chewed the succulent white meat, he weighed the young man's actions. He ate listlessly, eyes on the food. Nothing in his manner seemed to exude either guilt or innocence.

"High Fox," Panther said through a mouthful. "It's time to hear your story. Sun Conch went to great risk to bring me here. Did you kill this girl?"

"No. I already told you."

"Look at me. That's it. Eye to eye. I want to see your soul as you talk."

High Fox raised his wounded brown eyes and said, "I didn't kill Red Knot. She was . . . she . . ." He shook his head. "She was dead when I found her."

"Tell me, boy. From the beginning."

High Fox poked at his fish. "She didn't want him."

"Who?"

"Copper Thunder. He frightened her, repulsed her. She told me that the thought of him touching her was like having a snake crawl across her skin."

"Did she tell Hunting Hawk and Shell Comb how she felt?"

High Fox shook his head. "A woman in that family would never dare. Hunting Hawk is the Weroansqua, and Shell Comb, she's just as powerful in her way. In Three Myrtle Village, when they tell stories about Shell Comb or Hunting Hawk, they whisper. People fear those women."

"Because they are evil?" Panther plucked up another piece of flaky white meat and popped it into his mouth.

"Not like sorcerers or witches . . ." High Fox paused and glanced up, as if fearing he might have offended Panther, then continued, "It's just that no one crosses them. They wield a great deal of authority." He raised his head slightly. "I heard my father, Black Spike, say that when Hunting Hawk clapped her hands, even the thunder quaked in the clouds. It was like a joke, but not really. Do you understand?"

"I think I do." Panther stripped the bones of the first mullet, flipped them into the fire, and started in on the second. "And when did you first meet this Red Knot?"

"I guess, well, we've always known each other. We grew up in allied villages. We played when we were little." He glanced away, fidgeting. "Then things changed."

"When?"

"Last . . . last summer."

"Gull dung, boy, look me in the eyes." When High Fox did, he looked as guilty as Okeus after the Creation. "Spill it, boy. Right now. How did things change?"

High Fox tensed, his hands suddenly as active as ants with nowhere to go. "Just changed. You know. Like a man and woman. Not a boy and girl. We—we looked at each other differently."

Panther muttered dryly, "That happens between men and women."

"I swear, I never touched her!" High Fox blurted.

Panther's brows arched. "Indeed."

"He didn't, Elder!" Sun Conch came to High Fox's defense. "I tried to get him to . . . when I—I asked him to run away with me . . ." The words faded, and she lowered her gaze to the smoking fire. High Fox had squeezed his eyes closed, as if in pain. Sun Conch glanced at him, and added, "He wouldn't have dared, Elder. It would have cost him his life, and he knew it."

Without molars, Panther had to use his worn front teeth to chew his fish. While he did, he mulled over what they'd just told him about their own difficulties. "So, Red Knot was promised to Copper Thunder, but didn't like him and wouldn't complain about the marriage to her mother or grandmother, correct?"

"That's right."

"Well then, what were you going to do about it?"

"I was going to take her away. After the dance. She was supposed to meet me at Oyster Shell Landing at dawn."

"When did you tell her to do this?"

"I didn't . . . it was her idea."

Panther pointed with a hard finger. "You're a liar, boy. I won't be lied to." He glanced at Sun Conch, who sat watching with her whole heart in her eyes. "I've given him a hearing. He had his chance."

"No! Wait!" High Fox started forward, arms spread. "All right. It was me. I told her to meet me at Oyster Shell Landing."

Panther picked at his fish for a moment, allowing the boy's tension to rise. "Then why did you lie to me?"

"Because." High Fox slapped his legs. "It looks bad. As if I put her up to it in the first place. If a warrior would tempt a young woman to ignore her responsibilities, what else might he do? At least, that's how Hunting Hawk would look at it."

"Boy, tell me everything. I *don't* want any lies, you hear?"

When High Fox's shoulders slumped, Sun Conch reached out to lay a reassuring hand on his arm. They gazed at each other for a long moment; then she whispered, "Are you all right? You look ill."

"Tired," he whispered. "I'm so tired. I've barely slept since you left."

She squeezed his arm and turned back to Panther. "He's worn out, Elder. Perhaps we could hurry this along. High Fox—"

"Has to answer my questions, girl. First, he has to tell me how this was supposed to work."

High Fox let out a halting breath. "Red Knot was finishing the last of her dances, and saw me slip away from the fire. It took awhile, but then she came to our place and—"

"Your place?"

"On the sandy beach, just down from the canoe landing. We met there a lot."

"And that's when you asked her to run off with you?"

"Yes. We didn't have much time, you see. I told her I'd paddle around the neck, meet her at dawn at Oyster Shell Landing. We'd have a good solid day's head start, and even then, Nine Killer's warriors wouldn't know which direction to look."

"And she agreed to this? Just like that?"

"She was desperate. I swear it. Anything to keep from marrying Copper Thunder. She told me she'd be there, right at dawn. Or as soon as she could slip away. She hugged me, and then she ran back toward the village. That was the last time I saw her alive." High Fox rubbed his face with a nervous hand, staring back at that time and place.

Sun Conch shivered, wiping at a trickle of cold water that seeped out of her soaked cape.

Panther said, "What did you do next?"

High Fox straightened. "I made my way back to the

canoe landing, found my boat, and shoved it out into the water. After that I paddled all night, making my way around the neck. I landed at Oyster Shell Landing just before dawn. I guess I was tired . . . fell asleep until sometime just after dawn.''

"Did you tell anyone you were doing this? Even contemplating it?"

"No, Elder, I . . ." He paused and glanced at Sun Conch. "I told Sun Conch. But she's the only one. And I don't think Red Knot would have said anything. She wasn't that kind."

"But if she had told someone, could you guess who?"

"Maybe Quick Fawn. They were best friends. She's a little younger than Red Knot was."

"A chatter mouth?"

"No. Not really." He shrugged. "I don't know. If she was, I never knew it. I just thought she was sort of—well, you know, a pest. Always following us around when we wanted to be alone."

"I see. Very well, so you're at the landing, asleep in the boat . . ."

"That's right. I woke up and, um, I don't know, maybe the sun was a hand or two above the horizon. It was cloudy, so I couldn't really tell. The fog had risen, I know that. I was cold, so I paced up and down the landing, waiting, being nervous. I mean, I'd never done anything like this before, and a person starts thinking, you know, about what you're doing, and just where you will go and how you'll live. It's one thing to run off, another to find a place where you can survive.''

Panther cocked an eyebrow. "Did you think about backing out?"

High Fox shook his head resolutely. "I was Red Knot's last chance. Copper Thunder was there, in Flat Pearl Village. She was supposed to leave with him that day. We *had* to go."

"And when did Red Knot arrive?"

"She didn't." High Fox ground his teeth, a hardness in his eyes. "It was getting late and I couldn't help it, I started up the ridge, just to see if she was coming. I had this bad feeling, like we were in trouble. If she'd been seen, followed, I had to know, so I could fix it, you understand?"

"Yes."

"Well, I climbed up that high ridge, and almost walked past her. She'd . . . she'd been dragged off to one side, and just left there in a hollow behind this old hickory tree." He hesitated, his breathing strained. "As Okeus hears my words, she was just sprawled there. Broken . . . my pretty girl . . . all broken. Like . . . like something discarded."

"High Fox, what did you do? Touch her? Try to save her, what?"

"I wiped some of the blood off, thinking, hoping it was some silly game. A trick to make me worry. But the blood . . . fire and lightning, the blood . . ." He lifted his right hand, looking at it as if the skin were stained. "Her blood. It was so cold . . . all through her hair."

"Did you try to rouse her? To see if she was just injured?"

High Fox shook his head. "She was dead, Elder. No doubt about it. Her eyes were half-open—and had leaves in them."

"So she was dead. How was the body? Show me. Get down on the ground."

High Fox did, sprawling with his leg up, one arm outthrust, and slightly curled. "Like this. The blood was all over the left side of her head, and some had trickled down her face. Like this." He traced along the curve of his cheek.

"And was there anything with her?"

"No. Nothing that I saw." High Fox stood and returned to the fire, reaching out to the flames with trembling hands. "I didn't stay very long. I just turned and ran. I—I . . ." He winced. "I ran into a man on the trail. Flat Willow. He was halfway down the slope. I told him . . . well, I think I said my father wanted me. I don't know. I don't remember. I was scared like I'd never been scared before. So I hurried back to my boat and shoved off. Then I paddled like a madman for home."

Panther lifted his brows. "I thought you stowed your canoe in some brush and sneaked up to the village to hear the talk?"

"Oh, yes," he said, and jerked a nod. "I did do that. It was afterward that I paddled for home."

"And that's all there is to it?"

High Fox nodded. "I swear it, Elder. I didn't kill her— and I don't know who did. Maybe Flat Willow. He was out there. He was the only person I saw."

The Panther stared into those haunted eyes, and steepled his fingers. "You know, you're in a fix, boy. I can guess how Hunting Hawk and Flat Pearl Village are thinking. Not only were you running off with their woman—a woman promised to Copper Thunder—but you were seen running from the place where they found her murdered."

"Yes, I know." He stared at his hand again. "And I remember Flat Willow asking me about my hand. I told him I'd cut it."

"And why did you do that?"

"Because Red Knot's blood was all over it."

Sun Conch added wood to the fire, and Panther watched the flames lick around it. If High Fox wanted to save a lot of people a lot of trouble, he'd cut his own throat right now.

Bat droppings, that's how it's going to end anyway. Who'd believe the boy didn't do it? I'm not even sure I believe he didn't.

"And all I have is your word that you didn't kill her?" Panther asked.

"What else is there?" High Fox asked. "Maybe I was wrong to tell her I'd take her away, but I did it. And I think I'd do it again." He closed his eyes, shaking his head. "By the dark god, all we wanted was a chance. Is that too much to ask?"

"Sometimes, boy, it is." Panther sighed, and tucked his blanket tighter. "Well, let me sleep on it. I'll give you my answer in the morning."

As Panther curled up in his blanket beside the fire, he saw High Fox take Sun Conch's hand and lead her a short distance away. Panther slitted one eye, watching them.

High Fox stopped at the edge of the swamp, released Sun Conch's hand, and folded his arms tightly across his broad chest. Yellow eyes sparkled on the far side of the reeds, and Sun Conch saw a big wolf slink away into the darkness. She watched until it vanished, and put a gentle hand on High Fox's shoulder.

"What is it?" she asked. "What's wrong?"

"He doesn't believe me," High Fox whispered. "I could see it on his face, he thinks I—I . . ."

"No, he doesn't. You're imagining it. The Panther said he needed time to think about what you'd told him. If he'd already decided your fate, do you think he'd still be here?"

High Fox gestured anxiously, then pulled Sun Conch into his arms, and pressed her face tightly against his shoulder. "In the name of Okeus, I don't know what to believe. What am I going to do?"

The freezing mist seemed to draw closer, wrapping

them in icy folds, and she felt his lungs moving in and out in shallow breaths. Sun Conch slipped her arms around his waist. "You are tired, High Fox. You need to rest. Will you sleep better if I stand guard over you?"

She felt his hand moving down her back, and she could feel its warmth through her cape. The sound of his voice, his touch, skillfully opened doors she had tried very hard to close forever. Behind those doors lay the joy and warmth of their childhood together. A sad longing for them swelled her heart.

He pressed his face against her hair, and murmured, "Thank you for bringing him, Sun Conch. No one else would have been brave enough. I'm not even certain I would have been."

She lifted her head and saw grief in his eyes, grief that he kept under tight rein. She saw other things as well, the fear that choked him, and a desperation that verged on insanity. "I love you, High Fox. I would do anything for you."

A shiver climbed his spine, and his hands slid down her arms. "Sun Conch?" he said in a low hoarse voice. "Tell me about this old man. You have spent a few days with him. What do you know of him? Can we trust him?"

"What you're really asking me is if he's a witch, aren't you?"

"Yes. That's what I'm asking."

"I've seen nothing to prove it. But I don't think it matters. So long as everyone thinks he's a witch, his words will have Power."

High Fox nodded. "That's true. I just wish I knew if he thinks I'm innocent or—"

Sun Conch interrupted, "He will tell you in the morning, and if he decides to try and prove your innocence, you will need to be rested."

A fragile smile touched his lips. "Do you remember

when you had seen ten Comings of the Leaves," he said, and the sadness in his voice seemed to cast a spell over her. She could hear his careless laughter echoing from those long-ago days, and see his face shining for her, and her alone, as they ran deer trails, chasing each other through the forest. A tide of happiness swept through Sun Conch.

She rested her head against his shoulder, and said, "Yes. I remember."

He lifted her chin to make her look into his eyes, and the bright beauty of the moment was gone. Despair lay in every line of his face. "I never realized then how much I cared for you. I just knew you were the only one I could talk to. And you still are. Thank you. Thank you for always being there for me."

Sun Conch looked at him through blurry eyes. "I always will be."

He bent toward her, and she thought for a moment he might kiss her, but a tremor ran through his arms, and he released her and backed away. "You—you don't need to stand guard," he said. "You are as tired as I am. I'll be fine."

"I want to be certain of that," Sun Conch said as she reached beneath her feathered cape, untied his war club from her belt, and drew it out. "Why don't you roll up in your blanket beside the fire. I'll watch from here, where the shadows will hide me. Go on, now. You need to sleep well, High Fox, so that you will be able to think straight tomorrow."

High Fox took her hand and held it a moment, then walked to the fire.

After High Fox had rolled in his blanket, and had begun snoring softly, The Panther raised his head to look at Sun Conch. She saw sympathy in his faded old eyes. Was it directed at her, or High Fox, or, perhaps, both of them?

She sucked in a breath of frigid mist, spread her feet, and laid her war club over her shoulder, preparing for the long night ahead.

Nine Killer sat at the middle fire of his sister Rosebud's longhouse. He cupped a forgotten shell half-full of lukewarm tea. He had come here to discipline his young nephew, Two Birds, for talking back to his mother. That was the way of a matrilineage: a man raised his sister's children, for they were clan and family. His own children belonged to his wife, White Star. Since White Star belonged to Sun Shell Clan, her older brother, Half Moon, was responsible for the discipline and training of the children.

Nine Killer had grabbed the little boy by the shoulders, sat him down, and glared into his little black eyes, telling him just how a man of the People behaved, and all the terrible things he'd do to the boy if he didn't straighten up.

"Now," Nine Killer finished, "if I ever hear you've raised your voice to your mother again, I'm going to pack you up and send you off to The Panther! You hear me? He *eats* little boys, and then he curses their bones, and grinds them up. Then he leaves them around where his enemies can find them. Those bones make bad people bleed through their ears until they're dead. Hear me?"

Two Birds had swallowed hard and nodded soberly, his eyes half bugged out from his face.

"A bit dramatic, don't you think?" Rosebud had asked dryly after the tot had fled for his favorite toy, a corn husk doll, and the safer company of his big sister White Otter.

Rosebud was a sturdy woman of two tens and eight years. She generally wore her hair long, in a single braid that hung down her back. Her face was round, given to a generous mouth and a broad, straight nose. She went about life with a sense of competent efficiency that Nine Killer had always admired. Her most notable trait was her eyes, brown as berries, but with a depth that Nine Killer had never been able to fathom. When she looked at him, she had that knowing look, as if possessed of some deeper understanding of life that had eluded Nine Killer. It drove him half mad. When he asked her about things, she didn't seem any wiser than he, but, Okeus take him, she still *looked* like she knew.

Rosebud's once-narrow waist had thickened, and after five children her high breasts had begun to sag. She had just divorced her last husband, a man from Oyster Inlet, and was now swearing she'd never marry again.

As he sat by the popping fire, some portion of his mind was aware of the worried looks Rosebud and her family were giving him. Earlier, he had shrugged off their thinly veiled questions about what was going to happen next. Now the closest of them sat a respectful pace away, as if the distance would grant him a solution to this terrible mess.

The fire spat sparks as the damp wood smoldered in defiance of the freezing drizzle beyond the longhouse walls, its heat as futile as the options looming in his future. How could he possibly take High Fox from Three Myrtle Village? He would be making war on old friends, relatives, and people he genuinely liked and respected.

The moment the first arrow was released, no matter what the outcome of the battle, the damage to the alliance would be irreparable. Generations of trust would be severed as if cut by a sharp shell knife.

Nine Killer absently turned the cup in his hands, his

soul's eye focusing on his friends at Three Myrtle Village, the raids shared, the battles fought, the camaraderie they'd enjoyed. With each recollection, the sensation of emptiness swelled.

The hanging pulled back from the door, and he glanced up to see Hunting Hawk's hunched figure duck awkwardly through, balanced on her sassafras cane. The old woman straightened, winced, and hobbled forward.

Tension rippled through the people, their postures straightening. Fists tightened on kirtles and bodies shifted uneasily as they glanced back and forth.

"Miserable night out there," Hunting Hawk said by way of greeting. "Freezing rain. Foul stuff. You'd think it would have a care for old women like me who can't afford to take a spill. Why, if I fall down, every bone in my body will snap."

Rosebud stood hesitantly. "Greetings, Weroansqua. Can we get something for you? A cup of tea perhaps?"

"Yes, that would be fine." Hunting Hawk stopped before Nine Killer. The War Chief stood and nodded a respectful greeting.

Okeus himself might have just walked into the room, the way people fidgeted in the attempt to look at ease.

If Hunting Hawk noticed, she betrayed no awareness.

"Be seated," Nine Killer offered.

Braced on her sassafras cane, Hunting Hawk eased herself down with a crackling of joints and sighed.

Rosebud appeared flustered; she almost dropped the ceramic cup she used to dip warm tea from a pot on the cooking fire. She extended it to Hunting Hawk with anxious hands.

Hunting Hawk sipped the tea and nodded politely. "Thank you." She raised an eyebrow. "War Chief, I was wondering if we could talk?"

"If you'll excuse us." Rosebud shot a glance at her

family. "I think we'll take this opportunity to pay a visit to cousin Yellow Net." Like a flushed covey of quail, the children scuttled for the doorway and the stormy night.

Hunting Hawk's preoccupation kept her from noticing the panicked retreat. In the ensuing silence, the old woman turned her brooding eyes on the fire; her withered brown lips pursed as she watched the flames slowly win the battle with the damp wood.

Finally, Nine Killer asked, "What did you need to see me about, Weroansqua?"

"A bit formal, are we? 'Weroansqua'? And just the two of us alone?"

Nine Killer shrugged as he gave her a wary scrutiny.

She took a drink from the tea and wiped her lips with the corner of her soft deerskin mantle. "I need to hear your thoughts, War Chief. If we decide to go to Three Myrtle and retrieve this High Fox, what are our options?"

Nine Killer ran a hand over the back of his neck, trying to massage the frustration out of his knotted muscles. "What options are there? If we go after the boy, Three Myrtle will fight to protect him. Black Spike made that clear."

"Can you win?"

Nine Killer couldn't help it. He laughed. "Win, Elder? If I can take Three Myrtle, defeat Black Spike's warriors, and capture the boy, will we have won? If I attack and they beat us back, or fight us to a stalemate, will we have won? No matter the outcome of the warfare, the results will be the same." He met her hard gaze squarely. "The alliance will be destroyed, fragmented as completely as if you'd smacked a dry walnut with a stonc-headed hammer."

"Some things can't be avoided." Hunting Hawk made

a sour face. "I'm trapped, War Chief, like a squirrel in a cage. I keep reaching out through the gaps to claw a way out, but I can't find the latch string. Had it been any young woman but Red Knot, I could wiggle us out of this mess."

"Oh?"

She smiled crookedly. "Of course. I could put a little pressure on the aggrieved family, negotiate a deal with the culprit's clan, and impose a fine. I might have to surreptitiously funnel a couple of canoe loads of corn, copper, and puccoon to one side or the other, but I could buy off both parties and reach a compromise. I could have done it this time if Red Knot was marrying anyone but Copper Thunder, but I can't make a quiet fix of this. Not with Copper Thunder in the middle of it, and Water Snake out in the woods scheming against me."

"No, you can't." Nine Killer stared down into his tea. "Red Knot's death has created a crack in our alliance. At first opportunity, someone is going to wedge in a digging stick, and pry us apart."

"I think that will happen anyway." She pulled at the wattle of skin hanging under her chin. "I'm not accustomed to seeing this dullness in your eyes. You don't look excited about this raid on Three Myrtle."

"Elder, before I was Blackened and killed, I dreamed of being a warrior. And since I became a man, I've dedicated myself to my clan and my people."

"And very successfully, too."

"But for the first time, I wonder who I am fighting. Where is the enemy? These men I've shared the war trail with? The ones I've stood shoulder to shoulder with in battle against the Mamanatowick's warriors? The ones who covered my back when we drove off Conoy raiders?"

"The very same. Things change, War Chief."

Why was she here? Hunting Hawk always had ulterior

motives. This was more than her seeking her War Chief's opinion. She was probing, looking for something.

Nine Killer shifted uneasily. "And if I raid Three Myrtle, what have I protected? Have I saved any lives? Have I defended any territory? Is the Water Snake weakened? Is Stone Frog?"

"This isn't about those things." Hunting Hawk sipped her tea and studied him thoughtfully.

He knew that cunning look. She was hiding something. "Then what is it about? Glory? Honor? I feel a warrior's pride when I stand over a defeated enemy. I don't think I will feel that way when I stand over my cousin's bleeding body in Three Myrtle Village. I won't see it when I look into the women's eyes, and see them weeping for men I knew, and respected. So much for courage, and skill."

"I could almost think you didn't believe that High Fox was the killer. Is that what makes you hesitate?"

"Weroansqua, I have to be honest; too many questions about the girl's death are unanswered. Something about all of this isn't right."

"Exactly what isn't right? You've heard Flat Willow's account of what happened. Could it be any more obvious?"

"No, but, well . . ." He frowned, trying to put it into words. "I've got a stirring in my gut that we're missing something, some bit of information that would make it all understandable."

"And I'm supposed to trust your gut?"

He shrugged and glanced away. "It's the best I can give you for the moment."

"Would you prefer that I find someone else to lead this raid?" Her hard black eyes bored into him to read the secrets of his soul.

Was she digging for weakness? "No, Weroansqua. I am the War Chief of Flat Pearl Village. A man doesn't have to enjoy a duty to do it well. If this thing can be accomplished, no one is more capable of it than I am. If it is to be attempted, it must be done as efficiently, quickly, and cleanly as possible. We can't afford mistakes that would turn a bad situation into a disaster. The best we can hope for is to strike like lightning, grab the boy, and be gone with the least amount of damage done to Three Myrtle Village and its defenders.''

"Keep the anger and resentment to a minimum?'' Hunting Hawk's questioning eyebrow rearranged her wrinkles. "That, War Chief, might be our only hope. If you can enter, seize High Fox, and make your escape without killing too many, we might be able to reach a compromise in the aftermath. The trick is not to stir them up beyond the point where we can repair the damage.''

"To do so,'' Nine Killer whispered softly, "will take a miracle. We'd best pray that Okeus sleeps late on that day.''

"You'd do almost anything to avoid this, wouldn't you?''

"Wouldn't you? You know the risks.''

"To be sure, War Chief. Find me a clean way out, and I'll take it. I swear by Okeus.'' She drank the last of her tea, and waved him off when he tried to help her to her feet. She made a face as she straightened her back and said, "Sleep well, War Chief. Dream of ways to make this raid work. I want that boy, and without too much bloodshed.''

She gave him a curt nod, and pottered off toward the door, her sassafras cane making a ticking sound as it tapped the packed dirt floor.

After she'd stepped outside, Nine Killer stared after her, a frown lining his forehead. He could imagine her out in the night, her figure hunched in the misty darkness, crossing the village in her shambling walk—like a spider creeping along a deadly web.

Moments later, Rosebud's head peered in through the doorway.

"Is it all right?"

"No, sister. It is not. I fear Okeus is laughing at us this night."

Ten

The cold wind blowing down from the northwest sent white-capped waves scudding into the narrows of Three Myrtle Inlet. The water had a sullen green appearance, as if resentful of anything warm and alive. Undercut roots resisted its pounding, struggling to protect the fragile soil.

Low gray clouds billowed in the southeast. If anything, they made the winter-bare branches appear more bleak and questing.

Threads of mist blew over the palisade around Three Myrtle Village, moistening the weathered posts until they gleamed. The thatched longhouses, too, were mist-darkened and dreary. Curls of blue smoke eddied along the curves of roofs before being torn away by the wind.

This was no day for travel. A lone canoe bobbed and ducked, riding the choppy waves toward the village canoe landing. The solitary paddler had a cloth blanket wrapped over his feathered cloak, and his head was covered with a beaver skin cap. From time to time, he'd rest his paddle across the gunwales and use a conch shell cup to bail out the water that shipped over the gunwales. Then he would return to the struggle, driving his boat toward the landing's lines of beached canoes.

As the bow of his dugout slid onto the sand, a cry went up from the village. By the time the traveler sloshed ashore and pulled his slim canoe up the beach, several men had trotted out from Three Myrtle Village, bows strung and arrows drawn.

The traveler raised his hands, and cried, "I come with important news for Black Spike!"

Black Spike stepped out from the overlapping gate in the palisade, a blanket tucked to his chest. "I am Black Spike, Weroance of Three Myrtle. Who . . . Stone Cob? Is that you?"

"It is me, Weroance. I come with news!"

Black Spike stopped short, head cocked. "What news would the lieutenant of Nine Killer bring me?"

Stone Cob held his empty hands out to Black Spike. "Nine Killer's lieutenant brings you nothing; but Stone Cob, son of Blue Fish, of the Star Crab Clan, comes to warn you that Nine Killer is assembling warriors at this very moment to raid Three Myrtle Village."

Muttered curses broke out from the men surrounding Black Spike. The Weroance raised a hand to still them. "Very well, we are warned, Stone Cob. What of you? Why are you here?"

"My mother, my sisters, and brother live in Three Myrtle Village. No matter what I've sworn to Hunting Hawk, or to Nine Killer, I cannot make war against my kin."

"And what does Nine Killer plan?"

"He means to attack you by surprise. He seeks to accomplish by stealth and audacity what force of arms might fail to do. He hopes to strike in the hour before dawn, capture High Fox, and escape."

"And when we resist?"

"He hopes to be gone before you can organize a resistance. He would do this without killing anyone if he could." Stone Cob glanced uneasily at the trees that hugged the inlet's northern bank. They lay little more than a bow shot from the village's palisade. "He has told his warriors to land there in the middle of the night. As long as the wind is right, it will carry the scent away from the village dogs."

"I see." Black Spike scowled at the dripping trees. "Well, we can prepare for Nine Killer's attack." He glanced back. "Then, am I to believe you will join us? Fight against Flat Pearl Village's warriors?"

Stone Cob shook his head. "No, great Weroance. If it means my life, I'll never raise a hand against Nine Killer. He saved my hide more than once. Just as I cannot be party to the murder of my family and clan, I cannot carry weapons against my War Chief."

"Then what will you do?" Black Spike asked.

Stone Cob raised his hands in futility. "I don't know, Weroance. Just be warned that Nine Killer's attack is imminent. With that, I will take my leave. Perhaps when this is all over I will—"

"Oh, no you won't, Stone Cob." Black Spike made a gesture with his hand. Immediately, two warriors leapt forward, war clubs ready.

"What does this mean?" Stone Cob demanded angrily.

"It means that you might be here to mislead me. What kind of fool are you? Do you seriously think I'd just allow you to leave? To do what? Go back and report to Nine Killer that we are ready and waiting for him?"

Stone Cob took a deep breath, and stared at the soaked sand beneath his feet. "Are sense and honor gone from the world?"

"Bind him up," Black Spike ordered. "Then prepare! Nine Killer will come by water, seek to land his warriors in the trees in the night."

A warrior asked, "What if Stone Cob told us lies? What if Nine Killer cuts across to the south, approaches through the fields?"

"We'll prepare for that, too." Black Spike studied Stone Cob through half-lidded eyes as the warrior's hands were bound. "And if that's the case, we'll know that the *honorable* Stone Cob was sent as a spy to mislead us. Were I to discover that to be true, I'd bash his brains out myself."

Black Spike turned on his heel and strode back into the palisade. The warriors shoved Stone Cob after him.

Nine Killer could almost believe that Okeus had been against him from the very beginning of this raid. He'd been able to muster less than half of his warriors, the others gone mysteriously missing. Most were reportedly "out hunting." Then, just after they'd discussed the plan of attack, Stone Cob had disappeared. Stone Cob, of all people!

No sooner had Nine Killer launched his little fleet to paddle down to Three Myrtle Inlet than the weather had turned blustery, and then downright miserable. Two of his canoes had swamped, the warriors swimming their sodden boats to the safety of the shore before dumping them out and relaunching.

Wet, miserable, and shivering, they watched the night sky as the misty rain turned into slushy snow.

With his unerring sense of direction, Nine Killer had led them to the trees just north of Three Myrtle Village. Here, they huddled in the darkness, soaked to the bone, teeth chattering from cold, as dispirited as any band of raiders he'd ever led.

"What do you think?" Flying Weir asked as they crouched in the lee of an ash tree and peered out into the darkness toward Three Myrtle Village.

Nine Killer wiped water from his numb face and squinted toward where he knew the palisade stood. "I don't hear a thing. Only a mad idiot would be out in weather like this. Perhaps, after all we've been through, this weather is a blessing.''

"A blessing?" Flying Weir wrung out the fringes of his shirt, the sopping leather squishing in his hands. "My balls are sucked up so tight with cold that I have trouble swallowing."

"Well, I guess if you're the sort of man who swallows through his balls, you might not understand a blessing when you had one."

Another gust of wind blew in, spattering them with chill droplets. Nine Killer crouched down, wincing as the wind whipped off toward Three Myrtle Village.

He cocked his head. A nagging hesitation crawled around in his gut, trying to tell him something.

He searched the sky for any hint of light. Just how long did he have until dawn? The weather worked against the defenders of Three Myrtle Village, but it also worked against his raiders. When Nine Killer's party rushed forward, they had to be able to see their objective, negotiate the palisade gate, find High Fox —in Black Spike's Great House, no doubt—and then retreat to the canoes without getting lost. The one thing he couldn't afford was bumbling around in the dark.

He couldn't help but think about how terribly dark it was.

"All right," he growled at Flying Weir. "This wind is coming from the north, blowing right down our backs and toward the village. That will give us our direction. As I remember it, it's no more than a bow shot to the palisade. I want everyone to join hands. That way we can't be separated. I'll lead. At the palisade, we'll feel our way around to the gate and wait until it's just light enough to see. Then we can rush them."

"Right," Flying Weir muttered. He didn't sound convinced, but he passed the orders on.

"Let's go." Nine Killer took Flying Weir's hand and

stood, starting off into the murky night, feeling with his feet. The darkness pressed down on him, as if to smother his very soul. He could feel Flying Weir shivering; his own body shook so hard his teeth rattled.

Step by step they proceeded, worry building in Nine Killer's gut. What was it? There wasn't some ditch out here, was there? No, nothing he could remember.

In the back of his mind, an image formed, a memory of a summer day not so long ago: three laughing children chasing around with a pack of barking dogs. They'd been running back and forth across these flats, playing stick-and-ball shinny, the dogs barking and barking . . .

"Hold up!" Nine Killer hissed, squeezing Flying Weir's hand.

"What?"

Nine Killer cocked his head, realizing just what had upset him. "The wind . . . right down our backs, and not a dog barking at our scent."

"Maybe the dogs are inside?" Flying Weir had lifted a shoulder against the pelting flakes of snow.

Nine Killer could sense the unease among his wet warriors. His fears had carried all down the line. "Think, Flying Weir. You know Black Spike. He's expecting something like this. Would he take the dogs in?"

"I, uh . . . no. He wouldn't. Not the same man who fought with us against Water Snake."

Nine Killer chewed his lip. A cold trickle of water ran down the side of his head, and along his neck. "It's a trap," he decided. "Someone is muzzling those dogs. Turn around. Have the last man find our way back into the trees. We're going to have to do something different."

"Are you sure? If we—"

"He's *waiting* for us! If we go in there, we're going to be cut off, boxed, and shot down like the silly quail we are! Now, move!"

Nine Killer could feel his warriors' spirits sagging, any last optimism draining away like the water that streamed down their clay-cold flesh.

The chance of quick surprise had eluded him. The chance to use stealth was gone. All that remained was sheer brute force. An attack against a fortified enemy. And Okeus could skewer Nine Killer's soul with stingray barbs before he'd waste lives like that. No, the best course was to withdraw before first light, paddle southeast along the coast, and try a cross-country approach to regain the advantage.

It was only after they'd entered the little copse of trees that Nine Killer heard the anxious whispers of his men. At the urgency in their voices, he hurried forward, tripping over roots, demanding, "What's wrong?"

"The canoes," Split Rattlesnake called hoarsely. "They're gone! Someone has taken them!"

Nine Killer felt around on the shore, his fingers tracing the smooth tracks in the mud where the boats had been pushed out into the inlet.

And now, Nine Killer, how are you going to get out of this mess?

As he straightened, the first shout came to his ears. A man called, "We've got them cut off in the trees!"

Nine Killer and his warriors spun as another voice to their south cried, "We're ready if they come in this direction."

"Nine Killer!" The voice was hauntingly familiar to the War Chief's ears. "This is Black Spike! You are cut off. You may surrender, and take your chances, or die like a warrior should!"

Nine Killer muscled his way through his crowding knot of warriors, cupping his mouth to shout, "You come get me, you miserable excuse for a worm!" Then to his men, Nine Killer ordered, "Fan out. We've got until daylight to create some sort of defensive fortifications."

"And you think you can save us?" Flying Weir demanded too loudly.

"Of course. Oh, come. We've been in tighter fixes than this. We've nearly four tens of stout warriors, and one way or another, I'm going to get us out of this mess, and take High Fox for good measure." Despite the hearty tone of voice, he knew a lot of good men were going to die.

The Panther wasn't prepared for people. After watching ten Comings of the Leaves on his island, the thought of a village full of strangers took him somewhat aback. He'd done well with Sun Conch and High Fox, of course. They were two impressionable young people—but, bat dung and curses, he'd be surrounded by tens of people he didn't know!

That thought circled around his soul like a predatory hawk as High Fox and Sun Conch rhythmically paddled their way into Three Myrtle Inlet. Through the screen of trees, Panther could see irregular plots of land cleared from the forest. Little pickets, all in nice lines, protruded from the water to mark the location of fish weirs. No doubt about it, this was a place where humans lived.

Panther's stomach fluttered. To himself, he whispered, "Oh, come now, why are you afraid? These are just men and women like everyone else. No better, and no worse."

Sun Conch turned from her position in the bow. "Did you say something, Elder?"

"No," he replied, and scowled.

She blinked and returned to paddling, but he noticed that her shoulders had gone stiff.

After so long in exile, his nerves kept drawing tighter. They'd stare at him with horror in their eyes. He could see it just as in the past. That was the worst part, the suspicion and distrust. People thought him a witch, a night traveler, a baleful spirit that communed with dark Power.

"Face it, old man, you'll never sit around a fire again and laugh with others. You knew that when you left the haunts of men."

Sun Conch started to turn, but apparently thought better of it, and paddled harder.

Shouts carried on the eddies of wind.

"What's that?" Sun Conch asked.

High Fox shrugged, but Panther saw the tension building in the boy's muscular arms.

"That high-pitched wolf sound," Sun Conch observed. "I know that call. It's . . . a war cry."

"Big Noise," High Fox agreed, placing the voice. "He only makes that cry in battle."

"Hurry!" Sun Conch cried, her paddle taking a full bite of the murky water.

Hands braced on the gunwales, Panther swallowed hard. What would he find? And what would he do when he got there?

As the Three Myrtle Village warriors drew themselves into line and charged forward, Nine Killer drew his famous bow, figured the distance and drop, and shot. He watched the arrow rush up against the graying dawn, arch, and lance down toward the prancing figure at the head of the line. Perhaps Black Spike wasn't paying attention. At that range, he should have seen the arrow coming, would have had plenty of time to skip out of the way. He held his wicker shield high on his left arm, gesturing his warriors forward with his right as he checked his lines for the attack.

Thus it was that Nine Killer's arrow slanted out of the sky and drove itself through Black Spike's shield.

The Weroance staggered under the impact, stared stupidly at the bloody shaft that had driven through his shield and now protruded from his forearm. More from surprise than pain, he dropped to his knees and screamed.

At that, the line wavered in confusion.

Nine Killer smiled grimly to himself. He'd bought a little more time for his warriors. If he could delay the inevitable attack through the day and until dark, he and his men could attempt to swim the inlet. Perhaps then, at least, some of them might escape the death trap he'd led them into.

But not me, Nine Killer consoled himself. Someone had to pay for this debacle, and no matter what, his reputation was ruined. *Better to die here, bravely fighting a rear-guard action. At least that will save some shred of honor for my family and clan.*

"No!" Black Spike cried, refocusing Nine Killer's attention. The Weroance was struggling to his feet and waving his warriors onward. "Go on! Rush them! Kill them to the last man!"

Big Noise, to Black Spike's right, leapt and screamed his cougar cry, shaking his wicker shield and waving his war club over his head. "Onward! Kill them!"

Nine Killer glanced to each side, noting with satisfaction that his warriors were standing fast, bows strung, arrows ready. Some had boosted their fellows up into the trees, where they could shoot down on the attackers. Others had broken off branches, piled earth into crude breastworks, and used the trees to the best advantage for defense.

Three Myrtle Village could take them—would take

them before the day was out—but they'd pay dearly for the effort.

"Do you see!" Nine Killer called as he stepped from the trees to face the ragged line of warriors. "Do you see what happened to Black Spike? Come on! Who will be next?"

Nine Killer paced back and forth. "Who will die?"

The sullen line of attacking warriors had halted again. *That's it, buy time. Prolong the inevitable.* "I am *Nine Killer*! I have shot the first arrow, and drawn the blood of your Weroance. I didn't mean to kill him." A lie wouldn't hurt a thing here. "But you must know that we will kill you if we have to!"

"You can't escape!" Black Spike cried. Two warriors were working on the arrow in his arm. One snapped off the stone-tipped point, the other drawing the slim shaft back through the arm and woven willow. Black Spike's shield dropped to the ground as the Weroance cradled his bleeding arm.

"We don't *want* to escape!" Nine Killer thumped his chest proudly. "We came for High Fox! Give him to us, and we will leave!"

"How?" Big Noise demanded. "Walk on water?"

Hoots of derision rose from the Three Myrtle warriors.

Nine Killer raised a fist. "You know me! Give me the boy, and we'll leave! We don't want a war. We don't want to kill anyone. But Red Knot, daughter of Shell Comb, has been murdered!"

Black Spike struggled to his feet, one of the warriors binding a strip of hide tightly about the wound. "You came to kill, you worthless Flat Pearl dogs! Now, you'll reap the rewards."

Nine Killer rocked on his heels, seeing the resolve stiffening in the line of attackers. If only his arrow had cut through Black Spike's heart instead of his arm! With Black Spike dead, he might have been able to garner enough time to figure out a way to escape.

"Forward!" Black Spike cried, pointing at Nine Killer's warriors. "Nine Killer has taken his best shot! Yet here I stand, barely scratched! Okeus has granted his Power to our side! Go! Take them, and let no man live! You will be forever remembered for this day! Generations yet unborn will sing of your courage and bravery!"

A mighty shout broke from the lungs of Black Spike's warriors. Nine Killer swallowed hard. He'd seen that stiffening of spines, that raising of heads, and that hardening glint of proud eyes. Only an act of the gods would turn them back now.

"Here they come!" Nine Killer called, retreating to the edge of the trees. "Let's show them what we're made of, and we'll get out of this yet!"

But when he met Flying Weir's eyes, he could see the truth there.

"Within a hand of time we'll be overrun, wiped out to the last man. You know that, don't you?" Flying Weir asked quietly so the others wouldn't hear.

Nine Killer grinned humorlessly. "No one lives forever."

"No—but I curse Hunting Hawk for sending us on this fool's errand."

Across the flats, Black Spike called the fatal order. His unbroken ranks of warriors let out a wild whoop, then started forward.

Nine Killer pulled another arrow from his quiver, shouted, "Hold your shots until they close," and prepared himself to die.

Here they came, breaking into a trot. He could see the bright feathers woven into their hair. Painted and decorated loincloths swung with each step. Their skin was shiny with grease, each body painted dark red with puccoon root.

Glancing from the corner of his eye, he felt pride swell within him. His own warriors waited stoically, tense but resolute. None would run in these last fragile moments.

Shouts rang out from ahead, and to Nine Killer's surprise, the ranks of Three Myrtle warriors slowed, looking back toward the canoe landing. Like fibers fraying from a cord, the attack faltered as the enemy warriors stopped short to mumble among themselves. Word worked up the line until even Black Spike hesitated. Across the distance, Nine Killer could hear him calling out in disbelief.

"What's this?" Flying Weir asked warily, his bow clutched in a tight fist.

"I don't know." Nine Killer stepped out from the trees, looking south. A young warrior and a girl escorted an old man up from the landing.

"High Fox!" The name carried across the distance. Nine Killer craned his neck, his gaze hardening on his target. Yes, and the girl was Sun Conch, High Fox's faithful friend. But who on earth was that old man?

No sooner had the trio approached the first of the Three Myrtle warriors than the men recoiled as if from a rattlesnake.

Nine Killer's blood froze at the words that passed from lip to lip: "It's *The Panther*!"

Nine Killer instinctively made the warding gesture with his fingers.

"The Panther?" Flying Weir wondered as he stepped out beside Nine Killer. "The witch? What's *he* doing here?"

"I have no idea." Nine Killer's mouth had gone dry. "But look who he's with. That's High Fox. You see a witch walking with a murderer. How much worse do you think it could be?"

Flying Weir shook his head, his grimace that of a man who'd bitten into a moldy beach plum.

After all of Panther's worry about meeting strangers, the notion of walking into a battle left his stomach tied in an uncomfortable knot.

As he walked toward the shouting warriors, he cast a quick glance at each of his companions. High Fox still looked glum—as guilty as if caught in the act. Sun Conch appeared calm and stoic, but then she still believed she'd surrendered body and soul to a dangerous witch. She'd given herself up for dead days ago.

Panther squinted at the line of warriors. The closest man had stopped to call High Fox's name to his companions. Sun Conch shouted, "I have brought The Panther to look into the charges made against High Fox! He will speak for my friend!"

The nearest warriors melted away like snow from a fire, and Panther could see the rising panic in their eyes. At that moment, had the command but been given, they'd gladly have turned on him, skewering him with arrows until his flesh resembled a porcupine's.

Panther stalked forward and glared to the right and left. By Okeus' bloody balls, if they thought him a witch, he'd use the belief against them.

"What goes on here?" he demanded angrily. "Who is responsible for this mess?"

Warriors wheeled like a covey of quail to form up behind a tall man, his left forearm bound with a bloody strip of hide.

"Who are you?" Panther demanded, catching a glimpse of other warriors up in the trees. "And who are those people over there?"

The leader, his face ashen, whether from the wound or Panther's appearance, swallowed hard. "I am Black

Spike, Weroance of Three Myrtle Village. Those dogs hiding in the trees are Flat Pearl warriors belonging to the Weroansqua Hunting Hawk."

Panther stared at the trees, and shouted, "Who is in charge of the Flat Pearl war party?"

A short, burly man with shoulders like a ledge stepped out from behind a huge oak. He carried a thick-wristed bow, with an arrow nocked. His bandy legs might have been carved from stumps.

"You speak to Nine Killer, War Chief of Flat Pearl Village. What is your purpose here, witch?"

"Surly sort, isn't he?" Panther asked his companions.

Sun Conch came forward to stand beside him. "He's the most respected war leader among the Independent villages."

"Huh! He looks trapped, if you ask me." Panther raised his voice. "What is happening here?"

Black Spike took an uncertain step. "The raiders came in the night to take High Fox by force. We were warned that they were coming. Last night, in the darkness, two of my warriors, Big Noise and Wind, swam around behind them and pushed their canoes away. We surrounded them and waited for morning. When Nine Killer would not surrender, we decided to attack."

Panther turned. "You, Nine Killer, step out here!"

The squat warrior stood fast. "Why should I trust myself to you, night traveler?"

"Because I'm here to sort this matter out. And, from what I can see, you and your warriors are about to be killed at best, or captured, studded with slivers of pitch pine and set afire. Now, do you want to take a chance that I can save your life, and those of your men, or do you want me to sing an incantation that makes Black Spike's warriors invincible?"

"Save their lives?" Black Spike cried. "Impossible! We're going to kill them right here and now!"

Panther spun on his heel, glaring into Black Spike's eyes until they dropped. "Perhaps I will fester that wounded arm of yours. I think I could swell it up like a putrid corpse. The fever will burn your sense away while pus drips like rainwater. Why, you'd rave yourself to death in three days."

Black Spike wavered, worked his mouth, and nodded. "We will listen to your words, Elder."

"Fine, that's sense, for once." Panther indicated the warriors crowding behind Black Spike. "The rest of you, go away. Leave your Weroance here. He will be safe." Panther faced Nine Killer. "Come forward, War Chief. We will talk."

"I don't trust you!"

Panther pointed at the retreating Three Myrtle warriors. "Would you rather trust them? I'm here to determine the truth of the accusations against High Fox. If you have no interest in making that determination, Nine Killer, I might just as well let Black Spike kill you, and go back to my island."

Nine Killer hesitated, then handed his bow to a warrior who stepped out from the trees. The War Chief walked warily forward.

Panther waited, arms crossed, foot tapping the damp grass. When Nine Killer was within five paces he stopped, and his hands tightened into fists. The action made the thick muscle of his forearms swell and writhe. He shot a piercing glance first at High Fox, then Black Spike, skimmed over Sun Conch, and finally turned on Panther. "So, you're the famous night traveler? I've never seen a witch before."

"Hah!" Panther snorted. "That's what gullible fools claim. Myself, in all my years, I've never really believed in witches. Men and women with Power, yes. But witches, War Chief"—Panther tapped the side of his head—"it's all in here. A creation of the imagination."

Panther cast a glance at Black Spike, who scowled angrily at Nine Killer. The Weroance had his wounded arm tucked to his chest. He looked pale, all color drained from his face, as if the slightest breeze would knock him over.

"Imagination?" Nine Killer asked skeptically.

"Imagination carries its own Power, War Chief. A Power more intimidating than the combined forces of all your warriors with their bows and war clubs."

"This is empty talk. What are you here for, witch? What is your purpose with this deceitful dog?" Black Spike asked, his hot glare pinning Nine Killer.

Panther reached out and pulled the nervous High Fox forward. "This young warrior has been accused of murder. Young Red Knot is dead, as I understand it. Sun Conch came to me, told me that the Independent villages were about to come apart like an unfired pot in a rainstorm. And now, when I arrive here, I find that her words carried a great deal of truth. As I remember, Three Myrtle and Flat Pearl were the heart of the alliance that kept the Independent villages out of the Mamanatowick's grasp."

"Why do you care, witch?" Nine Killer crossed his arms.

"About the fate of the Independent villages?" Panther shrugged. "I don't. If the Mamanatowick captures all of you, it won't affect me. The sun will continue to rise, travel across the sky, and set in the west. The snows will come, followed by planting. Summer will nourish the plants and trees, and harvest will follow. The leaves will turn and fall and winter will come again. People will continue to be born, grow, live, and die."

"But not our clans," Black Spike added. "And if you don't care about that, what is your purpose here?"

Panther indicated Sun Conch. "This girl, Sun Conch, believes that High Fox didn't kill Red Knot. Maybe I'm here because of her." Then he paused and smiled. "Or, maybe I'm here because I'm curious. Who did kill Red Knot?''

''And if it was High Fox?'' Nine Killer demanded. ''What then, witch?''

Panther narrowed his eyes to slits and turned to the shivering High Fox. The youth had come forward to stand just behind Sun Conch's shoulder, his handsome face strained. ''Oh, if I find that he killed Red Knot—and lied to me about it—he'll wish he'd let you catch him in the very beginning, War Chief.''

Eleven

Nine Killer had camped his warriors in the little grove of trees that once had been his death trap. Gray scudding clouds could be seen through the stark branches overhead. Disgruntled, he frowned at the fire. The aroma of boiling corn, acorn, and fish stew rose from the cooking pots his warriors now watched over. In all of his life, he'd never undergone such rapid reversals of fate. That morning, he should have pulled off his most daring and audacious raid ever, only to be tricked, trapped, and confounded at every turn. Then, just as his enemy had massed to deal him a complete defeat, the witch, Panther, arrived to save him from disaster.

And now, here I sit, happily alive, but no closer to the solution of my dilemma, or escape from this impossible quagmire.

Two hands of time before, their canoes had been returned to them by sullen Three Myrtle warriors. So, not only had they survived at Panther's whim, but they could now extricate themselves from this stewing disaster.

A truly wise man would have packed up and run while the running was good.

Nine Killer scratched his ear and grimaced. He'd always believed himself to be a reasonably bright fellow. But no matter what the urgings of his heart, stubborn will kept him here, waiting to see just what would come of The Panther's arrival at Three Myrtle Village.

He plucked up a twig and used it to tap the damp soil. He'd been unhappy about every twist and turn in this Red Knot affair. As things progressed, the situation became ever more clouded.

"War Chief?" Flying Weir called, interrupting Nine Killer's thoughts. His lieutenant pointed out at the dusk.

Through the trees, Nine Killer could see The Panther walking toward them across the clearing that lay between the trees and the Three Myrtle Village. Young Sun Conch followed behind him, wary. She'd pulled her feathered cape back and hooked it over the war club tied to her belt. Her right hand rested on the handle. The weapon looked too big for such a small girl. Through the thin fabric of her red dress, Nine Killer could see her barely budded breasts. Did the girl seriously consider herself to be a warrior? In any other circumstances, Nine Killer would have laughed at the idea.

Nine Killer dropped his stick, stood, wiped his hands, and said, "Let them come, but Flying Weir, keep an eye on them. I want to know immediately if you see anything suspicious."

"Yes, War Chief." Flying Weir didn't seem reassured.

The Panther entered the trees and walked directly to Nine Killer's fire, nodding an absent greeting. Without ceremony, he seated himself before the fire and extended his bony hands to the warmth. The old man's skin looked like desiccated leather, dark, callused, and wrinkled.

Sun Conch stood behind him, the nostrils of her beak nose flaring. The Panther might act unconcerned, but Sun Conch remained on her feet and concentrated on the Flat Pearl warriors who glared at her from all sides. A brave girl, especially for one so skinny.

"It's going to be a cold night," The Panther said by way of greeting. "But actually a bit warm for the season. Could be worse, you know. I've seen snow hip deep to an elk this close to solstice."

"I've heard of such winters," Nine Killer replied. He crouched down and picked up his stick again, rolling it in his fingers, waiting.

The Panther rubbed his hands together, mused at the flames, and asked, "Have you ever watched the mist blow in from the ocean?"

Nine Killer lifted a skeptical eyebrow. "I have."

"This Red Knot problem, I think it's like a thick mist blew in. No one can see clearly. The girl is dead, and now people are blindly trying to see her death as they wish."

"You think so, eh?"

The Panther smiled. "Why else would two villages who have been friends for years be tearing at each other's throats?"

Nine Killer said nothing, his hackles rising.

"Ah," The Panther said knowingly. "From your expression I am supposed to think you wanted to die this morning?"

"Don't be silly."

The Panther studied him, seeming to see right through Nine Killer's skin and into his soul. Then the old man said, "Let's you and I be honest with each other. Of all the challenges men accept, honesty is the hardest to meet. So, tell me, War Chief, just this once, for this little moment, could you be honest?"

Nine Killer cocked his head. "Why should I be?"

"Why should you not? Or, is it because you know who killed Red Knot—and it isn't High Fox? Hmm."

"Absolutely not! That's . . . that's . . ." Nine Killer's protests died as he looked into the old man's unfailing gaze. In that instant, a grudging respect was born. "Very well. You may indeed be a witch, for you see a man's soul, don't you?"

The Panther shrugged. "Oh, I know you, Nine Killer. You gave yourself away when you didn't leave the moment your canoes were returned. Were you the killer, you would have left faster than a frightened duck—knowing full well you couldn't capture High Fox. The same if you were protecting the killer."

Nine Killer considered, hearing the sense of the words. "Maybe I'm just a smarter kind of killer. Maybe that's what I wanted you to think."

"Why?" The Panther steepled his hands. "What does it matter what I think?"

"It doesn't, I . . ." Nine Killer stopped. "You're very clever, witch."

"So, can we be honest, you and me? Your answer will depend on whether you really want to know what happened to Red Knot."

"I could tell you I was being honest, and lie anyway."

"You could. But, will you?"

Nine Killer chuckled and used his stick to tap the dirt. "Very well, witch, for this one moment, I will be honest with you."

"Then, if we are being honest, it bothers me when I'm called a witch. I've known a few, and I'm nothing like them. To be a night traveler, one must pay a terrible price. In the first place, I'm not prepared to give up that much of myself. In the second, I don't want the things most witches want. The possession of men's souls is a depressing and truly horrifying proposition."

"It is?"

"Tell me, War Chief, why would anyone with sense want to bottle a man's soul up in a jar someplace? What if it got loose, got mixed up with your own? I can't speak for you, but I'm perplexed enough with my own soul without having it attacked and confused by someone else's."

Despite himself, Nine Killer cracked a smile. "I'd never thought of it that way."

"No, I suppose you didn't. Most people don't." He paused. "Do you really think High Fox killed this girl?"

Nine Killer shrugged. "He was up on the ridge. She was running off to meet him. Who should I think killed her?"

Panther's attention had remained on the fire, but he said, "I don't hear conviction in your voice, War Chief."

"Just how much do you know about what happened that morning?"

"I'll tell you everything High Fox told me." The Panther went on to relate High Fox's story, ending with, "And, truthfully, I'm not sure he didn't kill her."

At that, Sun Conch shot a terrified glance at The Panther. As if the old man had eyes in the back of his head, he said, "I came here for Sun Conch, to find out the truth of what happened. I will follow that quest wherever it leads. For the moment, I will take High Fox's word that he didn't kill the girl. I even half believe him."

"He ran," Nine Killer pointed out.

"He's little more than a boy, Blackened or not. He panicked and lost all of his sense. He was already in enough trouble just asking the girl to run away with him. Like quicksand, he'd sunk up to his waist. When he found the girl's body, I think he was in over his head. Too much mud in his eyes to see clearly."

Nine Killer shifted uncomfortably. "Something hasn't been right about this from the beginning." He went on to relate the events of the morning Red Knot had disappeared: the decision to search; Copper Thunder's apparent nonchalance; Quick Fawn's discovery of Winged Blackbird; and the subsequent ambush of Corn Hunter's warriors.

"Flat Willow, a young hunter, found the body and reported it. We went up, looked around, found where the girl had been killed. She had a necklace in her hand. One made of drilled shark teeth, pearls, and . . ."

Sun Conch sucked in a deep breath.

"Yes, girl?" Nine Killer asked.

"Nothing, I—just a chill as the night settles." She pulled the front of her cape tighter, but her face had gone slack, her eyes huge.

Nine Killer continued: "Perhaps it's just that I don't like Copper Thunder, but I would have expected him to act differently about the murder of a woman promised to him. Hunting Hawk is playing her own deep game. She, too, didn't seem terribly distressed. Shell Comb, on the other hand, she's always been a firebrand, and she was ready to order an attack on Corn Hunter, convinced that Winged Blackbird's warriors had killed the girl."

"Copper Thunder didn't counsel war?"

"No. He's like a jumping spider, waiting, watching from his crack in the bark. He'll make no move until his prey is in range, and vulnerable."

"As the sun rises in the east . . ." The Panther sighed and rotated a shoulder, as if his bones ached.

"You were saying?"

"Oh, nothing." The Panther waved it away. "All those Comings of the Leaves out on my island, I'd come to wonder why I'd left the world behind. Now, I remember. It was people. The world never changes."

"We are the way we are, Elder. Descended from Okeus, living in the world he helped to mold."

"And for that I shall never forgive him." The Panther chuckled hoarsely. "So, you smell a pack rat in the nut cache, do you, War Chief? Well, I think someone is calling in the mist, seeking to keep us all from seeing.'' He scratched under his arm, firelight gleaming in his old eyes. ''Who would gain the most from her death?''

''The Mamanatowick. He'd have severed any potential alliance with Copper Thunder—and thrown the Independent villages into confusion in the process. But High Fox had reasons too, he was losing the woman he loved. Maybe even Copper Thunder—he might be playing a game we don't understand.''

''Flat Willow,'' Sun Conch whispered in a low voice.

The Panther turned. ''Flat Willow? The hunter who found her body?''

Sun Conch ran her hands over her war club. ''He . . . well, he, too, wanted Red Knot. He had been after her, trying to impress her. When she turned her eyes to High Fox . . . They had words. Flat Willow told High Fox to leave her alone or he'd make sure High Fox never set foot on Flat Pearl land again.''

The Panther arched a white eyebrow. ''I must have a talk with this young man.''

''A talk?'' Nine Killer asked.

The Panther smiled grimly, rubbing his hands together. ''But of course, War Chief. As I told you, I will see this thing through, no matter where it takes me. As I found this morning when I arrived, the mist has clouded everyone's vision—even your own, good War Chief. Now I am curious, and as you must admit, who else but The Panther can see this with clear eyes?''

''And what do you wish of me?''

Panther smiled cautiously. ''Two things. First, your help. And, second, the hardest thing of all, War Chief: your continued honesty.''

Things had a funny way of working out, The Panther thought as he and Sun Conch walked across the fallow tobacco fields toward the palisaded walls of Three Myrtle Village. Nine Killer could have been the blustery, arrogant sort of War Chief, the type whose blood pulsed with self-wonder and pride. Instead, the Panther had found him a sober and thoughtful man.

"What do we do now?" Sun Conch asked from a half-step behind. Dusk was falling.

"What anyone with sense does to a fire about ready to burn out of control. We splash a little water on it. How can we sniff out this girl's killer if warriors are killing each other and blood feud is being sworn?"

"Elder?" she said, and caught up to walk at his side. She'd plaited her long hair into a single braid that hung over her left shoulder. The style accentuated the roundness of her face and size of her eyes. "What you said back there, about High Fox—you don't truly believe he killed Red Knot, do you?"

Ah, what simple innocence filled Sun Conch's soul. "I told Nine Killer the truth; I'll take this trail wherever it leads me. I never promised that I would believe High Fox is innocent. If he is, I will do my best to prove it. If I discover that he really did kill her . . . well, no matter how much you might love a friend, he must suffer for his wrong actions. Or don't you agree?"

She frowned at her moccasins. "I suppose so, Elder."

"You *suppose*? My girl, there are three kinds of people in the world: the outstanding, the mediocre, and the truly hopeless. When you came to me, it was with the spirit of the outstanding. Then I hear you mutter such a thing?"

Sun Conch scuffed at the cold dirt of the tobacco field. "I have been asking myself what I would do if High Fox really killed her, that's all."

Panther shot her a glance. "And what did you decide?"

"Elder, I love him. I could not stand by and watch someone break his arms and legs and throw him headfirst onto a bonfire. I—"

"Nothing comes without its price, Sun Conch. We all must pay for our errors, as High Fox must if he killed this young woman. As you found out when you came to my island and gave yourself to me. Tell me, were the circumstances reversed, and you had been accused, do you think High Fox would have done what you did?"

"I would like to think so."

"Bah! You would like to think so? 'Would like'? What kind of words are those? To me, they sound like the kind of baby dribble that people use to fool themselves."

Sun Conch exhaled hard. "You don't think much of High Fox, do you?"

Panther stopped at the palisade gate. "No, Sun Conch, I do not. No matter that his father is the Weroance of Three Myrtle Village, or that he comes from a powerful clan, he will forever be one of those mediocre people, afraid to take the step that would make them outstanding. He will be a man without commitment, without the fiber in his soul to be a great leader. Unlike you, he won't pay the price to be outstanding."

Sun Conch frowned and fingered her war club. "I don't understand, Elder. He took a very great chance by asking Red Knot to run away with him. He was willing to give up everything for her. Isn't that paying the price?"

Panther pulled at the loose skin on his chin. "Answer me this, Sun Conch. Let's say you were in his position. You've asked the love of your life to run off with you. You find her, dead, freshly murdered on the top of the ridge. What is the first thing you do? Now, think before you speak. Be honest with yourself, and me.''

''I have thought about it, Elder,'' Sun Conch answered, ''But I really don't know. Assuming I didn't panic like High Fox, I think I would have . . . Well, but I'm not sure. Talking about it later isn't the same.''

''Ah, wisdom! Very good, Sun Conch. But I would wager that even if you'd run in panic—which I doubt—you would have turned back, accepted your responsibility, and born the consequences.''

''I hope you are correct, Elder.''

''Alas, if I am not, I've forgotten more about people and their ways than I think I have. And, now, let us go and see this Black Spike.''

They entered the palisade, through the narrow passage between the overlapping walls. From gaps between the posts, arrows could be fired from relative safety into exposed attackers. On the way, they passed four armed warriors who stood wrapped against the cold. Panther couldn't help but notice the warding signs they made with their fingers. The sight sobered him. Ohona help him if someone suddenly came down sick and died, or someone shot a deer that had no heart or liver. Humans could be violently irrational when it came to notions of witchcraft.

The muscular warrior named Big Noise met them at the opening into the village. ''What is your purpose, Panther?'' The man's eyes seemed to gleam, and he kept a safe distance between them.

''I have come to see Black Spike, Weroance of Three Myrtle Village.''

''Come this way, but be warned, at any sign of trouble, I will act to protect my chief and village.''

''I would expect nothing less of a responsible warrior,'' Panther agreed.

Big Noise glanced at Sun Conch. ''And what is your part in this, girl?''

Sun Conch's expression remained wooden. "I belong to The Panther. I do as he tells me."

Big Noise almost missed a step, his face stunned. "You belong—"

"Yes," Sun Conch replied mildly. "I have given him my soul. But it wasn't through witchery, Big Noise. I did it of my own free will. I will serve The Panther with my life. Do you understand?"

Big Noise gulped hard, and nodded, then led them quickly around the thatched houses, across the plaza with its big ceremonial fire pit and Guardian posts, in front of the House of the Dead, and to the high-roofed Great House that belonged to Black Spike.

"A moment, please," Big Noise said, gesturing for them to stop. "I will tell the Weroance of your arrival."

Big Noise ducked under the door hanging, leaving them alone in the cold evening. Panther said, "If I really were a witch, I'd take this opportunity to change into an owl and wreak havoc. What kind of incompetence is this, leaving dangerous fiends like us alone to commit mischief?"

"Elder, Big Noise is known for fighting. No one has much regard for his thinking."

"I see why."

At that moment, Big Noise emerged into the night, held the flap to one side, and gestured them inside.

Panther ducked into the warm interior and stopped, ambushed by the smoky scent of human bodies, the aroma of cooking food, the smell of tobacco and corn hanging from the rafters. A flood of memories ebbed from his soul: childhood, in a house like this, the noises of cooking, playing string games, laughter, and stories told. He could imagine his uncle, slapping his knee as he related the wild tale of the shark he'd tried to kill from his canoe with only a paddle for a weapon.

His own small house on the island had none of these

smells, engendered none of these memories. If it had any odor, it was the musty scent of mold in the thatch.

No, this odor was a thing of people, of the place where many of them lived, not just one lonely old hermit with a reputation for witchery.

Just how long has it been since you've been in a long-house? The question startled him. Had it been ten and two, or ten and three Comings of the Leaves?

Sun Conch asked. "Elder, are you all right?"

Panther blinked, realized that people were staring anxiously at him, and took a deep breath. With regret he shook off the memories and walked across the matting to the fire where Black Spike waited. High Fox sat to his right. Off to the side, three women—slaves, by the way they were dressed—huddled next to the sleeping benches, their eyes wary and frightened. One of the slaves, an older woman with gray hair and a horrible burn scar on the side of her face, squinted at him. Her eyes widened suddenly, as if she knew The Panther. But when he studied her, trying to place her, she turned away.

"Welcome, Elder," Black Spike said, his good arm indicating the mats across from the fire. His left arm was swollen and discolored from the wound, obviously painful. "Please sit and enjoy our hospitality."

"Thank you, Weroance. May Ohona guard and keep you." Panther winced as his joints crackled through the process of lowering him. Sun Conch stood behind him, her war club braced upon her crossed arms.

"I have business with The Panther. You may be excused, Sun Conch." Black Spike gestured with his hand. "I'm sure your family will want to hear of your recent adventures."

"She is with me now," Panther said evenly. "Sun Conch follows my orders."

Black Spike sat back. "What is this?"

Panther said, "You may tell him, Sun Conch."

"I have given myself to The Panther, Weroance. I no longer have a clan or family."

"It was the price of my service," Panther said. He took the moment to study the shocked Weroance's lean face. Black Spike had blanched, unease in those dark eyes. He was still a handsome man. Despite the years, and the gray streaking his pinned hair, muscle packed his broad shoulders. The lines of age enhanced the perfect nose, mobile lips, and fine features.

"I can read your thoughts, Black Spike," Panther added softly. "There was no sorcery involved. Sun Conch did this thing for High Fox." Panther shifted his gaze to High Fox. "So, we had better hope that you didn't kill the girl, for more than just your life is at stake."

High Fox dropped his gaze.

Black Spike shifted uncomfortably. "Well, if it was her wish, then Sun Conch is your responsibility. Now, what are you doing here, Elder?"

"I have come regarding Red Knot's death."

"My son didn't do it." Black Spike clenched his good fist.

Panther clasped his hands together and propped his chin on his knuckles. "If he didn't commit this act, then we must determine who did."

"We don't need your help," Black Spike said. "We didn't need your help this afternoon, either. If anything, your arrival here today was less than happy. Tonight we would be celebrating our victory over our enemies. We had everything under control until you—"

"Ah, your 'enemies.' Yes, I see. Correct me if I'm wrong, but aren't some of those warriors your friends? Didn't you and Nine Killer share raids, stand shoulder to shoulder in defense of your territory? Are you sure none of your relatives are within the Flat Pearl ranks camped beside the inlet?" Panther nodded seriously. "Indeed, everything is under control. So much so that you were about to murder your own kin."

"Things change!" Black Spike glared.

"Does that mean you must rush headlong through life like a pilot whale onto a beach?" Panther made an appeasing gesture. "Weroance, I am here to find out what happened. I will do that. But you must make a choice. Will you help me, or seek to hinder me? If you wish to hinder me, I might be tempted to wonder why. And if I wonder long enough, I might be tempted to consider you an enemy. Look at me, Black Spike. Do you wish to antagonize The Panther?"

Black Spike met Panther's gaze for the briefest moment, then looked away. "Only a fool would cross a night traveler."

"Especially a fool with a wounded arm," Panther agreed. "You never know what might creep into the wound. In fact, from the way it's already swollen, I would suggest that you take a bone awl and drain it. After that, I'd use a tobacco-leaf poultice to suck out the poison."

Black Spike seemed to deflate. "I'm sorry, Elder. Perhaps it's the wound that's affecting my judgment. I meant no offense."

Panther measured the fear in the man's eyes and gave him a benevolent smile. "There, we understand each other. Now, tell me truthfully, what do you know about this affair?"

Black Spike rubbed his face, glanced uneasily at High Fox, and shrugged. "I know that my son didn't kill Red Knot. He's not a killer, Elder."

"I see, and why is that?"

"Okeus alone knows why, but the boy has trouble killing a deer!" Black Spike cried. "He's . . . well, a bumbling incompetent! There's nothing of his mother or me in him! It's as if . . .'' Black Spike fidgeted with his good hand. ''As if he was born of . . .''

''Yes?''

''Nothing. I was just upset. No, I'm *always* upset with him. High Fox has never done anything *right*! He couldn't even find the right woman to fall in love with.''

High Fox hung his head, looking as crestfallen as a half-drowned puppy, and Panther heard Sun Conch take a step toward the boy.

''Sun Conch.'' Panther lifted his hand. ''Be still.''

She hesitated, shifted anxiously, and finally said, ''Yes, Elder.''

''My fault,'' Black Spike whispered. ''It's all my fault.''

''And where is the boy's mother?'' Panther asked, curious at the lack of women.

''His mother is . . . dead,'' Black Spike said, his eyes focused on the fire.

''And you didn't send the boy back to his clan? To his mother's people?''

''No.'' Black Spike gave him a nervous glance. ''High Fox's mother was of the Sun Shell Clan. Her family was from Duck Creek Village. I am of the Bloodroot Clan. I asked the Sun Shell Clan for the privilege of raising my son. As Weroance, I was perfectly suited to give him everything he needed.''

''I see.'' Panther pulled at his chin. ''And when did his mother die?''

''A long time ago. Just after his birth.''

''And you never remarried?''

''No. I had my son. My heart . . . well, it never had a place for another woman.''

''Grief is a powerful emotion.'' Panther gave High Fox a sidelong glance. He had his father's handsome features. Those broad shoulders, the thick muscles in the arms.

Those sensitive brown eyes might well be able to melt any woman's heart.

"As Weroance, I find it unusual that you didn't already have a second wife."

"I . . . I wasn't Weroance then. My brother, Monster Bone, was. Elder, High Fox was born while my wife and I were traveling, trading with the Susquehannocks up north. Something about the birth, well, I don't know. She bled . . . and bled. She never recovered." He glanced away uncomfortably.

"It must have been a difficult journey," Panther observed gently.

"Yes." Black Spike's gaze was vacant. "Okeus was against me. Only a day before my return, my brother, Monster Bone, was killed. His house caught fire in the middle of the night. Probably a spark in the thatch. He died in his bed. I came home to . . . emptiness. But for my son."

Panther glanced up at the thatch roof, soot-blackened and vulnerable. With any warning, the occupants could escape, since the house normally burned from the top down. On occasion, however, if the wind were right and the people sleeping deeply, families had been known to burn to death, many never even waking.

"So, you inherited from your older brother? That's how you became Weroance?"

"Yes, Elder." Black Spike steepled his fingers, smiling wistfully. "I have done my best for my people—even if it meant never remarrying."

"I want you to do even more for your people." Black Spike looked up in surprise. "I want you to provide a feast for the Flat Pearl warriors."

"A feast? For those—"

"You will do it."

"How dare you come in here and—"

"Think well, Weroance." Panther smiled. "Or would

you have me march out into the village and tell your people of the vision I've had? Empty houses, fallow fields returning to forest, the palisade in ruins. Weeds growing in the plaza. And where children play today, only the wailing ghosts walk, unburied and forgotten by their few enslaved descendants. Where once the proud Greenstone, Bloodroot, and Sun Shell clans passed, only the Mamanatowick's padding warriors stalk.''

Black Spike's face slackened. ''Is this the future you see, Elder?''

''One of them. There are many futures. I can also see one where the name of Black Spike is hailed as the man who saved the Independent villages from war and devastation through his mercy and wisdom. In that future, you feed your enemies, and forgive them for making a terrible—but understandable—mistake.''

''And then you will discover the real killer of Red Knot?'' Black Spike asked. ''You are offering us this as a way out?''

''I am.''

''Even if I agree, Nine Killer is another matter.''

''My impression of Nine Killer is that he is a most thoughtful and intelligent man. Like you, he is looking for a way out.''

''Nine Killer is only a War Chief, a tool, Elder. He is here following orders. In the end, you must deal with Hunting Hawk. She sent Nine Killer here, and she has made up her mind that High Fox killed her granddaughter. Do you seriously believe she will agree to peace?''

''I will handle Hunting Hawk when the time comes.'' Panther shrugged. ''As to what she agrees to, that is her decision. Like you, I can offer her an alternative. She can accept or decline my aid as her conscience wills.''

''And if she throws you out of Flat Pearl Village?''

Panther frowned. ''Not even Hunting Hawk would dare to throw me out.''

Black Spike sighed, spread his arms wide in acceptance, and said, "Very well, Elder. Tomorrow, we will hold a feast for Nine Killer and his Flat Pearl warriors." He paused, nursing his wounded arm to his chest again. "And I will forgive them, and try to make peace with Nine Killer."

"Good." Panther clapped his hands. "Now, let me see that arm. I myself will lance it and attend to the healing."

As he worked on the Weroance's swollen arm, he could feel the old slave woman's eyes upon him, her gaze gnawing at his soul like a rodent's teeth.

Empty Spaces

I do not speak of this with joy. No one has ever known where I am when my eyes seem far away. No one ever will know how much time I have spent wandering that empty space inside me. Pacing the walls of reaching arms, examining the trembling of the locked hands.

Space kept no matter the cost.

For her.

Are not all our lives molded around the empty spaces of arms left open for those we've lost?

Tender and tingling. Spaces brimming with warmth and laughter.

But the cost.

Blessed ancestors, the cost.

For five tens and three Comings of the Leaves, I wandered that space, and did not see him. The monster kept his gleaming eyes closed. His colors were mine. His pulse like an echo of my own.

Until one day, seven moons past, when I tried to unlock my hands. At last, I felt ready to let her go. I had kept her prisoner for so long my heartache had gone numb.

I tried to open my hands. I really did. But my fingers had frozen. Truly. I would not lie about this. I struggled, and screamed.

And he opened his eyes.

He must have lain in the walls from the beginning, watching and waiting.

When finally he moved, it was ever so subtly, a waver of the walls as his coils tightened around me like a huge fist.

Now . . .

All day. Every day. I sit afraid to move, staring into those savage glittering eyes.

Thinking.

There are many stories told around winter campfires, of heroes who slay monsters. Many end the same. When the hero thrusts his lance into the monster's heart, it falls to the ground, and begins a beautiful writhing Dance. In the throes, it transforms itself into a shining winged god, scoops the hero onto its back, and carries him into the heavens where the hero takes his place with the other gods.

And I wonder.

Is that what my monster is waiting for?

To see me, just once, brave?

Twelve

Later that night, when the star people first began to build their campfires, the call came, as Sun Conch had known it would. She jerked her head up when two of her cousins marched across the plaza toward her. A nervous flutter taunted her belly, but she did not rise from where she sat between Nine Killer and The Panther. She knew what Redbird and Whitesides wanted. They often acted as messengers for her uncle Sawtooth. As they closed on her, Sun Conch squared her shoulders and braced herself to meet them, staring them in the eyes. Twins, they had seen seven-and-ten Comings of the Leaves. They wore deerhide capes over their broad shoulders, and had twisted their hair into buns on the left sides of their heads. Both had wolfish eyes, with long hooked noses and full lips. When Redbird grinned, Sun Conch had to will herself not to shiver.

"You are wanted, Sun Conch," Redbird said.

"I knew you'd be coming sooner or later, cousins. Let me—"

"Who wishes to see Sun Conch?" The Panther said as he turned away from Nine Killer. He gave the twins a narrow-eyed appraisal.

Whitesides stiffened. "Her uncle, Sawtooth. He wishes to speak with her about this thing she has done—binding herself to you, witch."

The Panther started to rise, to go with her, and Sun

Conch said, "No. Please, I wish to go alone. Let me do this. I will return as soon as I can."

The Panther sank back to the ground, but his faded old eyes searched her face. "If you need me, you have but to call."

She nodded. "I will, Elder." And rose to her feet.

Her cousins silently led the way across the plaza toward her mother's small thatched house. As she walked, she held her chin high, and focused her eyes on their broad backs. She did not want to look into the faces of the people crowding the plaza. She could see them from the corners of her eyes, recoiling from her as she passed, pointing and whispering behind their hands, and knew what they must be saying. She had, after all, shamed her family by declaring her love for High Fox; then she'd returned home at the side of the most feared witch in the world. What had she expected? To be welcomed with open arms?

She shifted her gaze to the houses. Starlight glimmered on the thatched roofs, and frosted the palisade poles behind them. Clouds drifted through the midnight sky, their edges painted with the palest of silvers. As she neared her mother's house, she slowed down, letting her cousins go ahead, and fought the overwhelming urge to vomit.

"Pull yourself together," she whispered to herself. "Do it! You can't let them see you like this."

Her old ordered life had crumbled to dust before her eyes, and all of her sanctuaries had vanished. She couldn't run to her family, High Fox, or her clan. Warriors who had once been friends now stalked the forests, waiting for a chance to murder her and everyone else she knew. The only thing she had left, the only thing she could be certain of . . . was herself.

Sun Conch clenched her jaw as Redbird and White-sides pulled back the door hanging to her mother's house, and announced, "We have brought your niece, Sun Conch."

Sun Conch waited before the fire pit. Had it really only been four days since she'd sat there listening to her mother and aunt talk? It seemed like a lifetime.

Uncle Sawtooth, burly and tall, ducked out through the entry, followed by Sun Conch's mother and Aunt Threadleaf, the clan matron. The elders threw mats down around the fire, and sat. Not one of them looked at her.

Uncle Sawtooth brushed long white hair away from his brown eyes. Her mother's oldest brother, Sawtooth had seen three tens and nine Comings of the Leaves. He had deep wrinkles and a flat nose that spread halfway across his face. He said, "Redbird. Whitesides. You may go."

Her cousins turned and trotted toward their own longhouse, which sat near the eastern palisade wall, twenty paces away.

Sun Conch folded her arms beneath her cape, and hugged herself. The people in the plaza kept a respectable distance, but all eyes were on her. Even The Panther watched from his place beside Nine Killer. He had a curious, worried expression on his elderly face. It touched Sun Conch that he would care. She was, after all, only a slave.

She said, "I am here, Uncle, as you requested. What is it you wish to speak with me about?"

Aunt Threadleaf lifted her eyes and glared at Sun Conch with open dislike. "You are a headstrong, foolish girl, who does not know her duty to her clan! That is why you stand here."

Sun Conch said nothing. Her mother squeezed her eyes closed.

Uncle Sawtooth shifted to a more comfortable position, bringing up his knees, and wrapping his long arms around them. As always when he disciplined her, his voice came out soft and forgiving: "My niece, are you well? We saw you arrive and worried that you did not return to your family, as you should have."

"I am well, Uncle. But I am no longer bound to my clan. I have given myself to The Panther."

"Given!" Aunt Threadleaf shouted. "You had no right to give yourself to anyone! You are Star Crab! You are a child. You *belong* to your clan!"

Sun Conch stared unblinking into those white-filmed eyes. "Nonetheless, I have done it."

"And the witch accepted?" Sawtooth asked.

"He did, Uncle."

Her mother buried her face in her hands. Sun Conch longed to go to her, to comfort her, but she stood as if rooted to the hard-packed soil. It would be yet another breach of duty if she even sat down before her uncle gave her permission. She hugged herself tighter.

Uncle Sawtooth gazed up at her in concern. "Why did you do this, niece? To hurt your family? I know you must have felt trapped, your soul bruised, after all the shouting that went on in the plaza five days past. But why did you not come to me? You could have. I would have listened. Together we would have worked things out."

"Uncle," she said through a halting exhalation, "I bound myself to The Panther because it was his price for helping High Fox. And I—I love High Fox."

Aunt Threadleaf said, "You have seen four-and-ten Comings of the Leaves. You are not yet a woman. You know nothing of love! Not only that, your precious High Fox loved this Flat Pearl woman. Did you not know that?"

"I knew."

"High Fox never returned your adoration, not that I saw," her aunt continued. "Oh, you were friends, that's true, but nothing more. Anyone could see that."

"Even I saw it," her mother murmured, and gazed up

at Sun Conch through tear-filled eyes. Long black hair framed her oval face and highlighted the breadth of her cheekbones and the fullness of her lips. She lowered her shaking hands and clasped them in her lap. "I told you, Sun Conch, did I not? I told you that he was not the man for you. He—"

"Thank the gods," Aunt Threadleaf interrupted, "that my family would not allow me to marry the man I loved when I was a girl. He turned out to be a worthless, shiftless sort. Ran off to be a Trader for some unknown people among the western wild men. If I'd married him I'd be out there to this day, starving and sifting manure for seeds to fill my belly!"

Love for High Fox swelled Sun Conch's breast until she could barely breathe. "I would have gone with High Fox anywhere he wanted to go," she said in a shaking voice. "I would not have cared what he wanted to be, or do. So long as I was with him, I—"

"Then you are even more of a fool than I thought." Aunt Threadleaf's expression turned icy. "But then I have proof of that! First you run off and give yourself to the wickedest man in the world—a night traveler!—and then you come striding home acting as if you have no relatives! You must be a blithering imbecile!"

To act as if you had no relatives meant you were being selfish and prideful, and deliberately hurting the people who loved you most. Nothing worse could be said about a person—except an accusation of incest. Sun Conch lowered her gaze to the leaping flames in the fire pit, and mustered her courage. She could not let them see her pain. Aunt Threadleaf would pounce on her at the sight of weakness, like a gull spying a skittering hermit crab.

"Uncle," she said, stiffening her spine. "I cannot take back the words I told The Panther. I said them. I made my offering, and he accepted it. If you wish to go to him and tell him that he cannot have me, that is your right.

You are my family. But I ask you not to do that.''

Sawtooth tipped his wrinkled face up, and blinked sadly. ''And why is that, niece?''

''No matter how many Comings of the Leaves I have seen, I know my heart, Uncle.'' She removed a hand from beneath her cape and placed it in the middle of her chest. ''I made a promise to High Fox that I would help him. And I made a promise to The Panther that he could have me, body and soul. I will not break those promises. So, if you go to The Panther and tell him he cannot have me, I will still be his. I will go with him wherever he wants, and do whatever he says. I—''

''Body and soul?'' Threadleaf's filmy eyes widened. ''What does that mean? Has the old man shoved himself inside you, girl? Is that what you're trying to tell us? That you've shamed us again?''

''Oh, no. Blessed Spirits,'' her mother murmured. ''He hasn't, has he?''

Sun Conch's knees shook. ''If he wished to, Mother, I would not stop him. I *belong* to him. But he hasn't harmed me—hasn't so much as touched me. Not yet. He—he has been very kind to me.''

''She needs to be beaten!'' Threadleaf bellowed at the top of her lungs, and the entire world seemed to die around Sun Conch. Heads jerked to watch. The startled birds in the trees went silent. ''If I were your uncle, girl, I would thrash you with a green willow until you shrieked. I would leave scars that would never heal!''

''It would not make me break my promises, Aunt. Not to High Fox, or to The Panther.''

Tears streamed down her mother's face. ''I tried so hard,'' she said. ''After your father died when you were five, only you gave me a reason to live, Sun Conch. You needed me. And I—I loved you so much. I tried to—''

''And you see what a fine job you did,'' Threadleaf said, and thrust out a hand at Sun Conch. ''Girls are supposed to be obedient, modest, and hardworking. Sun Conch is everything but! Look at her standing there, that silly war club at her waist! You'd think she was like a Weroansqua, her nose in the air!''

Sun Conch's stomach churned. She had to fight to keep the contents from rising into her mouth. What her aunt said was true. She had turned against everything she'd ever been taught. Yet the more they belittled and humiliated her, the more determined she became. She felt as if some unknown person had been living, hidden, in her bones, and had just started to climb out.

She turned to Sawtooth. ''Uncle, if you are finished with me, I have duties to perform for The Panther.''

Threadleaf stood up, and her lips twisted into a cruel smile. ''Let her go,'' she said to Sawtooth. ''I do not know her. This child is unworthy of being Star Crab. She is no longer a member of my clan.'' And she started to duck into the house.

''Wait!'' her mother called. ''Threadleaf, you didn't mean that. Did you? Oh, Sun Conch, how could you do this to us? To me? If Threadleaf casts you out . . . oh, Okeus, pity me, I will not even be able to speak with you!''

Sawtooth rubbed his hands over his face. ''Please, Sun Conch, apologize to your aunt. Pledge to—''

''It's too late,'' Threadleaf said. ''I did mean it. Sun Conch is now outcast from our clan. As of this instant, both of you are forbidden to speak with her. Your eyes cannot look upon her. Your hands cannot touch her.'' Threadleaf's fist sliced the air. ''It is *finished*!''

Sawtooth rose and left the fire, walking across the plaza with his head down, elderly shoulders slumped. People rushed to him before he reached his own house, hissing questions, grabbing his arms.

Sun Conch stared at her mother. She was holding her

stomach and rocking back and forth before the fire, weeping silently.

Sun Conch marched across the plaza toward The Panther, forcing her weak knees to hold her. When she reached his side, she dropped to the ground and concentrated on the dull, nauseating thud of her heart.

The Panther said, "Nine Killer, might I speak more with you later?"

The stocky War Chief rose, glanced at Sun Conch's face, and said, "Of course, Elder. I will be around."

When Nine Killer had gone, Panther reached out and placed his fingers lightly on Sun Conch's forearm. "You only think you have lost everything," he said. "You haven't."

"I am outcast, Elder." Her voice was bleak.

"My dear girl," he said softly, his faded old eyes gleaming as if from some inner fire. "Listen to me. People spend most of their lives weaving cocoons inside their souls. Cocoons called 'clan,' 'family,' or 'self.' Most people clutch those cocoons to their hearts as if their very lives depended upon them. They won't let the cocoons hatch. They're too terrified of what might emerge. You have just been given a chance to see what will hatch. Don't throw it away. Wings are beautiful things."

Sun Conch wanted to open her mouth to respond, to ask him questions about what he meant, but opening her mouth would have meant screaming.

She just closed her eyes and nodded.

Thirteen

At sunrise, the men, women, and children of Three Myrtle trooped out of the village bearing their statue of Okeus on poles, singing songs of welcome, and escorted Nine Killer and his warriors into the palisade, where the lingering odor of a cooking feast hung heavily in the chilly air.

Nine Killer stood in the plaza, smiling uneasily, and wondering what had convinced Black Spike to do this. Giving a feast in honor of an enemy War Chief and his warriors wasn't the sort of thing Black Spike would initiate on his own—not that the Weroance wasn't at heart a good sort, but such clever political maneuvering just wouldn't occur naturally to him.

Black Spike stood up before the great crackling bonfire, his arm in a bulky wrapping, and called out:

"Okeus, hear my words! Divert your wrath around us. We, your people, honor your name and presence among us. Look into our hearts, and see the worth reflected there. Turn your wrath upon our enemies, and, if you must do harm, do it to those who are unworthy."

"Great lord, may you harm the unworthy," the people chimed in the ritual prayer.

Black Spike raised his good arm. "I welcome all of our friends and longtime allies to share our bounty. A mistake has been made, and now, with good will and understanding, we, of Three Myrtle Village, offer this feast in hopes that these last days will be forgotten."

A young woman stepped out of the House of the Dead, bearing a large conch shell, its contents steaming in the cold air.

Black Spike took the shell awkwardly, raised the rim to his lips, and drank deeply of the bitter brew. "I offer the sacred black drink to my friend, Nine Killer." He looked Nine Killer in the eyes, and extended the shell cup, balanced in his good hand.

Nine Killer stepped forward, took the shell, and drank deeply of the hot yaupon tea. As its warmth hit his belly, and the electric charge raced through his veins, he replied in his most gracious voice:

"To my friends and clanspeople of Three Myrtle Village. We happily accept your kind offer of food and friendship. The offering of a feast reminds us of the lessons taught by First Man, before he was raised into the sky to become the sun, and First Woman, who was carried up to become the moon. It was they who, just after the Creation, taught the twins, Okeus and Ohona, to offer food to visitors that their bodies might be refreshed.

"As your visitors, we accept your offer in hopes that our recent difficulties are behind us. We have faced many terrible troubles together. We have stood side by side through storms, sickness, war, and famine. As we endured those trials, and overcame them, so shall we weather this one. To the people of Three Myrtle Village, I offer my fullest cooperation in bringing this matter to a rightful and proper conclusion."

There, that should allow him to react to any future complications that Hunting Hawk might throw at him.

He walked over to where the statue of Okeus had been carefully lowered by the crackling bonfire, and poured some of the black drink into the bowl placed before the seated god. Those haunting shell eyes seemed to stare right through Nine Killer's soul, the painted grin mocking him.

After he returned the bowl to Black Spike, he nodded respectfully to the Weroance, and went to sit by the fire next to Flying Weir. Haunches of freshly roasted venison, steaming tuckahoe made from processed arum root, gourds filled with pumpkin soup, and a big wooden trencher of squash were brought and set before them after small portions had been offered to Okeus. At the edge of the fire, a pot of hominy bubbled.

The Panther ducked out of Black Spike's Great House, followed by Sun Conch. It was like a cloud passing before the sun. People went quiet and averted their eyes, many making warding signs with their fingers.

Appearing oblivious, The Panther met Nine Killer's gaze, smiled, and turned in the War Chief's direction. Nine Killer experienced that singularly unsettling jitter in his stomach. How could one relish the attention of a famous sorcerer when eating the first good meal in days?

"Greetings, War Chief," Panther called out as he approached. The old man groaned as he seated himself to Nine Killer's right.

As usual, Sun Conch stood on guard behind the old man, her hand on her war club. The girl had become such a familiar sight that Nine Killer barely noticed her now—except when she gazed at High Fox. At that moment her eyes shone like stars.

"War Chief, Elder," Flying Weir mumbled, "excuse me. I see . . . um, see an old friend over there." He beat a hasty retreat.

Nine Killer had to keep from making the warding sign himself. He wished he were anywhere but sitting across from The Panther, but he said, "You did this, didn't you? The feast?"

Panther inspected the bowl of squash, ran his fingers through it to scoop up a handful, and gratefully sucked the sweet mush from his fingers. "Ah, I love squash.

Especially on a cool day like this. Something about it warms the stomach like nothing else.''

"Did you do this?"

The Panther shot him a measuring glance. "What's this? Suspicion in your voice, War Chief? Am I to take it that we are no longer being honest with each other?''

"I asked the first question, Elder."

The Panther dived back into the squash, his expression radiant as he licked the yellow paste from his fingers, smacked his lips, and took another dip. "Yes, I thought it would be a good idea. Black Spike, when considering the alternatives, was only too pleased to take my humble suggestion and adopt it as if it were his own." Panther made a dour face. "Now, you wouldn't go around telling people I had any involvement, would you? It might, well, dampen the spirit of true brotherhood and reconciliation, much like a storm surge does a campfire on a beach.''

"I wouldn't think of it.''

"Good, I knew you were a man of uncommon sense."

Nine Killer glowered as the feasters closest to them picked up their dishes and drifted away. "Elder, you don't have many friends, do you?"

Panther, who was gumming another mouthful of squash, swallowed and said, "Oh, yes, I do. I miss my crows and my gulls. They tell me the most amazing things. Did you know that the moon is a world like ours, but without air and water?''

"No, I mean . . . Your crows told you that?''

"They did. And many other things, too.''

Nine Killer glanced up at the sky. What a preposterous idea! Everyone knew that the moon was First Woman. She'd been born as the second fruit of the tree of Creation, after First Man. She had been carried up into the sky by First Man just after she'd given birth to the twin gods. Together, they lived in the sky world along with the hunting star people.

"I mean you don't have many human friends."

"People come and people go. Friendship, now, that's a transitory thing indeed. Circumstances change and people change with them. Perhaps it is an experience that alters a person's understanding of life—say, an experience in war. Or, once, I knew a brave man who was elevated to the position of War Chief. He hadn't changed, not really, but his friends thought he had. Then, I knew a Trader once who crossed the Western Mountains, visited the great chieftains on their high mounds, drank their black drink, and ate from finely crafted dishes. When he returned, his closest friends called him crazy. They said he was a liar. Another time, two friends, a man and woman, married, each willing to do whatever was necessary to live as his mate wished. But once again, War Chief, the friendship that had lasted for years was altered forever. They divorced within two Comings of the Leaves."

"Nothing is constant, Elder. Only the sky above and the earth below."

"I wouldn't bet on them, either, War Chief."

Nine Killer scratched his jaw, squinted as he thought, and finally shrugged. "No, I suppose not."

They ate in silence for a while.

At last Nine Killer asked, "Don't you miss human companionship out on that island, or are those things beyond the needs of a . . . a man like you?"

The Panther lifted a white eyebrow. "You were going to say a witch?"

Nine Killer's guts crawled, but he said it anyway. "Witches have evil spirits to converse with, don't they?"

The Panther sighed, wrists suddenly going limp. The squash dripped from his fingers. "War Chief, I am going to need your help to see this thing through. I can't find Red Knot's killer by myself. I must have an ally in Flat Pearl Village. The murderer has cleverly hidden himself, and I will need you to help me weasel him from behind his cover.''

Nine Killer studied the steaming slice of venison in his hand. ''I have to tell you, for a sorcerer, you seem to have a basic lack of understanding as to what your duties are.'' He waved the meat to indicate the surroundings. ''A witch should be sowing discord, acting for his own self-interest. Not making peace.''

Panther resumed sucking squash from his fingers. ''Well, War Chief, don't tell anyone, but just for your information, I'm not a night traveler. Like I told you earlier, even if you offered me a witch's Power, I'd turn it down. It would cost too much of my soul.'' He jerked his head toward the statue of the god. ''He can have all the chaos he wants.''

''Be careful of what you say, Elder, witch or not.'' Nine Killer was uncomfortably aware that across the distance the god's shell eyes seemed to have fixed on him.

''My loyalty is to Ohona, War Chief. The dark god and I made our peace a long time ago.''

How could a man talk so blithely about Okeus? Nine Killer shifted the conversation to a safer subject. ''Then why do you let people talk? Why not do something to prove you're not a witch?''

The Panther met Nine Killer's gaze, a twinkle in his eye. ''Because only a witch could have stopped Black Spike from wiping out you and your warriors. Only a witch could have hinted horrible disaster to the Weroance if he didn't give this feast. And, when you finally take me to Flat Pearl Village, we're going to need a witch to smoke the murderer out of his hole.''

The Panther scooped up the last of the squash, gulped it down, belched, and added, ''But the greatest advantage of all is that when people think you're a witch, you can eat an entire serving of squash all by yourself.''

"Wait"—Nine Killer raised his free hand—"I'm not taking you to—"

"Oh, but you are. If you don't, I'll curse you in front of all your warriors. Do you really think anyone would follow you after that?"

Nine Killer blanched. "But you said—"

"Your warriors never heard me say it." The Panther wiped his hands clean on his thighs, eyes on the steaming pot of hominy across from him. "Besides, having a witch around is so exciting, I doubt they'd believe you if you told them otherwise. So, I guess you'll just have to take me to Flat Pearl Village, won't you?"

Nine Killer glared, but The Panther seemed nonchalant as he pointed at the hominy pot. "Could you pass that over in my direction?"

The Panther wrapped his blanket tightly about his shoulders and strolled out into the night, Sun Conch following quietly behind.

He sighed with relief as he left the palisade, and the stifling number of people within it. The presence of Okeus had bothered him, too. The statue hadn't been particularly well crafted, and that mocking smile had worn on Panther's nerves. More than once, he'd caught himself just short of throwing a bone at it. Had he, the simple-minded villagers would have nearly shed their skins in horror. The only thing that would have had him chucked headfirst into the fire faster would have been if he'd stood up and announced himself as born out of incest.

To be sure, when "in his moods," he'd thrown things at his own statue of Okeus, taunting the god, and nothing terrible had ever happened to him. What was it about his people's obsession with Okeus that irritated him so? The unfairness that Ohona had been virtually forgotten in the ceremonies and ritual?

"Maybe we deserve what we get?"

"Elder?" Sun Conch followed behind, keeping her place as surely as a shadow.

"Nothing. Just the mumbling of a cranky old man."

Overhead, light from the quarter-moon cast a faint glow on the last of the low clouds being blown out to sea. A few stars sparkled defiantly through the hazy air. Around the village, the dark fields were silent. The frosted cornstalks, beans, and squash vines reflected faintly.

Panther puffed a white breath and watched it rise before his face. The temperature was dropping toward a hard freeze. By morning the mist would rise as cold air rolled over the warmer waters.

In the village behind him, voices rose and fell in the babble of human conversations. He shook his head. Being around people rasped at his soul like sand on soft wood. The long moons of exile had wrought a change in him, made him brittle around mobs. He wanted nothing more than the solace to recenter himself, put his thoughts in order. Even the soft footfalls behind him irked.

Panther stifled a sudden urge to turn and growl at Sun Conch, but the girl's presence was Panther's own fault: a burden he would have to bear until this thing ended.

"We have done good work this day," Panther remarked to ease his conscience.

Sun Conch paused for a moment, then asked, "Why did you stop the fight, Elder? What difference would it have made to you if Black Spike had wiped out Nine Killer and his warriors? These aren't your people."

"I stopped it, girl, because it was foolishness—passion turned loose without direction. If Black Spike had killed Nine Killer and his warriors, the act would have been irrevocable. Remember this, my friend: When an arrow is loosed, you can't call it back no matter how desperately you watch its course through the sky. Human actions can be just as final.'' He frowned out at the night, craving the deathly stillness of the fields. ''And, we must see. Was Red Knot murdered specifically to start this war? If we are seeking to thwart the killer, we must try to do so in all ways, for an evil committed must not be allowed to flourish.''

''But, Elder,'' she said, ''we worship Okeus, and he's a capricious god.''

Panther snorted in derision. ''Yes, I know. Okeus is worshiped, and Ohona fades from memory like yesterday's mist. Have you ever considered that, Sun Conch? What does it tell us about people that they worship the god of chaos and pain, and forget the god of peace and goodwill?''

''Well, Elder, Ohona doesn't need us to placate him because he's already good. He wouldn't harm us, but Okeus would.''

''So?''

''So, since Okeus is the dangerous one, if you please him through your actions and offerings, he won't inflict disaster upon you.''

''Gull dung! How simple can you get?''

''Elder? I . . . I don't understand.''

''Well, think, youngster. Consider it from the aspect of Okeus. It matters not what he does, then, does it? If he brews up a terrible storm, the people suffer through it; then they provide him with offerings in hopes he won't do it again. So, he sends another storm, and they scurry around to lay twice as many offerings at his feet. Now, if that was the case, and you were Okeus, what would you do?''

Sun Conch said, ''Send yet another storm.''

''And you can imagine what Ohona feels. He spreads sunshine, helps people have a good harvest—despite

Okeus and his schemes—and who do these pesky people build a temple to?''

"Okeus."

"That's right, Okeus. It's a wonder Ohona sheds any of his grace on us, isn't it?''

"Yes, Elder. But, well, it's because it's his nature, isn't it? To be benevolent, no matter what?''

"It is. Now, think further. Where did Okeus and Ohona come from?''

"They were born of First Woman after she dropped from the World Tree.''

"Indeed. Twins. What does that tell us about Okeus and his nature?''

"That he, too, must do what his nature dictates.''

"Ah! So, what implication does that have for all of these temples raised to him?''

Sun Conch stood for a moment, her head bowed. "I see. That's why you have the two shrines on your island. That's why you said I wasn't ready for the answer.'' She paused. "But, Elder, why did you feed Okeus that day? Why build a shrine to him at all if he is always working against us?''

Panther waved at the night around them. "Because, in her infinite wisdom, First Woman understood that if the world was all good, it would wither and die. Just as Ohona hasn't abandoned us—no matter how we neglect him for his rascally brother. He still brings the sun after the storm. The same with Okeus. No matter how he makes us suffer, we're better off for a little suffering. It makes us stronger, makes the world work. For that, I honor him, no matter how much I dislike him.''

Sun Conch's eyes tightened and she tipped her face to watch the bare tree branches swaying above them. "I don't always understand what you're telling me, Elder, but I will think on this.''

"Yes, I know you will. You're a thinker, Sun Conch. Unlike your friend, High Fox, you . . ."

A shadowed form moved near the palisade. Sun Conch shifted on cat feet, her war club raised, and stepped in front of Panther.

"No!" came a gasped cry. "I surrender! Please, I'm no danger."

At the sound of the scratchy voice, Panther placed a hand on Sun Conch's shoulder. "I think it's all right. Who comes here?"

He could see an old woman detach herself from the darkness. "Elder?" her scratchy voice called out. "A word with you?"

"Do I know you?"

"Ah, once, yes, but that was two lifetimes ago. Two lifetimes, yes. Not now. Now your eyes barely see me."

"And who were you, those many lifetimes ago?"

"You knew me as . . . No, it matters not. That woman is dead. Her flower has passed from memory. There's no time, no time for remembering. Those thoughts are of pain. All that pain from long ago."

"You make no sense."

"Oh, no, great Elder, my words make a great deal of sense, but I didn't come to talk of the past. I came to talk of this life, and the trouble it brings. Let them suffer, that's what I said. What misery Okeus pours down on their heads is only what they deserve. Dogs that they are."

"Who are dogs?" Panther stepped closer, edging past Sun Conch and the war club clutched in her hard fist.

"These people," the old woman whispered, crabbing back into the shadows. "May their ghosts howl in the night, lonely and forgotten. May their spirits bathe in their own cooking blood as my man did. Let them burn, burn forever."

"I know you, don't I?" Panther said. "Please. Step out where I can see you."

"No. No. Great one, now I am a thing of shadows. He would kill me if he knew I was here, telling you about that woman. Bad blood! Forbidden blood! That's what this is all about. I am out of time. Must go. Get back before I am missed. I . . ."

Yellow light flickered as Big Noise stepped out from the palisade, a pitch-pine torch held high.

"Go now! Away from me! Away from Moth." The old woman scurried back, ducking down. "Don't let them find me."

"Wait!" Panther stepped forward. "You're in no—"

"She came!" she hissed. "In the night! The fire started at the bottom, rose around him like petals of a flower. His flesh bubbled and charred as he screamed."

The old hag scurried away, merging with the shadows as Big Noise approached in the company of four warriors. In the torchlight, Panther caught the faintest glimpse of the woman's face. The light shone on a patch of slick scar tissue.

"Say nothing of this," Panther said to Sun Conch, and turned toward the warriors. He strode forward, arms clasped behind his back. "Can I help you, War Chief?"

Big Noise stopped short, squinting in the torch light. "We missed you, Elder."

"Suspicious of a witch loose in the night? Fearful that I might be cavorting with the night spirits? Turning myself into an owl, perhaps?" Panther chuckled. "Oh, I'm out here listening to voices, all right."

Big Noise gave him a perplexed look, the warriors behind him fidgeting.

Panther waved it away. "Fear not, War Chief. Far from brewing evil, I just took the chance to walk out for air, to marvel at the stillness of the night, and think."

"I see," Big Noise said, though his voice indicated that he did not.

"Well, come then. If my presence is so reassuring, you may escort me back within the palisade."

The whisper of moccasins brought Sun Conch fully awake. She shifted in her warm deerhides, and lifted her head. Long black hair fell down her back. Panther slept nestled behind her, his back against the rear wall of the longhouse. She could feel the warmth of his body, the movements of his breathing.

Big Noise, the guard that Black Spike had posted to watch them, stood ten paces in front of her, his face gleaming in the starlight that poured through the smoke hole in the roof. Had he made the noise?

She looked around. This wasn't her longhouse, but she knew every person who lived here. Most were missing, spending the night with kin, as far from the witch as they could get. Twenty hands away, old man Lametoe had braved spending the night in his longhouse. He snored like an enraged bear, as he did every night, and Little Toad, his six-Comings-of-the-Leaves-old granddaughter, fidgeted in her sleep. She lay to the left of the old man, one arm curved over her head, her fingers opening and closing as though reaching out for someone.

Sun Conch longed to hold her. The child's mother had been killed six moons ago, and Little Toad had yet to recover. She had been whimpering earlier, the sound barely audible, but it had shredded Sun Conch's soul.

Moccasins whispered on the matting. Soft. Indistinct. The guard turned to look toward the far end of the longhouse.

Sun Conch silently reached for her war club, then

slipped it from beneath her deerhides. Hickory smoke spiraled up from the smoldering fire pits, crawled across the ceiling, and glimmered in the starlight shining through the smoke holes before being sucked out into the night. She rearranged the blankets so they wouldn't impair her movement if she had to rise and strike quickly with the war club. The wooden handle felt icy in her hand.

It's probably nothing.

Smoky air stung Sun Conch's lungs as she inhaled.

A shadow moved through the center of the longhouse, tall and graceful. As he neared, she could smell the scents of sacred tobacco and wood smoke.

"Big Noise," High Fox whispered. "It's me. I must speak with Sun Conch."

Big Noise replied, "Your father said—"

"He said you were to watch the witch, not me. I don't need your permission, Big Noise. I just thought I would inform you since you are standing guard."

High Fox silently passed Big Noise and knelt beside Sun Conch's bed.

She sat up, careful not to awaken The Panther, and laid her war club aside. The dim light revealed the bruise on the side of his face. "What happened?" she whispered, and reached to touch it.

High Fox caught her hand and held it in both of his. "My father, he—he was upset with me." His thumbs moved gently over her fingers. "I told him I thought it would be best for everyone if I just went away."

Sun Conch couldn't speak. One part of her wailed that after all that had happened, all she had gone through to help him, he wanted to just flee? The other part of her desperately whispered, *Run away . . . with me?*

She steeled herself, and said, "We discussed this, High Fox, that night on the shore of the inlet. You said we had to—"

"I know I did. But I've changed my mind." His grip on her hand turned hurtful. "Sun Conch, everybody thinks I'm guilty! I'll be killed!"

"Stop this," she ordered, and tugged her hand back. The expression on his handsome face went from terror to shock in less than a heartbeat. He sat in front of her with his fingers still clutching the air where her hand had been. Sun Conch whispered, "You are braver than this. What's gotten into you?"

"Sun Conch, I . . . I think my father may be turning against me." His mouth hung open, the lower jaw trembling.

"What! Why?"

"I heard him talking. He said that Red Knot was a stupid fool, that she should have known better than to show interest in a man like me." A swallow went down his throat. "It was the way he said it. The tone in his voice."

"That proves nothing, High Fox. He's worried about you, you know that. His son is in trouble. People say odd things when they're worried, looking for a way out."

He fumbled with the laces on his moccasins. "Yes, I . . . I know, but . . ." He paused for a long time. "Everyone thinks I did it, Sun Conch. Even The Panther! You heard him this afternoon! Please. There's something I need you to do for me. Something I can't do myself. I lost something when I was in Flat Pearl Village, up on the ridge overlooking the canoe landing. When you are in Flat Pearl, could you . . ." His eyes shifted to look behind Sun Conch, and he hastily rose to his feet.

"No, she can't."

Sun Conch swung around.

The Panther sat up, drew a blanket over his bony shoulders, and said, "What are you doing here?"

"I came to speak with Sun Conch, Elder."

Little Toad roused and woke Lametoe. Big Noise

stepped forward with his war club in hand to see what was happening.

Panther extended a hand in a calming gesture. Softly, so as not to wake anyone else, he said, "The stories of my sorcery are greatly exaggerated, Big Noise. I assure you, I am not so Powerful as my enemies would have you believe. Please. Go back to your guard position. This does not concern you."

Big Noise looked at High Fox, and when the young man nodded, the War Chief returned to his place by the wall, but he kept his club up and ready.

In the silvered light, Panther's gray hair resembled matted spiderwebs. He lowered his voice, and pointed at High Fox. "I *own* Sun Conch. I told you this, and she told you this. The next time you wish to speak with her, you will explain your reasons to me first." The words bit. "Do you understand?"

"Forgive me, Elder." High Fox glanced around. "I meant no offense. I just . . . I—I will leave and let you return to your rest." He swiftly turned and slipped away, head down, his movements reminding her of a whipped camp dog.

Sun Conch felt as if someone had struck her in the stomach with a blunt beam. She couldn't seem to catch her breath. She watched High Fox until he ducked beneath the door hanging at the opposite end of the house, and vanished into the darkness beyond.

She turned her wounded gaze at Panther. "Why did you do that?"

"He seems to think you are his slave, rather than mine," Panther said mildly. "I had to correct that misunderstanding."

Sun Conch lay back down and gruffly pulled her hides up. "You were too harsh, Elder. He's afraid. That's all."

"He's a coward, girl. He's been protected his whole life. First, by his father, and now by you. He doesn't know how to stand on his own two feet. Or won't. I don't know which, and it doesn't matter. A coward is a coward.''

Panther rolled up in his blanket again and turned his back to her.

Sun Conch lay awake long into the night, staring at the smoke that crept along the ceiling for the smoke holes. She alternately considered Panther's words and wondered what High Fox had lost at Flat Pearl Village that so terrified him.

Nine Killer woke to a dreary gray morning, the air almost solid with fog and his blanket hoary with frost. He sat up and puffed out a white breath that immediately merged with the surrounding mist.

Friendship might have been rekindled, but he'd nevertheless ordered his warriors back to their camp in the trees for the night. Better that than allow some hothead to undo all that had been accomplished.

He shivered and reached over to stir his fire for embers, but the damp charcoal was cold to the touch. Muttering to himself, he stood and peered around in the gray haze. His warriors lay in their blankets like logs.

Nine Killer rubbed his cold arms and bent down for his pack. From it he took a small bark container and used his fingers to dip out what was left of the contents. The concoction was made from rendered bear fat, ground puccoon root, and mint leaves for scent, the latter being his own addition. He smeared it thickly over his exposed flesh.

In the winter, the grease helped retain body warmth. In the summer it protected the flesh from the ravenous hordes of mosquitoes that rose in humming columns from the marshes. The little bloodsuckers could drive a man insane at best, and kill him at worst. In late spring and early summer they swarmed off the brackish water, the air screaming from their passage.

He was about to kick Flying Weir awake when he caught movement from the corner of his eye—a lone man picking his way through the wraiths of fog, staring down intently at each sleeper as he passed.

Nine Killer recognized the intruder. "Are you looking for someone, Stone Cob?"

The warrior started, glanced around, and located Nine Killer. "I was. It looks like I found you, War Chief."

"I thought you were out 'hunting' like so many of my other warriors."

Stone Cob walked reluctantly forward, his hands out, empty, in a gesture of trust. "Could we talk?"

"Say what is on your mind. But, in the process, you might tell me just what you are doing here. I thought you were sulking in the forest somewhere."

Stone Cob hung his head. "I did no sulking. I came here, to Three Myrtle Village. I couldn't let you kill them, War Chief. I have family here. They had to be warned."

Nine Killer tilted his head back and looked up at the gray heavens. Overhead, the bare branches of trees seemed to vanish in fainter and fainter patterns the higher one looked. "I understand. That's how they knew we were coming, when we would arrive, and where. That's how they trapped us here."

"Yes."

Nine Killer gave him a narrow-eyed inspection. "But I didn't see you out there yesterday."

"I couldn't bear arms against you. No more than I could have against my relatives and friends. When The Panther stopped the fighting, I ran, hid in the trees beyond the fields. I was out there all last night, trying to decide what to do.''

"And what did you decide?"

"To come to you, to explain what I did, and why. To tell you that I am not your enemy.''

"Nor my friend, I dare say.''

"You're wrong, Nine Killer. I will be your friend from now until I am dead and my bones stripped of their meat and placed in the ossuary with the rest of my people. You saved my life.''

"But yesterday you would have watched my death.''

He nodded sadly. "It would have been the most terrible thing I ever witnessed.''

"Again, I ask, what are you doing here, talking with me?"

Stone Cob straightened, head held high. "My honor demanded no less of me. I could not be party to the murder of my clanspeople, or my friends here. When you arrived, I could not be party to your murder, or the murder of my kin and friends accompanying you. That is over, but my part in it is not. I came here to serve you, to repay my debt to you. You may do with me what you will. Restore me to your side, cast me out, or kill me. Whatever serves you best, War Chief. The decision is yours.''

Nine Killer stared into those level brown eyes. His first instinct was to raise his war club and beat Stone Cob's brains from his skull. But he couldn't, not after all the times they had worked, fought, and laughed together. Nor could he welcome Stone Cob back with open arms. A betrayal, despite the circumstances, could not be countenanced.

Nine Killer rubbed his grease slick hands together. "You betrayed me, Stone Cob. No matter how justified your actions, I cannot—"

Sun Conch trotted like a ghost out of the fog, her face dour.

Nine Killer said, "What can I do for you this morning?"

She stopped, breathing hard. "The Panther requests your presence in the Weroance's Great House, War Chief. He asks that you come and discuss some matters with him before we depart for Flat Pearl Village."

Relief stirred Nine Killer's soul. The problem of Stone Cob wasn't solved, but at least he didn't have to deal with it this instant. "Very well, Sun Conch, I'm ready." To Stone Cob, he said, "I'll be back as soon as I deal with The Panther. Your fate will be decided then."

Stone Cob nodded and seated himself by the cold fire pit. When Nine Killer looked back, he could see Stone Cob pulling his blanket tight against the chill.

Just be gone when I come back, old friend. That would be best for the both of us.

Whatever Stone Cob had done, he had done it from an overwhelming sense of honor. And if Nine Killer told him to drown himself in the bay in penance, Stone Cob would do so. There would be no easy solutions, for either of them.

The Panther scratched and considered his night. The faint glow of morning shone through the smoke holes, like shining eyes through the soot. Low voices could be heard from the other room as the slaves went about preparing food for the day. Above him, the pole frame curved ever inward, like a rude webbing held together with dried roots. The wood had browned with age, trimmed knots swelling like old knuckles beneath the thatch.

Similar to a big basket, he thought. And considered it

an oddity that he'd never seen a longhouse from that perspective before. He shifted, feeling Sun Conch's bottom cuddled against him. The girl's warmth comforted him. He reached out and patted her gently, his soul oddly at peace.

What curious need did another human body fill when it lay close like this? He absently fingered a strand of her shining black hair, and watched as her chest rose and fell with gentle breathing. Not sexual, not at his age—and definitely not for an immature moonstruck girl like Sun Conch. This was some elemental craving, an emptiness that lurked in the center of the human soul. A need to touch, to hold, to feel another person close. It soothed—partially filled the gaping wound that had been torn in him so long ago.

Panther patted Sun Conch again and pulled back the musty deerhide, smelling of smoke, human, and must. The overhead light cast square beams through the smoke holes, blue and hazy in the smoke. The guard, a different man now, watched him with suspicious black eyes.

Panther had accepted Black Spike's hospitality in hopes that he might have a word with the old slave woman. Now, with the morning fires crackling and spitting sparks at the roof, he'd had no word with her, and worse, he'd had to listen to High Fox whine. How was he supposed to sneak over to the old woman when he and Sun Conch had been watched by guards the whole night through? The observation hadn't been subtle, either. An armed warrior had stood within feet of their sleeping platform, a strung bow in one hand, and a studded war club in the other. When Big Noise had started to yawn and blink, another, freshly awakened and vigilant, had replaced him.

In the coming years Panther would no doubt derive some amusement from it, but for now, he groused over the affair. In all of his life, he'd never tried to sleep with an armed, suspicious, and hostile man staring at him through hard black eyes and an expressionless face. How *could* a man sleep when the idea that the unconscious twitch of a lip, or the wrong gasping snore, might be the trigger for getting his head caved in?

Witchery definitely had downsides.

"I'll get a full night's sleep in Flat Pearl Village," he mumbled to himself, and rubbed his face with callused hands. Sun Conch stirred as Panther crawled over her and stood to stretch. She blinked awake, looked up at him, and smiled with innocent eyes.

"Girl, I want you to go and find Nine Killer. Tell him I would speak with him here."

"Yes, Elder." She yawned, stretching, her petite fists knotted. Gathering a blanket, she started for the doorway.

"And, come right back."

"Yes, Elder."

Immediately after she left, Black Spike ducked through the doorflap, having seen to his morning duties. The Weroance settled himself on the matting across the fire. "Our breakfast should be ready soon. My slaves are heating the remains of last night's feast."

"There didn't seem to be much left, from the empty bowls I saw."

"Those Flat Pearl men, they eat like bears in fall. They always have." Black Spike arched an eyebrow and then allowed himself a satisfied smile. "Actually, I'm just as happy to have fed them. Much happier, in fact, since I'd be brooding today had we killed them yesterday."

"Is that an admission that Nine Killer's head is better off on his shoulders than on a stick before your Great House?"

"Yes, I think so." Black Spike gave him a sober look. "Thank you for this chance."

"I just helped you to do what your heart wanted to in the first place. But, Weroance, we've still to cut our way through this mess. The mist obscuring this matter is as thick today as it was yesterday. In clearing our sight, we may well find ourselves faced with equally distasteful situations.''

''I suppose, but you'll be finding them in Flat Pearl lands. Not here.''

''Probably. Speaking of which, where is High Fox this morning?''

Black Spike reached into the pouch at his side and pulled out his clay pipe. From a bark container, he poured tobacco into the bowl and lit it with a burning twig from the fire. Puffing a blue cloud, he exhaled and considered The Panther. ''I sent him out to one of the outlying houses beyond the fields. I thought his presence there would be better for relations last night. Why wiggle your fingers before a snapping turtle's nose?''

''A wise decision,'' Panther said, and suddenly understood why the boy had come sneaking in last night. He wasn't supposed to be there. ''For the future, I want you to keep him here, inside the palisade at all times.''

''Is that necessary?''

''Did he kill Red Knot?''

''No, of course not. You already know that.''

''Then, Weroance, keep him here, in sight and accompanied by a guard, so that all may see him.''

Black Spike sucked deeply on his pipe, thoughtful eyes on Panther. ''You have a reason for this, don't you? Planning something again.''

''Of course. An innocent man doesn't run, for he has nothing to hide. And, if you will pardon my use of your own words, there are times when wiggling your fingers in front of a snapping turtle's nose can produce the most exciting results.''

''What? Getting your fingers bitten off?''

''Only if you are slow of reflex. That's why High Fox must be protected at all times. An armed guard to accompany him everywhere, even out to squat in the fields when he relieves himself. In the meantime, his being under guard will allow me to produce him upon request, a fact soothing to certain suspicious parties who still believe he killed the girl.''

''Were you always this clever?'' Black Spike grinned. One of his incisors appeared chipped.

''No, Weroance, for most of my life, I made a fool of myself in one way or another. For now, promise me you will keep him close.''

''Very well, he will stay here under close guard. If anyone tries to harm him, I will send word immediately.''

''And let me know who, that is the most important thing of all. By dangling our bait, we seek to discover exactly who the snapping turtle is. That in turn will take us to the murderer.''

''As you wish.''

Old Moth entered the house, followed by several younger women, each carrying a wooden trencher brimming with food. The old woman artfully avoided Panther's eyes. There was something vaguely familiar about her, but age and the terrible scar had changed her features. The younger women placed the round-bottomed cooking pots beside the fire to heat, and added wood to the blaze. Panther stoked his own pipe and puffed contentedly.

Only after the slaves had handed Panther a wooden plate heaped with mashed pumpkin and a bowl of hominy did they step back to their small fire by the doorway.

''The old woman,'' Panther asked as he put down his trumpet-shaped pipe and dipped pumpkin from the trencher with his fingers. ''You've always had her?''

''She was my brother's originally. Monster Bone captured her from the Mamanatowick many Comings of the Leaves ago. She was quite the beauty once. You'd scarcely know it now with her teeth knocked out and that burn scar.''

Panther's heart skipped, a sudden coldness chilling his heart. *From the Mamanatowick? Blessed Ohona, no, it couldn't be!* ''And that burn on her face?''

''Her husband was the Mamanatowick's brother. Monster Bone captured him at the same time he took her. We used pine slivers to burn him. As the fire consumed him, she broke loose, actually ran into the flames to hug him one last time. Monster Bone was so impressed with her devotion that he kept her alive, but the ordeal broke her soul. She's been deranged ever since.''

''Poor woman,'' Panther whispered, the sound of his voice coming as if from a long distance.

''Some are stronger than others.'' Black Spike shrugged. ''But beware of what she says. Moth will tell you the most curious stories.''

''Moth?''

''That's what we call her. For the time she flew into the flames.''

Black Spike studied Panther's ashen face. ''Elder, are you ill?''

''No—no, I was just . . .'' He shook himself, forced an easy smile to his lips, and said, ''The chill. Foggy days like this always send the cold right through my bones.''

Sun Conch, followed by Nine Killer, ducked under the doorflap and crossed the room. Panther took a deep breath and flogged his brooding memories back into the dark corners of his mind where he kept them hidden. He nodded as the War Chief settled cross-legged beside of him.

Sun Conch crossed, and competently rolled their blankets. These she secured with a cord before collecting the rest of their belongings. How long had it been since someone had cleaned up after him? Panther drove the thoughts away, knowing they would add to his melancholy.

"Good morning, War Chief," Black Spike said. "I hope you slept well."

Nine Killer gave him a smile. "I'm getting old. When I was young, I could sleep in the snow with only a blanket. Now, in a heavy frost, my teeth chatter."

"We are all older," Black Spike agreed. "Please, eat. You, too, Sun Conch. Partake again of my hospitality."

"The Weroance and I were talking," Panther began as Nine Killer and Sun Conch began dipping out hominy. "Black Spike gives me his word that High Fox will stay here in Three Myrtle Village under heavy guard. This way he is no more than a half day's journey from Flat Pearl Village if we need him, but still out of direct danger should others take matters into their own hands."

Nine Killer's jaw muscles worked under his smooth skin as he chewed. He didn't look pleased. "The Weroansqua ordered me to return him to Flat Pearl."

"Oh, I doubt the Weroansqua will take you to task for not bringing him back with us." Panther gave the War Chief a malicious grin. "She can turn her wrath on me, if she dares. You are just cooperating with me. Acceding to my requests."

Nine Killer continued to eat in silence, frown lines tracing across his forehead. "I want to leave someone of my own to assure this."

Black Spike stiffened. "Is my word not enough?"

Nine Killer said, "For me it is, Weroance, but I must answer to others who may not share my faith." And then he smiled, as if pulling the last cord loose from a perplexing knot. "The nice thing about two hands is that you can scratch both itchy palms at once." He paused. "What if the man I wanted to leave was Stone Cob?"

Black Spike shrugged. "He is on neither side in this matter."

"My thought exactly." Nine Killer nodded. "And it will give him a chance to choke on his honor."

Fourteen

Winged Blackbird stood before the fire, his features bronzed by the leaping light. Behind him stood Two Bones and Makes Water, his lieutenants.

The Great House where they stood was well furnished with deer hides, woven baskets filled with hickory nuts, chinquapins, and hazelnuts. Corn, tobacco, dried fish, and jerked meat hung from the rafters in long ranks. The red cedar burning in the fire gave the air a redolent odor.

The Weroance, Corn Hunter, sat on a golden cougar skin that had been draped over a stump, his raised seat giving him a commanding view of those coming before him. The only time Corn Hunter had his throne removed was when his brother, the Mamanatowick, came to visit.

As Weroance of White Stake Village, and the territory he commanded, he could levy great tribute from the surrounding clans. Most of this he passed on to the Mamanatowick, who lived three days' journey to the south.

Once Corn Hunter had been a warrior, younger brother to the Mamanatowick. Known for his prowess in war, he had been given White Stake Village, and responsibility for the northern frontier. For the most part, Corn Hunter's days were pleasant. The war with the Independent villages had ground into an endless stalemate that gave him enough stability to enjoy his position, but also sufficient danger to justify his larger than normal cut out of the tribute sent south.

The years had broadened his once muscular body, and the wealth of his position had covered him with a thick layer of fat. His tattoos had spread with his girth and faded. What had been sunbursts, bird's heads, and lines of dots now were nothing more than shadows under years of red puccoon root dye.

His heavy cheeks gave his face a thick, sagging look. Small brown eyes, mindful of a badger's, stared out from either side of a flattened nose. The story was that it had been mashed by a raider's war club when Corn Hunter had been a young man. He liked to wear finely woven and brightly dyed textiles rather than tanned hides, claiming that the cloth was warmer, lighter, and easier on his skin. Like so many in authority, he reveled in copper and tin jewelry. He sprinkled glittering antimony on his skin, and liked to weave colored feathers from painted buntings, kestrels, and blue jays into his hair. His seven wives kept the right side of his skull shaved, and spent hours creating his famous coiffure.

Winged Blackbird had always been leery of Corn Hunter, and since his elevation to War Chief his caution had increased. Something about those flat black eyes left an uneasy tickle at the base of his spine. No matter how Corn Hunter might smile, and praise his work, Winged Blackbird didn't trust the man.

The Weroance watched him with an inscrutable stare. He rested his chubby right hand on one oversized knee, his left holding Red Magpie's hand as she stood beside him, her attention also fixed on Winged Blackbird. Corn Hunter's first wife, she was ten years his elder, gray-haired, slim, and narrow of face. Behind them, Corn Hunter's six other wives waited, as did his older children.

"We could do nothing," Winged Blackbird said, hating the flush of embarrassment that crept into his cheeks. "Nine Killer had us surrounded before we could so much as raise a weapon. It was as if he knew we were coming."

"Indeed?" Corn Hunter said.

Winged Blackbird glanced around the packed longhouse. "I don't suppose that Barnacle is still among us?"

"No." Corn Hunter's only movement was to rub his thumb on the back of Red Magpie's hand. "He left the day after you did. Headed south, I believe. No doubt to fill the Mamanatowick's ears with stories about Hunting Hawk and Copper Thunder, and this coming marriage."

"You're sure he went south?"

Corn Hunter blinked slowly, the way a turtle did on a cold morning. He made no answer. He didn't need to.

"Well," Winged Blackbird sighed, "it would be nice to blame it on him."

"So, you were surrounded?"

"Yes, Weroance. I had no choice but to deliver your message to War Chief Nine Killer, since to press farther into their territory would have meant a hard fight, many deaths, and no guarantees that your message would have been delivered." Winged Blackbird smiled grimly. "The dead are not known for their elocution."

Corn Hunter's fixed stare ate into Winged Blackbird's very soul. Those eyes might have been made of polished rock for all the emotion they betrayed. Winged Blackbird locked his knees, refusing to show his unease.

After what seemed an eternity, Red Magpie leaned over and whispered into Corn Hunter's ear. The Weroance nodded ever so briefly, and a humorless smile appeared. "No, the dead are not known for their elocution. But then, neither, it seems, is my War Chief."

Winged Blackbird clamped his teeth and rocked back and forth on his heels.

Corn Hunter's smile widened. "Well, so be it. You were not appointed War Chief to tell stories, eh? You are

War Chief to win battles, and if you blurt your failures straight out, at least I don't need to worry about you plotting behind my back. Because of that, War Chief, I can trust you.''

"Yes, Weroance."

"Very well, so you gave Nine Killer my message. What did he say?''

"He said that he would tell Hunting Hawk word for word. This, I know he did.''

"I see, and how is it that you know without hearing with your own ears?''

"Because he is Nine Killer. Like your War Chief, he, too, blurts out the truth for his Weroansqua.''

The smile had frozen on Corn Hunter's face. "You take chances, Winged Blackbird. Especially for a man who failed in his mission. I would expect a War Chief to use a certain amount of initiative in fulfilling his duties.''

"Then, perhaps if the Weroance will allow me to finish my report, he will discover that initiative is not so foreign to his War Chief's ability.'' Rot it all, everything was going wrong! The tone was getting ever more formal and strained.

Don't goad him, or he'll have you roasted! Winged Blackbird smiled, seeking to ease the tension. "Weroance, please, hear me. Knowing that Nine Killer would send scouts after us to assure that we left his territory, we made it look good. We ran like rabbits—but just far enough to allay any of his suspicions. And then Two Bones and I doubled back, sneaking through the forest to see what was happening at Flat Pearl Village.''

"Ah.'' For the first time, Corn Hunter's expression seemed to warm.

"We crept close, Weroance, and saw the body of young Red Knot being borne into the palisade. She was hanging from a pole, limp, like a dead deer.''

"What?" For the first time, Corn Hunter looked mystified.

"That's what I really wanted to report to you, my chief. She's dead. And the Flat Pearl warriors were so demoralized by it that they forgot to post guards. Two Bones and I were able to creep close and listen that night. The best is, someone murdered her!"

For a moment, the only sound in the Great House was the popping of the fire as flames licked around the logs.

"Who?" Red Magpie asked, her eyes shining.

"I cannot tell you." Winged Blackbird shrugged. "Many suspected us, since our presence sent a scare into them. Some suspected High Fox, son of Black Spike. I heard mutterings behind houses. Some suspected Copper Thunder, and yet others Hunting Hawk herself. Since none of my warriors killed her, it has to be one of them, doesn't it?"

"And you saw no sign of other raiders? Perhaps the Conoy?"

"No, Weroance. The talk in the village that night was that Red Knot's body hadn't been violated. No trophies were taken. No sign was left. This wasn't war; it was murder."

For the first time that night, Corn Hunter threw back his head and opened his mouth. The laughter came rolling out of the depths of his belly, his fat sides shaking.

Nine Killer and Stone Cob stood to the side of the canoe landing, away from the other warriors who were preparing for the journey back to Flat Pearl Village. The fog had lifted, merging with the overcast sky. In the inlet, the water looked glassy, placid for once. Smooth water made for fast traveling.

Nine Killer cocked his head, watching Stone Cob absently chip at an ash tree that stood near the beach. The warrior seemed to take some perverse delight from driving his thumbnail into the bark and prying loose little half-moons from the stringy gray mass.

"I think I understand, War Chief. If you send me a piece of copper, I am to bring High Fox to you at Flat Pearl Village. If you send me a stone arrow point, I am to take the first opportunity to kill him. If you send me a bird's feather, you have found the real murderer, and I can return to Flat Pearl Village. In the meantime, if anyone tries to harm him, I am to protect him with my life. Then, I am to notify you immediately of the assailant's identity." He paused. "Curious instructions, War Chief."

Nine Killer propped his hands on his hips. "It's a curious situation—or I wouldn't be standing here, talking to you in this manner. No matter that I might have agreed with your decision to warn Black Spike in my heart, you still acted against me. Once, I would have trusted you with my life. Do this thing for me, and perhaps one day I can trust you again."

"I did what I had to to save my honor, War Chief."

Nine Killer waved it away. "I know what you did, and why. Were it not for your honor, I would be leaving another in your place. But know this, Stone Cob: For all that has passed behind us, this thing you do is between you and me. If the Weroansqua orders High Fox's death, I will not send you the arrow point. Understand? I will only send it if I have proven to myself that High Fox was Red Knot's murderer."

Stone Cob smiled, weary relief in his eyes. "You, I trust, War Chief."

"And in this matter, I trust you." Nine Killer gave the man a sober stare. "You must tell no one what I have told you. So far as Black Spike is concerned, you are simply here to watch after High Fox, to insure that he doesn't escape, and to see to the Weroansqua's interests."

"I understand."

Nine Killer lifted an eyebrow. "I have checked. None of your clan is involved in this."

"Thank you, War Chief."

"Be careful, old friend." Nine Killer hesitated before reaching out and slapping Stone Cob on the shoulder. "Let us pray that I send you a feather. If it's the arrow point, killing him might cost you your life."

Stone Cob frowned and chipped another piece out of the bark. "If he killed Red Knot, he deserves to die for what he did to all of us. My life will be well spent, War Chief." He gave Nine Killer a wry, sidelong glance. "And none shall say that I died without honor."

"No, none whatsoever."

Nine Killer turned, seeing that The Panther had hobbled down from the palisade and was seating himself in Sun Conch's canoe. Trouble might just be coming to a close in Three Myrtle Village, but it would really begin to brew when they landed at Flat Pearl.

Nine Killer gave Stone Cob one last nod, and strode toward his warriors where they pushed their canoes out into the gently undulating water.

Pray to Okeus you find the solution to this, old man. By making this arrangement with Stone Cob, he was acting without his Weroansqua's approval. Not even the dark god could help him if she ever found out.

The Panther sat with his chin braced on his palm, the water sloshing about his feet forgotten for the moment. To his left, the wooded shoreline passed in silence, the only sound that of the water on the hull, the dripping of the paddles, and the muted conversation of the warriors around them as the small flotilla paddled for Flat Pearl Village.

Panther should have been thinking about Hunting Hawk, and what he'd say to her. Instead, his attention remained on the old slave woman. It couldn't be her. It just couldn't!

Panther shifted, rocking the canoe. Sun Conch paddled with no more thought than she used to breathe.

"The old slave, Moth. What do you know about her?"

Sun Conch barely shrugged. "She was taken before I was born. Monster Bone captured one of the Mamana-towick's Weroances. She was the man's wife. Not of the Mamanatowick's clan, herself, but married into the family."

Panther knotted a fist. "The Weroance, do you remember his name?"

"Hmm. Let's see. Something about fire. There was a—"

"White Fire?" Panther asked, his voice barely above a whisper.

"Yes, that was it. The joke was that he might have been called White Fire, but when they burned him, he was greasy black."

"Blessed Ohona."

"Elder?" She stopped paddling and turned to peer at him, worried. She had removed her feather cape and laid it over her knees. The supple deerhide dress she wore had long braided fringes on the sleeves and hem, which accentuated the slimness of her body. Only her beaked face had any shape, and that was too round, the eyes too large. She frowned. "Are you all right, Elder?"

Panther took a deep breath and let it slowly out of his lungs. The feeling within him was as if a giant hand had reached into his breast and clamped onto his heart. "I'm . . . fine."

Panther gazed blindly at the passing water; Vs rippled out from the canoes as they lanced the waves coming in from Salt Water Bay.

How could a human being change so much? Nothing of that beautiful woman he had known remained in the burned old hag.

Or is it that you just didn't want to see?

What was it she had said? That lifetime was gone? Or something to that effect?

"Do you know how it happened, Sun Conch? How they were captured?"

"Water Snake had just become Mamanatowick, inheriting from his father. What was his name?"

"Blue Gill," Panther supplied woodenly.

"Yes, Blue Gill. He died, and Water Snake became the great chief. Rumor said that he wanted to make his own name for himself and he launched a war against all the Independent villages. At the height of the raiding, Monster Bone took a small party of warriors and slipped down to the south, to Appamattuck Village. No one expected them there. Monster Bone sneaked into the palisade and captured this White Fire and the woman."

"Her name was Sweet Stick?"

"I think so. The warriors brought them back, traveled right through the center of the Mamanatowick's territory, and brought them to Three Myrtle Village. Then Monster Bone sent a message to Water Snake, telling him he had his brother White Fire and this Sweet Stick. He offered to ransom them, trade them off in exchange for territory."

"And Water Snake said no," Panther filled in glumly. "Better a martyred brother to solidify his rule, than a potential adversary."

"I wouldn't know about that." Sun Conch continued paddling, never missing a beat.

I would. Panther let his arm dangle over the side of the canoe. The cold water began to numb his hand as it rushed through his fingers. *If only I could numb my soul the same way.*

But he couldn't. Not even after all these years. The wound was still there, ragged, ready to bleed.

Sunset cast a luminescent glow across the southwestern sky. Against the fading layers of orange, yellow, violet, and purple, winter's naked branches created a black tracework that reflected off the still water of Flat Pearl Inlet. Overhead, two flocks of brown geese honked and flapped across the heavens.

Hunting Hawk had heard the cry of the sentry over the chatter of the geese and ducked carefully under the doorflap of her Great House. She kept one hand on the frame, lest her balance fail her, and steadied herself with her walking stick. Once outside, she hobbled purposely forward, her sassafras stick tapping the hard ground. Shell Comb stepped out of one of the storehouses and cut across to match her mother's pace.

"What news?" Shell Comb asked.

"I've no idea. The sentry just shouted that the warriors are returning. Now you know as much as I do."

"It's not any too soon for me. This has taken too long."

Hunting Hawk growled under her breath. "War rarely provides instant gratification. If Nine Killer took an extra day, it was no doubt for a reason. Learn patience, girl, or you'll never be a leader."

"I thought you wanted me to learn discipline?"

"That, too, and you've exceeded my expectations recently. It's almost enough to worry me."

Shell Comb shot her a sidelong glance and said, "Mother, I can be just as coldly pragmatic as you can. I, too, can mute the voices in my soul, and deafen myself to the longings of my heart. I've tried to tell you that."

They passed through the palisade and walked down to where the crowd was gathering at the landing.

The canoes came in like a school of fish, the warriors calling greetings to friends and family as their paddles flashed in the fading light.

"One ten, two tens, three tens . . ." Hunting Hawk counted the bobbing heads as the canoes shot toward the beach. "Four tens, and four. That's two more than left here. What? Not a single loss? And none of them laid out wounded?"

"Maybe Nine Killer's raid was perfect?" Shell Comb propped her hands on her shapely hips. "He can do wonders when he puts his head and heart into it."

"Hard to believe. No raid is perfect. Do you see High Fox?"

"No. But, well, that's Sun Conch in that lead canoe. She's High Fox's friend. Who's that old man riding in back of her?"

Hunting Hawk squinted, studying the canoes as they beached and people swarmed around the warriors, slapping backs, laughing and joking.

Hunting Hawk caught the words "trapped . . . feast . . . good times." And then she heard the words, "The Panther! The witch!"

She was just stepping forward when the people pushed back, silence spreading through what had begun as a happy welcoming. Hunting Hawk drew up short with the rest when the old man was helped out of the canoe by Sun Conch.

He winced, rubbing his hips, taking careful steps, as if

his old bones ached from the long ride. His gray hair looked shaggy, wind-tousled, and wild. The tattered blanket draped about his thin shoulders was worn and smudged. But his fierce Power burned in his withered face.

Hunting Hawk hobbled forward, stabbing the damp sand with her walking stick. "What goes on here? Where is High Fox?"

Nine Killer collected his weapons from his canoe and looked around at the crowd, then at the old man, before he faced Hunting Hawk. "Weroansqua, High Fox is in Three Myrtle Village. There has been a change of plans."

"A change of plans?" Hunting Hawk throttled her first impulse to fly into a rage. No, she would wait to hear his story.

"I left him in Three Myrtle Village," the old man said, wincing as he came up to her. "Bat dung! I can't sit still that long anymore." He met her stony gaze, a grim set to his thin lips. In a commanding voice, he told her, "I am called The Panther."

People stumbled over themselves as they backed away.

Hunting Hawk's anger turned to fear. "The witch? What are you doing here?"

"I've come to make sense of this mess." He let his gaze travel the crowd. "I came here to determine the truth of Red Knot's death." He pointed at Sun Conch. "This girl came to me, asked me to see for myself if High Fox killed your granddaughter. She is now bound to me." His voice lowered in subtle threat. "Do you understand?"

Hunting Hawk tightened her grip on her walking stick. "We don't need you here, sorcerer."

"Indeed?" Panther gestured at the warriors grouped behind Nine Killer. "Would you rather that your young men be staring out of sightless eyes? It's hard to see when your head is fastened to a post on Three Myrtle Village's palisade.''

Nine Killer nodded warily at Hunting Hawk's questioning glance. "We were anticipated, Weroansqua. We . . . I walked right into a trap. Black Spike would have taken us all. The Panther stopped the massacre just as it was beginning. I . . . we all . . . owe our lives to him. When others had lost their senses, he spoke with wisdom. I urge you, Weroansqua, hear what he has to say.''

Hunting Hawk's stomach felt hollow, her legs suddenly weak. Pride forced her to meet the sorcerer's probing stare. "So, what will you do here?''

"I have told you. I will find your granddaughter's murderer.''

"Why?'' Shell Comb demanded. Her voice sounded raw. "What is our business to you?''

"I was asked to do this.'' Panther spread his bony feet and locked his wrinkled knees to keep standing. "If you were to demand that I leave, I might be tempted to ask why. Such a demand might stir a great many curiosities.''

"We have nothing to hide!'' Shell Comb's fists knotted at her sides. "Search, for all I care.'' And with that, she wheeled, and shoved her way through the clustered people.

Hunting Hawk sighed wearily. Any advantage she might have had had melted like ice in spring. "I don't want a night traveler in my village.''

Panther's eyes seemed to glow. "There will be no witchery within the walls of Flat Pearl Village.'' He paused. "At least, not on my part. I give you my word before Ohona and Okeus. I have told you why I am here.'' A slow smile crossed his face. "And, from what I have heard and seen with my own eyes, I think you need me.''

Hunting Hawk struggled with the sick feeling in her

gut. Did she dare say no? Terrible stories circulated about this man, about his dark Power.

"I honor his word," Nine Killer said, placing himself solidly at The Panther's side. "But, as always, Weroansqua, I will do your bidding."

Hunting Hawk's mind raced. What was it that bound Nine Killer to this dreaded witch? People were watching her, waiting for her decision. Did she dare tell him to leave? Okeus take her soul, any turn in Flat Pearl's luck would descend on her head like a weight of stone. Turn him away, and there was no telling what evil he would work against her.

She wet her lips. "I will hear what you have to say, Panther. Then I will decide what to do with you. You have one day to convince me."

With that, she made a gesture of dismissal, then pointed to Nine Killer. "You will stay, War Chief."

People drifted off slowly, talking in low voices as they eyed The Panther. When they were far enough away, Hunting Hawk said, "Now, War Chief, what is this about?"

Nine Killer related the events at Three Myrtle Village, omitting nothing. "So, I brought him here, Weroansqua."

Through it all, The Panther's eyes never wavered, and wary young Sun Conch studied the departing villagers. The girl had grown a full hand since the last Coming of the Leaves, but she had yet to develop a woman's curves. In her green dress, she resembled a moonfaced willow stalk.

"So, it seems I must thank you for saving my warriors," she said. "But I still don't want you here."

The Panther sighed and looked toward the village, where people gathered around the palisade. "Oh, I can understand that, Weroansqua. Were I you, I wouldn't want me either, but I am here. In the beginning, I didn't really wish to take on this task; however, my curiosity has been piqued. Too much of this sad event makes little sense. High Fox is the likely killer, and indeed, he may yet prove to be the culprit, but too many people of fair judgment do not believe him responsible.'' He paused. ''How about you, Weroansqua? Who do you believe killed Red Knot, and why was she killed?''

''High Fox,'' she growled. ''Because Red Knot was promised to another.''

''Too easy,'' The Panther replied. ''And, talking to High Fox, my soul can't seem to place him as the murderer.''

''Your soul?'' she countered. ''You place things with your soul? I have heard that animals tell you secrets.''

Nine Killer tensed at Panther's frown. *Ah, that prodded a sensitive spot!*

''Sometimes,'' The Panther conceded. ''But not in this instance. No, my crows only told me about Sun Conch's arrival. They have been mute about who killed Red Knot.''

''Too bad. Perhaps you should go ask them, and leave us alone.''

The Panther was staring up at the last light. Absently, he said, ''If they discover the truth, they will come and tell me. Really, I would rather beat them to it.''

''Weroansqua,'' Nine Killer begged. ''Please, we have enough difficulties as it is. If The Panther can make sense of this, why not let him try?''

She pinned him with her hard glare. ''I don't understand your part in this, War Chief.''

Nine Killer hunched his shoulders, as if expecting a blow. ''I trust him, Weroansqua. And you told me yourself that if I could find an alternative to war with Three Myrtle, you would take it.''

Yes, she'd said that, hadn't she? Sworn on the name of the dark god—and look what good it had done her!

She wet her thin lips. "I give you one day, witch." Her stomach crawled at the admission. "But, I don't want you sleeping within the palisade. Do you understand? And, War Chief, he is *your* responsibility. I want him watched, constantly."

She turned, jabbing the ground angrily with her sassafras stick. No good would come of this. No good at all!

Fifteen

Sun Conch sat on a stump, shivering. The night had fallen clear and cold. Her breath clouded each time she exhaled. They had made camp in the narrow band of trees that lined the inlet just south of the canoe landing. Just behind them, the winter-fallow fields, spiked with burned stumps, stretched toward the wooded ridge. Their camp lay but a short distance from the palisade—close enough that they could hear each voice that called out from Flat Pearl Village. People must be cooking supper. She heard laughter, and children shrieking to the barking of dogs. Wooden plates clunked, and a golden aura of firelight haloed the palisades. It made Sun Conch long for home and family. And High Fox . . . her precious High Fox.

Panther hummed to himself as he diligently arranged kindling in the fire pit they'd hacked into the frozen soil. He looked frail and old. The tattered brown blanket he wore around his shoulders highlighted his gray hair and bushy eyebrows.

Sun Conch cupped her hands around one knee and

listened to the sounds beyond the village. Owls hooted as they glided over the treetops, their eyes flashing. Owls: the familiars of night travelers.

"Elder?" she said. "May I ask you a question?"

"Questions are good things. Of course you may." He placed his last twig on the kindling pile and lifted a small ceramic pot of hot coals, given to him by Nine Killer, from his pack. He sprinkled the coals over the carefully arranged kindling and crouched down to blow on them.

Sun Conch said, "Do you recall when you talked about cocoons hatching? I didn't really understand. I was hoping you could give me some answers about that."

Smoke curled up from the kindling. Panther kept blowing and the coals flared. Bright yellow flames licked up around the tinder. He sat back to catch his breath. Sun Conch shivered at the sudden warmth. Light leaped through the bare branches above their camp.

"People," Panther said, "are always searching for answers, Sun Conch. Answers. They all want answers. And that's what cocoons are."

"Answers?"

"Oh, yes," he said, and nodded somberly. "The worst kind. They're absolute truths. Lifeless and worthless, but absolute. The clan is mother. The village is family. The world was created by the great tree that grew out of the mud in the first days before giving fruit to First Man and First Woman. Boys are carefree warriors. Girls are responsible managers. The moment we come into the world, the first threads are woven into our souls, and meant to be the foundation of who we become. And so they are. From those cocoons we can hatch many grand things, but humans usually kill them before they have a chance. A few Comings of the Leaves and those precious cocoons have been turned into nothing more than hollow husks."

Sun Conch clutched her feathered cape close at her

throat and studied the way the firelight flowed into his deep wrinkles. "What does that mean?"

He smiled, and the few teeth in his mouth shone orange in the gleam. "You have to stop wanting answers. Let them go. You can't grow wings with a belly full of answers. Wings are born only when you start living your questions."

"Living . . . questions?"

Panther added a larger branch to the fire. Sparks crackled and spun upward in a blinking twirl. "Oh, yes. Whenever you truly take the time to look at a trembling leaf, or watch a stone being tumbled along the bottom of a river, you are living a question."

Sun Conch's brows pulled together. "You're confusing me, Elder."

"Hmm?" He looked up.

"What question are you living when you look at a trembling leaf?"

Panther tucked his blanket around his moccasins, and heaved a sigh. "You want me to give you an answer?"

Sun Conch sensed she'd said something wrong. She wet her lips. "Yes."

He made an airy gesture with his hand. "Answers are not shiny rocks that you can dig from the ground, Sun Conch. They are the cool air in your lungs, and the warm blood pulsing in your veins. If you live your questions, sincerely, with all your heart, the answers will smile at you from every grain of sand and drifting cloud. Answers, my girl, are not found. They are lived."

She fumbled with the war club tied to the side of her belt, pulling it around to the front, and checking the knot to make sure it would come loose with one quick tug. "So . . . you're not going to answer me?"

His bushy silver brows arched. "I could. But it would be my answer. Not yours. The answer has to be yours, or it isn't an answer at all."

"And"—her eyes darted about uncertainly—"I will only find answers by living my questions?"

"Correct."

Sun Conch scratched her calf while she considered this. The breeze changed, blowing sweet hickory smoke in her face. She had no clear idea of what he meant, but the discussion fascinated her. "How do I live questions, Elder?"

"You want me to give you an answer?"

Sun Conch bit her lip. "Does that mean you don't really want to talk to me?"

"On the contrary. I am enjoying our talk very much. I guess I'm just not very good at it these days." He stretched out on his side by the fire and propped his head on his hand. His gray hair touched the ground, and the lines around his eyes drew tight. "There *is* one thing I can tell you about living your questions."

"What, Elder? I would really like to know."

"Well, I'm not certain how to say it so that you will understand."

"Please, try." She swiveled around on her stump and leaned forward to get closer to him. "I may not understand now, Elder, but someday I might. My mother used to say that when I got older I would . . ." Her voice trailed off. Every time she thought about her mother, she felt as if she'd eaten flakes of mica, and her stomach was being cut to pieces.

Panther gently said, "Seeing inside the empty cocoons is one of the hardest things you will ever do, child. But it *is* all right to look."

She wiped her eyes on the sleeve of her deerhide dress, and croaked, "About living questions: You said there was one thing you could tell me. What is it?"

He smiled. "Well, let's start at the beginning."

"Very well."

"You must first realize that life is not days, or weeks,

or moons. Certainly not Comings of the Leaves.''

''Then what is it?''

''Life is instants.''

''Instants? Like . . . the blink of an eye?''

''Yes. A single blink of the eye. That is all we have.''
Panther reached out and tapped the toe of her moccasin
with his finger, as if trying to get her full attention. ''You
will know you are living your questions, girl, when you
see life that way. As precious, fleeting instants, uncon-
nected to anything else, with no promise of another instant to come.''

She straightened up slowly, frowning, and caught sight
of Nine Killer slipping out of the palisade. The stocky
War Chief walked toward them, his hand on his war club.
Sun Conch said, ''I will think on your words, Elder. I
promise. But for now, you should turn around.''

Panther followed her gaze and got to his feet.

Nine Killer had a distinctly queasy feeling in his gut as
he led The Panther and Sun Conch toward the village.
The night had turned bitterly cold, nipping at his exposed
skin like tiny teeth.

''War Chief, is your stomach bothering you?'' Panther
asked.

''Yes, I . . . How did you know?''

''From the expression on your face.''

''The Weroansqua is frightened. I've never seen her
this way. I can hardly believe that she didn't have me
run you off this afternoon. Or kill you on the spot.''

''She had no choice.''

''You don't know the Weroansqua.''

''Perhaps, but I know her kind. Tell me, who was that

younger woman? Tall, attractive. The one who stalked off like a mad she-bear?''

"That was Shell Comb. The Weroansqua's daughter."

"Ah, the girl's mother. The one who thinks Winged Blackbird's warriors killed Red Knot."

"That's her."

They slowed at the overlapped gap in the palisade, an unusual number of people loitering by the opening. Nine Killer waved them away. "What are you going to do for food?"

"We have some dried fish in our packs. It will be enough."

"You could . . . that is, I would be happy to provide for you. Rosebud, uh . . . my sister no doubt has a pot of hominy warming. After all, the Weroansqua never said anything about eating inside."

"You might draw more of her wrath."

Nine Killer sighed. "She'll call me when she's ready. I was Blackened and killed once when I became a man. The worst she could do is kill me again."

"Indeed," Panther noted. "But it's the way that she'd kill you that would be most unpleasant."

Nine Killer scowled at the reminder. As they passed through the narrow defensive passage, his skin prickled. An odd sensation to experience coming into his own village, but his place here had been compromised. How easy it would be for a frightened or worried villager to drive an arrow through him.

No, not yet, he reminded himself. *We just got home. But in a couple of days, when fear of The Panther begins to eat at their souls, then they will become dangerous.* He cast a nervous glance at The Panther and Sun Conch. The girl moved like a warrior, each step careful, eyes searching for danger. She'd draped her cape over her shoulders, and the red and blue feathers glinted in the tree-filtered light.

He led them across the gloomy village, people watching from a safe distance. How often was it that a Powerful witch entered their sanctuary?

"You know, Panther, this might not have been such a good idea."

"Life is full of bad decisions, but right now I'm more concerned with my empty stomach than a friendly reception from your people."

Nine Killer noticed his sister peering out beneath the doorflap, and belatedly realized that, after all, it was her house. *She wouldn't refuse me entry, would she?*

To forestall a scene, he called out, "Rosebud, Nine Killer brings guests with him!"

"A word with you, brother?" Rosebud called out hesitantly. For once, her eyes had lost that vexing look, replaced by an uncertain sheen. She set her strong jaw, fists on her hips.

"If you would excuse me." Nine Killer smiled to lessen the strain. "My sister is probably concerned that she hasn't prepared a feast worthy of a guest." There. If she flat refused him entry, he could simply say that nothing was cooked, take a pot full of something cold, and feed Panther and Sun Conch outside the palisade.

He ducked into the warm interior, and found himself face-to-face with Rosebud. She wore a mantle over her left shoulder, her right breast bare. The soft hide was belted at her waist, and hung in gentle folds. Her generally spare movements were nervous for once, and her hands twisted at the hem of her mantle.

Two fires shed their light over the interior. At the rear fire, White Otter, Slender Bark, and the rest of the children watched wide-eyed. Nine Killer could smell the enticing odors of squash, tuckahoe, and steaming wild rice cakes.

"Greetings, sister. I can't tell you—"

"Is *that* the witch?"

"Sister, between you and me, no. He's not a witch. He's an elder, that's all."

"Who are his people? What is his clan?"

"Well, I . . ."

Her dark eyes seemed to widen, and she threw up her hands. "What *is* it, brother? What happened out there? Stories are flying around like sparrows!"

"And I'll tell you the whole story, just as it happened. But for now, I *need* you to welcome him to your house. Will you do this thing for me?"

"My children *live* here! Do I need to remind you that—"

"*Please*, sister? Trust me . . . just this once?"

She stood like wood for a moment, face grim. Then her resolve melted into stubborn reluctance. "I'll feed him. But just this one time."

He grinned, then took her hands and kissed them. "Thank you, sister."

Rosebud shook off his hands, gave him a reproving look, and said, "If I ever collect all that you owe me . . ."

But Nine Killer was ducking outside, returning to Panther and Sun Conch. "My sister is looking forward to meeting both of you."

Panther chuckled. "You know, I've visited people where the men own the house and the food. At first, I thought it a little peculiar. Over the years, however, I've come to believe there might be something to it."

Nine Killer paused, considering. "I, too, have heard of such peoples. Met some among the Traders who pass through. But, tell me, if the men own everything, and clans and families are traced through the men, how can a man be sure that any given child is his? A man would have to guard his woman most jealously, wouldn't he?"

"Believe me, they do," Panther answered, and walked toward the entrance.

If Nine Killer had any qualms, they passed quickly.

The Panther, it seemed, could charm the fur off of a beaver. He shed his aura of Power like the old blanket he carried and beamed at Rosebud as if she were one of his oldest and dearest friends. His warm smile, gracious manner, and cheery disposition reminded the War Chief of everyone's favorite uncle.

Panther scooped a mixture of boiled squash, sunflower seed, and walnut from a bowl as Rosebud said, "I didn't hear your clan, Elder."

He gave her his sunny smile. "Oh, I doubt you've ever heard of them. The High Steppers, from down south of here."

"The High Steppers, Elder? I've heard of many clans, but—"

From outside, a voice called, "Welcome home, War Chief. A visitor comes to see you."

Nine Killer tensed, glanced at his sister, and responded, "You are welcome here, Great Tayac." A lie if ever he'd said one.

Copper Thunder ducked through the doorway, followed by two of his warriors. The man wore his spider gorget over his chestful of copper necklaces; they tinkled musically as he walked. A lustrous bear robe hung about his shoulders. His forked eye tattoos seemed to catch the wavering firelight. The two warriors stopped at the doorway, both standing rigidly, arms crossed.

Copper Thunder gave Nine Killer a shallow smile as he approached—and then his eyes met The Panther's.

The Tayac seemed to miss a step. His smile faded. Utter surprise registered on his face, then a faint flicker of fear.

"So," Copper Thunder said, his voice going low and deadly. "They call you a witch now."

The Panther's sunny expression didn't change. He smiled and sucked squash from his fingers. Only after he'd swallowed did he say, "I hear they call you a . . . what is it? A great something?"

"Great Tayac," Copper Thunder supplied in a threatening voice.

"Hmm." Panther scooped another handful of squash, ate it, and smacked his lips appreciatively. "That's quite a change. From a Grass Mat to a Great Tayac."

"You will never use that name again!" Copper Thunder's expression blackened.

Panther frowned, as if searching his memory. "Seems to me I never did. I was called a great many things, but never Grass Mat. Nor would I ever want to call myself that. That was your name, after all."

Copper Thunder crouched before The Panther, his muscles bunched as if to spring. "Don't toy with me, old man. I'm not the young boy you once knew. Things have *changed.*"

"Oh, things always change, Grass Mat, or Copper Thunder, or whoever you are now. Very well, you will be Copper Thunder, the Great Tayac. After all, they're only words, aren't they? You and I both know that down under the skin, wrapped in the muscle, bone, and blood, the soul remains as it was, and will be."

"You mock me!"

For the first time, the Panther's eyes hardened. "Never. Not when it comes to the soul. What have you done? Masked yours, curtained off those parts of it you wanted to forget?"

Nine Killer watched in fascination as Copper Thunder glowered his hatred.

"It took me many Comings of the Leaves," Panther said, "before I was willing to pull back the curtains and stare down into my own black depths. I wonder if you'll ever have the courage to look closely into yours?"

"I have all the courage I need, old man."

"Aptly put. Ask a coward, and he'll tell you he has

all the courage he needs, too. Oh, I don't doubt your willingness to face death, or to risk your life and fortune. But like a quartz crystal, that's only one facet of courage, Tayac.''

"Great Tayac."

Panther dipped up another handful of squash. "I keep forgetting."

"How I have dreamed of this day!" Copper Thunder struck like a snake, his hands closing on Panther's neck. "I am going to crush you like the insect you are, Raven. Feel your life drain away as I squeeze my fist.'' The thick fingers began to tighten on Panther's skinny neck.

"No!" Nine Killer lunged forward as Panther was pulled off balance and toppled against Copper Thunder. Sun Conch leaped to her feet with her war club raised over her head. She danced from foot to foot, seeking the right angle to strike.

To Nine Killer's surprise, the old man waved them both back with one hand, then gestured for Copper Thunder's attention. When the Great Tayac looked down, he started, his fingers releasing their deadly grip. A slim bone stiletto dimpled the skin just beneath Copper Thunder's breastbone.

"Another couple of moments, Tayac, and you would have sent your soul to Okeus," Panther whispered hoarsely, the stiletto still in place. "The two of you deserve each other. Remember that, Grass Mat. Kill me, and I swear on your mother's soul that I'll take you with me. Do you understand?"

Hatred glittered in Copper Thunder's eyes, but he jerked a nod. Panther slipped the slim length of deer bone back into his breechclout. Copper Thunder stood, his hands still working, as if strangling the old man in his imagination. He tossed his head, flipping his high-roached hair to one side. "A great many things are unfinished between us, Raven."

Panther stared up at him sadly and dipped another handful of pasty squash from the pot. "I suppose they are, Great Tayac. But, in the meantime, I ask you this: Wouldn't it be better if you simply let them be? A man who rakes the coals in yesterday's fire pit runs the risk of burning his fingers."

Copper Thunder stalked toward the door, gestured to his startled warriors, and ducked out into the night.

Sun Conch slowly lowered her war club, and clutched it to her chest, breathing hard. "Blessed Ohona," she whispered. "That was close."

Rosebud stroked her throat with shaking fingers, terror slowly fading from her eyes. For his part, Nine Killer's heart was only now recovering from its frantic beat.

Panther sucked his fingers clean, expression mild. "Rosebud," he said, "did I tell you how marvelous your squash is?"

That will be all, thank you, warrior." Hunting Hawk waved her dismissal. Flying Weir rose to his feet and beat a hasty retreat from her Great House. The door hanging swayed back and forth after his passing.

Hunting Hawk fingered her chin absently, staring down the house to the front room. There, the slaves sat by the first fire, talking among themselves in low voices. Now, with Flying Weir's departure, they stood and began their evening chores.

They were a mixed lot, some taken from the Mamanatowick's land, others from the Conoy, and two, oddly enough, from the Susquehannocks once when they raided this far south. Taking slaves was a mark of triumph, a trophy of a battle hard fought or a raid perfectly executed. The men, of course, were killed outright. Only the women and children were kept, being, by nature, more pliable.

Hunting Hawk watched the flames leap and dance for a moment. The mellow light cast a tawny glow on the grass matting of the interior walls. It sent eerie shadows flitting across the sooty rafters overhead. Slavery for her people was what she was trying desperately to avoid.

Instead of High Fox safely in her grasp, the situation was ever more out of her control. Her fire barely held the night's chill at bay, and couldn't possibly illuminate the darkness in her soul.

Shell Comb sat by her side and, next to her, Yellow Net. The slaves shot them surreptitious glances as they went about rolling out the sleeping robes. From Flying Weir she had heard the entire account of the expedition against Three Myrtle. What should she do with The Panther? Shower him with gifts in thanks, or have someone sneak up behind him and bash the brains out of his skull?

"Tell me, just what were you trying to do down there?" Hunting Hawk asked her daughter. "Prove to the world that you're a mindless fool?"

Shell Comb gave her a steely glare. "We have nothing to hide. We've done nothing wrong."

Hunting Hawk closed her eyes, taking the moment to collect herself. "Daughter, it's not a matter of what we've done, or not done. It's a matter of controlling our own affairs. Don't you understand that?"

"He's not going to find anything."

"Good! Well, why not invite the Mamanatowick inside our gates to dig into our business, too? He won't find anything either, will he?"

"It's not like that!" Shell Comb protested. "Don't be ridiculous!"

Yellow Net stood then, wiping her hands on a rag. "If you will excuse me, Weroansqua, I think I'd better—"

"What? Not interested in another family quarrel?"

Hunting Hawk asked bitterly as she studied Shell Comb through half-lidded eyes.

"It's late," Yellow Net pleaded. "Quick Fawn should have everything ready for bed. Good night, Weroansqua. We'll talk in the morning."

"Good night, niece." Hunting Hawk rubbed her shivering arms and reached for a softly tanned deerskin blanket, its surface covered with blue *peak*, the highly prized blue shell beads. This she wrapped tightly about her, as if to ward off more than the cold. After Yellow Net had ducked out into the night, she said, "Shell Comb, the only time I'm ridiculous is when you make me look that way."

"I wasn't near the problem Nine Killer was. If you have wrath, I'd turn it his way instead of at your own family."

"Don't you see what's happening here? We're about to come apart. Whoever killed Red Knot is trying to kill us all! I took a gamble by pledging the girl to Copper Thunder. With an alliance by marriage, I hoped to play him against Water Snake and Stone Frog, use him as a big ugly bear to take swipes at the wolves snapping at our flanks. And now what? Eh? I ask you?"

Shell Comb lowered her eyes.

"I'll tell you what," Hunting Hawk continued. "Now I've got that very same bear here, lingering, watching, learning our weaknesses while he lives in our midst. I can't throw him out! He's here as our guest. If I tell him to leave, he has all the excuse he needs to turn his warriors loose on us."

Shell Comb nervously creased the hem of her doeskin dress, her mouth pursed.

"And to the south, the Mamanatowick licks his lips, fully aware by now that disaster has struck and the Independent villages are about to lunge for each other's throats. Do you think he'll just sit down there in Appamattuck Village and roast hazelnuts on his fire? While to the north, you know that word will reach Stone Frog, and his Conoy warriors will be asking questions, just to see how disorganized we are." She pointed a finger. "And do you think that our people don't understand this? That they're not frightened by the consequences?"

"Mother, I—"

"Wait! Let me finish. All these things that you should know—that should be as normal to a leader as the very breath in her lungs—seem beyond you! And when even a fool should have a grasp of our situation, you give a notorious witch access to our village." Hunting Hawk slumped. "Okeus have mercy on us."

Shell Comb spoke slowly, deliberately, desperation in her voice. "Wasn't it you who constantly beat into my head that there is no setback that can't be turned to an opportunity if a little thought is given to it?"

"That sounds like something I would say." Hunting Hawk shifted. "I'm surprised you listened."

Shell Comb ignored the sarcasm. "Well, I have given thought to our current situation. There is an opportunity here, perhaps a better one than we had with Red Knot. And The Panther can play a role, too."

"Oh, have you another unmarried daughter to offer the Great Tayac?"

"No. But you do."

"I do? But, I don't . . ." Hunting Hawk gaped at Shell Comb's resolute expression. *"You?"*

"Me."

"You're much older than he, almost past your bearing time."

"I still spend my three days in the Women's House. Look at me, Mother. When have you ever seen a woman of my age look so young? And I've seen the look in Copper Thunder's eyes when he watches my breasts and the sway of my hips."

Hunting Hawk frowned. "It's been so long since I gave you any serious thought that it never occurred to me the Great Tayac might."

Shell Comb scowled. "You can call on your sister's family to rule after you. I don't have to be here. Yellow Net is your closest living relative after me. And, following her, there is your nephew Tall Deer and great-niece Quick Fawn."

"That's assuming you stay with Copper Thunder. You wear out husbands faster than most people wear out moccasins. Each time I marry you off, you come home, divorced and pregnant again."

"If I can conceive his child, we'll have Copper Thunder in our camp, and he can savage our wolves for us." Shell Comb was smiling to herself, absently fingering a ringlet of her long black hair.

"I'll consider it." Hunting Hawk sat pensively. "And The Panther? Where do you see the advantage of having *him* here?"

"What if we do all we can to help him? If, rather than harass him, we make him welcome?"

"Welcome a witch?"

"Mother, please. Let's see what he's like. He may not be so bad."

"He's a night traveler! What do we have to see?"

"You're not thinking clearly about this, about our options. What if he can be molded, turned to our purposes?"

"I don't follow you."

"He already saved the Three Myrtle raid from disaster. So, suppose that we win him to our side. As much as our people fear him, think how much the Mamanatowick's people would fear him."

"We don't even know who he is, what he wants."

"But if he could be persuaded to work with us, help

us, wouldn't that be a weapon to use against our enemies?''

''You're talking about a witch, girl, not some duty-bound warrior. You don't just give them orders like you do a War Chief!''

''Of course not, but if we could persuade him to help us, it would strengthen our position. Handled properly, he could hearten our warriors, and strike fear into the souls of our enemies. Nine Killer and his men are already in his debt.''

''You scare me sometimes.''

''Mother, wasn't it you who told me that nothing worthwhile ever comes without risk? Wasn't it you who said that sometimes, we have to deny the inclination of our hearts, and use our heads?''

A sorcerer of their own? Hunting Hawk considered the implications. Nine Killer had clearly supported The Panther. But what did they know about him? The stories that circulated through the villages told of a man with terrible Power, one who conversed with animals, could charm even the most resolute opponent. Some young warriors who had traveled to his island to kill him had been found floating in their canoes, shot dead. Others had simply disappeared, never to be heard of again.

Then, on the other hand, if The Panther could be persuaded to join them, to work with them, he would be a Powerful weapon indeed. In spite of her better judgment, the idea appealed to her feisty nature. Of late, she'd grown tired of moderating the endless squabbles among the Independent villages. The growing threat of Water Snake's warriors had sent her to Copper Thunder in an attempt to break the age-old equilibrium between the Independent villages, the Conoy, and the Mamanatowick. Suppose she could have Copper Thunder and The Panther to boot? Wouldn't that be a legacy to leave behind? People would speak her name with awe for generations.

"I don't know. I need time to think about it." Hunting Hawk tucked her blanket over her legs. The possibilities raced through her head like little mice. "There is more to this than . . ."

The deer hide hanging over the entrance was thrown back, and Copper Thunder ducked through with two of his warriors. He strode across the floor like a brooding thunderstorm. His necklaces clinked with each step.

"Weroansqua, a word, please." He stopped before her, chest heaving, and propped both of his hands on his hips.

"Speak, Great Tayac." Now what? He looked as if someone had slapped his face, and it set her blood to prickling. Not for the first time, she wished she had a guard standing at her back.

"I want that old man cast out of Flat Pearl Village tonight!" His jaws clamped, the muscles knotted.

"That old man?" Hunting Hawk kept her expression blank. Shell Comb at least had the wits to remain silent.

"The one who calls himself The Panther. I want him out of here. Now!"

Hunting Hawk stiffened. How dare he order her as if she were some lesser chief? "Great Tayac, he is a guest here, as you are. If his presence offends you, I will do all that I can to minimize his contact with you."

"You don't—"

"No! You don't order *me* in my village. Were I in your village, I would never presume to use the tone of voice you just used with me." She raised her hands in a calming gesture and lowered her voice. "We are both upset, Great Tayac. Please. Let us not lose our heads over a triviality. We are better than that."

He fumed for a moment, but when she said no more, he took a deep breath. "Yes, you are right. I apologize for my outburst. However, if that old serpent crosses me, I will not be responsible for the consequences, do you understand?"

Hunting Hawk's curiosity roused at the mixture of anger and uncertainty in his eyes. What had the old man done to fracture the iron will that had dominated Copper Thunder's actions during their association?

"Great Tayac, I cannot control The Panther any more than I can control you. But, tell me, what has he done to upset you so?" She gave him the mild look of curiosity and challenge that had worked so well for her in the past.

"Nothing's changed! He's still the same old arrogant reptile he's always been. A troublemaker, meddling in other people's . . ." Copper Thunder stopped short, a clenched fist raised. His gaze sharpened, the cunning returning to his expression. "Well played, Weroansqua. Your reputation for competence is deserved indeed. You almost made me forget myself."

"And my curiosity is stirred." Hunting Hawk made a gesture. "Please, seat yourself, Great Tayac. Someone, bring my guest a cup of hot tea."

Copper Thunder gave her an amused smile and seated himself with the smooth agility of a cougar. "A cup of tea will do me quite well, thank you."

One of the slaves scurried to comply with her request. Shell Comb stirred for the first time since Copper Thunder's entrance, watched from behind large dark eyes.

Copper Thunder arranged himself, straightening his strings of beads and the spider gorget. He smoothed his breechclout flap and smiled as the steaming mug was handed to him. "Mint tea. My favorite. And what is this? Blackberry added for extra flavor?"

"I find it a soothing mixture on a cold night like this." Hunting Hawk waited, the chill forgotten.

The Great Tayac sipped the brew, grunted his pleasure, and cradled the gourd cup in strong hands. "Yes, I knew him before. On the other side of the Mountains-of-the-Setting-Sun, far to the southwest on the great river called the Black Warrior. He and I crossed paths. At the time I was traveling with my father, a Trader. The man you know as The Panther was called Raven then, a wandering magician and rumormonger. No, that's too strong. Let's call him a storyteller, a man who made his way by entertaining the great chiefs with incredible stories. The greater the flights of fantasy, the more they liked it. The stories he told became more and more fantastic.''

''That doesn't sound like the sort of thing to prompt his being thrown out of Flat Pearl Village.''

''No, but he was also known for poisonings, assassinations, spying for other chiefs. He would report on their defenses, on the comings and goings of war parties. It was whispered that he betrayed several of the towns to their enemies.'' Copper Thunder's eyes slitted. ''Keep one thing in mind: No matter what he tells you about himself, about his past, it will be a lie!''

Hunting Hawk studied him as he talked, seeking any hint of deception. Copper Thunder betrayed none.

''I will watch him, Great Tayac. I assure you. At any sign of treachery, I shall have him removed at best, burned alive at worst.''

Copper Thunder's lips twitched. ''Weroansqua, one last word of advice, if I may. Though I tread on delicate ground, I would not necessarily trust your War Chief to 'remove' him. Raven has a habit of blinding those closest to him. Perhaps he truly is a witch in this regard. However, should you need help with this problem, you need but ask.''

And you will be more than happy to kill him yourself. ''In the unlikely event that I need your help, I will not hesitate.''

Copper Thunder drank deeply of his tea and shot a quick look at Shell Comb. Hunting Hawk noted that her daughter had turned slightly so that the light accented her lustrous black hair, and if anything, her eyes had enlarged, as if to drink his very soul.

Yes, look, he is interested. The revelation surprised her as much as any of the day's events. She could feel that subtle sexual tension between them like the crackling of rubbed fox fur.

"So," Copper Thunder said to Shell Comb, "High Fox eludes us again?"

"Even the worthy have to wait for fate to drop the ripened plum into their hands," Shell Comb reminded him. "You, of all people, should know that war doesn't always grant victory on the first skirmish. The best rewards are those hardest won. And there is always a price to be paid."

He studied Shell Comb over the rim of his cup. "If you wanted something badly enough, what price would you pay?"

Shell Comb spoke with unusual bitterness. "Perhaps I have already paid, Great Tayac. I have given up everything for my clan, my people. But the price is for me alone to know." She gave him an enigmatic smile, one that teased and challenged.

Hunting Hawk saw the glint in his eyes as he laughed aloud, sharing some secret communication with Shell Comb. "No doubt you have. You're a deep one indeed." He glanced at Hunting Hawk then, his expression calculating. "I don't know which of you is more dangerous, Weroansqua, you, or your daughter."

"We manage, Great Tayac," Hunting Hawk replied, half-expecting Shell Comb to say something ridiculous. But Shell Comb's only response was to mock Copper Thunder with a lifted eyebrow.

"I thank you for the tea," he said, rising. "It is late." His face turned stony. "Do heed my warnings about this Panther. He's trouble. Don't trust him. And, well, I wouldn't let him around the food. You never know what he might put in it."

"Thank you." Hunting Hawk inclined her head. "We appreciate your warning and will be on guard. Have no fear."

She watched him go, collecting his warriors at the doorway and disappearing into the night.

"So, he thinks I'm dangerous," Shell Comb said softly.

"A most interesting night," Hunting Hawk agreed. "Very well, I shall give this Panther, or Raven, or whatever he is called, a chance. Play him off Copper Thunder, if nothing else."

"And my other suggestion?"

"Yes, he is interested in you, rather fascinated, in fact. But beware of him, daughter. He's not like the others you've toyed with through the years."

Shell Comb's eyes gleamed as she stared at the fire. "No . . . he's not, Mother."

At her daughter's expression, a cold shiver traced down Hunting Hawk's spine. But she hadn't time for Shell Comb, not now. Plans spun through her like the filaments of a web. She had things to do.

Sixteen

It *was him! It was really him, after all of these years! Who would have thought?* Panther had wondered about the upstart from the Pipestone Clan, but he had refused to believe his own gut instincts.

"He called you Raven," Nine Killer said as Rosebud cleared away the dishes and the empty pots and laid them out for the dogs to lick clean. Two of her daughters supplied wood for the fire. The flames licked up around the branches, popping and snapping as they cast their light on the inside of Rosebud's longhouse. The wood support posts took on an amber hue, and the shadows leaped through the corn, tobacco, and sacked goods hanging from the rafters.

Sun Conch sat to Panther's right, turning her war club over and over in her hands. Her eyes looked far away. Perhaps she had discovered that being a warrior wasn't all that easy.

Panther worked to control the excitement and fear that surged within him. Taking a deep breath, he slumped into a more comfortable position and filled his pipe bowl with tobacco. He studied the chopped brown weed and shrugged. "A man must be called something. At the time, that was what I was called."

"I can't believe you baited the Great Tayac the way you did. I thought for a moment he was going to kill you." Nine Killer shook his head.

"And in *my* house!" Rosebud cried. "Think of it. I would have had to move. Who could live here after a witch was killed in the house?"

Panther responded, "Trust me. After that wondrous meal you fed me, my soul would never harass you, dear woman."

"He took me by surprise," Sun Conch said glumly. "He lunged for you so quickly, Elder, I couldn't do anything."

"I was in no danger. Sun Conch, if you learn nothing else from me remember this: Appearances can deceive. Never ever underestimate an opponent. Only a fool acts against another man without thinking through the ramifications. Copper Thunder, for all of his bluster and cunning, is still a fool. That part of his soul hasn't changed.''

''The best challenge is the one never issued,'' Nine Killer added thoughtfully.

Panther smiled and bent forward to light his pipe. His wrinkled cheeks worked in and out as he puffed a billowing cloud of blue smoke. ''Such sense is generally wasted on War Chiefs.''

''Not if they want to win.''

Panther sighed as the tobacco worked its magic on his tired body. The excitement of battle was thinning from his blood. Grass Mat! After all these years!

Blue smoke rose from his pipe. It was said that Okeus gave the world tobacco as a reward for good behavior. For the life of him, Panther couldn't figure out the catch. Such a thing just wasn't normally in Okeus' nature.

Rosebud cast suspicious glances at Panther as she collected the shiny pots. The dogs had finished and now wandered off to rest their noses on their paws.

''I have missed this,'' Panther said. ''A man forgets what it's like to live in a snug house and share a fire of an evening.''

''Then why did you run off to that island?'' Rosebud asked, beating Nine Killer to the question.

Panther again watched the smoke curl from his pipe. An image of Grass Mat's mother lingered, her shining black hair spread over the robes as he looked down into her dark brown eyes. Not once in all the long nights when she warmed his robes had she ever uttered a sound. No emotion had crossed her face as he spent himself inside her. For all the warmth her naked flesh imparted to his, her soul had been forever cold and alien to him.

Grass Mat, here!

Panther sighed wearily. ''I went for many reasons. I wanted time to study the world, to know why it was made the way it was. I needed time to find myself, to reflect on who I was and how I came to be that way. Mostly I just needed to think." *And to deal with the ghosts.*

"And what did you find?" Nine Killer asked as he pulled his own stone pipe from a leather pouch at the foot of his bed. He resettled himself and studied Panther with thoughtful brown eyes.

"I found that truth can be as slippery as an eel in greasy hands. That humans are as treacherous as sea nettles in summer waters, looking so delicate and fragile but delivering a very painful sting. I learned the easiest person of all to fool. Do you know?"

"No." Nine Killer frowned.

"Yourself." Panther pulled on his pipe and glanced at Sun Conch to see if she'd understood. To his chagrin, she still seemed to be fretting about Copper Thunder's attack. "To answer your question, Rosebud, that's why I went. To figure out what had happened to me—what I had done to myself. And, I hoped, maybe in the process I would learn something about why the world is the way the world is."

"Elder, the world is the way it was made to be, isn't it?" Sun Conch asked. "How could it be any different?"

Panther gave her a sly look. "Sometimes I think your optimistic innocence is my greatest weakness. I wish . . ."

A stick tapped outside and the flap to the doorway lifted. Hunting Hawk peered inside. "I thought I'd find him here."

Rosebud instinctively lowered her eyes. "Enter, Weroansqua."

Hunting Hawk ducked through, wobbled, and caught herself with her walking stick. She crossed the mat-covered floor and lowered herself amid grunts. One by one, she studied them. To Panther's eyes, Nine Killer clearly looked the most uncomfortable, as if caught in a breach of etiquette.

"I just had a visitor," she said, gazing levelly at Panther. "The Great Tayac objects to your presence in my village. Ordered me to make you leave."

"Brash of him." Panther puffed on his pipe and sent another cloud of blue toward the roof.

"I thought so, too." Hunting Hawk's gaze narrowed. "But he told me fascinating things about you. Said you betrayed villages to their enemies. Poisoned people. Said you did a lot of terrible things."

Panther gave her a dry smile. "No doubt he did. There is no love lost between us."

"Why are you here? What do you want?"

Panther ran his fingers along the stem of his pipe. "I have told you."

"You came to find out who murdered my granddaughter. Yes, so you've said. Why should I believe you? Why shouldn't I believe Copper Thunder? He says you committed all sorts of mayhem."

"I did." Through the smoke from Panther's pipe, they stared at each other. "I'll not engage in sneaky little games with you, Weroansqua. I have no need of them anymore. Across the mountains, to the west, along the mighty rivers and down toward the south, are great chieftainships. Tribes who raise mountains of earth and still greater temples atop them. They trade, make war, and conduct their affairs with a passion and dedication we can barely understand. A long time ago, I left this country and traveled among them. I served some of their leaders, traded, and even gained some fame as a War Chief. The kind of authority they wield is an intoxicant, heady and wondrous. For a time, I fell under the sway of that giddy Power. In the end, I found it hollow, for it devours the soul."

He glanced at Nine Killer. "When I became aware of

what I had become, of how much I had lost of myself, I left. Alone in the night, I walked away from the great wealth and the authority I had accumulated. That was when I escaped to my little island. And there I would have stayed had not Sun Conch come to me and asked me to speak for her friend. Had she offered me wealth, or status, or slaves, or lands, I would have turned her down. Instead, she offered herself. She did that because she thought a man was being blamed for something he didn't do."

"You want me to believe that you no longer crave these things?" Hunting Hawk asked suspiciously. "That you are here because this girl asked you on behalf of her friend?"

Panther shrugged. "Believe what you will, Weroansqua. I have told you the truth." He chuckled. "Curious. Once I spun lies the way a spider spins a web, and now I offer truth and find it less palatable to people than a good lie. What does it tell us, Weroansqua, when complex lies are easier to accept than simple truth?"

"You don't deny Copper Thunder's accusations?"

"Why should I? A story is like a corn plant. It grows over time, rises tall and sprouts new leaves, but at the root, there was a kernel to start it. Grass Mat saw only a few of the seeds I sowed."

"Grass Mat?" She cocked her head.

"He was called that once. I take it that he doesn't announce his humble beginnings these days. Great Tayac does have a better sound to it, doesn't it?"

Nine Killer shifted uncomfortably, glancing back and forth between them. Rosebud had slipped away, increasing the distance between them. Only Sun Conch seemed unafraid. She sat with her war club across her lap, and her young face expressionless.

"Enough of the past," Panther said. "I have survived a long time, and done a great many things that I must live with. Those things, good and bad, made me who I am, Weroansqua. Just as the things you have done have made you who and what you are today. It is the present we must deal with."

"And you are that concerned with the present?" She seemed unconvinced.

"I dislike chaos. A disagreement between Okeus and me." He realized his pipe had gone cold and knocked the dottle into the fire. "Here you sit, Hunting Hawk, squarely mired in the present, and around you, a great tempest is gathering. Isn't this correct? You're an old woman and death is reaching out to caress your soul. Throughout your life you've worked, schemed, and sacrificed for the security of your family, clan, and friends. But now, of a sudden, everything is about to come apart. You fear that your life's work will be for nothing—that your world won't survive your death.

"Your most terrible fear is that your ghost will have to watch the dissolution of your dreams. You couldn't bear that thought, so you sought an alliance with Copper Thunder, figuring that was the last great gift you could give your people. A chance to survive the growing influence of the Mamanatowick. You would marry your granddaughter to Copper Thunder, because he was the most promising counterbalance to Water Snake."

Hunting Hawk swallowed hard, her eyes vacant, but she listened to Panther.

"And then, just when it seemed that everything was going to work out, Red Knot is murdered, and the situation is worse than if you had done nothing. You are desperate, teetering on the edge of a black pit, clawing for balance in one last desperate chance to save yourself."

"So you sent me against Three Myrtle Village," Nine Killer whispered.

"How do you know?" Hunting Hawk demanded.

"I know." Panther watched the leaping flames, his soul stirred by the memories he'd hidden for so long. *Once, I'd have done the same.*

"Then you are a witch." Hunting Hawk rubbed her face, her withered hands pulling the wrinkles this way and that. "No one else could see so clearly into the soul of another."

"You know little of witches. They don't peer into people's souls. They tend toward more exciting things." Panther reached for Nine Killer's little ceramic pot and pinched tobacco from it to relight his pipe.

"But what can I do?" Hunting Hawk demanded. "How can I save us?"

"First off," Nine Killer said, "let's find the murderer. Find him, and we've discovered our most dangerous enemy."

Hunting Hawk took a breath, straightening. "Yes, and we can determine a course of action against them."

"Them?" Panther asked.

"Of course," Nine Killer replied. "The killing of Red Knot destroyed the alliance with Copper Thunder, and threw the Independent villages into chaos. Water Snake and Stone Frog are immediately suspect. They had the most to gain. Given what we know now, Shell Comb may have been right, Winged Blackbird and his warriors could have killed her. They left her unmutilated to mislead us into thinking it was murder instead of assassination."

Panther raised a hand. "Perhaps, War Chief. But all in due time. For now, the greatest danger is to leap to decisions. You did that and ended up trapped at Three Myrtle Village. I would advise that you not stick your hand into the same hole again. The last time you did, I was barely able to keep the serpent from biting you."

Nine Killer grinned sheepishly. "Your warning is heeded, Elder."

"I came here to decide what to do with you. I still don't trust you," Hunting Hawk announced, as if coming to a decision. "But I am willing to allow you to stay, in the village. Under close guard, of course. Nine Killer will be responsible for you."

"Why did you change your mind?"

"Partly because the Great Tayac ordered me to cast you out, and partly because you might be able to help me."

"As you wish." Panther nodded politely.

"But I don't want you making trouble, do you hear me?"

"I am not here to make trouble. It makes itself readily enough." Panther puffed contentedly. "Once I determine who killed your granddaughter, I am going home."

"Yes, you are," she told him firmly. "Having you around here makes me uncomfortable."

"And you must understand something else. I will go where I must to find the murderer. No matter who he is. Is that understood? I am not interested in your politics. I will not be used for your purposes."

"I wouldn't dream of it."

Panther gave her a grim smile. "Good. In the past, others have not had as much sense."

Hunting Hawk fingered the hem of her robe, skeptical eyes on Panther. "Why did Copper Thunder call you Raven?"

Panther lit his pipe, puffing reflectively. "It was a name I was given when I was War Chief to White Smoke Rising, one of the Serpent Chiefs on the Black Warrior River. In their Creation stories, Raven picks flesh from the bones of the dead. He called me that because when I was done, only the bones remained."

"So, he is going to stay?" Copper Thunder gave Shell Comb a sidelong glance as they walked along the beach just after first light. The day was dawning clear and cold, with a blustery wind blowing down from the northwest.

Shell Comb nodded to the slaves waiting as they approached the sweat lodge where it was built into the hillside just up from the water. In the early morning it resembled a pile of dirt with a leather door curtain. The fire outside was burning, the stones already hot.

"For the time being," Shell Comb told him, "he's more of an asset than a liability. He may come in handy." She dismissed the slaves, who lowered their heads and hurried back toward the village.

"Listen to me." Copper Thunder placed a hand on her shoulder, turning her to stare into his hard eyes. "You don't know what he is. I do. He is a monster disguised as man walking on two legs."

So, the invincible warrior has a crack in his shell. She smiled as she laid a hand over his. "We will deal with him, Copper Thunder. He's an old man."

"He's a monster," Copper Thunder repeated. "A venomous insect that will crawl through your village and inject its poison wherever it can. Kill it now! Swat it dead before it destroys you."

She arched an eyebrow. "Such words reserved for that old wreck of a man? Maybe I ought to give him a second look?" She parted her lips, stepping closer to him. "I thought you were dangerous enough."

For a long moment he looked into her eyes, enough of a hesitation that she wondered if he'd forgotten just how close she was. She could smell his musky odor, feel the warmth from his body. He reached out with his other hand and ran his fingers down the glossy black length of her hair.

"You are dangerous," she whispered. "I didn't think you'd look at an older woman."

"You fascinate me." His fingers were twining in her hair now. "I never met a woman who could see things as clearly as I do."

"I'm my mother's daughter." Shell Comb taunted him with a smile and slipped agilely out of his grasp. "If I didn't know better, I'd say that was desire in your eyes."

"How do you know it isn't?" He remained where he was, watching her check the stones in the center of the fire.

She used a stick to roll one of the stones out and dripped water onto it. The droplets exploded in white steam. "I'd say this is hot enough, wouldn't you?"

A wary smile bent his lips. "You and fire seem to have a lot in common."

"Men have burned themselves on me before." She used two sticks to lift a white-hot rock. "Would you raise the door hanging?"

He held it to the side, allowing her to slip into the dark interior of the sweat lodge. As she entered, she brushed him with a hip, just enough pressure to tease. One by one, she carried the hot rocks inside, piling them on the dirt where they glowed like ruddy eyes. Finally, she picked up the water pot, filled by the slaves, and set it inside.

He watched her every move the way a hunter did a deer. "So this is the dance?"

"The dance?" She looked up at him as she lifted a shell necklace from her shoulders.

"The one you and I shall dance," he said flatly, his expression revealing nothing. The forked eye tattoos gave him a predatory look.

She stepped up to him, gaze inquiring. "Are you up to it?"

"Am I . . . ?" He laughed. "You asked me to walk with you, told me you had things you wanted to discuss. Very well, here I am, cold, nearly shivering, and you want to use the sweat lodge? Why do I think you had all of this planned? It couldn't be the fire, the water ready and waiting.''

She flipped her long hair over her shoulder. ''I need several questions answered. First, I need to know if I attract you as a woman does a man. I think I just saw that in your eyes.''

''Yes, you did. You're no fool, Shell Comb. Neither am I. You said 'several questions.' Where is this going?''

''You can't marry a corpse, and I don't have any other daughters.''

''Then why didn't you simply ask if I would marry you?''

She cocked her head. ''I don't marry just for the good of the clan, or simply to obtain an alliance. I'm worth more than that, and I know it.''

''Ah, the hot-blooded Shell Comb.'' His expression reflected appreciation.

''Does that bother you?''

He shook his head, stepping close. ''On the contrary, I respect that quality in you. You will not be taken for granted. I pity the poor man who does.''

She ran her hands over his muscular chest and watched his eyes widen. ''Pity them all you want. I'm here with you, and they, well, they're somewhere else. Without me.''

His hands were on her again, sliding over her shoulders and down her sides to the swell of her hips. She could see the pulse quicken in his neck, sense the tension in his chest as his breathing increased.

''So,'' she whispered as she fingered the rising hardness beneath his breechclout, ''even an old woman like me can stir your passion.''

''I've never thought of you as old,'' he said hoarsely.

She led him to the doorway. ''I had my slaves place several blankets inside. No one will disturb us.''

"I still haven't said I'd marry you."

"Nor I you. Marriage is a broad and deep territory." She looked up at him with half-lidded eyes. "Shell Comb doesn't just marry a man—even if he's called Great Tayac. Before I agree to this, I have to know if you can satisfy me. I'd hate to grow bored with you."

"And I with you." He removed his bearhide cloak, peeled off his leggings, and tugged his breechclout down. "For all of your looks, you might have dried up inside."

Shell Comb slipped out of her dress, standing before him, a provocative tilt to her hips. "Does this look like an old woman to you?" And she laughed as she followed him into the darkened interior, her body alight with the thrill of a new conquest.

Shell Comb sat cross-legged in the darkness beside Copper Thunder. The stifling heat worked into her flesh. Sweat trickled across her naked body. The lovemaking had been good. He'd met the challenge, joining with her no less than three times to prove his virility to her. But while he'd demonstrated stamina, he hadn't exactly been imaginative.

Nevertheless, I think he will do. And who knew, perhaps his seed would catch.

She tilted her head back, panting in the wet heat. Every muscle in her body had turned limp, relaxed from the copulation, and further loosened by the steam that boiled off the hot rocks.

"So, he will try to discover who killed the girl," Copper Thunder mused. She could feel him shift as he rubbed a hand over his tattooed face.

"My mother has agreed to let him try." She paused thoughtfully. "I wonder who he will name as the killer?"

She could sense Copper Thunder's smile in the darkness. "Oh, I have no doubts. It will be me. This is a perfect opportunity for him. A settling of old debts."

"And if he accuses you?"

"Let him. He can't touch me. Besides, what reason could I have for killing Red Knot? I *wanted* this alliance."

"You shall still have it." Shell Comb paused. "Provided I satisfied you. Or, was I all dried up?"

He chuckled. "Tell me, where did you learn those things? I never knew a woman could make a man feel that way."

"That was just the beginning." She smiled grimly, delighted with the moans she'd coaxed from his tight throat. How typically male he was; but he'd been willing to learn. How many men over the years had cared less about her art, preferring to rush to their climax and be finished?

"If I had any doubts, you have disposed of them this morning." He wiped sweat from his skin and rose to his feet. Hunched inside the low dome, he stepped to the doorway and pushed the flap aside. Sunlight reflected on the blue water of the inlet. His skin steamed as the cool air blew across it.

With a warrior's grace he ducked outside. She followed him, shading her eyes against the brightness, and admired his muscular body as he waded into the cold water and dove in. He struck out, swimming vigorously.

She fought the urge to follow him. Best take no chances with his seed so recently planted within her. Instead she waded out to knee depth and splashed the cold water over herself. When her skin began to prickle, she headed for the fire. She had shaken her wet hair out when a cold Copper Thunder emerged from the water and trotted up the beach. Shivering and goose-bumped, he used his bear hide to dry and crouched naked over the fire beside her.

"Be careful," she teased. "You wouldn't want to set fire to anything."

"It's had fire enough for one day," he admitted. Then he shivered, his muscles rippling under pebbled skin.

"Feeling alive?" she asked.

"Indeed. Such things are good for the heart."

"They can also be dangerous. We have jellyfish in these waters. Sea nettles in summer, winter jellyfish now."

"Are you always so careful?"

"No." She smiled wryly. "I thought seriously about following you."

"Jellyfish, hmm?" He stared out at the water. "If Raven becomes too much of a problem . . ."

"You were saying?"

"Oh, nothing." He glanced up at her, dark eyes flashing. "My belly tells me it's time to eat . . . that is, if all of your questions have been answered."

"I think so." She watched him turn and look back at the water again. "We will need a couple of days to work out the details, allow people to get used to the idea, and then we can return to your village."

"Yes," he mused. "There are a great many things to be done."

Panther and Nine Killer walked side by side across the plaza with its great fire pit and trampled dance ground. The Guardian posts stood equidistant from each other and the fire. Each was capped by a carving in the form of a person, or animal, the wood supposedly inhabited by a spirit Power that kept watch over the people and ceremonies. Sun Conch followed a step behind, one hand, as usual, atop the war club on her belt. Thus far the morning sun had made a poor job of vanquishing the chill from the air.

"I want to see the body," Panther repeated. The pained look in Nine Killer's eyes amused him. Did the War Chief think that The Panther, of all people, was unaware of the things that took place within a House of the Dead?

"Elder, it's a matter of . . . of . . ."

"The sensitivities of the family? Bat dung! Those were smashed flat by the blow that knocked the life out of her head. You said that Green Serpent is going to prepare her today. I will help."

Nine Killer shot him a worried look. "Help? How? I mean, what do you know about—"

"Ah, yes, what does a man who is feared to be a witch know about the dead?" Panther chuckled and shot a measuring glance at the suddenly pale Sun Conch. "Evidently, not what you think. I'm not going to trap her soul, or steal parts of her body for secret rituals. Your Green Serpent and his priests will be there, doing the work. I suppose that you could come along if you'd like. See how it's done. Quite fascinating, actually."

"No." Nine Killer gave him a flat smile. "My ancestors are all resting outside the village in the ossuary. That's where I'll be. I have no business mingling with the ghosts of chiefs."

Panther slowed and studied Nine Killer. "I've been many places, done a great many things, and seen all the different ways that men raise themselves above their fellows. Some of the chiefs I have known have called themselves gods, others said they were born of the sun, their souls composed of a blinding shaft of light that would blind mere mortals with its brilliance. In the end, War Chief, they are just as ordinary as you and I. Their spit is just as wet, their belches caused by the same indigestion. Heat them and they sweat, feed them and they defecate. Their supposed Power of soul and spirit can't even stop a simple thing like wrinkles and gray hair. They die of the same wounds and poisons that would kill their lowest slave. Besides," he added. "The people resting in the House of the Dead are your relatives. It *is* your business."

Nine Killer shook his head. "You've had the most unusual life, Elder."

"Indeed. And now let me turn my experiences to this latest of curiosities. Hunting Hawk said I could search for the girl's murderer. I can't do that unless I can learn everything that happened, War Chief. I must begin with the girl—be there when Green Serpent prepares her body."

Nine Killer cast a quick glance at the Weroansqua's Great House, and nodded. "This way."

Together they walked to the curtained entryway to the House of the Dead. Panther ducked and entered. Nine Killer hesitated.

"Come, War Chief," Panther waved him in. "You are to guard me, observe all of my actions. If you're not inside with me I might steal all of Greenstone Clan's treasures."

"I don't know, I—"

"Are these your ancestors, or not?"

"Well, yes."

"Then you've as much right to be in their presence as anyone else."

Nine Killer stepped inside.

"What of me? I'm Star Crab Clan," Sun Conch asked. She'd worn her long hair loose today, and it shimmered in the wan sunlight. "Do I have to go in?"

"I'll protect you," Panther said. She gritted her teeth,

and entered. Once in the anteroom, Panther called, "Is anyone here?"

"Who comes?" a scratchy voice returned.

"It is The Panther, come to watch the preparation of Red Knot's body. It is all right, Kwiokos. The Weroansqua knows I am here."

"The Panther?" Green Serpent appeared from behind the first mat wall. He squinted, and stepped forward. "I had heard that you were coming here. The ghosts told me. I was going to go and see you, see if I had to fight you in order to protect my people from your sorcery."

Two younger men followed the elder out, each wearing their priestly garb of feather cloaks, necklaces that clattered with a wealth of shell and copper, and perfectly tanned deerhide clothing. Panther figured the tall one to be Lightning Cat, the short muscular one Streaked Bear.

"You have no need to fight me," Panther replied as he walked past the first smoking fire pit. The eternal fire had burned down to a bed of glowing coals. "I am here to help; not to harm. Red Knot has been murdered, and I have come to find the killer."

"This death of Red Knot . . ." Green Serpent frowned, his white eyebrows drawn together. "This is a problem. I have been looking into the coals"—he gestured at the eternal fire—"and have seen nothing but shifting images of the murderer. I don't know if it's because Red Knot's killer has used Power against me, to blind me, or whether it's Red Knot's ghost getting in the way."

"Her ghost is getting in the way?" Panther asked, intrigued. "How? Why? This is most unusual."

Green Serpent cast him a sidelong glance. "Indeed it is. That is why I suspect that something is blinding me. What would the terrible Panther think of that? Hmm?"

Panther stroked his chin. Nine Killer and Sun Conch stood watching uneasily from across the room.

"She may be trying to help you, not hinder," Panther

replied. "Have you asked her if she's displeased?"

Green Serpent nodded. "And when I do, the image wavers even more."

"Have you tried rubbing sacred datura paste on your temples? Sometimes that can clear the vision."

The Kwiokos nodded. "Oh, I have. I used the paste until I was sick, my soul floating out of my body. I saw many wondrous and frightening things, but this murderer eluded me. It was most peculiar . . . but, I'll tell you what, there is a terrible crime involved in this. Nothing else would have the Spirits so upset."

Panther cocked his head, frowning. "How do you mean, great Kwiokos? Something worse than murder?"

"Yes." Green Serpent pursed his lips, his tufted white eyebrows rising. "It's close, I tell you. When I drift off to sleep, I can almost feel it, malignant, dark, and dangerous. Close . . . so close that the ghosts are milling and frightened. That's why I can't quite see it. Like knowing that people are waving to you from the other side of the room, but the mist is so thick you can't quite see them, only their shadowy movements. The ghosts are horrified. I think Red Knot is, too. Terribly upset . . . yes, terribly . . ."

"You'd think that the House of the Dead had been profaned in some way."

"Yes." Green Serpent watched him through narrowed eyes. "You know your craft well, sorcerer."

Seventeen

Panther shook his head and made a dismissive gesture. "I'll not try and fool you, great Kwiokos. I'm no sorcerer, no witch. I have made a study of the plants and their Powers. I have listened to, and studied under, men and women with great Power. I have practiced magic tricks and sleights, and even played the god on occasion."

Not everyone was allowed to play the god. In the ceremonials, strings were often tied to Okeus, so that when the hidden operator pulled them, the god would move his arms, turn his head, and stand in his shrine. A Kwiokos kept that knowledge secret unto himself.

"I see." Green Serpent took a step to the side, shooting a quick glance at Nine Killer and Sun Conch where they stood just inside the doorway. "And what is your purpose here, Panther?"

"I told you, I came to find—"

"No. Your *real* purpose? What made you come to this place? What will you *do* here?"

He took a deep breath, considering his words. "I am not sure yet. Hopefully I will come closer to maintaining the balance that has eluded me for years."

"An act of goodness to counter the bad?"

"Something like that."

"Tell me, Panther, are acts more important than beliefs?"

"I don't know, Kwiokos, but acts have a Power all

their own. I have seen that a child's smile is worth a lifetime of worshiping before a shrine. An insult shouted across a river can fire the blood of a thousand warriors in lands you've never heard of. That is the Power of actions. Be they for good or evil, they spread like ripples upon a pond.''

"Like the murder of our Red Knot," Green Serpent mused.

"Exactly." Panther lifted an eyebrow. "I wonder if the murderer understood just how many ripples would spread from that blow to the girl's head?''

Green Serpent shook his head. "Oh, that is never understood, Panther. Not until the act is done can the ripples be seen spreading. Only then does the murderer begin to see that his life will never be the same.''

"Then come, let us take a look at the girl." Panther smiled warmly at the Kwiokos. "I would like the War Chief to accompany us. Nine Killer was there at the place where the girl was killed, and Sun Conch is bonded to me.''

Green Serpent glanced at them, no doubt seeing the fear on their faces. "It is most irregular, but I will do as you wish." He glanced at Lightning Cat and Streaked Bear, who had been listening intently. "There will be no trouble over this. Come, all of you. Let us attend to Red Knot.''

Panther followed the Kwiokos back past the mat partition, past the storeroom with its graven guardians. As he passed, Green Serpent raised a finger to touch each one, calling for their blessing. Beyond the final mat wall, they entered the sanctum where Okeus sat on his perch, the painted wooden statue covered with *peak* shell necklaces, polished copper, and fine dress. The shell eyes seemed to gleam with an inner light, but only reflected the fire. His outstretched arms held a shock of corn in the left, and an ornate war club in the right: the dual nature of the fickle god obvious to all.

Above Okeus, on the platform, lay the bundled corpses of clan leaders. Each corpse had been rolled in its own fabric shroud. They rested in a ranked line. Forever silent to this world, they were the repositories of the honored ghosts of the Greenstone Clan.

On the floor to the right of the fire lay young Red Knot, her body swollen from decomposition. She had been placed on a woven cattail mat.

Nine Killer stopped short as he followed Streaked Bear into the room. The War Chief's gaze fastened on the god, then took in the platform, and finally stopped on Red Knot. He seemed to be having trouble with his breathing.

Panther made a respectful gesture to the god, then crouched down over the girl, the taint of corruption and smoke filling his nostrils. He had been told that she was a pretty girl, her body just blooming into a full-busted figure. Now her half-open eyes had sunk into her face, the lips drawn back over the teeth.

Panther could imagine her, young, alive, and vivacious. He could see those dark eyes flashing, sense her saucy smile. Her blood must have raced as she hurried off to meet High Fox that fateful morning. How excited she must have been. That shining black hair would have swung with each anxious step.

But here she lay, dead and cold, her flesh swollen with rot, the eyes sightless. The pulsing blood had blackened to clot in her veins.

Who did this to you, girl? And, why did they do it?

"War Chief, could you come here?" Panther could see bits of leaves in her hair. As Nine Killer bent down beside him, Panther asked, "You saw her up on the ridge. Could you lay her out just as she was?"

Nine Killer flinched as he touched her cold skin. Her body gurgled as he rolled it over. Despite some remaining rigor, Nine Killer placed the limbs appropriately.

"She was laid out thus, Elder. This leg drawn up, the hand clasped so."

"That was the hand clasping the necklace?"

"Yes, Elder."

"I have the necklace," Green Serpent said from where he watched in the rear. "Would you bring it, Lightning Cat?"

The priest nodded and stepped from the room to return with the necklace dangling from his hand. Panther studied it in the light, looking closely at the stone shark's tooth. "I've seen these. From the bluff down by Piney Point."

Sun Conch made a small forlorn sound.

Panther looked up. "What is it, Sun Conch?"

"That necklace, Elder. I wasn't sure when Nine Killer first mentioned it, but . . . it belongs to High Fox."

"You think this is what he said he 'lost'? The object he wanted you to look for when you got here?"

Sun Conch looked as if she'd swallowed poisonous swamp laurel. "Yes. Probably."

Nine Killer exhaled wearily. "It was in Red Knot's hand. So, High Fox is the killer after all."

"No!" Sun Conch shook her head violently. "He isn't! I swear, I would know if he—he could do something like this! It isn't in him!"

Panther held up a hand to calm the girl, but he spoke to Nine Killer. "Remember, War Chief, High Fox might have given the young woman the necklace as a gift. She was, after all, running off to meet him."

Nine Killer looked unconvinced.

"Think. How many explanations can this have?" Panther held Nine Killer's gaze. "Did she clutch it to her breast? Perhaps to hold it close while she died? Like a warrior does a Power bundle?"

"That is possible."

"By itself, the necklace does not indicate guilt. It is only another of the curious facts we must sort out."

"Yes, Elder." Nine Killer relented.

Sun Conch stepped sideways to lean her shoulder against the wall, and Panther noticed that she seemed to need the support. Her legs were shaking.

"I need more light." Panther turned to study Red Knot's matted hair. Streaked Bear hurried to place more wood on the fire.

The flames leapt up, and Panther examined the blood-stains on the dress, and the way the girl's head lay. "Come, let's remove her clothing."

"Her spirit must be placated," Green Serpent insisted. "You dare not bother her until she knows your purpose. The dead can be most easily offended."

"Of course, Kwiokos," Panther agreed. "If you will inform her of our mission as we work, I would deeply appreciate it."

Green Serpent grinned, exposing his stubby brown teeth. Then he removed his large gourd rattle from his belt, shaking it in a shish-shishing motion as his old voice quavered in a sad song to Red Knot's ghost.

Only then did Panther and Nine Killer lift the girl, slipping her dress over her head. Panther took the garment and studied it in the firelight. Red Knot had danced her last dance in this beautifully tanned deerhide dress. Chevrons of dark blue *peak* decorated the front. At the point of each, a bit of copper had been sewn to gleam in the firelight. A line of pearls, each carefully drilled through the center, had been tacked to the neckline, and long fringes had been cut from the hem.

Panther turned his attention to the ominous dark stains. "The smear of blood on the left shoulder is interesting. From the way it's feathered across the deer hide, it was carried there by her hair. Brushed onto the leather of her dress. Take a look, War Chief. What do you think?"

Nine Killer stepped forward to look at the deerhide that Panther held up. "There's a difference in the way the blood is smeared from the front to the back."

"Indeed." Panther cocked an eyebrow. "The blood on the back smeared when it was wet and fresh. The blood that pooled on the front cooled and dried there. It's dark, thick, and clotted."

"I see," Nine Killer whispered as he leaned forward. "That's because she was lying on her front."

"And the blood on her back?" Panther queried.

Nine Killer narrowed an eye. "She fell that way first." He walked around the dress as Panther held it for him. "Yes, the first blood that leaked from the wound would have drained into her hair, then smeared the back of the dress like that. Then, when she was pulled over and buried in the leaves, the blood drained out of the wound to cake the front of the dress."

"Very good, War Chief. That mind of yours is keen indeed."

Nine Killer bit his lip, glanced uneasily at Green Serpent, and said, "Why didn't I see that before?"

Panther chuckled grimly. "Because in the passion of the moment you weren't looking, War Chief. Now, let's see what else Red Knot has to tell us about her death."

Panther crouched down, studying the girl's skin. "No sign of bruises or cuts." He lifted her curled hands, peering at the fingernails. "No evidence that she scratched or fought."

"How can you know that?" Green Serpent asked as he bent forward.

Panther rocked back on his heels. "If she'd struggled with him, we should see evidence of it. Torn nails, maybe skin or blood under them. But her skin is unblemished. She wasn't struck, or cut, or punctured. Not even a bruise."

He rolled her head to the side and carefully probed the

depression on the side of her skull. "She was struck on the left temple." He glanced at Nine Killer. "What would that indicate to you, War Chief?"

"That whoever hit her was facing her. That's where I try to hit an opponent. Even a glancing blow will disorient, allow for a fast follow-up."

Panther's fingers traced through her hair, around the edge of ragged bone that had broken the skin. The wound was . . . "What's this?" He pulled the hair back and frowned. "Kwiokos, do you have a pot of water? And perhaps a strip of cloth? There's so much blood and hair here that I can't see."

Green Serpent made a gesture, and Lightning Cat hurried away, only to return an instant later with a large pot of water and a piece of fabric.

Panther crouched, wet the fabric—it was a piece made from hemp—and dabbed at the blood-matted hair. It took time to sponge the area clean, but at last he was able to see the wound, a nasty depression just above the ear.

"Here, look here"—Panther pointed—"a second, smaller dent a bit further in front."

"She was hit twice?" Nine Killer looked closely. "Wait, something's not right about that."

"Indeed." Panther considered the wound for a moment. "It would be unlikely that she was struck twice, wouldn't it?"

Nine Killer exhaled thoughtfully. "The wounds I have seen would make me think so. If the first hit was the forward one, she would have staggered, probably lost her footing. Generally the warrior steps up and smashes the blow downward, right through the top of the skull."

"That isn't what we're seeing here."

"What does it mean?"

"Oh, we'll find out. Everything will come clear, War Chief. Red Knot has told us a great deal already." Panther cleaned the bloodstains from the girl's chest and inspected her breasts. Then he spread her legs and stared thoughtfully at her vulva. The pubic hair had been plucked, as was customary for a woman's first menstruation. "No sign of a man's seed was seen?"

"No. Flat Willow said that she hadn't been used like that."

With equal care, Panther inspected her legs, buttocks, and back. Then he used a stick to pry her mouth open and looked inside. Blood had trickled down her cheek and across her lips, and caked the outside of the teeth. "There's no blood on her tongue, no evidence that she bit anyone. None of the teeth are snapped off from a blow."

Sun Conch made a deep-throated sound and turned away, her eyes moist.

Panther washed his hands in the pot of water and glanced at Green Serpent. "Very well, Kwiokos, you may begin your duties."

"With you here?" Green Serpent shifted uncertainly. "You're not of her clan."

"No, but I must see her as you skin the body." Panther glanced at Sun Conch. "Out of respect, however, I will ask Sun Conch to leave us and guard the front entrance."

Sun Conch nodded gratefully, and ran for the entrance.

Panther shrugged. "I believe we were about to lose her anyway. I'm not sure that she's used to seeing the aftereffects of violent death. Especially with a girl she knew."

Nine Killer's grim expression reflected agreement.

Green Serpent nodded, and Lightning Cat and Streaked Bear stepped forward holding a ceramic pot decorated with cord marks and punctations. As Green Serpent sang in time to the shaking of his rattle, each priest removed a sharp chert flake, and bent over the girl.

Panther and Nine Killer stepped back as the War Chief

said, "I'm not sure I'm supposed to see this."

"Why is that, War Chief? She's a member of your clan. Her soul won't mind that you're here. After all, you are working for her."

"Our being here, it won't taint the ritual?"

Panther waved it away. "Just between the two of us, no, it won't. The Kwiokos and his kind like to keep certain privileges to themselves and the gods."

Green Serpent shot him a reproving look and continued with the task of removing Red Knot's skin.

"What we are doing here is making a familiar place for her ghost to reside." Panther inspected his hands, watching the lines deepen in his palms as he flexed the fingers. "Whether her ghost stays here is up to her, no matter what rituals we do to bind her to the body."

Despite periodic inspections by The Panther, Red Knot offered no more clues. He studied her arms in particular, even pulling back the muscles to feel the bones. She had no bruises, no other evidence of violence under the skin, or in the organs. Only the bloody indentations in her skull remained as cause of death.

In the end, she lay supine, garishly vulnerable as the last of her skin was carefully cut loose. What had been a girl looked monstrous: exposed red muscle, white tendon, and mottled blood. The sunken eyeballs stared sightlessly up from the stripped meat and cartilage on her face. Black bruises surrounded the wounds in the side of her rounded and naked skull.

"Kwiokos," Panther said gently. "Please, be very careful in the preparation of her skull. The muscle must be picked away with the greatest of care. If you find anything unusual, please, send for me immediately."

Green Serpent bobbed his head thoughtfully. "Yes, after watching you work, I think I understand."

It was late afternoon when Panther led Nine Killer out

of the temple, and collected a pale Sun Conch at the doorway.

"Your color looks better," Panther lied as he greeted the girl.

"I hadn't expected . . . to see her . . . not this way, Elder." Sun Conch glanced away uncertainly.

Nine Killer took deep breaths of the clear cold air, watching the sun as it slanted down toward the trees in the southwest. "One thing I don't understand. Why were you so concerned with her arms?"

Panther whirled, his face twisted in rage. "You filthy dog! I'm going to kill you!" And he swung his fist, striking at Nine Killer's head.

The War Chief threw his arm up as a shield. And at that, Panther danced back, saying mildly, "That's why, War Chief."

Nine Killer stood in a half-crouch, tensed to spring, confusion on his face. "Have you lost your senses?"

"Just proving a point. The instant you thought I was attacking you, you couldn't help but raise your arm to parry the blow. Think, War Chief, in battle, how many arms have you broken with your war club?"

The anger cleared from Nine Killer's eyes. "A great many, Elder. A man's first reaction is to raise his arm to block the blow."

"A woman's, too, I'd wager. But Red Knot never did so."

"Then she was killed from ambush!" Sun Conch cried. "She never even knew she was in danger!"

"No, and yes." Panther saw the light come to Nine Killer's eyes. Yes, the War Chief was a quick one; he already understood where Panther was headed.

"You see, Sun Conch," Panther said as he began walking across the plaza, "had I not shouted at the War Chief first, he would never have had time to raise his arm. Red Knot's death came so quickly, she never had time to react to the danger.''

"And the ambush?" Sun Conch asked. "Why do you rule that out?"

"From the nature of the wound," Nine Killer said grimly. "Her killer was facing her."

"So if the killer was facing her, and she never raised her arm in defense, she wasn't anticipating an attack. And that means . . . it was someone she knew." Sun Conch's young brow furrowed.

"And trusted," Panther added.

Nine Killer watched The Panther demolish a bowl of boiled squash, hominy, and periwinkles. Rosebud had seasoned the whole with beechnuts to give it a subtle tang. They washed the meal down with draughts of walnut milk poured from gourd cups.

They were quiet, lost in their own thoughts. Sun Conch had barely picked at her food. Even to Nine Killer's tongue, it tasted flat. Only The Panther, his forehead lined pensively, ate as if he'd never tasted such a feast.

The fire popped and crackled while Rosebud told her children stories of the first days, when First Man and First Woman, and deer, raccoon, skunk, and turtle, roamed the world in the form of men. She told of how chipmunk got his stripes and how First Man became the sun. And finally of the first terrible crime, when Okeus brought incest, murder, and war into the world.

Did she have to tell that last? Nine Killer listened halfheartedly, images from the day's activities popping into his mind. He felt unclean, the taint of death clinging to his body like the odor of smoke.

Relax, he told himself. *You're just not used to the ways of priests. You saw things today that you shouldn't have seen.* A good sweat bath, that's what he needed. And afterward, he'd take a long swim in the cold waters of the inlet. Yes, sweat the musk of death from his soul and then wash it clean.

Nine Killer pictured Red Knot's skull. He saw it after it had been skinned, the bone blood-blackened and broken. The two indentations mocked him. It wasn't just the violation of that delicate skull, but the way the wounds were situated. How could two blows be made so close together, the fractures running into each other, as if . . .

He stopped in midchew, and gave Sun Conch's war club a sidelong glance. The handle was as long as a man's arm, made of white ash, stained by sweat and dirt. The war head consisted of single stone, ground into a point and bonded to the wooden shaft by dried ligament stripped from a deer's hock. His own war club had been made much the same way.

But there were other ways to make a war club. Some had spikes—like Copper Thunder's. His had a stone head, and a copper spike set into the wood.

Two indentations?

"Rosebud? Could you come here?"

Panther and Sun Conch gave him inquisitive looks as Nine Killer's sister walked over, asking, "Do you need more? I thought that was enough food to feed half of your warriors."

"No, I need you. Come." He stood, placing hands on her shoulders and facing her toward the fire. "Were you the same size as Red Knot?"

She gave him an uneasy frown. "I think she was a little shorter, but I'm not sure. She grew like a thistle in the cornfield this last year."

Sun Conch stood, facing Rosebud. "She came up to here on me." She held a hand level with her brow. That made Rosebud a finger shorter.

"That's good enough," Nine Killer said. "Sun Conch, hand me my war club. It's over there next to the sleeping platform. That's it." Sun Conch brought it, and Nine Killer hefted his club in his right hand, testing the familiar balance. "Now, suppose that I was Red Knot's murderer, and—"

"No, you don't!" Rosebud snapped, stepping back warily. "I'm not going to stand in for a *dead* woman! Her soul would never forgive me!"

Panther's expression lit with sudden excitement. "Yes! What were you thinking, War Chief?"

"The two dents in the skull. What if they weren't two separate blows, but one. A war club can have two heads. The larger usually goes on the end of the club, correct?"

"That's right," Sun Conch said as her gaze measured the frightened Rosebud.

"Oh, hold still!" Nine Killer cried, grabbing his sister just before she turned to run. "Do you want to help us, or not?"

"Not if it means standing in for a murdered woman!"

"We could tie her up," Panther pointed out. "Hang her from the rafters so that we can make the height just perfect . . . even if she's on tiptoes."

"You wouldn't!" Rosebud wriggled in Nine Killer's grasp. Since his sister was taller than him, he had to look up at her, but she was no match for his thick muscles.

"Red Knot's ghost won't mind, Rosebud. I promise you." The Panther stood, and gave her his best fatherly look. "She's as anxious as we are to have her murderer exposed."

Rosebud relented, her hard eyes shooting poison at Nine Killer. "Just this once, I'll do it. What do you want me to do?"

Panther walked over and squinted at the left side of her head. "About here." Rosebud flinched as his finger touched the side of her head. "And here. Can we mark those spots?"

Sun Conch scooped up two gobs of yellow squash and dabbed them on the side of her head. "Like that?"

"Yes, just." Panther nodded.

Nine Killer extended his club, lining it up with the two dots, and determined that he needed to raise his hand but little to match the arc of the swing. "A short man?"

"Beware," Panther warned. "The head is the most active part of the body. Even if she didn't have time to lift an arm to ward the blow, she still might have jerked her head at the last minute."

"Look at the angle," Sun Conch noted. "She couldn't have been struck from behind. Not unless the attacker was above her."

"Or exceedingly tall," Nine Killer noted. "No, I've been all over that ridgetop. It's flat—unless the assassin hung from a tree."

"So," Panther concluded. "She was facing her attacker, and yes, given the way the skull broke, it was most likely a double-headed war club." He pulled at his chin. "Most interesting. All we need to do now is determine who has a two-headed war club, someone that Red Knot would allow close to her."

"Then that excludes the Mamanatowick's warriors. Winged Blackbird couldn't have done this to Red Knot." Nine Killer shook his head. "I'd rather it was him. I'd much prefer to take it out of his hide than someone here."

"You can't discount him!" Sun Conch declared adamantly. "How do you know that he *didn't* do this? If not on his own, then perhaps he used someone here to do his work for him?"

"Used how?" Nine Killer demanded. "The Mamanatowick doesn't just say 'Have someone kill Red Knot' and have one of our people jump to his pleasure."

"No," Sun Conch countered, "but it could have been more subtle. The Mamanatowick has a great many of our people from the Independent villages captive. What if word came to one of your people that a slave was to be freed? Perhaps someone's mother, father, or child? That would be a pretty strong motivation for murder.''

"Never discount the Mamanatowick," The Panther agreed. "He hasn't kept his alliance of Weroances without a great deal of cunning and intelligence. Were he an idiot, he'd have been replaced years ago.''

"And Copper Thunder, or Grass Mat, as you call him?'' Nine Killer asked, reading the wary look in The Panther's eyes.

"He, too, is worthy of your most careful attention, War Chief. He was always bright, but forever impetuous. If he has learned patience to complement that intricate mind of his, he would be a most challenging adversary.''

"He was here, you know.'' Nine Killer crossed his arms, trying to sift all the information through his mind. An element of clinging doubt was tangled up somewhere in the bottom of his soul. They were missing something, some vital bit of knowledge that would make all the pieces fit together.

"And he was out in the night,'' Rosebud stated. "My daughter White Otter saw him come through the palisade gate just at dawn. She said his leggings were wet, as if he'd been out in the fields.''

"White Otter?'' Nine Killer called. "Come tell us about this.''

She was the eldest of Rosebud's daughters, and his favorite of her five children. Whip thin, with shining black hair, she had a narrow face that accented large brown eyes. She'd be a beauty in a few more years, and no doubt a heartache for her mother to marry off.

"This is true, Uncle.'' White Otter gulped at being the focus of such serious adult eyes. "Mother sent me out for water for the morning stew, knowing that we would have to provide something for the Weroansqua's house. She was feeding all of those guests. I was on my way toward the palisade with that big clay jar over there. He came through the opening, looked around, and walked right toward the Weroansqua's Great House.''

"Did you see anyone else?" Nine Killer asked. "No one was with him, or followed him into the palisade?"

White Otter shook her head. "No one. Well, people were about, you know. It was first light, after all. I didn't think much of it. Just that he'd gone out to relieve his night water. The only thing odd was his wet leggings. I wouldn't have noticed if it hadn't been Copper Thunder.''

"Thank you." Nine Killer reached out and patted her fondly on the shoulder. "If you think of anything else, you be sure to come tell me. All right?"

"Yes, Uncle." But she didn't give him the usual smile.

"My, my, so our old friend Grass Mat was up and about." Panther narrowed an eye as he stared at the fire. "Now, isn't that a coincidence?"

"You know, the Great Tayac has a war club headed with stone, and just below that is a copper spike.''

"Yes, I know," the Panther replied softly. "I wonder if it would match the holes in Red Knot's head?''

Eighteen

Flat Willow was working on a clam rake when The Panther and Sun Conch finally located him the following morning. The young hunter sat on an overturned canoe down at the landing. As water lapped at his feet, he bent over his work. A thoughtful frown etched his forehead as he concentrated on lashing a wooden peg to his rake. Beside him lay a roll of flax cord and a supply of sharpened clamshells for woodworking.

The day was gray and cloudy, and a north wind drove white-capped chop into the inlet. Despite the weather, Flat Willow wore only his loincloth and a feather cloak. A thick layer of grease protected the rest of his body from the chill. He'd pulled his hair up tight on the right side of his head and held it in place with a slender deer-bone hairpin cut from the length of a cannon bone.

The rake itself consisted of a thin pole cut from a sapling twice the height of a man. Finger-thick branches as long as a man's arm had been attached to the bottom in a fan shape and braced with a crosspiece. The resulting tool would claw clams and oysters loose from the muddy inlet bottoms, and scoop them into the canoe.

"Going out for shellfish, I see," Panther said.

The young hunter barely glanced up, nodded, then realized who had spoken. Startled, he muttered, "I, uh, yes. I'm about ready for a change from chasing deer." His smile died when he met Sun Conch's bland gaze. "Hello, old friend."

"It is good to see you, Flat Willow." Sun Conch smiled thinly, clearly uncomfortable. Panther gave Flat Willow his most unsettling grin—the death's-head one he'd long practiced.

Flat Willow glanced at him uneasily and twirled the shaft of the clam rake in his hand. "I was missing a few teeth on the end." He pointed absently. "Had to replace them."

"Bound them up with cordage, I see. You don't use sinew?"

"No, Elder. No one does. I mean, well, in the water the sinew loosens. Cordage is much better."

"It will be a cold day out there. The water's rough." Ranks of waves marched across the inlet. "You're not going out into Salt Water Bay itself, I take it?"

"No, Elder, Fish River will be rough enough. Even then I expect to be cold. I imagine I'll ship enough spray to put out my fire." He indicated a slim dugout across from the one he sat on. A charred wooden bowl was set amidships in the floor. Fishermen built fires in the hardwood bowls for warmth, and for attracting fish to their nets at night. If the fire was cared for properly, a fisherman never had to build a new one, but could nurse the coals over long distances, and cook fish and fowl as he traveled.

"I hear that you were the one who found poor Red Knot's body." Panther pulled his old fabric blanket tightly about his shoulders. He wished they'd done this next to the fire in the longhouse rather than down here on the exposed beach.

"That's right, Elder. I tracked High Fox back up to where her body was hidden in the leaves." He shot a quick glance at Sun Conch, his expression pained, as if in guilt.

"Oh, fear not," Panther said mildly. "I know that Sun Conch and you have been friends from a long time back."

Flat Willow nodded, lips tight as if biting off words.

"And you and High Fox, you used to spend a lot of time together as children. Best of friends when the clans came visiting here, or you went to Three Myrtle."

Flat Willow nodded.

Panther gestured again at his companion. "Yes, Sun Conch has told me a great deal about you and High Fox. She also told me that you wanted to marry Red Knot. That you, too, fell in love with her."

Flat Willow glowered at Sun Conch, reddening as the

anger of betrayal was stifled by clamped jaws. "My *friend* seems particularly loose of tongue these days."

"Why, my good hunter, if tongues don't loosen, we will never understand just what happened to Red Knot." Panther stepped closer, using his aggravating smile to mock Flat Willow. "It must have bothered you to hear that lovely young Red Knot was marrying Copper Thunder."

Flat Willow took a deep breath and lowered his eyes, fingers tracing the grain of the wooden handle. "I do my duty, Elder. She was the Weroansqua's daughter. We all knew that. Everyone but High Fox." His lips quirked. "He liked to live dangerously."

"That's a curious way to put it. When I met High Fox, he was fairly well subdued, scared half out of his skin."

"Was he? Ask your friend there. Go on, Sun Conch, tell him. High Fox figured he could get away with anything. He was Black Spike's son. He could take chances with the Weroansqua's granddaughter!"

"Take chances?" Panther glanced skeptically at Sun Conch, and then at Flat Willow. "I'm afraid Sun Conch never mentioned that."

"Of course not, she is covering for her friend. She's particularly fond of him, you see. She thinks she loves him, will forgive him anything. They're in it together. Or hadn't you figured that out yet, Elder? Are your witch's Powers that limited that you can't tell when you're being lied to?"

Sun Conch's hand dropped to her war club, but she said nothing.

"Lied to? Me?" Panther gave him a startled look, then jerked a thumb toward Sun Conch. "By Sun Conch? That's ridiculous."

"Ridiculous?" Flat Willow mimicked his tone of voice. "I'll tell you about being ridiculous. High Fox was the ridiculous one. Did you know he was lying with Red

Knot? As long ago as last summer? What was that? Six moons *before* she became a woman?''

Sun Conch took a half step forward, clutching her club, her face stormy. Panther tugged her back with a restraining hand, muttering, ''Easy, there.''

''Oh, yes, easy, Sun Conch, you silly grouse. Or didn't you know he was wetting himself in her sheath?''

''If you knew this, why didn't you say something?'' Sun Conch growled. She allowed Panther to drag her back.

''Because, *old friend*, I figured that in time, events would catch up with him. I just never thought he'd kill her.'' Flat Willow looked away, the wind teasing loose strands of black hair out of the bun on the side of his head.

''You must have really hated him,'' Panther said softly. ''And her, too.''

Flat Willow shot him a sidelong glare. ''No. Not her. I thought she was a fool for letting High Fox pump himself dry inside her, but I never thought she'd suffer for it. He was a man! Blackened in the *Huskanaw*! By blood and bone, a *man* does not couple with a child! Not among our people.''

''You didn't try to protect her? To drive him off?'' Panther chided.

''For what?'' Flat Willow cried. ''She'd have hated me for it! Hated *me*! She . . . she thought she *loved* him!''

''And you loved her?'' Panther countered. ''Indeed, if that's love, you're—''

''How would *you* know?'' Flat Willow leapt to his feet, throwing down the clam rake. ''You come in here, stick your old nose in our business! What do *you* know of love, old man? About the burning in my breast when I'd look at her? How my guts went watery when I knew that she was with him, letting him drive that pitiful penis of his into her when I . . . I . . .'' He clenched his fists, and turned away.

Panther watched the thick muscles in Flat Willow's chest knot and writhe, then said, ''So you would have done anything to get her.''

''That's right,'' he grated, struggling to control himself.

''It must have been terrible for you when she was going to run off with High Fox. Your plan hadn't worked. No one had discovered that High Fox was lying with a girl. He wasn't disgraced and punished, and Red Knot's status hadn't been diminished enough that you, a lowly hunter, could hope to marry her. All of a sudden she was a woman, running off with the man you hated. They were free. On their way. She was out of your life completely, and you couldn't stand it, so you picked up a club and beat her brains in.''

Flat Willow, eyes glazed, stepped toward Panther. ''Killed her? Beat her . . . No. No! I never!''

''If you couldn't have her, then neither could any other man!''

''No! How dare you!'' Drawn with rage, Flat Willow stood face-to-face with Panther. ''If you only knew what lengths I was willing to go to. What I'd sacrificed to . . .''

But he stopped short. His mouth gaped, as if he was struggling for breath—and then he chuckled nervously. ''Oh, you're very clever, Panther. You thought you'd get me to admit to something, make me lose my sense and tell you . . .''

''Tell me . . . what?'' Panther prodded.

''Why, about Red Knot's death, that's what.'' Flat Willow folded his arms across his chest. ''Sorry, old man. Take your tricks and games to the Weroansqua. I've told everyone what happened up there. I was hunting deer and High Fox came running down the trail. We had words. He had blood on his hand, and he ran off, jumped in his canoe, and paddled away like a madman. I was curious; I backtracked him and found Red Knot.''

''And what did she say to you?''

''She was dead. Had been for a long time.''

''How do you know?''

''I'm a hunter, Elder. A body loses heat quickly on a cold day like that one. She was stone cold. She'd started to stiffen, and her eyes were dried. Even the urine that leaked out had started to dry.''

''Any sign of a struggle?''

''No. None. And she hadn't been with a man, either. There would have been stains.''

''But her body had been dragged from the middle of the ridge, to the side, and covered with leaves?''

''That's right.'' He studied Panther with half-lidded eyes. ''High Fox did that. Tried to hide his crime. He thought that scattering a few leaves would keep her from being discovered.''

''Indeed?'' Panther nodded slowly. ''Do you carry a war club, Flat Willow?''

''Sometimes. What business is it of yours?''

''Do you have it with you today?''

''I do. I could show you how it works.'' His eyes narrowed. ''In fact, I think I'd get a great deal of enjoyment out of doing just that.'' He squinted at Panther's skull, as if judging just where to land the blow.

''Perhaps later.'' Panther ignored the threat and gestured. Sun Conch stepped over to the canoe, looking inside. She boldly bent down and lifted a thick war club from the bottom of the boat. Like most of the war clubs in Flat Pearl Village, it bore a single knob on the end, this one carved from the wood itself.

Panther shrugged as Sun Conch replaced the club. ''Well, good fishing to you today, Flat Willow. I guess that whenever Red Knot becomes the center of attention, your hunting is disrupted.''

"It would seem so," Flat Willow replied crossly.

Panther nodded and started up the canoe landing toward the village, Sun Conch following. Then, on a hunch, he turned on his heel, head cocked. Flat Willow hadn't moved. He stood glaring after them. "Tell me, Flat Willow, that morning, you shot at a deer?"

"That's right."

"Did you ever find the arrow?"

The hunter shook his head. "No. And if you think that's what killed Red Knot, you can go find it yourself."

"Pleasant sort," Panther muttered out the side of his mouth as he resumed his walk toward the palisade opening. "But one never knows what he will find when he goes looking, does he?"

"No, Elder, but make no doubt of it, there was murder in his eyes."

"Oh, yes. And he's hiding something. Like a snake in a bag, it's wiggling around down next to his heart."

"Let's just hope it doesn't come out and bite us, Elder." Sun Conch gave Panther a worried look. "Don't underestimate Flat Willow. I thought I knew him, but he's so different now. I think he'd kill you without a breath's hesitation."

In the center of the plaza, the bonfire greedily devoured the stack of piled wood. Around it, Flat Pearl Village's warriors danced in time to Green Serpent's high-pitched and wavering song. To each side, Lightning Cat and Streaked Bear shook their large gourd rattles in time, adding their deeper voices to the Song of Thanksgiving. They sang facing the fading glow of sunset, the direction of war and death.

Led by Nine Killer, they danced, leapt, and stomped,

ducking their heads, and raising their voices to mingle with the priests' song. They looked up toward the night sky, where the sparks twinkled out and the thin smoke carried their words of praise up into the air, bearing it toward Okeus' ears, that he might know their gratitude for allowing them to return safely from the raid.

In the fading light, the carved faces of the Guardians seemed to blink as the shadows of cavorting warriors masked the yellow firelight. Behind them, the people watched, clapping and stamping in time to the shishing rattles. For most of the observers, this was an expression of relief rather than the out-and-out joyous abandon that followed a successful raid with captives and trophies. Then, the celebration would have lasted for several days instead of this single evening.

Shell Comb closed in on her quarry, moving stealthily as she circled the celebration. She stepped up beside him where he stood in the shadows, leaned against the bark of the House of the Dead. "Good evening, Elder. I hope you are enjoying the dance?"

Oddly, he showed no reaction to her approach, responding in a conversational voice: "That Flying Weir, he seems particularly light on his feet for such a large man. When he and Nine Killer are side by side, I sometimes think they are twins to Lightning Cat and Streaked Bear."

Shell Comb watched the warriors whoop and jump. "You seem to have made quite a stir with your arrival here. My mother is unsure whether to have the Great Tayac's warriors drive you from the village, or to simply surrender her position to you."

The Panther was moving his fingers in time to the music, his head bobbing in time to the beat. "You must be Shell Comb."

"Indeed, I am." She studied him in the glowing firelight. "But, who, I wonder, are you? I've heard no mention of your clan, your family, or where you might have come from. You are simply referred to as 'the witch.' Unless, of course, it is Copper Thunder speaking. He calls you Raven.''

"That is how he knew me; but it was a long time ago, Shell Comb. And far, far from here.'' He gestured off to the west and the last darkening of the sky. "Clear across the mountains, on the great rivers. I suppose you've heard of the Serpent Chiefs and the temples they raise to the sun.''

"You are one of them? They are your people?''

"I lived among them for a time.''

"Your accent,'' she told him, "would lead me to believe that you were raised here. You don't speak like a foreigner.''

"I said I lived among them. I've been a great number of places.''

"A perpetual mystery, aren't you?'' Who was this man who talked so easily of himself, yet said nothing? "I heard tell that you called your clan . . . let's see, yes, the High Steppers?''

"That was a bit of a joke, I'm afraid.'' He smiled wistfully. "Oh, I had a clan a long time ago. To them, I have been dead for over five tens of Comings of the Leaves. That's quite an odd notion to your ears, isn't it? That a man could live without a clan? After all, that's how we place ourselves, define ourselves to the rest of the world. Our kinship gives us everything, our rules, our obligations and responsibilities, our mates, our friends, even our afterlife. It defines who we *are*.''

"Without family, we are nothing.''

"Then I am nothing, Shell Comb. My clan is dead to me, and I to them. So here I stand before you, a bit of human flotsam, a blob of living flesh without obligation to any clan, family, or village. I am completely free.''

She took a deep breath, twisting a curl of hair around

her finger. "Actually, Elder, I may be the only person in this village who can admire you." What would it be like, this total freedom? She caught his slight smile as he read her thoughts.

"Frightening," he answered simply. "To be completely free is terrifying. Especially after having been raised in the careful nurturing arms of a respected and influential clan. I never wanted for anything, Shell Comb. Just like you. Someone was always there to help me, to make a place for me at their fire. If I was sick, they cared for me. The same with you. If you are hurt, they will nurse you. If you are threatened, they will come running with their war clubs raised on high, for you are of the clan. They have given you everything, and you are obligated to give them everything back."

She felt herself drifting under the soothing spell of his words. The great hollow emptied under her heart, a yawning abyss into which she could fall very easily. Her voice dropped to a wounded whisper. "Oh, yes, Elder. I've even given them my heart, ragged and bleeding. But I fought with them, the whole way. I've struggled to make my own rules." She caught herself, angered at her vulnerability. "But why do I tell you this?"

He chuckled, amused by her reaction. "Because no one else will listen to you. No one else understands that longing in your voice." He pointed off to the west. "You could go, you know. Pack up and leave. The whole world is out there."

She rubbed her arms, thinking of Copper Thunder, of the upriver villages, and then her thoughts took her back, into the past. "I went north once, a trading expedition to the Susquehannocks." She glanced at him, measuring his reaction. "I was . . . No, they were, well, different. As if they weren't really human at all. The things they did, the way they lived, the same, but so . . ."

"Frightening," he answered, eyes veiled. "That's the

reason you will never go, Shell Comb. For all of your chafing at the restrictions of your clan, the most important thing they do for you is make you safe and secure.''

The abyss yawned, and she had to fight to push it back, to block the past before it overwhelmed her control and left her broken and sobbing on the ground. She stiffened, reminding herself that she had been renewed, accepted a fresh start. To look back caused pain. She'd sworn she'd never look back again. ''It comes at a price, Elder. A terrible price.''

''Most things in life do.''

She hardened her heart, looking down at her right hand, flexing her fingers. The muscles tightened under her smooth brown skin. Power lurked there, hidden in the memory of flesh and bone. The rules were clear— and some were absolute. Some she would not break, no matter what price her soul paid. ''Tell me, Elder. Are people different from the animals? Are we better off with our clans, kinship, and obligations?''

''I don't know.'' He mused for a moment. ''The deer, raccoons, bobcats, and chipmunks have no one to rely on but themselves. Humans, with their clans, villages, and tribes, can accommodate an individual's disaster. That is a strength we have that they don't.''

''But they are free,'' she countered, ''to follow the longings of their hearts. Why did First Man create us with longings and desires? Why did he give us such hungers of the soul, and then establish the clans?''

''Is that how you see life? A conflict of desire against responsibility?''

They passed through the palisade gate. She nodded to Crab Spine, who stood guard, and noted the reserve in his eyes as he stepped back to let The Panther pass. Once they had entered the plaza, she said, ''The way I see it is meaningless. That's how it is. Follow the urgings of your soul, Elder, and sooner or later you will run afoul of the clan and its rules.'' Unnerved, she quickly added, ''That's why you are dead to your people, isn't it?''

His thin lips quirked. ''I was young and foolish once.'' He hesitated, studying her from the corner of his eye. ''Have you ever been foolish, Shell Comb?''

''Everyone has been foolish at one time or another.''

He stopped short, apparently lost in thought as he studied the trampled dirt under his feet. The soil had been discolored by charcoal from the fires. Bits of broken pottery, bleached clam and oyster shells, and cracked nut shells dotted the surface. ''I am sorry about your daughter, Shell Comb.''

''So am I,'' she told him. When she met his gaze, her chest seemed suddenly starved of air. Her heart began to race. How could just looking into his eyes turn her stalwart control into such confusion? Against the rising grief, she smiled. ''Enjoy your stay here, Elder.''

Get away, Shell Comb. Now, as quickly as possible. As she turned, he called, ''I look forward to speaking with you again.''

Nine Killer sat cross-legged on the cattail matting before the fire in Rosebud's longhouse and puffed on his clay pipe. His legs ached from the dancing, but a gentle satisfaction filled him. The dance had brought an ending to the Three Myrtle raid, a sort of healing for his wounded pride. He studied the blue smoke rising from his pipe. The tobacco crop this year had only been fair; before they could be picked off, worms had chewed holes in many of the leaves. Nevertheless, the weed had produced enough to satisfy his clan's tribute requirements to the Weroansqua, and still leave them a year's supply.

The hominy had been devoured, and the main course

of squash and pumpkin had been eaten. The last of the walnut milk had been drunk. Rosebud had finished stacking the wooden dishes after the dogs licked them clean. Now she rustled about the sleeping benches, rolling out soft deerskin robes.

Nine Killer looked at The Panther and Sun Conch. The old man had been thoughtful all evening. From the wrinkles on his forehead, his mind had been knotted around the problem of the girl's death.

Sun Conch seemed moody, and withdrawn. Most of the evening she had stared absently at the fire, eating as if her food had no taste. White Otter had attempted several times to draw Sun Conch into a conversation, but something had changed between the girls. Once they had been close friends, but now Sun Conch seemed older, more a woman than a girl.

Noting that Rosebud was out of earshot, Nine Killer asked, "What did you discover today?"

"Oh, a great many things." Panther rubbed his face with a leathery hand. "Tell me, War Chief, what is the penalty for a young man who is caught sleeping with a girl?"

Nine Killer shrugged. "That would depend on who the girl was, how old, and which clan she belonged to. And, of course, it would depend on who the man was."

Panther reached out and pinched tobacco from the small ceramic pot beside him. He packed the cut leaves into the bowl of his old stained clay pipe, glanced at Sun Conch, and indicated the fire. To Nine Killer's surprise, it took a moment for the girl to realize what she was being asked. Sun Conch jumped, looking startled and somewhat guilty, and reached out with a twig to light the Elder's pipe.

Only after The Panther puffed a blue cloud did he say in low tones, "Let us suppose the young woman was Red Knot."

Nine Killer took a deep breath. "The Weroansqua's granddaughter?" Nine Killer shook his head, imagining the hot anger that would have brewed in Hunting Hawk's eyes. "That would have been bad indeed, Elder. Only a fool enrages an old sow bear as possessive of her cubs as Hunting Hawk is."

"Granted, but say the youngster was High Fox, son of Black Spike. This wouldn't be quite so impermissible as, say, Flat Willow?"

Nine Killer's pipe was forgotten in his hand. Panther could read the shock on his face. "This coupling was forced, or with her consent?"

"According to my sources, she wasn't forced."

"Good. If she had been, not even you could have stemmed the Weroansqua's rage. Oh, Black Spike's Bloodroot Clan might have been able to buy off some of Hunting Hawk's anger—provided suitable tribute was offered. High Fox would still have to be punished, of course, but he might have been spared his life. On the other hand, if someone like Flat Willow forced her, Hunting Hawk would most likely have tortured him until he died, or broken his arms and legs and thrown his body on the bonfire to burn to death."

"But if she wasn't forced, and freely coupled with him?"

"That's different," Nine Killer said slowly. "In Flat Willow's case, she might have ordered him beaten to within an inch of his life. Maybe his legs would have been broken and he'd have had to live on the mercy of his clan. Catch her on the wrong day, and she might still have ordered me to brain him and toss his body into the Fish River at high tide."

Sun Conch bit her lip.

Nine Killer gave her a questioning look. Panther noticed, and explained, "It seems as if young High Fox lied to me. In the process, he placed Sun Conch at a disadvantage.'' He turned to the chastened girl. ''How much of this did you know?''

Sun Conch dropped her head to stare at her slim brown hands. ''I *didn't* know, Elder. I swear. I . . .''

''You suspected?''

''Well, they—they used to disappear. You know, just up and slip away. Sometimes a person doesn't ask . . . doesn't wish to know.'' She spread her hands wide. ''Besides, they thought they would marry. No one anticipated this match with Copper Thunder.''

Nine Killer considered the implications. To think, the Weroansqua's immature granddaughter dallying with a man—and right under his nose!

Nine Killer growled to himself, realized his pipe had gone cold, and snagged up the twig to relight it. Very well, it had happened—and Red Knot was dead. So, how were these things related?

The Panther gave the fire a baleful look, his fingers gripping his pipe stem until the nails had gone pale. ''I told him I would skin him alive.''

''Pardon? Skin who?'' Nine Killer asked.

''High Fox! I told him what would happen if I discovered that he'd lied to me.''

Nine Killer exhaled through his nose, watching two threads of blue smoke wind upward from his nostrils. ''Perhaps we have yet another reason for murder. Was this something Red Knot was using to control him? To manipulate him to her ends? After all, her word against his would be a powerful incentive. Perhaps he thought the only way to keep Red Knot quiet was the most permanent way?''

Panther stared into the distance, eyes vacant. ''That makes a great deal of sense, War Chief. More now than at any time before. If she married Copper Thunder, she would hold that club over High Fox's head for years. Oh, gradually the seriousness of it would fade, but at eighteen summers and blinded by the impetuousness of youth, did High Fox understand that?''

Sun Conch shook her head, answer enough.

"It appears, Elder, that rather than champion High Fox, you may have just killed him.''·

"Oh . . . but . . .'' Sun Conch's eyes blurred. "Elder?''

The Panther raised a cautionary finger. "Not yet, War Chief. Flat Willow claims that Red Knot's body was cold when he found it. He said her urine was even drying out. Now, let us consider. Flat Willow sees High Fox charging down the trail. They talk. Not the best of friends anymore, they have a quick conversation, and High Fox wants to escape as quickly as he can. Flat Willow's curiosity is stirred, so he backtracks High Fox to the ridge-top to find the body. How long would that take, War Chief?''

Nine Killer pictured the trail above Oyster Shell Landing. "Say that Flat Willow was halfway down the slope, I'd say it would take about as long to scale the ridge as it would take to smoke the tobacco in your pipe bowl. I saw High Fox's tracks where he ran down the trail. His was not exactly a difficult trail to work out, and Flat Willow, I hear, is an excellent tracker. Once on top, not knowing what he was looking for, Flat Willow finds Red Knot's tracks coming up the other side. Now, he knows those tracks were not High Fox's, so he would scout around, trying to identify the person High Fox met. All in all, I'd say it took less than half a hand of time for Flat Willow to find the body.''

Panther nodded. "You think as I do, War Chief. It's much too soon for the body to cool.''

"If you take Flat Willow's word that it . . .'' Nine Killer shook his head. "No, that doesn't make sense. Why would he lie about how long the body had lain there?''

"Why indeed,'' Panther agreed. "It's a flaw in his

otherwise perfect story. If he wants us to believe that
High Fox killed the girl—and I think he does—he
slipped up when he told me she was cold to the touch.''

''He's hiding something!'' Sun Conch blurted. ''You
saw him, Elder. You called it a serpent around his heart.''
She glanced at Nine Killer. ''Flat Willow even threatened
the Elder! Said he'd like to use his war club on him.''

Panther raised a hand to calm Sun Conch. ''What can
you tell me about Flat Willow, War Chief? What sort of
man is he? My impression is that he's looking for recognition and glory, but unwilling to do the work such
rewards entail.''

Nine Killer resettled himself, glancing quickly over his
shoulder to insure that their talk was still private. ''A
potter couldn't make a better impression in soft clay with
a cord-wrapped paddle. He's all of that. His clan, Star
Crab, is respected, if not influential in Flat Pearl Village.
His mother and father were killed by the Mamanatowick's warriors when he was a boy of four. He went to
live with this mother's brother, Green Starfish. Green
Starfish went out fishing one time, and never came back.
Drowned, we think. Flat Willow would have been six
then. After that the boy shuttled from family to family,
never quite fitting in.''

''In trouble?'' Panther asked.

Nine Killer shrugged. ''What boy isn't? But, yes. He's
unruly, loudmouthed, and as abrasive as wet sand on
greenstone. He has a reputation as a scrapper—generally
picking fights he can't possibly win. You know the
type.''

''Elder?'' Sun Conch said, and tucked her fingers beneath her arms, as if suddenly chilled. ''Flat Willow used
to tell such lies. When he was a boy. Things we couldn't
believe. Stories about huge fish he'd caught—but no one
ever saw the fish. Or, he'd tell of seeing deer that jumped
over whole trees, and flying monsters. If one of us said

no, that it was just a story, he'd start a fight to prove himself right.''

Panther stared at the embers in his pipe bowl. ''Not the most reliable of people to find the body, but in this case, do you think he would have lied to me? You said you ran straight up there. How long after dawn was it?''

Nine Killer sighed. ''Sometime around midday. It took a while to determine that Red Knot was missing. We organized a search, and were warned of Winged Blackbird's approach. We intercepted the raiders, and it wasn't too long after that when Flat Willow called that he'd found Red Knot.''

''You saw the girl.'' Panther winced and resettled himself, as if his bones were aching. ''How long would you say she'd been dead?''

Nine Killer shrugged. ''I'd say she died sometime around dawn.''

The Panther frowned. ''That fits what both High Fox and Flat Willow have told me.''

''Indeed,'' Nine Killer agreed. ''But, the question remains. Did either of them tell the truth?''

Darkness grayed into dawn, softly illuminating the forest beyond the palisade of Flat Pearl Village. Here and there, scruffy dogs ambled about, sniffing at bits of broken pottery. Sun Conch sat with her back against the side of Rosebud's house, her war club beside her, watching the tatters of mist that floated by. A few of the star people still gleamed, but most had closed their sparkling eyes to sleep.

Sun Conch yawned and folded her arms. Restless, she had left The Panther snoring in his blankets, and come outside to greet the morning. The cold breeze ruffled the red and blue feathers of her cape and fluttered her long black hair. From this place, she could survey the entire length of Flat Pearl Village. A finger of time ago, an old man had stumbled around the corner of a longhouse and spilled his night water; then Copper Thunder and two of his warriors had slipped out of the village with their bows. To hunt for breakfast, she assumed.

Sun Conch tipped her head back to watch a tuft of mist curl over the thatched longhouse roof. She had slept poorly. Throughout the night, images of High Fox's pleading face had assaulted her. She had never seen him look so pitiable. Who would he turn to now? Red Knot was dead, and Sun Conch was gone. Was there anyone left in the world to comfort him? For the first time, High Fox had no one.

And, given the things Panther had discovered, he was in the worst trouble of his life.

Her soul kept replaying the happy, joyous days of their childhood together, and she longed to go to him. Just to—to talk. She *needed* to talk with him.

When they'd been children, she had followed him around like a happy puppy, often embarrassing him in front of his friends, who thought that a girl demeaned their approaching manhood. Sun Conch smiled to herself. Despite the taunts from his friends, High Fox had never shouted at her, or told her to go away. Of course, none of the other children had really liked him, either. Oh, he had ignored her on occasion, but then, later, when they had been alone, he'd apologized for it, and promised to make it up to her. And he always had. Many mornings she had awakened to find treasures deposited near the foot of her bed—the farthest he could reach without actually coming into her house, which would have been impolite—flowers, beautiful seashells, brightly colored autumn leaves. Things he knew would please her.

The past two Comings of the Leaves, however, had

been much harder. After his Blackening, the pressures on High Fox grew extreme. People expected more of a man than they did a boy, and High Fox never seemed able to meet those expectations. Especially his father's. He hadn't been free to see Sun Conch as often, but she'd understood. When they did sit together, she had been content.

Sun Conch cocked her ear.

Panther had awakened. She could hear him speaking softly to someone inside the longhouse. She sighed. As soon as he found her, there would be work to do. Not that she minded. He had kept his part of the bargain. She would certainly keep hers.

She turned when Panther rounded the corner of the house. His gray hair was wild from sleep, and he looked only half-awake. He stood yawning and scratching his side. His gaze landed on her, and he walked forward.

"You are up early," he said.

"I couldn't sleep, Elder."

"Homesick?"

"No," she said vehemently. "I never wish to see my family again."

He gave her a wan smile, as though she'd told him she was dying from a strange fever that he knew would pass. "Then you must be fretting about High Fox."

Sun Conch lowered her gaze to the damp toes of her moccasins. How could he say High Fox's name with such distaste? "You don't know him, Elder. If you did, you would respect him."

Panther sank to the ground a pace in front of her. His faded old eyes had a puffy look, and his wrinkles etched his face so deeply, it appeared sculpted from brown clay. The worn blanket around his shoulders didn't hide his shivering.

Panther said, "Do you want me to tell you the truth? Or would a decorous lie be better?"

"I'm not sure, Elder. Your truths usually leave me feeling bludgeoned with a war club."

"They're meant to."

Sun Conch waved a hand. "Go ahead. Tell me the truth."

For a time, Panther watched the birds chirping and hopping across the thatch roof. Their songs had just begun to serenade the dawn, and he seemed to be enjoying them.

"You can tell a good deal about a man by the way he treats others, don't you agree, Sun Conch?"

"Yes, Elder. I do."

"Good." He kicked at a stone lodged in the frozen earth near his feet. "High Fox is a user. He uses whomever he can, whenever he can. He's just used you for so long, you think that's the way it's supposed to be."

"Elder," she said, exasperated, "have you ever loved someone?"

"Yes. I have. Deeply."

The tone in his voice made her stomach muscles go tight. She felt as if she'd just plunged a deer-bone stiletto into his belly and twisted it. "Then why don't you understand my love for High Fox?"

"I do understand, Sun Conch. I understand that young love is a very powerful thing. It is also, too often, very foolish."

Her mouth gaped. "Elder, how can you say that? All I want in life is to give myself to High Fox. I want him to have my whole soul. I would already have given it to him if . . . if . . ."

Panther waited, and when she said no more, he calmly finished for her, "If he'd wanted it. But, he didn't. You should be very grateful for that."

"But—"

"Sun Conch, do you know what would have happened

if he'd allowed you to give yourself to him? And I don't mean in body, child. I mean your soul."

Half-angry, she snapped, "What?"

"First of all, he wouldn't have known what to do with it. He doesn't know what to do with his own soul, let alone yours. He would have played with your soul like a toy, tossing it about, seeing how much it could take, until he finally broke it. Then he would have cast your soul aside, Sun Conch. What man wants something broken?"

She hesitated. "My love wouldn't have been broken, Elder. Wouldn't he have still wanted that?"

Panther closed one eye. "You speak of love as if you think it's easy."

"It is. I mean, for me. Loving High Fox is the easiest thing I have ever done."

"Loving is work, girl. And hard labor, at that. The hardest any human being can ever attempt."

Incredulous, she whispered, "Perhaps it was for you."

Panther sat back and tugged on his blanket, pulling it down over his exposed knees. "Sun Conch, doesn't it disturb you that High Fox's necklace was found in Red Knot's hand? That he was coupling with her when she was a girl? That last is certainly not the action of an honorable man."

She fingered the hide of her dress. She had all but asked the same thing of High Fox when she'd begged him to run away with her and told him she could be his wife. She had no right to condemn High Fox for loving Red Knot. Though the discovery of his necklace *had* bothered her. "The coupling . . . that wasn't honorable. You are right, Elder. But there must be a reasonable explanation for the necklace. High Fox would never have hurt Red Knot. I know it."

"You don't think it's possible that Red Knot grabbed

the necklace in a fight for her life? That she tore it from his throat trying to protect herself?''

Sun Conch's spine went rigid. She stared at Panther. ''No. I don't.''

''I see.'' But he acted just the opposite. His mouth had set into hard lines. ''Then who do you think murdered Red Knot?''

''I don't know, Elder! It could be one of ten people!'' She made a sweeping gesture with her arm. ''Nearly everyone in Flat Pearl Village has a motive!''

Panther frowned at the mist. As the morning warmed, it seemed to fall apart, fragmenting into patches, then wisps. Soon it would rise and transform itself into low clouds. ''Well, that's true. We need to uncover more of what happened here before we can begin to judge.''

The eastern sky had started to glow. Gulls flapped across the luminous blue, their hoarse calls echoing. Sun Conch smoothed her fingers down the polished wood of High Fox's war club, the club he had forced her to take, despite the fact that it was his life that was in danger. ''Elder,'' she asked, ''why do you hate High Fox so much? He's never done anything to you.''

''No,'' Panther said. ''But he will if I let him. He'll hurt anyone who gives him a chance.''

''He's never hurt me.''

''Never?''

She started to give him a hasty answer, but he'd know she was lying. ''Well, even if he has, I still want to marry him, Elder. Do you think that's wrong? To want to love someone forever?''

''Not wrong,'' he answered wistfully. ''But there is nothing more difficult than loving another person, Sun Conch. Lovers so often want to consume each other, to draw the other inside their hearts where they can keep them caged like a beloved pet—''

''I don't want High Fox as my pet!''

Panther looked up at her from beneath bushy silver brows. "Perhaps not, but I'm sure he wants you as his. He already treats you like his second-favorite dog. Now, let me finish what I was saying."

She clamped her jaw.

Panther leaned toward her to peer into her eyes. "Do you want to know how to avoid becoming a pet?"

"Not really. I don't think it will ever happen to me. I'm too strong-willed."

"I'm going to tell you just the same, because someday you'll be glad I did." He brushed at a speck of dirt on his blanket, gently, as if it were alive and he feared to hurt it. "Never strive to be one with another person, Sun Conch. You will want to. The heart can be very demanding. But don't do it. Love only succeeds when two people realize they can't be one, and learn to nurture the distance between them. Distance is what makes it possible to see another person for who they really are, whole, and naked against a clean blue sky. That is the beginning of real love."

"Distance! But I . . ." Sun Conch stopped, and checked to see if Panther wore his evil squint. He didn't. In fact, he looked a little sad. "Elder, I promise you that I will remember your words, though I will surely never learn to appreciate such a distance. More than anything, I want to be close to High Fox." The closer the better.

Panther looked away, and his eyes glinted with a silver-silk flash of dawn. "You will learn. Or you will spend your life alone." He abruptly rose to his feet, said, "As I have," and hobbled off as if each step hurt.

Sun Conch flopped back against the house wall. He had a way of conversing that felt a lot like being pelted with rocks. She shook her head.

The pungent scents of the newborn day rose powerfully, wet thatch and burning oak, the mist-soaked feathers of her cape. Several people were up and about. Two girls walked toward the opening in the palisade, water jugs cupped in their brown arms, their voices loud in the morning stillness. A dog trotted happily at the heels of a boy with an armload of wood.

An odd pain spread across her chest as she wondered at Panther's last statement. Did it mean that he had never learned to nurture the distance? Was that why he wasn't married? Why he lived on his island in the middle of nowhere?

As Panther neared the opening in the palisade, Sun Conch suddenly realized he intended to go outside. She grabbed her war club, sprang to her feet, and dashed across the plaza, calling, "Panther? Wait! Don't go out there alone! I'm coming!"

The Solitary

Blessed gods, my gods, I am so alone.

I stare at the firelit roof above me, and try just to breathe.

How curious that the sudden awareness of my coming death has awakened me to the fact that I have no one, that I spent my life discarding loved ones like broken pots along the way.

Faces flutter across my soul, and guilt overwhelms me when I must struggle to put names upon their smiles. Images whirl like snowflakes around each face, falling, falling . . .

Now I even understand how I did it.

As I grew older, piece by piece, I chose to move outside myself those ideas and people that cluttered my solitude. Old friends. New friends. They were all the same. I did not have the stamina for them. I truly believed that. Like bits of granite, they weighted my soul, demanding attention, gobbling more and more of my precious internal moments. I was fighting for my life! For the lives of other people! I could not afford such draining ties. I thought that if I set them aside I would have the strength for greater, more profound efforts. Not just for myself, but for everyone.

But that is not how it happened.

You see, I was a solitary for the sake of the work, and the work required me to create a magnificent self. All of my strength went into that. The splendid impostor.

For many Comings of the Leaves, I have been telling myself that doing battle with him is too difficult, I am too old and tired. Surely I can postpone the battle for another day. A day is nothing. Tomorrow I will begin the hunt. Tomorrow I will stalk him until he leads me into myself.

But as I blink up at the firelight dancing on the ceiling, I realize there may be no tomorrow.

. . . There may be no tomorrow, and I am condemned to spend my last moments with a man I do not know at all.

A soft desperate laugh escapes my throat.

Blessed gods, my gods. What a vast sparkling wasteland I carved in my heart.

For the sake of the work.

Nineteen

Hunting Hawk hated mornings like this. She stepped out of her Great House and squinted up through the naked myrtle branches at the gray sky of morning. The misty chill already pierced her thin flesh. Her rickety old bones soaked up cold the way old fabric absorbed rainwater. And once it leached into her bones, she couldn't seem to get warm no matter how many hours she spent next to the fire.

Patches of low cloud hovered over the arched roof of her home like vultures over a dead deer. How close they were: a strong warrior could have shot an arrow into their fluffy bellies as they drifted above the frosted palisade posts. She didn't need her breath puffing whitely before her nose to know that winter lay heavily on the land.

Hunting Hawk flexed her aching fingers and took stock of Flat Pearl Village. People did morning chores. Some ran errands. Others walked beyond the palisade to relieve nature's demand. Girls hauled water from the inlet while the tide was low and the water fresh. A group of sleepy-eyed boys plodded toward the gate, no doubt sent out to scout for firewood. The old lightning-riven oak would be scavenged yet again for its dwindling supply of fuel.

She took a deep breath, nose and throat rebelling at the cold air, and tapped the frozen ground with her sassafras walking stick. Her hips ached, and her knees and ankles pained her, too. Even the small of her back gave her twinges. Winter did that to her, made every joint ache. Not even rubbings of hemlock and teas of roasted and chopped poke root seemed to help anymore. Perhaps later today she would call Green Serpent to the sweat house and have him perform an herbal steam cure of cedar, bull thistle, and dwarf sumac.

She waddled toward the House of the Dead to offer tobacco and corn to Okeus, and her ancestors.

Lost in such thoughts, it took her a moment to recognize the gray-haired elder who stepped in from the palisade gate, his lanky form shadowed as usual by Sun Conch.

Hunting Hawk twitched her lips, considered, and changed course to intercept The Panther. She was within hailing distance when he saw her, stopped, and smiled.

"Greetings, Weroansqua," he called respectfully. He had his old fabric blanket wrapped around his bony shoulders, and raccoon-fur leggings covering his calves and the tops of his moccasins. "A good morning, wouldn't you say?"

She snorted, annoyed. "Good? My legs ache, my fingers ache, my feet ache. The colder and damper it gets, the worse I feel."

The Panther gave her a knowing smile and raised his thick eyebrows. "Ah! Been taking the usual cures, I suppose?"

"Them, and others. That old heel bone, Green Serpent, said he was fixing to rub me all over with sturgeon oil and sweat me until my meat cooked."

"Sturgeon oil?" Panther fingered his chin. "That's a new remedy."

Hunting Hawk narrowed an eye. "If you ask me, he's tried everything else. Lightning Cat told Flying Weir, who told Walks-By-Trail, who told Yellow Net, who told me, that Green Serpent had muttered something about never seeing a sturgeon that had bone-joint disease." She gave him a crafty look. "How would you interpret that, old witch?"

He huffed at her to show his displeasure at being called an old witch, then said, "I'd say he's run out of remedies and doesn't want to tell you so."

"I think that, too."

Panther studied the swollen joints on her fingers. "I want you to try something. Send one of your youngsters after willow. Strip the bark, dry it and pound it, then make a tea from it. It will help you for a while. It will taste vile, but it works on most pain. The Power in the willow is very strong. Don't take too much of it, or it will affect the stomach."

"Oh, yes. Always the stomach." Hunting Hawk rubbed her gaunt belly. "That's another problem."

"Perhaps I can help."

"Where did you learn so much about healing? From those Serpent Chiefs on the other side of the mountains?"

"From them, yes, and others as well." He tilted his head. "You seem to be well informed of my doings. The War Chief is reporting, I suppose?"

"Oddly, he's not talking about you with as free a tongue as I'm used to." She made a face. "I think he likes you. And, to tell the truth, Nine Killer has never been the trusting kind. It makes me suspect that you really do travel by night."

This time, The Panther smiled in amusement. "He's a good man, Weroansqua. I'd use him wisely. Such as he don't just pop up like ears of corn in a well-kept field."

Sun Conch stood to the rear, her attention apparently on everything but the two of them.

Hunting Hawk gestured toward the girl. "Your companion doesn't seem the trusting kind. That wouldn't be related to Flat Willow's threats, would it?"

"Who told you Flat Willow had threatened me?"

"Oh, he was bragging that if you didn't leave him alone, he'd be roasting your body in the bonfire some night soon. Funny thing is, I was watching Copper Thunder at the time. The Great Tayac was seated at my fire, apparently more entertained by Flat Willow than he was by Shell Comb."

"Indeed, and is he entertaining her?"

"They are talking." Hunting Hawk left it at that, wondering at The Panther's complete lack of concern about Flat Willow's threats.

"I see." The frown lines tightened on the old man's face. "And Greenstone Clan thinks this marriage is a good idea?"

"What Greenstone thinks is of no concern to you, Panther. In fact, I've had people asking around. No one seems to know anything about you, who you are, where you come from. It's as if you came out of thin air."

"Been looking for owl feathers in my bed?" he asked mildly.

"Should I be?"

He laughed. "No, but you have been sending Streaked Bear to peek into Nine Killer's doorway off and on for the last couple of nights. Has he reported that I've been in my robes each time?"

"He has," she growled to herself, irritated that the young priest had been so clumsy as to be discovered.

The Panther's lips twitched, as if controlling a grin. "Tell him that next time he might want to sneak over to the hole on the south side of the lodge. That's where the girls go to gossip with their friends when they've annoyed Rosebud into punishing them. That brown-and-white dog of Nine Killer's sleeps over by the doorway, and he growls every time Streaked Bear sneaks up."

"No wonder Nine Killer likes you. You have the same foul sense of humor." She paused, evaluating him. "Have you found my granddaughter's murderer yet?"

"No."

"But you have suspicions?"

"Of course, but so do you."

"You talked to Flat Willow yesterday. Do you think he did it?"

"Perhaps." Panther cast a sidelong glance in the direction of the longhouse where the young hunter lived, a ramshackle thatch building just behind the Women's House. "You saw him on the day they brought Red Knot in. Tell me, how did he look?"

She sucked at her cheeks, remembering that day, seeing the grim procession approaching through the fields, Red Knot's body swaying from the pole. And there was Flat Willow, following . . . "He was last in line." That thought hadn't occurred to her then.

"And that is significant?"

"For Flat Willow, yes." She nodded, one eye narrowing. "Normally, he'd have been right up front, smacking his chest and making a show of himself."

"He does strike me as that sort. And during the ceremony marking Red Knot's womanhood? Did he act oddly?"

Hunting Hawk thought back, fingers to her lips. She remembered seeing him, didn't she? Where was it that he'd been? Something a little odd had caught her attention, but . . . "He did, come to think of it. Had you not mentioned it, I wouldn't have given it a second thought."

"Well, odd how?" Panther demanded.

"That's just it." Hunting Hawk gestured helplessly. "I can't remember. Something about that last night at the dance. He was . . . He was . . . Oh, bat dung! It will come to me. These things always do. It just didn't seem important at the time."

"Did it have to do with Red Knot? Or maybe High Fox?"

"No, of that I'm certain. But I can tell you that I saw

High Fox and Red Knot together that last night. They were talking off to the side. It was just before her last dance. At the time, I thought little of it, since, after all, she had a right to say farewell to her friends.''

''What other friends did she have? Flat Willow?''

Hunting Hawk hesitated. She realized that he read the tracks of her thoughts as if they'd been made in fresh mud. ''You know something, don't you?''

The Panther shrugged, expression veiled. ''I may, and I may not. Weroansqua, I'm not going to contribute to your problems by revealing my every suspicion to you. Were I to do so, you'd be looking askance at everyone in the village.''

''I would, would I?''

''Indeed, including yourself.'' His sudden smile sent a shiver down her back. ''Where were you that morning, Weroansqua?''

''Me?'' She stiffened, mind racing back to that morning, to the things she'd done before she entered the House of the Dead. ''I was around. In my house, checking on things. Taking care of my guests. You know as well as I that there is a lot to do with a village full of . . .''

His face had turned oddly blank, eyes intent as if to probe past her sudden defense.

''I *was*!'' she declared heatedly, unsettled for the first time. She felt her control beginning to slip. ''Look, you don't come in here and question *me*! I am Weroansqua!''

She put a hand to her heart, aware that it hammered against her thin breastbone. Her blood raced, and in that instant, her balance deserted her. Only Panther's quick hand stabilized her. As quickly, the dizziness passed.

''I—I'm all right.'' She shook off his hand, and glared at him. ''Okeus curse you!''

''But you see, don't you,'' he replied calmly, ''that you, too, could have killed her.''

''That's ridiculous!''

"Is it? The Weroansqua has made an agreement to marry Red Knot to Copper Thunder—but, when she reconsiders, she finds herself in water over her head. How does she stop this alliance without angering the Great Tayac? She can see no way out, but, with the stakes so high, and driven by desperation, she orders her granddaughter killed the morning she is supposed to leave with Copper Thunder. In the process, High Fox is sacrificed, but how great a price is that? Black Spike can fume for a moon or so, until the arrival of canoe load after canoe load of tribute, along with an apology."

He fingered his chin, glancing up speculatively. "I'd word it something like this: 'Most honored Weroance, I wish to beg your forgiveness. The grief of my granddaughter's death drove me to rash actions. The counsel I received from the Great Tayac, and from others close to me, led me to believe your son had murdered my granddaughter. Please, take these gifts and forgive an old woman a foolish mistake!' "

Hunting Hawk swallowed hard. By dint of her leather-tough will, she kept control of herself. *Okeus eat his soul! How does he know me so well?*

He watched her without change of expression, as though he already knew what she'd say.

"All right," Hunting Hawk growled, goaded by self-disgust. "If I'd had her killed, I *would* have said something like that."

"Weroansqua, assuming she hadn't been killed, but had run off with the boy, what would you have done?"

"Sent Nine Killer and every whole-blooded man here to drag her back!"

"And Red Knot knew this? Knew you would react that way?"

"Of course! She's *my* granddaughter! She knew I'd be angry enough to uproot trees to get her back. The women in my family face up to their responsibilities. We do our duty.''

"Apparently, Red Knot didn't agree with you. After all, she was running off to meet young High Fox.''

"Or to tell him she wasn't going with him.'' Hunting Hawk uttered a low growl. ''I can't believe my granddaughter would be fool enough to think that she could escape the net of warriors I'd send after her.''

The Panther cast a curious look at Sun Conch, and said mildly, ''Well, one never knows about the gullibility of young love.'' Sun Conch lowered her eyes, but her face flushed hotly. Turning back, Panther said, ''And when they'd been returned to you, what then?''

Hunting Hawk narrowed her eyes. ''It would have cost me plenty, making restitution to Copper Thunder, paying for the affront of Red Knot's running away like that. That girl should have cut off her right arm rather than disgrace her clan that way.''

"So, once the act was committed, assuming that she was running off with High Fox, perhaps it was better that she come back dead than in disgrace?''

"By Okeus' wooden balls, you're a crafty one.'' And it came to her. *Perhaps too crafty.* A story like that could ruin her, filter off all the respect she'd worked so hard to earn over the years. Rot and death! The old fool had just speculated himself into an early grave.

Besides, The Panther was believed to be a witch. While Nine Killer might not have the stomach to brain him, she'd seen Flying Weir's reaction. At a word from her, that hardy warrior . . .

"Don't even think it,'' Panther said gently. ''It will make matters worse for you.''

"Think what? Make what worse?'' The screaming spirits take him, did he truly see into a woman's soul? Another cold shiver crept down her aching back.

Panther gave her a chiding look. ''Don't you think that

the Mamanatowick and that fat old Stone Frog will have already thought of that story? They aren't fools, either one of them. If I can think it up, so can they. And, yes, your situation will be worse with me dead. Every chief with holdings along the Salt Water Bay will be saying, 'When The Panther got close to the truth, Hunting Hawk had him killed—just like she did her granddaughter!' ''

Angrily, she drilled her sassafras stick into the frozen mud. ''And use it against me, they will!''

''Only if I find out that you ordered her death,'' the Panther reminded. ''If you have me killed, you will have proven it in my place. And defeated your own purpose, since Copper Thunder will hear of it, and you'll have all three alliances against you, for I doubt the Great Tayac, Grass Mat, will forgive you for what you've done to him. At least, the man I once knew wouldn't.''

''Then I'd better keep you alive,'' she muttered dryly.

He shrugged. ''I'm an old man. Death is a longtime companion of mine. We know each other well. Besides, in the end, what are another couple of winters, more or less?''

''Go on, get out of my sight! And you keep that silly story all to yourself! You hear me?'' She poked at him with her walking stick, a new rage born inside her.

The Panther grabbed the end of her stick with a quick hand, meeting her stare. ''So, tell me, Weroansqua, did you have Red Knot killed?''

''No! No! And, *NO!*''

''Then, you shouldn't be so worried about what I'll find, should you?'' And with that, he released her stick, turned on his heel, and set off across the plaza, the nervous-looking Sun Conch following. ''Oh,'' he called over his shoulder, ''don't forget to send someone for that willow bark!''

''I won't!'' she snapped, then, under her breath, muttered, ''Lick dog spittle, you old crank!'' And imagined

all the ways she could get Flying Weir to snuff the pesky
life from that bony old body.

Should you have goaded her so?'' Sun Conch peered
over her shoulder at the angry Weroansqua. ''You didn't
really mean that she could have killed Red Knot . . . did
you?''

''Why not?'' Panther studied her. ''She had every reason to act just the way I said. Put yourself in her position.
What if you had made the marriage proposal, and then
found out just how dangerous Copper Thunder really is?
Like a boulder rolled off a ridge, this marriage alliance
had picked up speed and was rolling toward the bottom.
How could she stop it without ending up in a war with
the upriver villages?''

''But her granddaughter?'' Sun Conch shook her head
in bewilderment. ''She couldn't just tell someone to beat
the brains out of a member of her own family! Red Knot
was born of Shell Comb's womb. By all that's holy, Elder!''

''Well, if you're still thinking of Okeus as holy, he'd
like the idea. Really appreciate it, in fact. It's just the sort
of thing he'd do.''

''But, Elder—''

Panther raised his hand, stopping short to stare into
Sun Conch's disbelieving eyes. ''Why do you still surprise me, girl? I thought you'd seen and heard enough in
the last few days to begin to understand just how people
think and act. Would Hunting Hawk kill the girl to save
the Independent villages? Yes, in a heartbeat.''

''How do you know?''

Panther rubbed his brow, sensing a brewing headache.
''Because I've seen it often enough. Seen it. Lived it.

Been part of it. Why, in the name of Ohona, do you think I went out there to that island in the middle of the bay? It was to get away from the plotting and scheming that comes with authority and influence. When the stakes are that great, men and women become obsessed, driven to the point that they know nothing but the need to control others. Life becomes . . . well, skewed, like looking at the world from the bottom of a clear pond. Everything is distorted, unreal from the outside, but, oh, so real on the inside. Do you understand that?''

Sun Conch gave him a clear-eyed look and shook her head.

"No, I suppose you wouldn't, would you?" Panther threw his hands up in disgust. "Why am I stuck with you? You're so pure and honest, you might have been born of Ohona's right testicle! I worry about being close to you! You're bad for me!"

"I thought I was helping you, Elder, by watching your back. I gave you my life. No matter what it takes, I am yours—''

"Enough!" Panther waved her down, searching for any thread of understanding in Sun Conch's eyes. "What I was trying to say is that being close to you is starting to affect the way I think."

"The way you think?"

"Sun Conch, if you were looking for Red Knot's killer, you'd never find her. You are completely incapable of doing so."

"I am?"

"You are. Goodness runs through your blood. It blinds you to the flaws in people. Take your friend High Fox. On his word you came to me and offered your very soul to save him. But, Sun Conch, I'm not the slightest bit sure that he *didn't* kill the girl! He's a leech. Don't you understand? For the rest of his life, he'll live off of others, forever mediocre at what he does. He takes, but he never gives back.''

Sun Conch's face fell. ''Please. Don't talk about him that way. I—''

''In the name of evil Okeus, girl. Do you realize that because of you, I almost didn't accuse the Weroansqua?''

''I can't believe you did.''

''That's the whole point. I almost didn't. I was having such a pleasant conversation, and you were there right behind me, and I knew it was going to disturb you. Because I knew you would be upset, I almost didn't say it.'' He winced, rubbing his temples. ''And that bothers me a great deal.''

''Elder, she's the most respected of the chiefs. In every village they speak well of her. She sent food to Three Myrtle when I was a child and we were starving. And to the other villages, too. Her warriors have placed themselves between us and the Mamanatowick countless times. At her word, Greenstone Clan has adopted orphans into their households, and—''

''Quiet!'' He raised a hand to the gray sky. ''All of my life, I have beseeched Ohona for aid. And now I have him walking in my shadow.'' He rolled his eyes and sighed. ''Come, let's see how Nine Killer has made out with his inquiries.''

Behind his growing headache, he considered Hunting Hawk's reaction when he questioned her whereabouts. Cunning old leader that she was, she'd barely controlled herself. Panther couldn't convince himself that she'd acted that way out of indignation that a stranger dared to doubt her.

You're hiding something, Weroansqua, and before this is over, I'm going to find it.

Unless, of course, she made good on her threat to have him killed.

The girl was working on hemp when Nine Killer found her. White Otter used a short wooden club to pound the long stems, loosening the silken fibers before stripping them from the long stalks. These she laid straight beside her. The lengths of fibers would then be sorted, separated into threads, and twisted. Half were twisted to the right, and half to the left; then the threads were in turn twisted together to make cordage for nets, snares, and bindings.

Nine Killer smiled in greeting and dropped down beside her, crouching on his haunches. "That looks like good cord. Making a new net for your uncle?"

She gave him one of her special smiles, eyes sparkling. "Why would I give him a new net? If I made you a net, you'd fold it up and forget it until the mice chewed it up."

"Well, maybe. I always seem to be busy." He cocked his head, suddenly realizing just how long it had been since he'd been able to while away a couple of days netting mullet from the canoe, or taking a party and sneaking up through the ridges in search of deer, bear, or turkey. Instead, his warriors had been giving him gifts of fish, meat, and fowl—enough that, now that he thought about it, he had been shirking his duties to his family.

"Busy? With the negotiations with the Great Tayac? The business over Red Knot? White Star was mentioning just the other day that she hadn't seen you in ten days' time. You might want to spend some time in her longhouse, Uncle. Mother always says that first a woman complains, and then she acts."

Nine Killer gave her a suspicious squint. "When did you gain such insights about men and women? You're not even . . .'' But then he noticed just how fully budded her breasts were, and now that he thought about it, her hips had begun to round. Within the year, she would be visiting the Women's House for her first menstruation.

''I've survived fifteen winters, Uncle.'' She arched a slim eyebrow. ''Adults never want to believe a child is as old as she is. Why is that? Why do you want us to stay little for all of our lives?''

''And why do you want to grow up so quickly?'' he countered.

She shrugged. ''Who wants to be treated like a child forever? I want to be a woman and take on my responsibilities.''

''I wouldn't get in a big rush, White Otter. You might think that you take responsibility. It's more like it takes you. Once you have it, you can't get rid of it again.''

''Most of my friends have grown into women.'' She had always been a precocious girl, and Rosebud had remarked more than once that her friends were all older.

''That's one of the things I came to talk about. That morning that Red Knot died. How well do you remember it?''

''Very well.'' She gave him a sober gaze, unsettling him with her big brown eyes. ''I hadn't slept well. I should have been dead tired, but my stomach bothered me. I think I ate too much and then danced too hard.''

''When did your mother send you out, just after dawn?''

She hesitated and glanced down at the soft threads in her delicate brown hands. ''Yes, Uncle.''

Nine Killer's brow lifted. ''What's this? Come, girl, look at me.''

She raised her pretty face, expression subdued.

''Don't be coy with me, White Otter. This is your uncle. Remember him? I always told you to come to me if you had a problem.''

She pursed her lips, saying nothing.

"Ah, let me guess. You had just barely come in, hadn't you? You were out with your friends, perhaps? Maybe you went in, rolled out in your bed, and then sneaked back out?"

He could read the truth in her guilty eyes. "I see."

"Uncle, I didn't . . . I mean . . ."

He sighed, then chuckled. "I was young once, too. Besides, you are almost a woman—but not quite!"

She'd lowered her head again, so he raised her chin with his fingers to look into her eyes.

"My father said it was all right." Her eyes pleaded.

"Your father isn't responsible for your behavior. As your mother's brother, I am. Are we understood?"

She nodded.

"I can tell White Star's children anything I want, but their discipline is up to Half Moon. He's responsible for raising them, and I'm responsible for raising you. That's how we do it. We're not like some of those people out west where responsibility for the family lies with the father."

"Sometimes I think that would make more sense."

Nine Killer quirked his lips. "They're barbarians. Our ways were given to us by First Woman, who bore the children. Responsibility lies with the clan. In your case, that means your mother and me."

"I know, Uncle. But Red Knot was leaving, and we just . . . Well, I wanted to be with my friends is all. My time is coming soon. I just wanted to be out, hear what people were saying. I didn't do anything wrong, I just—"

"You were supposed to be in bed." He smiled then. "Let's make a bargain, you and I. I agree, you are almost a woman, but, until the day when you walk out of the menstrual house, you still answer to me. Understood?"

"Yes." She squared her shoulders. "What bargain?"

"In the future, if you want to spend time with your friends, you come to me. Unless I have a very good reason, I'll let you stay out." He paused. "Provided you can still attend to your responsibilities the next day."

She gave him the old familiar smile. "Thank you, Uncle."

"Now, let's get back to the problem. You were out, and then sneaked back in before everyone awakened."

"That's right."

"What did you see?"

She glanced around and leaned close. "It was just before dawn. Still dark, but the bonfire hadn't burned down. It cast enough light that I could see the plaza. I was walking back to the longhouse when I saw the Great Tayac. He was talking to someone by the palisade gate. I couldn't see who it was, but I know it was a young warrior."

"One of his?"

She shook her head. "One of ours. I could tell by the way he dressed, and his hair. The Great Tayac's warriors have taken to wearing their hair like he wears his. This man had his hair wrapped in a bun and pinned on the left side of his head."

Nine Killer frowned. "One of ours? The Great Tayac's men are staying in our village, after all. We'd been dancing together all night long. It's only natural that we'd be talking to each other."

"I know." White Otter's brow lined. "It was the way they were talking, heads close together. It was like, well, like they were being sneaky."

"Go on."

"That's what made me suspicious. I ducked into the shadows and watched, and the warrior slipped out of the palisade. Then Copper Thunder looked around as if to see if he'd been observed. He walked over to the side of the Weroansqua's Great House and listened for a moment with his head against the wall. Then he looked around again, and hurried for the gate. He took one last look, then trotted out through the passageway."

Nine Killer sat back, puzzled. "Why would he be furtive? He's a guest here."

"Maybe he didn't want anyone to know he was talking to that warrior?"

But what did it mean? Who had the warrior been?

"I see. Anything else?"

"No. Not then. I came home, and made sure that no one had missed me. Everyone was asleep. I didn't think anything of it, because no one else mentioned that Copper Thunder was gone, or that anything was wrong. Not until Red Knot was found missing. But then, I couldn't tell because . . ."

". . . Your mother and I would have known you slipped out," he finished for her. "White Otter, there's a lesson in this for you. When you do these things, it's like toying with a jellyfish. You're not supposed to do it, and periodically you'll get stung when you do."

"I'm learning that, Uncle." She ran the soft fibers through her fingers, combing them out.

"All right, what's past is past." He fingered his chin, thinking, seeing Copper Thunder sneaking out in the predawn. "So, the Great Tayac slipped out of the palisade on the morning when Red Knot was murdered? I wonder if she'd already left Flat Pearl Village by then?"

"No. She was behind the House of the Dead talking to Quick Fawn just before that. I think they were having an argument. I could tell that they wanted to talk alone, so I left them. That was just before I saw Copper Thunder. Red Knot had to leave after Copper Thunder did."

"But he was here the next morning. He ate—"

"But I saw him come back! It was when Mother sent me for water. I had stepped out of the longhouse with the water pot, and he came through the gate."

"Did he look suspicious?"

"Not really. He just looked as if he'd stepped out and made water. But, well, I don't know for sure . . ."

"Go on."

"When I saw him, I thought he had been out the entire time. He just, well, he didn't look . . ." She made a face.

"Look like what?"

"It's nothing I can be certain of. I think what I want to say is that he didn't look as if he'd slept. He was, yes, too alert. You know, he didn't have that sleepy look a person has when they just get up."

Nine Killer tucked that thought away the way a squirrel did a plump nut. "What else did you see?"

She closed her eyes. "Let's see. Old man Mockingbird was walking across the plaza. And Hunting Hawk's dog was sitting by the Weroansqua's doorway. Then Shell Comb came out of the House of the Dead and walked toward the Weroansqua's Great House. I passed her going across the plaza. Then, I walked down to the canoe landing and dipped the pot full of water. After that, I carried it to Mother. Just like every morning."

Nine Killer shrugged. "That sounds pretty normal."

"What about Shell Comb being out? She usually sleeps late. She was coughing, too, as I recall. Old man Mockingbird told her to be careful of her health in the cold."

"Niece, Shell Comb's daughter was being married that day. Shell Comb had been responsible for a great many things. With the visitors in the Great House, she might have been in the House of the Dead for any number of reasons."

"You've always been too easy on her, Uncle. Mother says it's because you wish she was from another clan."

Nine Killer narrowed an eye and shook a warning finger. "Don't even jest about such a thing! She's a friend, that's all. And I'd never even think of her in any other way. Shell Comb is my cousin! Even the thought would be the most horrible calamity that could befall our clan.''

Nevertheless, White Otter's words unsettled him. Shell Comb had always had an effect on him, and his interest ran so far beyond friendship that he made extra sure never to be alone with her for more than a moment's time. It wasn't that he didn't trust himself . . . but, well, when it came to Shell Comb, he *didn't* trust himself.

White Otter's lips might have been mute, but her eyes said, *I've seen how you look at her when you think no one is watching.*

''You're changing the subject,'' he growled. Then he paused, sudden inspiration coming to him. ''Wait! Who was guarding the gate?''

She shook her head. ''No one. I didn't think it strange because of the dance the night before. The whole village was up for most of the night.''

Nine Killer frowned fitfully. ''Stone Cob would have set the guard that night. Maybe, with all the excitement, he forgot.''

Nine Killer didn't like things to be forgotten, not when it came to keeping the Flat Pearl Village safe.

''Thank you, White Otter. If you think of anything else, please, come and tell me.''

She smiled up at him. ''Yes, Uncle, I will.''

Nine Killer rose to his feet, and clasped his muscular hands. So, Copper Thunder had followed a warrior out into the night? Which warrior? All the men from the Independent villages wore their hair tied off on the left side of the head.

Then a chill ran down his back. Yes, all the men. Even the Mamanatowick's warriors!

Twenty

The ridge turned out to be steeper than Panther had anticipated. Each foot had to be placed with care on the narrow trail that led straight up through the trees.

"Oh, be assured, War Chief, Grass Mat—or Copper Thunder, as he calls himself now—is entirely capable of arranging a marriage with Greenstone Clan at the same time he's scheming with the Mamanatowick," Panther declared between puffs as he stopped to catch his breath.

Sun Conch wasn't even breathing hard, nor was the War Chief. Only Panther's lungs labored.

Nine Killer didn't seem to see the forest, or the steep ridge they climbed. He stood there, expression clouded, his right hand resting on the war club that lay over his broad shoulders.

"Scheming *what* with the Mamanatowick? The destruction of his new wife's people?" Nine Killer shook his head. "That doesn't make sense. Why marry Red Knot at all? If he was scheming, why not just ally with the Mamanatowick, and crush us?"

"Then the man White Otter saw had to be one of yours."

"I just can't make myself believe it."

"War Chief, only your heart doesn't want to believe it. Your head knows better. You, and your allies, have shared the war trail, taken care of each other. If one of your men is dealing with the Great Tayac, you feel betrayed. Such a betrayal frays the very fiber of your soul, but you must never forget that nothing lies beyond human capability.'' Panther propped his foot on the steep slope and looked up the game trail. ''You need only remember your loyal lieutenant Stone Cob. Who, I remind you, was supposed to post the guard that night.''

They had climbed halfway to the top of the ridge, following the route of Red Knot's ill-fated morning journey. Panther wished he hadn't insisted on seeing the spot for himself.

''I can understand Stone Cob warning Three Myrtle Village.'' Nine Killer fingered his war club and glanced reassuringly at Sun Conch. ''He had kin there. Everything we do is for the clan.''

''Everything for the clan,'' Panther mused as his eyes roamed the old trees that rose from the steep slope. The way the naked branches wove together over his head, he might have been in a huge lodge supported by a thousand mighty posts.

From the inlet, he could hear geese and ducks. Without seeing them, he knew the loons were diving for young menhaden in the shallows. The forest around him echoed in birdsong. Not the boisterous chatter of summer, but a mellow chittering that filtered through the trees. He watched a nuthatch prance up the bark of an elm, which led his eye in turn to a flight of tundra swans winging overhead, the air rasping with each beat of their powerful wings.

The girl whose trail they now followed would miss the migration of her namesake come spring. She wouldn't see the hordes of red knots swarming the beaches for helmet crab eggs. She would never see the return of the ospreys in the new year's third moon. Such visions had died just up above him.

Everything we do is for the clan. He resumed his climb, pondering that terrible truth. The clan was everything: the rule and guide of the people. That thought needled him, as if a thread lay in it, somehow, some way. All he had to do was pull it, and the knot would come unraveled for him.

Nine Killer looked preoccupied, unhappy with the thoughts circulating behind his eyes. He climbed easily, the muscles rippling in his short legs.

Sun Conch followed along behind them, looking through every gap in the maze of trees, peering up the trail to ensure that disaster didn't descend from above.

Panther's lungs heaved, his old heart thumping solidly against his breast bone. The age-flaccid muscles in his legs were already sapped, and now they complained in unison with his joints. Despite the chill, he wore his blanket open, thankful that he wasn't climbing this ridge on one of those sticky hot midsummer days that rolled over the Salt Water Bay country. But then the forest would have been alive, the buzzing of insects covering all hint of approaching sound.

Panther had liked the summers as a boy. On those warm nights he'd walked out beyond the palisade and felt the world pulsing and vibrating with life. With it came the swarms of mosquitoes that had floated around his greased body like a personal mist. Grease kept them from sucking a man dry, but it didn't stop them from clogging nostrils or filling his throat when they flew into his open mouth.

Maybe winter was a better season after all. The harvest was in, the bugs were gone, and white perch could be collected from the fish weirs. The hunters had traveled up the peninsulas to drive deer into their surrounds. Big baskets of nuts had been collected from the ground or shaken from trees. During those cold, blustery months, a man could sit by the fire and tell the old stories, gossip with his friends, and watch his family through contented eyes.

But not me, oh no, I had to leave all of that behind.

Irritated with his sudden longing, he pushed himself that much harder. From what hidden corner of the soul had all of these long-stifled desires arisen? Was it sitting by Nine Killer's fire that stirred the embers of memory?

He was gasping for breath as he climbed up next to a great spreading beech tree, and finally topped the ridge. There, he bent double, puffing like a toadfish hauled from the water.

"This is where it happened," Nine Killer said as he stepped past Panther and looked around the flat ridgetop. He tapped his war club on his left palm, making a smacking sound.

"Are you all right, Elder?" Sun Conch asked, bending down to peer at him. She laid a cool hand on his hot shoulder, and patted him encouragingly.

"Lost my wind." Panther waved her away and straightened on his rubbery legs. "Youth is wasted on the young. Red Knot no doubt ran up that, completely unaware of how desperately some of us would crave that ability."

"Few know what they have, Elder, until it is taken away from them," Nine Killer concurred. "You're not going to fall over dead, are you?"

"No. I'd hate to make you carry another corpse back from this place." Panther coughed, his throat rasping from the effort.

"You're assuming I'd carry you back." Nine Killer prodded the leaf mat with his war club. "I might just leave you here for the crows and raccoons."

"They'd have a poor feast, I assure you." Panther had caught his breath. "Very well, show me where it happened."

Nine Killer followed the shallow rut of the trail. He stopped about midway across the narrow ridge. "We think she was killed here. That someone stepped out from behind that tree." He indicated a gray-barked walnut.

Panther stepped up to the walnut, its trunk so thick he couldn't quite reach around it. If the hard wood knew any secrets, they remained hidden in that cracked and lined bark. Then he walked back to the big beech tree, and studied it. The thick roots had knotted and flexed from the bottom of the wide trunk. "Look here, War Chief. Since the tree is perched on the lip of the edge, a person could crouch down here in this hollow and watch the trail below."

Nine Killer and Sun Conch came over and studied the little leaf-filled hollow between the thick roots. From there, the trail could be seen snaking down into the trees, and the branches overhead would have broken a watcher's silhouette.

Nine Killer bent down, with Panther looking over his shoulder, and carefully picked out some of the leaves that had drifted into the hollow. "I think this is fruitless. That morning was damp, so the leaves would have been flexible. None of them are broken or crushed from a person's weight, and I can't tell if the ones that are stuck together are that way from being stepped on, or from being frozen and thawed since they blew in here."

Panther pointed to a spot where the smooth gray bark had been slightly polished. "Did someone lean there?"

"Maybe." Nine Killer shrugged. "Do you know of a way to tell if that was rubbed by Red Knot's killer, or by children playing around the tree over the last moon?"

"No, I don't." Panther straightened and stepped thoughtfully back, looking between the beech and the walnut. No more than six paces separated the two. "The beech is a big thick tree. But rather than wait there, the killer retreated to the walnut."

"I would," Sun Conch volunteered. "It's closer to the trail, and being but little wider than a person, the victim has less time to react when the attacker steps out from behind cover. Not only that, the victim would let his guard down after having topped the ridge and determined the way was clear.''

''You're learning.'' Panther approached the walnut and studied the relationship between the tree and the trail. ''Sun Conch, come here. Pretend you are going to ambush Nine Killer. War Chief, you're a little shorter than Red Knot was, but I want you to drop over the crest of the ridge, and then act as if you were Red Knot crossing toward Oyster Shell Landing. Can you do that?''

Nine Killer gave him a skeptical shrug and trotted past the beech and over the edge.

''Now, Sun Conch, you know she is coming, so hide yourself and ambush him in the most logical way.'' Panther stepped back, watching.

Nine Killer climbed up to the crest, couldn't help but glance around the beech tree, and then trotted across the ridge. Panther noted the sounds as his moccasins rustled the leaves. When Nine Killer passed, the walnut tree was no more than two paces on his right. It wasn't until he was past that Sun Conch stepped out and mimicked bashing him on the head.

''Hold!'' Panther came forward, studying the situation. ''Where was the blood spot, War Chief?''

Nine Killer frowned, and glanced about. ''A step or two behind me.''

Panther pulled thoughtfully at his chin. ''Sun Conch and I would have struck you right where you stand, War Chief. As Sun Conch just pretended, she would have bashed you right in the top of the skull. From the momentum of the blow, the knees would have buckled, and you would have fallen on your face. The bloodstain would have been at least a pace in front of you.''

Nine Killer turned around, seeing where Sun Conch stood, how she held her club. ''I see what you mean. So, if the bloodstain is back there . . .''

''Indeed.'' Panther rubbed his hands together. ''Let's

do it again, but this time, Sun Conch, I want you to step out from behind the tree just before he passes.''

Once again, Nine Killer retraced Red Knot's path across the ridge. This time as the rustle of Nine Killer's trotting moccasins came close, Sun Conch stepped out from behind the tree, war club raised.

Nine Killer came to an immediate stop.

''Hold still, right there.'' Panther stepped forward, comparing where Nine Killer stood and where he said the bloodstain had been. ''Now, step out, Sun Conch. Just one step, as if you were talking to him. That's it.''

Sun Conch closed the distance.

''Now,'' Panther said quietly, ''strike him dead.''

Sun Conch swung the war club slowly through its arc, the deadly stone-weighted end reaching just past Nine Killer's head.

''Close enough,'' Nine Killer said. ''And, if Sun Conch were truly talking to me as she stepped out, I would have turned, thus.'' He faced Sun Conch, the extended war club next to the left side of his head.

''If Sun Conch were to strike you down, the blow would pop your head to the right, setting you off balance as your knees buckled. You'd fall in a heap . . .''

''Right where the bloodstain was.'' Nine Killer stared down speculatively at the leaf mat as though seeing it again in his mind: fresh and red. ''So she did know the killer. He stepped out and said something to her. Then struck before she could react.''

''Only someone Red Knot trusted could have walked that close to her.'' Panther dropped to his haunches, picking through the leaves.

''You won't find any blood, Elder,'' Sun Conch said. ''With the rain and storms, it's long washed away.''

''Oh, I know.'' Panther continued lifting the leaves away and brushing his fingers over the ground. ''Here, let's sift this anyway. It would surprise me if we found anything, but perhaps Red Knot had something in her hand besides the shark-tooth necklace.''

As they picked through the leaves, Nine Killer said thoughtfully, ''She expected to meet High Fox, so he would have . . . What's this?'' Nine Killer lifted a small wedge-shaped chunk of wood and held it up to the light. It was no longer than a thumbnail; one side had been rounded, obviously carved and polished. The wedge shape came from the fact that it was broken, splintered off of a larger piece of wood.

Panther settled next to him, taking the piece. ''Well, if I was a guessing man, I'd say that was hickory wood, War Chief. And part of a tool. That rounded side was worked.''

Nine Killer examined the grainy side where it had broken off. ''And not so recently, Elder. Look. The worked side is dark, stained. Where it broke, the wood is light, as if freshly cracked.''

''Anyone could have dropped that,'' Sun Conch said, pointing to the trail. ''This trail is used a lot. It's the quickest way from Oyster Shell Landing to Flat Pearl Village without paddling all the way around the neck. It's customary to drop a runner off here to let Flat Pearl know they have company coming. The runner will be in the village two or three hands sooner than the fastest canoe can make it. I've run this myself more than once for Black Spike. Anyone could have dropped that.''

Nine Killer shrugged, on the verge of tossing the chip.

''No,'' Panther said thoughtfully. ''I want to keep it. It may come in handy.''

Nine Killer handed it over and Panther dropped it into his belt pouch before continuing to sift through the leaves. The rest of the search proved fruitless.

Panther stood, smacking his hands clean. ''Enough of this, War Chief. Show me where the body was dragged to.''

Nine Killer rose and pointed northward along the ridgeline. "Over there." He led the way no more than thirty paces to a shallow depression behind a hickory tree. There, leaves were still scattered from where Red Knot's body had been.

Panther cocked his head, squinting back toward the trail.

"This doesn't tell us much, does it?" Nine Killer propped his hands on his hips. "Anyone could have dragged her here."

Panther said nothing as he studied the spot, then studied the shagbark hickory that blocked the view from the main trail. Like the walnut, it remained a mute witness. The hollow had been formed years past when a tree had blown down, the roots tearing a hole in the ridgetop. Over the many years since, the deadfall had rotted back to the soil from which the tree had once sprung. Even the earth had, for the most part, healed the scar.

Once again, Panther crouched down and searched the leaves for anything that Red Knot or her killer might have dropped—and found nothing. He sighed and rubbed his sore knees.

"Anything else?" Nine Killer asked.

Panther winced as his bones crackled through the effort to stand. He hobbled painfully back to the trail and stared down the east side toward Oyster Shell Landing. "Yes, I suppose so. I should go down where High Fox says he was waiting."

"If you wish." Nine Killer tapped his fingers rhythmically on the handle of his war club. "The only thing down there are huge piles of oyster shells. It is said that they date back to the days when First Man walked the earth."

"I can believe it," Sun Conch agreed. "It would take lifetimes to eat that many oysters."

Panther made a face as he stared down that long slope.

"Once down there, I suppose I'll have to climb all the way back up?"

"We could send a canoe around for you." Nine Killer gave him a crooked smile.

"If you have trouble, I think I could carry you up, Elder," Sun Conch said seriously. "You're not that heavy, and I'm a strong girl."

"If it comes to that, Sun Conch, I may let you." Panther took the first step onto the steep descent. Aspects of determining the identity of Red Knot's killer—like climbing such slopes—just didn't fit him anymore. "Who knows, perhaps we shall find Flat Willow's missing arrow?"

Hunting Hawk sat beside the fire in her longhouse and breathed deeply. Pounded willow bark! What a godsend! She flexed her fingers. Not in years had she been able to clench her fist tight—let alone do it painlessly. No matter what other trouble he might be, The Panther had brought her the first relief she'd had in years. For that, she could almost forgive him his accusation.

But not quite.

Slaves and servants bustled about behind her, feeding Copper Thunder's remaining warriors. Out of courtesy, the Great Tayac had sent home three canoe loads of his men, reducing the demands made on Hunting Hawk's food stores.

That was tactfully played, for not even at threat of death would she have complained about his men eating her winter food supply. To do so would have demeaned herself in the Great Tayac's eyes—insinuated that she couldn't care for honored guests.

Normally, this wouldn't have been a problem. She

would have sent out messengers asking for donations from the Independent villages, but at this strained time, with the bad blood between Flat Pearl and Three Myrtle Villages barely patched, she had no desire to push her luck.

The ten men who remained with Copper Thunder had been helping to make their own way by scouting, hunting deer, raccoon, opossum, muskrats, and rabbits, as well as working the fish weirs and casting nets for the killifish that invaded the shallows on warmer winter days.

Copper Thunder sat across from her now and used a piece of damp leather coated with sand to polish the gleaming copper spike on his war club. With each movement, his thick muscles rolled under his smooth bronze skin.

To her right, Shell Comb wove a section of cloth at her small loom. She had dyed the fibers different colors, red from puccoon, black from squid ink, yellow from woodland sunflower, and purple from black cherries. Her nimble fingers worked each thread through the warp before she packed it tightly with a fine-tooth bone comb. Hunting Hawk was more than aware of the sidelong glances Shell Comb and Copper Thunder kept casting toward each other.

"So, the old man went to see where the girl was killed today." Copper Thunder chuckled. "Tell me, what has he found, poking under rocks here and there? Any delightful morsels?"

"He found my wrath," Hunting Hawk snorted. "He had the nerve to say that *I* would have benefited from Red Knot's death! *Me*, her grandmother!"

"Surely, Weroansqua, you shouldn't have to put up with that kind of insolence."

Hunting Hawk bit off a hot retort, needled by the Great Tayac's voice. A hint of mockery lay just below the point of perception. As a result, it took her a moment to recognize the odd look in Shell Comb's eyes.

"Don't stare at me with those wide eyes, girl," Hunting Hawk growled. "I won't have it. I had nothing to do with the girl's death."

Shell Comb's expression cleared. "I—I know that, Mother. I'm just surprised, that's all."

"I'll tell you what I'd do." Copper Thunder squinted at the gleaming spike on his war club. "I'd have him removed from my village. He was always trouble."

Hunting Hawk sighed. "As a witch, he could cause me more than a few problems. Especially if he shouted out a curse as we were shoving him out the gate."

Copper Thunder cocked his head as he ran his hand along the smooth wood of his war club. "He could indeed . . . if you shoved him out the gate. There are other ways. He could be carried out. Feet first."

Hunting Hawk considered that. "Odd as it may seem, the man I usually depend on for such things appears to be unwilling to take such a step."

"War Chiefs can always be replaced. Especially if their loyalty is compromised."

Hunting Hawk stared into the crackling fire. Had the old buzzard truly blinded Nine Killer to his duty to clan and family? If he had, should she replace her War Chief? Or try to talk him out of his delusion?

"If you allow the old man to stay," Copper Thunder continued, "he will slowly poison your people. Turn them against you. He can't help it. It's just the way he is. The way Okeus made him."

She worked her hand again, remembering his advice. "What did he do for the Serpent Chiefs?"

"War Chief, and advisor, among other things. Mostly he skulked around their councils sowing discord. The thing I remember about him the most was how his enemies always seemed to come up dead. Sometimes without a mark on them." Copper Thunder tapped his fingers on his war club. "It was said that he knew plants, and their properties. I heard once that he was particularly fond of water hemlock. But he knew the uses of other plants as well. Some that killed instantly."

"I don't think I'll share a meal with him." Hunting Hawk ran her tongue over toothless gums as she remembered his words. "But poison comes from more than plants."

"He has a way about him," Shell Comb declared. "But I don't think he's that dangerous."

Copper Thunder chuckled. "Never underrate him."

"If he is so dangerous, what's he doing here?" Shell Comb asked, an eyebrow arched. "Why isn't he a chief somewhere?"

"Probably fled for his life when one of his little plots was uncovered." Copper Thunder shrugged. "It wouldn't be the first time a man fled just ahead of a Serpent Chief's wrath. And one thing about my old friend Raven, he was always clever enough to save his own skin, no matter how many of his friends lost theirs."

Hunting Hawk propped her chin on her hand and frowned. "He did save us from a war with Three Myrtle. Like it or not, that would have been a disaster."

"But, at what price, Weroansqua?" Copper Thunder smiled at her, the action automatic and humorless. "So you lose an old ally? You have other options now. Different strengths to look toward."

She kept her face straight. "I am always open to new alliances, Great Tayac. At the same time, why ruin old ones? The future is a perilous place at best, especially these days."

Then she saw the look traded between Shell Comb and Copper Thunder. Ah! He'd taken the bait. And suddenly, the old plan had new life blown into it. Maybe, just maybe, she could salvage something for Greenstone Clan—and the future.

"Daughter?" Hunting Hawk asked, her stomach oddly queasy.

Shell Comb shrugged, struggling to appear at ease. "The Great Tayac and I were talking the other day."

More than talking, I'd say, from the look of you. Hunting Hawk straightened.

"With Red Knot's death, we have no other eligible woman within our clan. Quick Fawn would be a candidate for marriage, but she is not yet a woman, and may not make the change for some time."

"So, naturally, you thought of yourself." Hunting Hawk decided to cut short the elaborate tale Shell Comb would have told.

"Copper Thunder is willing, Mother." Shell Comb tilted her head, seeking to regain the advantage. "And so am I."

The only sounds were the chatter of the slaves serving the warriors behind them, and the metallic rasp of the sandy leather on the copper spike.

Hunting Hawk studied the Great Tayac through half-lidded eyes. He seemed completely at ease, careless of her response to so sudden a proposal. What game was he playing? Why did he wish a woman of Shell Comb's age? She might bear him a child. Perhaps two, but her loins had almost dried up.

"Shell Comb would bring a great many advantages to my people," Copper Thunder said at last, looking up from his work. "She knows the Independent villages, understands the machinations of the Mamanatowick. While Red Knot would have given me youth and many bearing years, Shell Comb brings experience."

And you think she'll be Weroansqua after my death. Hunting Hawk felt the final piece fall into place. A marriage to Shell Comb would place Copper Thunder that much closer to the center of Greenstone Clan and its influence over the Independent villages. So, she wasn't going to have to maneuver him into an agreement after all. Instead, his testicles were leading him right where she wanted him.

"I suppose I could appoint Yellow Net as Weroansqua in your absence," Hunting Hawk said to gauge her daughter's reaction. "You'd be too far away to serve here."

Shell Comb nodded, apparently undisturbed, but Copper Thunder shot her a measuring glance.

Hunting Hawk nodded to herself. Copper Thunder was playing a deep game that she still didn't quite understand, but Shell Comb, as usual, was ruled by her passions instead of her head.

"I shall think about it," Hunting Hawk said. "In the meantime, The Panther will stay and poke about under the rocks."

In her heart, she wasn't happy with this new permutation of an old plan. Using Red Knot hadn't been as much a gamble as sending the impetuous Shell Comb off with Copper Thunder. The problem with summoning a storm was that you never knew where lightning would strike.

Twenty-one

Panther stepped into the dim interior of the House of the Dead and stamped snow from his feet. On the heels of the mild clear days had come a cold west wind that blew a bank of clouds down from the mountains. The temperature had plunged, and the first flakes of snow spun out of the sky.

Panther loosened his wet threadbare blanket before nearing the fire that burned in the central pit. He shook it out and rewrapped it over his shoulder. Glancing around, he could find no one in the anteroom, so he approached the mat divider and called down the hallway, "Hello? Anyone here? Kwiokos, could I have a word with you?"

Tall, lanky Lightning Cat appeared, trotting down the hall. The guardians watched him pass with expressionless faces.

"Elder?" Lightning Cat said. "May I help you?"

"I have come to see Green Serpent. Perhaps I might have a word with him. It's about Red Knot, and what we found up on the ridge where she was murdered."

Lightning Cat glanced around, uncertain, then bobbed a quick nod. "Come. This way." He led Panther back down the hall.

Oddly, Lightning Cat ignored the guardians, but Panther nodded to each in greeting. He could sense their appreciation that a stranger offered what a familiar servant did not.

Once past the storerooms with their piled goods, he was led again into the sanctum with its statue of Okeus and the platform of Greenstone Clan ancestors.

Okeus seemed to glare at him, his eyes shining with malice. His copper necklaces gleamed in the firelight, and his painted limbs seemed possessed of the strength to spring. The corn in his left hand looked wilted, brown, and desiccated—but the war club in his right, with its twin war heads, looked polished. A copper skewer glinted in the light where it ran through the hair bun on the top of his head. His mouth might have been mocking, or filled with humor. Panther couldn't quite tell which.

"Greetings, Dark Lord," he murmured ritually, and

bowed to show his respect. Only then did he turn to the form laid out to the right of the fire.

Red Knot's body lay supine on its mat, as it had the last time Panther had seen it, but now only a skeleton remained, the flesh having been carefully cut from the bones. The joints remained attached, bound by wraps of brown ligament that had dried hard in the heat of the fire. That was as it should be. Red Knot's skeleton would serve as the framework for the reconstruction of her body as soon as the skin was tanned. Grass straw would fill out her body where once muscle and viscera had been.

Panther stopped short, glancing at her skull. Something about the girl's irregular rictus bothered him, prickling uneasily at his soul, as if familiar.

"Panther?" Green Serpent asked, rising from a large round-bottomed pot that he oversaw. "You have come back?"

"Yes, Kwiokos. I was wondering . . . But, what are you doing there?"

Green Serpent glanced back at his pot. "Tanning her skin, of course. I was just attending to the mixture, seeing that the juices were right. I had a pot spoil once. Terrible thing to have happen to one's kin. In that case I was able to dry the skin before mold discolored it. But now, in the dead of winter, that would be impossible."

"Indeed it would, and worse, it's snowing outside." Panther jerked a thumb back at the door. "I'm afraid your work would freeze solid."

"You're not supposed to be here," Green Serpent said, bending down to wash his hands in yet another pot. "The Weroansqua said that we were not to help you anymore. Apparently, you angered her."

Panther gave the old man a disarming smile. "Apparently she didn't tell you the rest."

"The rest?" Green Serpent's forehead wrinkled. The

action made his mousy white eyebrows lower. "What rest?"

"Ah, well, I had no choice but to hint that she might have benefited from Red Knot's death. I have my reasons, you see. The killer must think that everyone is suspect. Even the Weroansqua. How else can I smoke him out?"

Green Serpent's frown deepened. "Well, I'm not sure. But I do know that the Weroansqua was infuriated. Is that what you did? Accused her of murdering her granddaughter?"

"Do you think she could have had the girl killed? After all, it was a way to avoid having the Great Tayac marry into Greenstone Clan. She might have figured out just what a cold-blooded spider he really is."

Green Serpent raised his hands helplessly. "I've known her for years, since she was a little girl and I was an even littler boy. She was always smart. Like a crafty bobcat. It wasn't just her birthright. I *knew* she would be Weroansqua one day. Everything she did was right. No mistakes like so many of us make. When her uncle, the old Weroance, died, and he had no brother, leadership fell to Hunting Hawk as the heir of Greenstone Clan. She accepted the duty and became Weroansqua. At the time, some among the Independent villages scoffed at her. She was so young, you see. Barely out of the Women's House after her first menstruation."

"It must have been difficult for you," Panther agreed.

"Oh, yes, but Hunting Hawk, she wasn't like most women. Not at all like that daughter of hers." Green Serpent touched his forehead with an index finger. "She was centered, Panther. Here. Her soul knew what it was about, what it wanted, where it was going, and how to get there. Before we could even get the skin off of her father's body, she sent out war parties. That was under old Blood Heron. He was War Chief then. He spread the word that Hunting Hawk was in charge—and then he raided the Mamanatowick.''

Green Serpent grinned, seeing back through the years. ''Yes, she was something. There wasn't anyone who thought that little girl was anything but Weroansqua, clear down through her blood and muscle to her bones.'' The Kwiokos shook his head. ''Blood Heron brought back prisoners from his raid on the Mamanatowick. Two warriors, cousins of the Mamanatowick's. Hunting Hawk called everybody together and walked up to those two warriors. They stood there, being brave, and sneering down at her. They called her names, told her that no little girl could kill the likes of them.''

Panther glanced away. ''But she had them burned, didn't she? Thrown on the fire out there in the plaza. I heard they screamed and writhed, and one actually got up on his feet before his hair burst into flames and he fell kicking and screaming in the coals.''

''Yes. It was just like that. Were you there?''

''No. I just heard about it. That's all.'' Panther indicated Red Knot. ''What about her? Do you think Hunting Hawk would have had the girl killed to stop the alliance with Copper Thunder?''

Green Serpent sucked at his lips while he inspected the skeleton that stared sightlessly up at the sooty roof high overhead. Then he slowly shook his head. ''No. Not her. Hunting Hawk, hard woman that she is, would have just said no. Maybe offered another girl. Maybe one of Yellow Net's brood, or some other clanswoman. And she would have sent enough canoes of food and gifts that Copper Thunder's pride would have been satisfied.''

''What about in revenge? Punishment for running off and disgracing her clan in front of Copper Thunder? I can't imagine the Weroansqua enjoying the prospect of telling the Great Tayac that Red Knot had run off with a callow youth on the eve of her marriage.''

"Oh, my, Panther, that would have been bad. Bad indeed, but the children would never have escaped. No, no, Nine Killer would have had them within the day, no matter that High Fox had a day's head start. Knowing Hunting Hawk, as I do, I'd say that she'd cast Red Knot out, disown her, and give her to Copper Thunder as a slave rather than kill her. The Weroansqua is never one to let an opportunity pass to teach a lesson to her enemies. And, had she wanted the girl killed for disobedience, it would have been a most public execution. Not what we have here—all loose ends and suspicion." The Kwiokos paused. "You see, the Weroansqua is smarter than to do something like this."

"But, someone, it seems, did it anyway."

Green Serpent nodded, crossing his arms. "So perhaps you need only find someone stupid? That's not the Weroansqua."

Panther smiled grimly. "To kill in this fashion, Kwiokos, isn't a matter of being smart. No, no, you misread the mind of a murderer. Red Knot wasn't killed because of craftiness."

"What then?"

"Tell me, Kwiokos, have you ever seen the Weroansqua desperate?"

Green Serpent glanced uneasily at Lightning Cat and Streaked Bear where they waited by the doorway. He made a subtle gesture, saying, "You two. Check the fire in the front room. I wouldn't want it to go out. And after that, make sure we have a good supply of wood in. This snow might last awhile."

Reluctantly, the two younger men glanced at each other, nodded, and left.

"Desperate?" Green Serpent said when the priests had retreated beyond hearing. He waved his gnarled old finger back and forth. "Ah, yes, Panther, I have seen that in her eyes, but only when she looks at Shell Comb. The

Weroansqua's only great fear is turning the affairs of Greenstone Clan over to her daughter.''

"Shell Comb?"

Green Serpent stepped over by the fire and seated himself, gesturing Panther down opposite him. From the pouch at his side, Green Serpent produced his pipe, and with his other hand, pinched tobacco from a bowl. This he offered to Panther, who in turn retrieved his own pipe and tamped it full.

The Kwiokos raised his pipe in humble offering to the statue of Okeus, then used a twig kept for such purposes to light his bowl. Panther repeated the offering to Okeus and lit his own pipe. Smoke sanctified words, sent them to the Spirits, and validated conversations such as this.

"If any single thing has disappointed the Weroansqua it is Shell Comb." Green Serpent gave Panther a knowing look. "Of all the quickness of wit and craftiness that runs in Hunting Hawk's veins, none of it was passed to Shell Comb. She is like the wind, blowing one way one day, and another the next. As focused as the Weroansqua is, Shell Comb is scattered, forever slave to her passions and desires.''

"I see."

"Do you?" Green Serpent puffed, blue smoke curling about his head in a wreath. "Hunting Hawk is like a sharp chert blade, cutting through life with a single purpose. Shell Comb is like an otter, playing here and there, forever hunting new game. Take them to a ceremony, and Hunting Hawk will be appraising each of the participants for their value to her, and what she can gain from them. Shell Comb will be assessing what lies under their breechclouts, and what trinkets they would be willing to string around her body.''

Panther glanced sidelong at Red Knot's naked bones. "Then Shell Comb has always disappointed her mother?"

Green Serpent shrugged. "Only in the last couple of years has Shell Comb seemed to show the slightest interest in ruling. I think it was because she finally realized just how old her mother was getting. In the last year, Shell Comb has really tried to show some responsibility. But, were I to guess, I'd say she's not going to be a very good Weroansqua."

"That worries you."

"I will be dead soon." Green Serpent stared pensively at the fire. "The problem will be Lightning Cat's, or maybe Streaked Bear's." He glanced at Red Knot's supine skeleton. "Some of us thought that perhaps Red Knot would be more like her grandmother. But what I saw, she was another one like her mother, letting her desire outweigh her good sense."

"The Weroansqua could name Yellow Net as her successor."

"Maybe she will." Green Serpent studied the clay bowl of his pipe where the tobacco had stained it. "It is being said that Shell Comb might marry Copper Thunder."

Panther straightened. "Indeed? And the Weroansqua has agreed?"

Green Serpent blew smoke out through his nose. "I have heard that she will think about it. So, if she says yes, then it would appear that one of your reasons for Red Knot's murder is gone. The Weroansqua really did want an alliance with Copper Thunder and his fierce warriors."

"*If* she agrees." Panther's pipe stem tapped the few teeth left in the front of his mouth. "She might not want to say no too quickly. The Great Tayac might take offense. With time, she has room to maneuver." He glanced at Red Knot's skeleton again. "What of it, girl? Does any of this make sense to you?"

"She tried to tell me," Green Serpent said, his sad gaze on the rendered bones.

"Tried to tell you?" Panther asked gently. "When?"

"The morning she died." Old Green Serpent rubbed his face. "Her ghost walked through the House of the Dead. I was asleep in the front room, and she walked past me. I saw her in my dream. I think she came to join her ancestors. She's been here ever since." He looked up at the platform of bodies encased in their wrappings. "She's up there now. Sometimes, when I'm half-awake and the soul loosens, I hear her. She's trying to tell me something, but she's sobbing so hard that I can't make out the words."

Panther stared up at the platform, wishing mightily that Red Knot would simply appear and speak out. If only she would, he could name the murderer, and have Sun Conch return him to his island.

Too many memories are stirring. You've your own ghosts to worry about, Panther. But unlike Red Knot's, yours are malevolent.

Panther snorted in irritation and stood, thinking that the time had come to leave. It was then that he saw Red Knot's skull again in the flickering firelight. He stepped close, bending down. "Did you do something to these teeth?"

Green Serpent was staring into the fire, his eyes unfocused—seeing the ghosts, no doubt.

"Kwiokos, did you do something to these teeth?" Panther said, a little louder.

"I, ah, what? What did you say?" Green Serpent blinked to clear his vision. "What was that?"

"There is something wrong with these teeth," Panther repeated. "Here, look. Right here in front. She's supposed to have those two big flat teeth. But the one next to it on the right side ought to be smaller, and flat, like its match on the other side of her mouth. Instead, it is just a peg. Did you break it?''

Green Serpent stooped over the girl's skull and squinted down his nose. "Oh, no. That's not broken. I noticed that tooth when I was cleaning her skull. It just grew that way."

Panther bent close, aware of the odor of decay that hung on Red Knot's picked bones. Now he could see that indeed the tooth wasn't broken, but rather just malformed.

"Well, good." Panther straightened. "I thought for a minute that she might have been hit in the mouth. A blow that we missed."

"No, no. There are only the dents in the side of her head." Green Serpent tilted his head to peer at the fractures. "I had to be very careful when we pulled the brain out. You said you wanted those wounds left just as they were. I did my best to leave them unaffected."

"You did just fine." Panther straightened. "In fact, I couldn't have done better myself." He cocked his head, still studying the girl's grinning skull. "So, Red Knot, your mother is going to marry Copper Thunder? Isn't that a curious turn of events."

"It would keep the alliance," Green Serpent reminded.

"Yes," Panther said thoughtfully. "But an alliance with what?" And his gaze fixed on the two indentations in the side of Red Knot's skull.

Panther walked behind Nine Killer, placing his feet in the footprints the short War Chief left in the snow. Sun Conch followed a pace behind, her wary attention fixed on the ground that rose to their right. To their left the water of the inlet rippled, cold and gray in the reflected light of the clouds. Across the inlet, Panther could see the distant tree-covered shore.

Panther puffed out a breath that rose frosty before his face. The snow crunched underfoot. The only sign of life was the ducks that huddled in tens of tens on the water.

"Elder, I am asked to escort you to Shell Comb," Nine Killer had told him. "She said for me to take you to the sweat house. She will talk with you there."

"Indeed?" Panther had said, interest kindled within. And so he had come here to the low structure next to the water. As they approached the building, he could smell smoke from the fire out front and see small streamers of steam slipping around the gaps in the roof.

Nine Killer slowed and called out, "Shell Comb? I bring you The Panther, as you instructed."

She answered from inside: "Thank you, War Chief. That will be all. You are dismissed."

Nine Killer lifted an eyebrow, gave Panther a look of worried amusement, and whispered, "Good luck," as he passed by.

Panther nodded to Sun Conch, who gave him an equally worried look, then took her position beside the building.

Panther pulled back the hanging and ducked inside into the muggy heat. For the first couple of steps, breath stuck in his throat, the steam choking him. As the flap fell back in place, his snow-bright vision could see nothing in the blackness. A hand reached out and took his.

"Come, Elder, sit here beside me." Shell Comb led him to a mat and helped him to be seated.

Panther gasped for breath, fighting the smothering steam, and slipped his old blanket from his shoulders. "Excuse me," he rasped. "It's been a while since I've been in a sweat lodge. It will take a while for my old skin to adjust."

"I come here a lot," she told him. "It helps me to

think." Then she added, "You might want to undress. You'll roast. Or worse, step out into the cold in damp clothing and become sick."

He grunted, and pulled his hide shirt over his head before pulling the flap of his breechclout out of its belt. Shell Comb took his garments and set them outside the doorflap as he removed them.

He rubbed his hands over his arms. "The stories tell us that in the beginning, First Woman lived in a place bathed by steam, that it cleanses the soul, and renews the body. It is said that a person can never be truly refreshed unless they sweat in the steam and wash in cold water."

"Do you believe that's true? About First Woman?"

"Sometimes."

"I believe it," Shell Comb said. "I think that's why I've kept my health, and my youth." She paused. "Tell me, Elder, do you think I'm an attractive woman?"

He chuckled. "At my age, I think that all women are attractive. But that's all I can do . . . just think."

She laughed with him, then was silent. Panther took the moment to catch his breath, his skin prickling from the heat. Moisture had begun to bead on his bushy eyebrows, and he could feel the heat working into his old joints.

"You sent for me," he finally said. "Since the charms of my body have long since faded, I assume you have something else in mind?"

He could almost see her now, a dim figure in the darkness and swirling steam. She seemed hunched, head down. "Have you discovered who my daughter's murderer is?"

"No." He tilted his head back. "The curious thing is that everyone I talk to appears to have a reason for killing her. This daughter of yours seems to have stirred a great many people's passion." He turned his head to look at her. "I hear that you wanted to go to war with the Mamanatowick the morning she was killed."

"I was upset, Elder. Desperate to do anything, to strike back. Winged Blackbird was out there. It seemed only logical that he'd killed her." Shell Comb paused. "What would you think if it was your daughter? I'm still not sure that he didn't do it. The way she was left, unmolested, that might have been cleverness on Winged Blackbird's part."

"You sound like you are still trying to convince yourself, Shell Comb. Why is that?"

She shrugged. "It would make things a great deal easier, wouldn't it?"

"Would it?" He waited for her to answer her own question. "Why?"

"Because . . . well, we wouldn't have to face the truth." She sounded uneasy. "I wish we could just start over, make believe this never happened, and give everyone a second chance to do things right."

"Give the murderer a second chance?" Panther frowned. "What makes you think he wants one? Red Knot's killer was driven to an act of desperation, Shell Comb. That's why Red Knot was killed. She was doing something, or knew something that compelled someone to kill her."

He heard Shell Comb's breath stop short, and her shoulders slumped miserably. A moment later, he heard sniffling sounds and reached out to pat her shoulders. "There, there. Grief, like all things, eventually passes."

"I—I'm sorry," she mumbled, and sniffed. "All this time, I keep trying to be the dignified woman that everyone expects me to be. What you said . . . it just . . ."

He snorted half-derisively. "Well, to tell you the truth, your lack of apparent grief had begun to bother me. A mother generally doesn't lose a daughter without weeping, hair-pulling, and hysteria."

"Not when you are the Weroansqua's daughter," Shell Comb said wearily. "Such things are for others, not for the pride of Greenstone Clan."

At the tone of her voice, Panther asked, "So, tell me, do you think your mother could have had Red Knot killed?"

Shell Comb's head remained bowed. Only after a long moment did she say, "No."

"And why not? Surely she understood just how dangerous a marriage with Copper Thunder would be."

"Dangerous?" She shifted, staring at him through the darkness. "You don't understand, do you? We're losing, Elder. Cycle by cycle, the Mamanatowick tightens his control on our southern borders. Stone Frog and his Conoy raids from the north are taking a toll. We can no longer spare the warriors to send on punitive expeditions. With the growth of the Great Tayac's strength on the upper river, the balance has been changed."

"The way Okeus made the world, it is supposed to change." He paused. "And, I think if you decide to go ahead and marry the Great Tayac, you'll have plenty of opportunity to live dangerously. In a very short time, you'll regret that decision."

"I've lived dangerously all of my life, Elder." She straightened her back, arms braced on her knees. "I've paid for my mistakes. Oh, have I paid. Sometimes, I wonder how I managed to do the things I've done, but I tell myself, *'I am the Weroansqua's daughter!'* I do what I have to. The cost has been greater than you could know."

"So, you will add another mistake to a long list?" He paused, weighing his words. "Copper Thunder isn't any different than the Mamanatowick. If anything he's more ambitious than the other chieftains. He's seen the Serpent Chiefs, and pictures himself as one."

She paused thoughtfully, then asked, "What happened between the two of you?"

"Many years ago, I killed his father and captured him and his mother. His father was a Trader. The man's timing was bad. He was visiting and trading in a village I overran for my chief." Panther shrugged. "If Copper Thunder's father had stayed out of it, I might have let him go. Instead, he felt an obligation to stand by the chief, a man called Stalks-By-Night. Grass Mat's father picked up a war club and joined the fight. He killed my lieutenant, and I killed him. After the battle, I claimed Copper Thunder and his mother for myself. They went back to my house as slaves."

"How did he get here?"

"Ran away most likely. I'm sure he's not keen on having the knowledge spread that he was once a slave." Panther sighed. "I might have done you a favor, that long-gone day, by cutting off his head instead of taking him back to carry water and firewood."

"That's why he hates you?"

"I can't blame him. I ruined his life."

"And his mother?"

"She served my needs while I was there. After I left she went to another and I don't know what happened to her. Dead I suppose. Originally, she was a woman from the upper villages. The Trader arrived one day and they fell in love. She went with him, back across the mountains to trade on the great rivers. She was used to being well treated, and never adapted to being a slave. Grass Mat was still young. A boy is more flexible, but those days of beatings and living like an animal soured something inside him, made him what he is today."

She clapped her hands together and leaned forward to spill more water on the hot rocks. As the steam rose, she asked, "What about all of those tattoos? Do they have a meaning?"

"Those are the marks of a Serpent Chief. Your Copper Thunder is trying to make himself into the very man he hated so passionately as a boy. Envy, like the bite of a copperhead, can dispense the most deadly of venoms.''

''He says that you poisoned your enemies, that you were very good at making your rivals disappear.''

He took a deep breath. ''You have told me that in your life you have made more than your share of mistakes. As a young man, so did I. And like you, I have paid for them.'' He barked a harsh laugh. ''Anything that Copper Thunder tells you about me, well, if it's not true, it ought to be.''

''So, you were a great, influential War Chief. What did you do? Dally with the Serpent Chief's wife? How does a feared War Chief end up as a witch on an island in the Salt Water Bay?''

He closed his eyes, seeing himself as he had been, tall, strong, wearing brightly dyed fabrics, his body decked in necklaces of shining copper. From his house, high on its mound on the western end of the plaza, he could see out over the shining Black Warrior River, across thatched houses among the cornfields beyond. His ranks of slaves knelt at his feet, heads down. His hair was festooned with feathers of blue, yellow, and orange, held in place with a burnished copper hairpiece.

There, at the foot of his high square mound, stood a pyramid of human heads as tall as a man, all rotting in the bright sunlight. Even now, so many years after, and so many days' journey away, the smell cloyed his nostrils. He could still hear the buzzing of the flies.

He wiped at the trickling sweat on his face, looking back into the past, into that dark room, the moonlight streaming in through the little square window. He could hear the hooting of owls out in the forest, smell the dank water and mud of the Black Warrior. ''I had a dream. First Man, Wolfdreamer, came to me. He said, 'Who are you, Raven? What have you become?'

''I answered him, 'I am the mighty Raven, War Chief

for the renowned White Smoke Rising, Lord of the Three Rivers. Before me, all the world trembles, for I am my lord's sweeping right arm.'

" 'You are polluted,' the Wolfdreamer told me sadly. 'You were born under the sign of the Wolf, and here you are, perverted by the Raven. Look inside, great man, and tell me what you see.' "

Panther wet his lips, staring into the darkness of the sweat house. "So I did, brash and headstrong as I was. What did I, of all men, have to fear? I . . . I looked inside . . . and saw what I had become." He shook himself, casting off the dangerous memories. "That night, I argued with my chief. Then I went a little crazy. And later . . . later that night, I walked away. Told no one I was going. I just walked out of the great gates, across the cornfields, and into the forest. I never looked back. Hungry, dirty, and alone, I traveled north, following the Black Warrior River to the crest of the mountains, and then followed them east, from peak to peak. From them I descended to the lands of my birth. Alone, in defeat and silence, I came home."

She waited patiently.

"That's about it." He smiled grimly at the hot swirling steam. "I went out to my island to find myself."

"And did you?"

He worked his fingers. The stiffness of old age had been driven from them by the heat. "Oh, yes. It frightened me to my very bones."

She shifted uncomfortably. "So, why are you here?"

"Because of innocence," he replied.

"I don't understand."

He straightened. "I wouldn't expect you to. You can't find yourself until you've become lost. In order to see, you must become blind. To seek goodness, you must become evil. To achieve great wealth, you must seek poverty. To be truly free, you must first become a slave."

"That makes no sense."

"It makes all the sense in the world." He cast a side-long glance at her. "What about you, Shell Comb? Have you ever looked deeply into your soul?"

He could feel her fear when she said, "Of course."

"You are a liar," he told her evenly. "But then, most of us are at heart."

"I know," she said, voice low. "But, sometimes it hurts too much to tell the truth."

Twenty-two

Nine Killer hunkered down on his heels in the snow, watching the clouds scud eastward toward the ocean. The spot he'd chosen gave him a good view of the inlet. On its slate-colored surface, choppy waves marched relentlessly toward the narrow beaches, where they would curl, slap the earth, and die. He rested with his back against an elm, the rough bark scarred by the years and the periodic fires his people used to clear weeds from their fields.

From here he could see over to the far shore with its gray-furred winter forest, but his attention centered on the sweat house and the girl who stood guard before the doorway.

After the Panther entered, Nine Killer had loitered beside Sun Conch, and heard most of what had passed within. Only when Shell Comb had stepped out into the weak afternoon light, her naked body glistening with sweat, did he step self-consciously away. She'd twisted her damp hair into a thick knot and walked out to splash in the cold water just below the lodge entrance.

For the briefest of moments, Nine Killer had let himself admire her lithe body. Those athletic curves would have blessed a woman half her age.

What was it about her that captivated him so? Of all the women he'd ever known, her body, the sultry look in her eyes, attracted him like no other. Was it the way she moved with sensuous grace or the rapt attention with which she listened to a man talk that made her so irresistible? She'd enchanted him more than once when he spoke to her. He'd seemed to fall into her gaze, his heart racing as he became the center of her attention. Then her lips would part the slightest bit, and his senses would swim. As if she could discern his attraction, she'd smile at him, teasing him just beyond his ability to respond.

She'd stepped from the water, dripping and shivering, her nipples taut, and wrapped a blanket around her shoulders. Only after she'd dressed, caught his gaze on her, and given him one of those flashing smiles, did she turn and walk toward the palisade. At that point, Nine Killer had retreated to the old elm to sit and think.

With an effort, he dragged his thoughts from Shell Comb, and settled on the fascinating things he'd been able to hear through the thin sweat house door hanging.

The Panther had been a war leader for the Serpent Chiefs? He would never have guessed. The implications startled him. Nine Killer might pride himself on being a responsible war leader for the Weroansqua, but from the stories told by the Traders, the Serpent Chiefs made a different kind of war—one where entire tribes were pitted against each other, and warriors numbered in the tens of tens. All those warriors did was practice their art. When they marched, their bodies were bedecked with bright feathers, wicker shields, and finely made arrows. Those warriors, he had been told, left on dedicated battle walks, each group traveling like an appendage of the whole.

And The Panther had been the brain for an organization like that? He chewed thoughtfully on his lip, recalling the defeats Copper Thunder had inflicted on the Mamanatowick, and Stone Frog, the Conoy Tayac. Was that the sort of chieftainship Copper Thunder was building on their very borders?

What fate would befall Nine Killer's people if Copper Thunder consolidated his territory? That thought rolled around in his mind. How could his warriors—a collection of hunters and fishermen—compete with those nearly mythical warriors of the Serpent Chiefs?

Down by the sweat house, Sun Conch turned suddenly, and reached out with a slim brown hand to help The Panther through the low doorway. The old man shivered in the cold air, blinking in what was, to him, blinding light.

Nine Killer rose, winced at the stitches in his knees and ankles, and walked down to the shoreline, where The Panther splashed water on his antique flesh.

Nine Killer gave him a skeptical inspection. Withered skin, now flushed with heat, hung from a bony skeleton. Strings of muscle were only a memory of what had once been strength. Here and there, an old scar still puckered whitely. Even the testicles seemed to hang tiredly beneath the gray thatch of pubic hair. Had this old man really been *that* kind of War Chief?

"I've not done this in years," The Panther said, rubbing his shivering hide with his blanket. "I think it's time for a cup of warm tea and a nice fire."

Nine Killer gestured toward the village as The Panther pulled on his old hunting shirt, arranged his breechclout, and slung his blanket around his shoulders. Sun Conch took up her place behind them.

For a moment, Nine Killer walked, lost in thought.

Then he caught Panther's knowing eyes on him, as if the old man were peeling away the layers that protected his thoughts.

"Yes, War Chief?"

"I couldn't help but overhear."

Panther's lips quirked. "I expected as much. It must have been the heat, it ate into my self-control."

"You served a Serpent Chief? The one called White Smoke Rising? Even I have heard of him."

"It was a long time ago."

"I heard you say that Copper Thunder was trying to be just like the Serpent Chiefs. You said that was why he adopted their tattoos."

"A great many people want to be what they are not. With Copper Thunder, I think it goes back to when he was boy." The Panther hesitated. "You heard that I captured him? A child is such a curious creature, strong and resilient, yet so very fragile. Grass Mat was all of those."

"I don't understand."

The Panther gave him a thin smile. "When I killed his father and captured young Grass Mat and his mother for slaves, my warriors and I destroyed his whole world. From those shambles, he had to make a new one, one that he could understand."

"That doesn't make sense, Elder," Sun Conch said from behind. "He should have hated the Serpent Chief who took him captive. I would have."

"Oh, Grass Mat did, but he admired him, too." Panther glanced over his shoulder at the girl. "Sun Conch, you must put yourself in the boy's place, see the world through his eyes. Can you imagine that?"

"I think so, Elder."

"Well, some of us have problems with that." He cast a sidelong look at Nine Killer. "Despite what the Kwiokos claims, that he can beat the boy's soul from a body, and chase it away with his rattle, if a man can't remember his life as a child, he is either a liar, or was hit on the head harder than he recalls.''

Nine Killer grinned at that, knowing full well that after being Blackened, no man would consciously talk about anything that happened in childhood. The Panther was picking at another of his people's self-imposed rules. Aloud, he said, "Is nothing sacred to you, Elder?"

"Many things, War Chief. But not the rituals of men.'' Panther took a deep breath. ''So, what do we have? A boy whose whole world is crushed. His father is dead, and for that, the boy will never forgive him.''

"Why?" Sun Conch asked. "His father couldn't help being killed in battle.''

"Does a young boy understand that?" Panther asked. "Sun Conch, Grass Mat's father was a very influential Trader. He didn't have to join the battle for Stalks-By-Night's town. The boy worshiped his father—thought the man invincible—and no matter how he died, Grass Mat couldn't forgive him for not living up to expectations. Children do that, especially if they are taken into slavery along with their mothers—whom they also love. It has to be someone's fault.''

"So the boy turned all that rage against his father?" Nine Killer shook his head.

"Being dead, and unable to defend himself to his son, he made the best target.'' Panther glanced at Sun Conch. "And, naturally, Grass Mat hated me, and my chief, White Smoke Rising, but because we won, he couldn't hate us too much. After all, the one thing Copper Thunder wants today is to win.''

"I heard you telling Shell Comb about the tattoos. If he hated the Serpent Chiefs, why try to look like them? And, if he did, why come back to Fish River and the Salt Water Bay?''

"War Chief, answer me this: What would you say if

I told you I wanted to be the next Weroance for Flat Pearl Village?"

"I'd tell you that you were crazy. It's impossible, and you know it."

"Absolutely."

"You're not Greenstone Clan, Elder," Sun Conch reminded.

"Exactly, and Grass Mat didn't belong to any of the ruling clans among the Serpent Chiefs. He was forever an outsider."

"So, when he came back to his mother's people on the Fish River," Nine Killer mused, "he had a place."

"Now he wants to build a chieftainship on the Salt Water Bay that will be like the ones he knew on the Black Warrior, or the Serpent River, or the Father Water." Panther kicked at the melting snow.

"Can he do it?" Nine Killer asked.

Panther shrugged. "I would think, War Chief, that the answer to that lies with you, the Mamanatowick, and Tayac Stone Frog."

Nine Killer tightened his grip on his war club. "I heard you say that anything Copper Thunder accused you of was probably true."

Panther peered intently into Nine Killer's eyes. "I told you once that the hardest thing to share was honesty, War Chief. I haven't forgotten that I made that bargain with you. I said that to Shell Comb for a definite reason: I want her to know exactly what sort of man I was."

"Why?"

Panther shrugged. "In due time, War Chief, I will tell you. I'm not ready to yet, and I'm not even sure why that is. Just a hunch—an itch that tells me it will be the right thing at the right time. But getting back to the point: Yes, I did murder, assassinate, poison, and otherwise eliminate my enemies. Unfortunately for us, here today,

Copper Thunder knew, or at least suspected, most of those terrible murders.''

''But that was part of your duty as War Chief, wasn't it?'' Nine Killer asked.

Panther snorted irritably, rubbing his chilled arms for warmth. ''Some were killed on orders from my chief. Others I killed because I feared them, or disliked them, or wished them punished from some slight or another.'' His gaze hardened. ''The point is, War Chief, I killed them. And yes, sometimes a man can kill from duty, and it is all right. But mostly those people died—some horribly—because I wanted them to.''

Sun Conch paled, a stricken look on her face.

Panther noticed and turned. ''You may relax, my friend. None of them died by witchcraft. Those that I killed, I killed deliberately, with weapons, poison, or suffocation. None of them were witched, or had their souls driven away by sorcery. I give you my word.''

Sun Conch whispered, ''Thank you, Elder.''

Nine Killer swallowed hard, shaking his head. ''You told Shell Comb that you had a dream? That First Man came to you?''

Panther's lips twitched, voice softening. ''Yes, that part was true, too.'' He glanced at Nine Killer. ''You heard those things I told Shell Comb, about losing everything to find everything? I meant that, War Chief. That is the most important lesson I can teach anyone.'' He smiled wistfully. ''But so few people understand just how important that lesson is.''

The old man gestured for silence and continued plodding his way through the snow for the palisade. Sun Conch hesitated long enough to give Nine Killer a questioning look.

He frowned, then raised his shoulders in a vague shrug. The original bond had been forged between the two of them. If Sun Conch didn't understand, Nine Killer couldn't be expected to, either.

"Oddly enough," Nine Killer whispered for Sun Conch's ears, "I still trust him. I'm not sure why, but I do."

"I think it's because he's seen through the eyes of Okeus," Sun Conch whispered. "And what he saw there sent lightning bolts through his soul."

Half Moon, Nine Killer's brother-in-law by marriage, was waiting for him inside the palisade gate. Nine Killer gestured to The Panther, saying, "This looks like family business. Why don't you and Sun Conch go and warm yourselves. Rosebud will have tea for you."

Panther nodded gratefully, shivering from the cold. Then he shuffled off across the plaza toward Rosebud's longhouse. Sun Conch walked just to one side, casting about as usual for any sign of danger.

"Busy day?" Half Moon asked. He stood a full two heads taller than Nine Killer. Long ropy muscles covered his limbs, and his shoulders, though stooped, were built for endurance rather than brute force. Half Moon's lower lip tended to stick out, and his rounded nose and perpetual squint gave him a perplexed look that caused people to underestimate him on first acquaintance.

Nine Killer fingered the handle of his war club, tied to his breechclout. "Very. It started first thing this morning with errands for the Weroansqua; then I had to carry some baskets of corn out to Aunt Windleaf. She refuses to live inside a palisade now, claims the air loses its spirit, whatever that means. I guess she thinks it gets worn out being breathed by so many people."

"And him?" Half Moon twitched his lips to indicate

The Panther. To Nine Killer's amusement, no one seemed to grant Sun Conch any recognition. As the witch's servant, she might have become invisible.

"I just took him to a meeting with Shell Comb. She wanted to talk to him."

"About what?" Half Moon crossed his arms, uneasy eyes watching the old man hobble past one of the Guardian posts outside the House of the Dead.

"I don't know," Nine Killer lied. "I don't listen to the Weroansqua's business."

"Ah, the Weroansqua's business!" Half Moon grinned. "So, Shell Comb wasn't just being sociable?"

"Brother, I don't know. Maybe, or maybe not. She wanted to talk to him in private. I serve my clan, just as you serve yours. Now, what can I do for you?"

"Go and see your wife." Half Moon scratched at his ear lobe. "How long has it been? A week, maybe two? White Star is starting to think she's a widow. You've been spending all of your time at your sister's."

"Red Knot's murder unsettled too many things. That's clan business. Then we had the raid against Three Myrtle Village. You know how that went."

"Old friend, if we never find ourselves in that kind of mess again, it will be too soon. That raid should never have taken place. It was wrong—ill advised from the beginning. Only that old man saved us ... saved us everything, in fact."

Nine Killer smiled up at his brother-in-law. They'd been companions and warriors long before they'd become kin through marriage. In fact, had they not been such good friends, Nine Killer wouldn't have married White Star. She was nearly six years older than he, and a widow. After her husband's death, it was found that part of his intestine had broken through the gut wall and into his right scrotum. There it had choked itself, and ruptured, and rot had festered throughout him.

White Star should have remarried to a more prestigious man than a young unknown Greenstone warrior. At that time, Nine Killer was a mere youth, and hadn't even earned his name in that daring raid on the Mamanatowick's Weroance at Mattaponi Village. But, because of Half Moon's influence, and because he came from Greenstone Clan, the marriage was arranged. The youngster who would become War Chief Nine Killer married the most beautiful woman in the village—save, of course, Shell Comb. But in those days, his cousin was still married to Monster Bone, and was living at Three Myrtle.

"Friend, I have to tell you, I don't know about this Panther." Half Moon crossed his long arms. "He might have saved us at Three Myrtle, but people are nervous. What's he doing here? What is he after, brother?"

"If I told you, you wouldn't believe me."

"Oh, come on. This is your brother-in-law that you're talking to—if not your oldest friend."

Nine Killer gave Half Moon a conspiratorial look. "He's here because of Sun Conch."

"What?"

"I told you you wouldn't believe it."

Half Moon gave him a disappointed look.

"All right, I'm supposed to come home and warm White Star's robes tonight. Good, tell her I'll be there. Late, but I'll be there." He winced. "Unless, of course, some kind of problem pops out of nowhere to ambush my best intentions."

"Like your sister throwing the witch out of her house? Don't you dare bring him to your wife's. White Star loves you, but she doesn't want her children exposed to the likes of him. It's bad enough that you do that to your sister's children."

"Oh, even I am smarter than to bring him into White Star's longhouse."

Half Moon hesitated, kicking at the dirt.

"What is it, brother? Speak up. The time for minding one's tongue is long passed for us."

"It's my nephew, Rabbit," Half Moon said, meaning Nine Killer's son. "He's got it into his head that he's going to run off and join the Great Tayac's warriors. Apparently there is some story going around about Shell Comb marrying Copper Thunder. If so, there will be an alliance. Rabbit thinks he's going to pack up and travel upriver so he can fight for the Great Tayac."

"Tell him no."

Half Moon sighed. "Oh, I did that. White Star and I both told him no. He is adamant, almost to the point of insolence. You can see the defiance in his eyes. He is your son, Nine Killer. Just as buck-strong and thick-headed. When I told him that, I saw the satisfaction in his face. That's when I got to thinking, perhaps, if you had a word with him . . . ?"

Nine Killer pursed his lips as Half Moon talked, and nodded. "I will, old friend. If you think it will do any good. I can't forbid him, I don't have the right. It's your clan business, what he does."

"Yes, I know. But he admires you more than anyone. In spite of the fact that you spoiled him rotten, turned him into this incorrigible monster, he still thinks you're the most important man on earth. At least, he did until the Great Tayac showed up. Now, he wants to be tattooed like that—that forked eye design—when he's Blackened. As if the Sun Shell Clan designs weren't good enough!"

Nine Killer chuckled and crossed his arms. "I'll speak to the boy, tell him that if he doesn't listen to his uncle, I'll hunt him down and whack him—even if he is sprung from my loins. And, after I've done that, I'll trade you straight across. Rabbit for White Otter."

"No, you don't." Half Moon raised his hands in defense. "Your seed grew nothing but boys in White Star's womb, but, thankfully, no daughters!"

"Girls aren't so bad."

"Aren't they? Says who?"

"And whose house do you think you'll live in when you get old and outlive your wife? Do you think the woman Rabbit marries is going to let you freeload when your teeth have fallen out?" Nine Killer thumped his chest with a fist. "Now, me, I can wear out White Otter's hospitality, and then go mooch off of Slender Bark, and when she finally throws me out, I can go to Little Shell's. If I'm still alive when she's tired of feeding me, there's always Sea Rice. See the benefits of four nieces? You always have a place to live."

"Then, as an old man, I shall curse you for giving White Star no daughters, and, since it's your fault, I'll come live with you and your nieces."

"Done!" Nine Killer reached out and shook Half Moon's hand.

They chuckled together for a moment, happy with their well-established friendship, rocking back and forth on their heels as they watched the doings in the plaza. Nine Killer studied the people who went about their duties.

She would have glanced back from the palisade gate, taken a look at the plaza. Nine Killer turned enough that he could see the gate. *Yes, she would have stopped here, just in the shadow of the post, and looked back. What did she see?*

"What's that?" Half Moon asked.

"What did she see?" Nine Killer repeated. "Red Knot, that last morning. She left through the palisade gate. Stood right here where we are. What did she see when she looked back? If only I could see through her eyes. Was anyone there, watching her go?"

"The man who killed her, perhaps?" Half Moon shrugged. "I don't know. No one will ever know. The dead are dead, brother. What they know dies with them."

"I suppose."

"Rabbit wants to cut his hair like the Great Tayac's."
Half Moon made a face. "He wants to cut it all off on
the sides. He's still a boy. I told him, when he goes
through the *Huskanaw* he can do any silly thing he
pleases, but so long as he lives in our household, he must
follow Sun Shell Clan rules. Is that too much to ask?"

"He's just a boy."

"Oh, he's all of that." Half Moon agreed. "He's too
much your son, that's what. All that energy, and I'm the
one who has to turn him into a human being, not a wild
weasel."

"Weasels are great hunters. You'll never have to
worry about him being hungry."

"Weasels are savage fighters, and bloodthirsty to
boot!"

"I'll talk to him," Nine Killer said in reassuring tones.
"But, keep in mind. He *doesn't* have to listen to me. I'm
only his father."

"I know, but I think he will." Half Moon reached out
and clapped Nine Killer on the shoulder. "I think your
wife would appreciate it if you weren't too late tonight.
I think she'll cook up something special for you."

"Thanks. I'll be there."

Nine Killer watched Half Moon walk away, headed
toward his sister's longhouse. He had been neglecting
White Star, but then, the needs of family and clan came
first. His wife knew that; she'd always understood the
things he had to do. He was one of the lucky ones. Ever
since their first night together, they'd grown to love each
other.

A man could do worse.

And—when Nine Killer considered the union of Red
Knot and Copper Thunder—so could a woman. How had
she felt, being promised on a moment's notice to a man
like Copper Thunder? He started rethinking the entire
problem of Red Knot.

As he worked through each of the little clues he and The Panther had uncovered, the voice in his soul whispered: *He's got it into his head that he's going to run off and join the Great Tayac's warriors . . . to be tattooed like that—that forked eye design—when he's Blackened. As if the Sun Shell Clan designs weren't good enough!*

Was there a key in this that would help unlock the riddle of Red Knot's death? Or, was this just another blind trail in the woods that would lead him back to the beginning?

Panther was sipping rosehip tea when Nine Killer ducked through the doorway, a perplexed look on his face. The short War Chief strode across the matting, shrugged off his feathered cloak, and untied his war club. Dropping them into a pile, he seated himself to Panther's right.

"You look preoccupied," Panther noted as the War Chief reached out and warmed his hands at the crackling blaze. "You're still not mulling over if I'm really a witch, or perhaps poisoning the Weroansqua's broth so I can step into her moccasins when she keels over dead, are you?"

"Hmm? No. At least, not at the moment."

"Well, perhaps you will in the next moment."

"What's that?"

"Worry about if I'm poisoning the Weroansqua so that I can take over and step into—"

"Yes, yes, I heard that." Nine Killer's expression cleared, and he lifted an eyebrow. "What are we talking about?"

Panther sipped his tea, and started over. "What has you so perplexed? I thought perhaps you were still ruminating on what you overheard this afternoon. About what a black-hearted and evil serpent I used to be."

Nine Killer shook his head, the frown deepening again. "No, well, yes, I suppose it's related." He reached out for an empty gourd and dipped up some of the tea that steamed beside the fire in a ceramic pot. "I just came from talking to my son. His name is Rabbit."

"Good name for a son." Panther rolled his gourd, watching the weak tea lap at the edges.

"He's perhaps a year shy of his *Huskanaw*, but he's been listening to Copper Thunder. It seems as if the Great Tayac has been spending a lot of his time here visiting with the boys."

"Indeed?" Panther squinted into his tea. "I never knew him to be interested in youth."

"Apparently he is." Nine Killer sipped at the hot liquid, made a face, and sucked air to cool his scalded lips and tongue. "And what he's telling them is that when they become men, they are more than welcome to go off and join him and his warriors. After all, he tells them, each of the clans have members in the upper river villages. Further, he offers them wealth, advantage, and promotion. Lands for the taking. To hear Rabbit tell it, Copper Thunder has already given away half of the Mamanatowick's territory."

"I see." Panther pulled thoughtfully at the loose skin on his chin. "I'll bet Grass Mat forgot to tell this to Water Snake."

Nine Killer set his tea aside to poke at the fire with a smoking stick. "He's got most of the boys ready to cut their hair into his roach. Not the traditional people's cut, with the right side shaved and the left pinned up. According to what Copper Thunder told Rabbit, the Serpent Chiefs cut their hair that way so that it can't come undone in war."

"There's some truth to that," Panther muttered. "But those warriors drill and practice all day long. They don't take time off to hunt and fish, unless it's just for the pleasure of it. All they do is practice war.''

Nine Killer gave him a clear-eyed stare. ''That's exactly what Copper Thunder tells the boys. If they will come to him, they can be full-time warriors, and live as such, their every need met.''

Panther put down his gourd and steepled his fingers. ''My, my, little Grass Mat is ambitious indeed. But how on earth does he suppose he's going to support this army of his?''

''Pardon?'' Nine Killer gave him a grim stare.

''The Serpent Chiefs have many warriors, it is true, but among them, only one in ten tens is a full-time warrior. He must be supported, War Chief. He must be given a house, a wife, and his food, clothing, and adornments. For that, it takes nearly thirty farmers and craftsmen.''

''Why not three warriors for every ten tens, then?'' Nine Killer asked. ''You could have an even bigger army.''

''Ah, but who flakes the arrowheads, makes and fires the pots, attends to the rituals, monitors the celestial observations, organizes the workers, supervises the sowing, weeding, and harvest of the fields, builds the canoes, raises the mounds, cuts the trees, and repairs the houses? War is but a small part of a great chieftainship. The priests, carvers, Traders, weavers, and others all must do their part, and many of these must also be supported by others.''

Nine Killer made a face. ''Then, Copper Thunder really can't do things as he wishes—at least, not right now.''

Panther shrugged. ''I'm not sure he can ever do them. The lands around Salt Water Bay are not like the great river floodplains in the interior. Their cornfields look endless, all tended by laboring clanspeople. Here, the land is a-jumble with ridges and steep slopes. The rich soil is often restricted in extent and depth, easily exhausted. The bottoms are swampy, and flood often. No, the difference here, War Chief, is that we must collect so much of our food. The Serpent Chiefs have masses of people to grow theirs for them. They don't rely on the fickle nature of the fish, the deer, the nuts, or the shellfish. To them, corn is life—and they can grow a great deal of it.''

"Then we should discount the Great Tayac's stories?''

"I'm not sure.'' Panther frowned at the gourd he picked up in his gnarled hand. "You know, this would be pretty if you painted it. Maybe a picture of a deer?''

"I'll consider it. I'm more worried about Rabbit wanting to run off and become a warrior for the Great Tayac.'' Nine Killer jabbed his stick into the fire, rolling it in his fingers, watching the flames char the end. "He's doing the same thing that happened to him as a boy, isn't he? Trying to impress the little boys. Seeking to make them want to be like him.''

"I believe so.'' Panther glanced down the length of the longhouse to where Rosebud was bustling around the cooking fire. "Do you think she's making squash again tonight? That stuff that she made last night was wonderful. I could have eaten that until I burst wide open.''

"You almost did.''

Panther sighed, returning his attention to the fire. "I think, War Chief, that we've come to the point where we have asked the normal questions, and found enough normal answers. Lots of people have reasons for murdering your cousin Red Knot. High Fox because she might have decided to expose his dalliance with a girl forbidden to him by age. Flat Willow for thwarted love. Hunting Hawk because the girl's death eased her out of a dangerous relationship with an ambitious spider. Copper Thunder . . . well, he's still a random clap of lightning—we don't know if he struck, but if he did it could be for a multitude of reasons.''

"And the Mamanatowick's warriors? Winged Black-bird was here to stop the marriage."

Panther narrowed his eyes. "Oh, I don't know. Perhaps, War Chief. But somehow, no. I think I'd know his odor if it were involved in this, and I can't smell him."

"Easy for you to say, Elder. I've been living too close to him for too long." Nine Killer glanced to the rear where Rosebud was adding the final touches to dinner. "You should know, Elder, that I'm going home to my wife tonight. I'm leaving you in the capable hands of Rosebud. I doubt that she's as skilled in the arcane uses of plants as you, but I think she's over the urge to poison you."

Panther raised a hand, gesturing Nine Killer to be off. "No, indeed, War Chief, I think she's rather come to like me. But, well, don't you worry. I think you can leave me here with a clear conscience. Unlike so many of these ill-mannered serpents these days, I respect the hearth and hospitality of my host, and wouldn't dare creep into your sister's robes unless she invited me most adamantly."

Nine Killer, halfway to his feet, stopped short in a half-crouch, expression startled.

Panther looked up blandly, refusing to betray the smile that tugged at his lips.

Twenty-three

Frost silvered every blade of grass, every twig and weed, with a white crystalline lacery. Thick mist had rolled in from the warmer waters of the Salt Water Bay, pushed up Fish River, and billowed through the trees and over the fields. Now it hung low in the air, masking Flat Pearl Village in ghostly gray.

The Panther could barely see across to the palisade as he passed the Guardian posts set around the plaza with its ritual fire pit. Each of the carved faces looked gloomy, as if their spirits, too, were dampened by the thick fog. From inside the House of the Dead, he could just smell the smoke from the eternal fires. Lightning Cat and Streaked Bear had been dutiful in fueling them.

Panther walked unsteadily this morning, his joints aching from the damp cold that, despite the fires Rosebud had maintained, had still managed to penetrate his old hide.

As he walked, he could hear Sun Conch's wary tread behind him. The girl was keeping an eye on his back, as usual.

Panther missed Nine Killer's company. The sawed-off War Chief had proven a good companion. Not only insightful, the man had a well-balanced sense of humor, and a genuine concern for his people and what Red Knot's death meant for them.

And, to be honest, that expression on the War Chief's face as he'd left for his wife's had been priceless. To Panther's absolute delight, the War Chief had seriously worried that an old chunk of human flotsam like him might crawl into Rosebud's blankets.

A figure materialized out of the mist, tall, muscular, and it took Panther a moment to identify Flat Willow. The hunter had his head down, his expression anxious.

Panther came to a stop. Flat Willow almost walked into him, and started, his eyes going wide with recognition. "Oh, it's you."

"Sorry to intrude. You looked as if your clan had just disowned you."

Flat Willow gave him a disgusted glare. "Are you still

around, stirring the pot to see what floats to the top?''

"I found you."

"Yes. Now, leave me alone."

Flat Willow started to step past, and Panther said, "If you didn't kill her, why don't you tell me what you were doing out there that morning? I find it curious that you would have picked that morning, of all mornings, to pack up and go hunting."

"That's what real men do, Elder. We hunt. Someone has to bring in food. Men hunt and fish. I realize you never have to. You just move into someone's house and they feed you. But for some of us, it's a full-time occupation."

"Oh, I've done my share of hunting. It's good practice for war." Panther studied him in the half-light. "Why, you've shaved the left side of your head. If I was to guess, I'd say it was to look like the Great Tayac's warriors."

Another bit of the puzzle dropped into place. But, did it fit?

"How I cut my hair is my business. I've been through the *Huskanaw*. No one tells me what to do."

"Yes, I've heard." Panther lowered his voice. "And I think I understand."

"Understand what?" Flat Willow crossed his arms.

"Living without parents, being passed around the clan like a basket of walnuts. It's a lonely way to live, never quite being one with a family. Always apart."

Flat Willow's expression softened, then the hardness returned. "You have nothing to tell me, Elder. You and your fawning puppy, Sun Conch, can dive to the bottom of Salt Water Bay and be fish bait for all I care."

Sun Conch crossed her arms, glaring malignantly at Flat Willow.

"You could help me, Flat Willow. I'm not your enemy. I'd say, right off hand, that none of this would have happened if Copper Thunder hadn't arrived. You're misplacing your loyalty."

"The Great Tayac recognizes talent when he sees it. Unlike so many around here, he has vision, a plan for the future."

"I see, but have you asked what the Independent villages will be like when his plan ripens?"

"Like the fields in fall, old man, we'll be a lot better off than before the harvest." He took a quick breath. "We're stale, all of us. The Mamanatowick and the Conoy are squeezing us between them. I don't want to end up with my skull resting in some Weroance's House of the Dead with the other war trophies. I have kin in the upriver villages that will welcome me." He glanced around at the rolling mist. "I've listened to the Weroansqua, heard her ramblings in council. This place, well, it has had its day."

"What about your duty to your clan? They were the ones who took you in, fed you, gave you a place to live, and filled your belly. Don't you owe your family something? That's part of every warrior's honor and duty."

He narrowed an eye. "If you're so intent on stirring the pot, Elder, why don't you try stirring Greenstone Clan's? If you're so interested in honor and 'right' behavior, see what you dig up in the muck they hide behind all their forthright speeches."

"For example? Go on, I'd like to hear it from your mouth."

"I'll bet you would, wouldn't you, witch? Well, then listen, like I did. You're just as enamored with Hunting Hawk and Shell Comb as the rest of them. I'll tell you what's at the center of Greenstone Clan. Rot, that's what."

"And you wanted Red Knot? To marry into that clan?"

"She . . ." He hesitated. "I thought she was different.

At least in the beginning. But then I found out differently, and it was right before my eyes the whole time. Like mother, like daughter. I found that out the night I saw her rutting with High Fox. It's in their blood, Elder. They can't help it.''

"What's in their blood? Just what are you trying to tell me?''

He gave Panther a bitter smile. "I'm not going to make it easy for you. You're so smart, you figure it out. See, if you can, just why the Weroansqua was so interested in going to war with Three Myrtle. After all, if Black Spike was dead, the last traces of the crime could be buried. What better cover for last year's tracks than a fresh layer of ash?'' Flat Willow snorted his disgust and walked off.

Panther stood where he was, feeling the cold moisture on his face. "Sun Conch, what did that mean, about the ashes?''

She looked up at him, her eyes wide and perplexed. "I don't know, Elder. But, I've heard about Flat Willow. It is said that he often creeps around at night, listening at the walls. There is no telling what he overheard, or where.''

Nine Killer studied the horizon as the canoe pitched on the gray waves of Fish River. He kept a careful watch in all directions. The midmorning breeze had blown the fog into patches, sending it inland to rise into ragged clouds. He and Flying Weir had taken the opportunity to paddle out to the center of the river. Beside them, Many Dogs and Crab Spine bobbed in their canoe, paddles flashing in the light as they maneuvered into position. They had located themselves by line of sight, navigating by points of land that jutted into the water. The canoes had to be at just the right spot.

In midwinter, the tides were the lowest of the year. Mudflats that were normally covered by water lay exposed for shellfish collecting. While the women and children attended to them, the men paddled out to fish the deep channels.

Now, their canoes at just the right place, the men could lower their nets into the deep hole where the fish had retreated. The water was warmer down deep, and the white perch concentrated there. If they did this right, they could net a canoe load of fresh fish in a short time, but the nets had to be worked perfectly.

Flying Weir stood at the front of the pitching canoe, helping Nine Killer sort out the folds of net with its stone sinkers. As each fold dropped over the side, the two men kept the net from tangling. Across from them, Many Dogs and Crab Spine reeled in the ropes that pulled the large net between them.

The chore was complicated, for along with the intricacies of the net, a man had to keep his balance, and each canoe had to be headed into the waves. With each freshening of the breeze, Nine Killer glanced apprehensively out toward open water. If the swells grew too high, they would have no choice but to reel in their net and paddle madly for shore before the canoes were swamped.

"That should do it," Flying Weir said as the last fold of hemp net slipped over the side. He caught up the guide rope as Nine Killer got a grip on his. Now he had to hold the rope, let it out coil by coil, and use the paddle to keep their course and the proper distance from the second canoe.

Bit by bit the long rope played out, and Nine Killer took his bearings from the point of land that marked the deep water. The breeze at their backs was taking them right over the deep hole with its winter-torpid fish. This had to be timed correctly. Precisely at low tide the currents were still. The net acted as big sea anchor, slowing their drift as it settled in the water. If the tide were running, the net would drag them along with the current.

Flying Weir had been monitoring the length of rope that played out, his practiced eye judging the angle at which it trailed into the water. "Back water!" he cried. And Nine Killer back-paddled, glancing across to measure his progress against that of Crab Spine in the rear of the second canoe.

"There," Flying Weir called as the ropes hung down at the proper angle. "Another three coils to go, and we should be right on top of them."

Nine Killer nodded, checking his position. They were on a straight line between the point on one side, and the old gray tree that marked the skyline of the peninsula occupied by Flat Pearl Village.

The last of the rope played out and Flying Weir clutched the knotted end. He judged the distance between the two canoes and said, "Close up a little, let the net settle to the bottom."

Nine Killer used his paddle only to keep them moving with the waves, allowing the weight of the net to pull the two canoes closer. He could feel the change in the drag as the net settled on the bottom.

"Paddle!" Flying Weir called, taking up a loop on his rope.

Nine Killer clamped his rope to the canoe bottom with his right foot, and took a deep bite with the paddle. Across from him, Crab Spine did the same, angling his canoe away. A fine sweat broke out on Nine Killer as his muscular arms propelled them forward.

He could imagine the net down below, the top held up by the forward ropes, the stone weighted bottom skimming the mud. Like a giant maw, it scooped the fish into the netting.

Flying Weir had likewise clamped his rope and plied his paddle to drive them forward and away from the other canoe.

Stroke by stroke they pulled their net ahead, each paddler panting as he struggled onward. Paddle as he might, the weight of the net pulled the battling canoes inexorably together.

"That should be it," Nine Killer called as the net lined out behind them. "Let's haul it up." He could feel the freshening of the wind. When he looked over his shoulder, he could see how it scalloped the waves.

Hand over hand, they pulled up their catch, the canoes crabbing sideways toward each other under the load.

Nine Killer strained until the muscles knotted in his arms and shoulders. His fingers began to cramp from the cold water, and the smell of wet hemp mixed with the salt breeze blowing in from the bay. From long practice, he laid out the rope in soggy coil after soggy coil. Water was puddling in the canoe bottom.

The corner of the net appeared from the depths, and Nine Killer stole a quick glance to see that Crab Spine, too, had reached netting. Together, they began pulling the knotted cord into the canoes. The vessels were almost knocking gunwales, only the thick cluster of loaded net keeping the boats apart.

"Watch it," Flying Weir reminded. This was the point when people lost their balance and tipped over.

Between them, they began putting the net into the center of the canoes, and the first wiggling fish could be seen as they splashed and fought the restricting mesh.

"All right," Many Dogs called. "Half and half."

In unison, they heaved, the bulk of the net, heavy with fish, caught between the canoes. Nine Killer reached into the cold water and lifted the burden past the gunwale. Silver scales gleamed in the light as they spilled netted fish into the canoes.

"Looks good," Flying Weir said through a smile. "We filled a lot of bellies with this load."

"And I for one," Many Dogs crowed, "am tired of smoked fish."

"Well," Nine Killer joked, "with as many hungry mouths as you have in that misbegotten Star Shell Clan, I think your part of the catch is spoken for. But don't be disheartened, I'll save a skeleton or two for you."

"You just have to remember to ask him nicely," Crab Spine joked. "Or, he might just let you have the heads."

"Oh, be quiet," Many Dogs answered, "or I'll slap you with a wet fish!"

Nine Killer found the bottom of the net and turned it inside out, spilling perch, rockfish, and at least one winter jellyfish. Nine Killer paused long enough to skewer the beast and flip it overboard. He could even see a couple of catfish—lured into the depths by the fresher waters of low tide—squirming in the mass at his feet.

Balancing carefully, they transferred the net, heavy with water, to Crab Spine's canoe.

For a long moment, all they could do was bob on the waves and grin at each other as fish flopped ankle-deep in the canoe bottoms. Then Nine Killer glanced back at the open bay. The wind had picked up enough to raise the swells they rode. "I think it would be prudent to head for home. If these waves pick up, it will be the fish eating us for supper."

Nine Killer snaked his paddle up from the bottom and turned his canoe for shore. As he paddled, he took a moment between strokes to club this or that particularly vigorous fish that threatened to flip itself overboard.

Now they paralleled the swells, each heavily laden canoe cresting the waves with but a finger's width to spare at the gunwales.

From the bow, Flying Weir said, "You've been spending a lot of time with the witch."

"We've been working together on the matter of Red Knot's death." Nine Killer glanced at the shoreline, measuring the rising waves and wind against the distance they had to travel to the inlet below Flat Pearl Village, and safety. Could they make it?

"Well, what's he doing? Everyone's talking about it. The stories are rampant, that he's accused the Weroansqua, that he's going to challenge Copper Thunder, all kinds of things."

"I'm surprised people haven't said he's turning himself into an owl at night and flying around."

"They have." Flying Weir shook his head. His eyes were riveted to the rough water.

"Well, he's staying in Rosebud's longhouse. I've been there most nights. I haven't seen him become any owl, and, to tell you the truth, for the amount of squash he eats every night, he couldn't fly if he wanted to."

Flying Weir chuckled. "Well, it isn't often that we have a witch who's looking into a murder to talk about. You've got to expect these things."

"I know." A wave sloshed water over the gunwale as they crested the peak. Many more like that, and their fish would be swimming again. Nine Killer paused to whack a rockfish as long as his arm. The paddle made a sodden sound as it thumped the purple-striped body.

"So, there's nothing to report?"

"Not really, but I have a question for you."

"For me?" Flying Weir looked back across the mass of writhing fish.

"That last night of the dance, a warrior should have been appointed to guard the palisade entrance. Do you know who?"

Flying Weir paddled in silence for a moment, and Nine Killer could tell by the set of his shoulders that he was suddenly tense, more so than the rough water would warrant.

"Yes, I know." Flying Weir said at last. "Stone Cob was responsible for posting guards that night. He told me about it later, griping about Flat Willow . . ."

"Flat Willow?"

"The same—our bit of bright sunshine. Stone Cob told me that when he asked Flat Willow to guard the gate, he was almost insolent. I think Stone Cob's words were 'I thought I was going to have to smack him in the head. He said he had things to do.' Or something like that."

"I see."

Flying Weir spared a glance over his shoulder. "The Panther's been talking to him, hasn't he?"

"Just do me a favor, all right. Keep this between you and me."

"Why would Flat Willow want to—"

"Flying Weir?"

"Yes, yes, between you and me."

They crested a tall wave, the wind kicking spray to soak Nine Killer. The exertion of his body almost evened the cold bite of wind. Water trickled down his greased skin, slowly winning the battle for his body heat.

"Well, it looked like a good chance to fish, but we could have had a better day," Nine Killer muttered. He glanced back, seeing the second canoe plowing along in their wake, their situation just as perilous with the heavy net mounded amidships.

"Good thing we didn't go out into the bay, we'd be swimming. And in water this cold, not for long." Flying Weir wiped spray from his face. "Do I need to take the gourd and bail yet?"

"No, but some of the fish are swimming again." Nine Killer cracked another rockfish with his paddle. "I think if we push hard, we can make calmer water before we have to bail."

If things became serious, they could pitch some of the

fish, but Nine Killer decided he'd rather sink first. The catch had been as good as he could remember for a deep-water netting.

They made the shallows just as rain began to pelt them from the dull sky. Around his feet, half the fish floated on their sides; the others, smaller, splashed about in the shallow canoe bottom. The water was up above Nine Killer's ankles, and his flesh was pebbled with cold. He suffered through his first shiver, and tightened his grip on the wet paddle. When he glanced behind him, he could see angry white caps on the water.

"You know, we just made it." Nine Killer grinned in spite of himself. Fishermen plied open water at their own peril in winter. Rough water swamping canoes wasn't the only risk. Fishermen had been known to grow so cold that their wits deserted them. Disoriented by shivers, they forgot to bail their boats, or would be swept out to sea on the tide. Some died, and others, luckily rescued, couldn't even name their clans.

Flying Weir snared the bailing gourd as it floated by and scooped water over the side. Behind them, Many Dogs was doing the same.

Nine Killer shivered again and bent his back to the chore of sending them homeward.

"This Copper Thunder," Flying Weir noted, shivering himself, "he's been talking to the younger warriors."

"Uh-huh, promising them glory and fame on the war trail."

"What do you make of that? Is there anything to what he's been saying? Can he really push the Mamanatowick out of his lands and claim them?"

"Not according to The Panther. Did you hear that the elder was a War Chief for the Serpent Chiefs once? He says that Copper Thunder might train his warriors, but he can't support them."

"Why is that?"

Nine Killer pointed at the fish sloshing in the bottom of the canoe, then realized Flying Weir couldn't see the gesture. "Because we have to spend so much time fishing. Like today. Our people can't be full-time warriors."

"That makes sense, but who are the young going to listen to? The Panther, or Copper Thunder?"

"Will it matter in the end?"

"I don't know, War Chief. I just don't know."

"Flat Willow was on guard that night?" Nine Killer considered the implications. "White Otter told me there was no one guarding the gate when she went through just after dawn. So, if Flat Willow wasn't at the gate, where was he?"

"He was the one who found Red Knot's body," Flying Weir added. "Remember? He said he'd been hunting, seen High Fox, and backtracked him."

"Yes," Nine Killer added grimly. "I remember."

"I think you should add a little more squash," Panther said. "Maybe one or two at least."

Rosebud sighed and gave Panther a cross look. "I think the hominy will be fine for tonight. I've seasoned it with beechnuts—you like those—and added mint leaves for good measure."

"What's boiling in that pot over there?" He peered anxiously down his long nose.

"That is what's left of two muskrats I was given today. I cut them into pieces to boil with chinquapins. And, lastly, I've spent the entire day boiling acorns until they were leached. I spent the last hour pounding them into flour. That's the bread baking there in the ashes." She crossed her arms. "And, just for you, I burned some stickweed root. When the acorn bread is ready, I'll mix the ashes with deer grease so you can slather it all over the acorn bread and eat like a Weroance. . . . Any complaints?''

Panther sat back and screwed his face into its most pensive expression. "Well, I suppose not. For acorn bread covered with stickweed grease I suppose I could pass up squash for just one night.''

Rosebud smiled and shook her head. "Didn't anyone ever feed you out on your island?''

"The only person who fed me was me. And, after you've eaten oysters and clams, and clams and oysters, and oysters and clams, well, I suppose you can imagine what a wonder it is to come into your house, Rosebud.'' He sighed wistfully. "The problem with being a warrior all of your life is that you learn how to boil corn, meat, and fish. Other than that, everything you eat is dried or smoked. Food, especially food like this, is just—well, you can't imagine the effect it has on me. I can't tell you how much I appreciate these meals.''

She chuckled then. "I think I see it in your face. It is a pleasure when your smile lights up like that.'' She paused. "Didn't you ever have a wife?''

He spread his hands. "Somehow, I never quite got around to it.''

"Surely your clan would have made you marry.''

He hesitated, unsure what to say.

She read his sudden wariness and cocked her head, an arched eyebrow asking the question.

He glanced across to where Sun Conch was meticulously twisting hemp into a cord.

Rosebud lowered her voice. "Panther, you've lived here for days, and I've never asked. Among our people, the most important question is: Who are you? A human being has a clan, and relatives. Surely you didn't just appear out of smoke. Who are your people? Rumor has it that they threw you out, that you are a pariah whose relatives won't even claim you. Is that true?''

He looked into her probing brown eyes, measuring his response. Gull droppings and bat dung, she had a right to know. He'd been living under her roof, and because of her brother's respect for him, she hadn't asked the most burning question these people had.

He lowered his voice. ''I wasn't thrown out by my people. I left. It was my decision . . . my fault. I found myself trapped in a situation I couldn't stand. I was young, barely more than a boy. One night I packed up and walked away. It was that, or kill myself. I'm sure that they gave me up for dead long ago. I doubt that my people even remember my name.''

She reached out, placing a sympathetic hand on his arm, concern mirrored in her eyes. ''Panther, that doesn't mean you don't have a clan. It was a long time ago. You could go back, you know. A family doesn't cease to exist just because of a mistake made when you were a young man.''

He patted her hand. ''Precious Rosebud, how naive you are. That angry youth died that night. He turned his back on his world and went out to find a better one. Oh, I tried, believe me, I did. My travels took me a great many places. I rose among the highest, and fell to the lowest, and look as I might, I found people to be the same every place I went. Some might be a little meaner than others, some braver, others happier, but as a whole, people everywhere are people. We are indeed the children of Okeus, all wretchedly flawed and noble at the same time.'' He chuckled. ''Even when we're at our best. Which isn't often.''

''Is that why you never married? Because you were a man without a family, without relatives? Would no one make a place for such a man?''

''Hah! Gain enough fame, Rosebud, acquire enough wealth and influence, and people will forgive you anything. They see only the gauds of a War Chief, not the man beneath the feathers and copper. But a man ought to be able to stomach himself. I awakened one morning with the knowledge that what I had become was a loathsome monster. In the end, the only person I betrayed was myself.''

''You still didn't answer my question. You're very good at that, you know. Avoiding answering.'' She leaned over, checked the acorn bread with a fingertip. ''Why didn't you marry? You hinted that you could have if you'd wanted, that people would have overlooked your being kinless.''

Once again her patient gaze defeated him. ''I loved a woman. I couldn't have her. She was promised to another. Unlike Red Knot and High Fox, I didn't have the courage to run off with her.''

He glanced down at his callused old hands, knotty with swollen joints and flaccid skin. ''I could never see beyond her. No other woman would do. She became, well, an obsession. People with obsessions are never quite sane, not whole, like a bird flying with only one wing. In the end, they tend to fall out of the air.''

She nodded. ''So this affair with Red Knot is more than just a simple puzzle to you, isn't it? It's still part of your obsession.'' She gave him a measuring glance. ''Does Nine Killer know?''

He shook his head, eyes still on his wrinkled hands. ''Sometimes I think Ohona sent Sun Conch to me on purpose. If I can solve this thing, make sense of it, perhaps I can lay my obsession to the side for once.''

''And maybe it will blind you. Have you thought of that?''

''Oh, yes, I have, Rosebud. If anything, it has made me more cautious in dealing with Red Knot's death.''

''I see.''

He finally met her eyes. ''I would appreciate it if you

would keep this conversation between the two of us. There are already enough rumors passing from lip to lip. What I have just said is because of the kindness you have shown me. I thought I owed you an explanation.''

''I will keep your confidence, Panther.'' She glanced cautiously at Sun Conch, still obliviously twining her cordage. ''And the name of your clan?''

He shook his head wearily. ''They are dead, Rosebud. In reality, if not in fact. No, I'll suffer your belief that I am a pariah rather than allow that name to cross my lips again.''

''As you wish,'' she said in clipped tones.

He wondered why her words stung, and why the open wound in his soul hadn't closed, even after all these years.

Twenty-four

Snow fell from the sky in big fluffy flakes as Panther walked across the plaza, Sun Conch at his heels. The cold nipped at Panther's bones. The snow fell so thickly it coated his shoulders, and whitened his already gray hair. Each step crunched underfoot.

Around him, the longhouses looked like humped whales, their arched roofs blanketed in white. The sooty thatch around the smoke holes looked as if the monsters puffed blue wreaths of smoke through their blowholes.

''I have my doubts about this, Elder,'' Sun Conch said uneasily.

''It was inevitable,'' Panther confided. ''The biggest

surprise is that the summons was this long in coming.''

"I still don't like it. Why now? Why in the Weroans-qua's Great House? It doesn't seem right.''

"Because there is no other place, Sun Conch. This meeting must occur where authority can be demonstrated. Given what's between us, we must meet in a setting that at least hints of equality.''

Panther paused outside the Weroansqua's doorflap long enough to knock off most of the snow, and bent down to duck into the warm, smoky interior.

A big fire crackled in the hearth. The front room was empty, save for its single occupant. The sleeping benches were made, every robe laid out neatly. The storage baskets were all hung, and supplies stacked. Panther smiled grimly to himself as he strode forward, well aware of Sun Conch following so protectively close that her toes brushed Panther's heels.

Copper Thunder had placed a single section of log behind the fire and covered it with finely tanned deer hides. This he sat on like a Weroance, his arms braced on his knees. With a stony expression, he watched Panther cross the mat-covered floor. The firelight gleamed and danced on the polished copper necklace, and cast a ruddy light on the spider gorget. Perhaps to make his appearance more formidable, the Great Tayac had greased his thick roach of hair so that it stood up straight, contrasting with his shaved scalp. His heavy war club sat propped within easy reach of his strong right hand.

"Well, you've come at last, Raven.'' Copper Thunder gestured to the mats spread on the ground across the fire from him. "Be seated. You and I must talk.''

Panther glanced around nonchalantly, removed his blanket from his shoulders, and snapped the melting snow from it. Sun Conch stood to the side, her war club clutched in both fists.

Panther cocked his head, taking his time. "Thank you,

Grass Mat, but I believe that I shall stand. It's this weather . . . hard on the joints. Funny, isn't it? You'd think that joints would move more easily with age rather than stiffening. Most things tend to loosen with time and use.''

"I want you to sit!"

"But I will stand. Or, is that all that you wanted? Just for me to sit? If that's it, I shall return to Rosebud's and sit there. Not only will I not have to rise again, but she cooked a wondrous breakfast this morning. Nine Killer made a good catch yesterday. Fresh fish roasted to perfection, the succulent white meat steaming as I plucked it from the bone. If I'm going to sit, I want something like that to pick at.''

Copper Thunder's enraged eyes seemed to burn. "I warn you that I've had enough, Raven. All you are doing is making trouble. Up to your old tricks. These people don't know you as I do. They don't understand that where you go, you spread your poison until it eats away at all that is good and peaceful.''

"Pardon me if I'm wrong, Grass Mat, but isn't that a spider that you're wearing around your neck? Last time I watched a spider, it killed its prey with a venomous bite." Panther's faulty memory flashed, and he said, "I've seen that spider motif before: it was being worn by a Natchez warrior, as I remember. Night Spider society, isn't it? Are you one of them, Grass Mat?''

"Raven, you try my patience. I ordered you here to—''

"Ah! You just *copied* that design!'' Panther took a step to the side, making Copper Thunder turn his head to keep him in sight. "I didn't think you'd voluntarily undergo the initiation. It takes years of brutal training. To be a full initiate and wear the Night Spider gorget, you must kill eight men in one-to-one combat—one for each of the spider's legs—and then drink a tea made of datura to be granted a vision. Those few who survive are bled, scarified, and tattooed. Once they take a vow on a battle walk, none will retreat until they are killed or they kill their opponents. I think that's why there are so few Night Spiders, and why they are so honored and revered up and down the rivers.''

"Enough!" Copper Thunder bellowed, rising to his feet. The coals of anger had burned free now, his face contorting, jaw muscles jumping. "The last time you entered my life, I swore I'd kill you. By the Longnosed God, I wanted to.'' He raised a knotted fist, his face twisting the forked eye tattoos. "Then I come here and find you, a broken old man, but still spinning your little intrigues. Dung and fire, you old bloodsucker, you disgust me.''

Panther locked his hands behind his back, casting a reassuring glance at Sun Conch, who seemed strung tight enough to vibrate. The nostrils of her short beak of a nose quivered. "Disgust you, do I? Why, Grass Mat, at least I don't come here under false pretenses.''

"I *came* to claim a wife. Now I find you defending the man who killed her. Curious coincidence, isn't it?''

"As curious as the fact that the daughter is dead, and now you seek the mother as wife?'' Panther raised a taunting eyebrow.

"That was *her* idea. Shell Comb's. She came to me! These people *want* this alliance. They need it! Without it, they are dead. It's only a matter of time. Better to ally with a winner than to be crushed by a conqueror. You, of all people, should know that.'' His eyes narrowed. "Or have you forgotten how we met that day?''

"I remember it quite clearly, Grass Mat. That was the day you and your mother became my slaves, wasn't it?''

Copper Thunder stepped around the fire, thrusting his face within a finger's width of Panther's. The firelight danced eerily on his forked eye tattoos and the black stripe around his mouth. "I've lived and relived that day, Raven. When I close my eyes to sleep, it's to have that nightmare bleed itself into my dreams. And finally, here you are, delivered to my hands, as if by Okeus himself."

"I don't quite understand what you're doing with the young men here." Panther, unconcerned, waved Sun Conch back with one hand while he pulled at his chin with the other. "Are you trying to sell them on the idea that you're a Night Spider so that they'll follow you? But how? If that was your plan, why murder Red Knot? She was your key to the youngsters here."

"Murder Red Knot?" The question caught him off guard. "I came to marry the girl. Why would I kill her?"

"That's what I just asked." Panther gave him a sober look. "Grass Mat, you've always been the logical one. Try this: You kill Red Knot, and then make it look as though High Fox did it. Confusion spreads, old alliances are suddenly suspect. The Independent villages fragment, tear themselves apart, and you sweep in before the Mamanatowick's warriors snap them up. You unify them under your protection without having to risk your fake Night Spider identity."

"You old fool!" Copper Thunder shouted. "The marriage was enough! Why do by war what I could by marriage? To think I killed her, that's . . . well, it's insane! You're even crazier than I thought you were."

"Then, who killed her? Surely you don't believe that sleight about Winged Blackbird's warriors doing the deed, do you? It wasn't their style to leave her like that. I *know* those people. They'd have at least wanted to take the head back to Corn Hunter. He in turn would send it— with due ceremony and substantial groveling—to Water Snake."

"High Fox killed her!" Copper Thunder backed away to stomp off around the fire. "Who else?"

"Oh, I can think of lots of people. Flat Willow, for

one. He could have done it for you. He wanted Red Knot, and lo and behold, she's promised to you. A bruised lover might have been just the person you needed for the deed. Desperation makes people do odd things that don't make sense on the surface. It twists the logic.''

"Flat Willow?'' Copper Thunder stopped short, a puzzled look on his face. "But he . . .''

"He told me he'd have done anything to win her love. He even thought of killing High Fox—or at least exposing the fact that she was letting him warm his favorite arrow inside her. But Flat Willow was afraid she'd hate him for it. You were the unexpected stone cast into his pond.''

Copper Thunder frowned, his confusion palpable. He looked at Panther, as if casting about for explanations, and then a slow smile spread across his lips. "Some things never change, do they, you old weasel? Always casting your dung into other people's drinking water. Then, you see just how much you can stir it up before people realize they are drinking your shit.'' He shook his head. "Why, you even had the gall to accuse the Weroansqua.''

"If it wasn't you, why not her? She has as much motive as anyone else. She might have finally figured out what a vile little serpent you are at heart, Grass Mat. With a dead Red Knot, she avoids losing her territory to your expanding chieftainship. I know this is beyond your ability to believe, but there are people who will do anything within their means to keep clear of your filthy intrigues.''

Copper Thunder said nothing, his hands alternately grasping and flexing. His mouth had thinned to a bloodless line.

"So, you see,'' Panther summed up, "the shit in the water isn't mine. But by stirring it, the innocent may discover who fouled the water in the first place.''

Copper Thunder glared at Panther from across the fire.

"I called you here to tell you that I've had enough of your games. Two of my warriors will take you back to your island when this storm breaks."

"The Weroansqua agrees to this? She has ordered me to leave? Oh, I doubt it, Grass Mat. She has more self-respect than that. Were she to throw me out, it would cause her a great deal of grief in the end. She knows that, and she's smart enough to avoid those pitfalls."

"Indeed, old man? And why is that?"

"Because too many people know that The Panther is here. The story has already circulated through the Independent villages, and no doubt beyond to the Mamanatowick, and to Stone Frog and his Conoy Confederacy. If she throws me out before I name a murderer, it will appear to the other interested parties that I uncovered something so rotten that she couldn't let it out. Now, think, Grass Mat—though I know that's not your strength. What reason do you think will circulate from mouth to ear? Hmm?"

"I could not care less."

"You could not care less? Ah. Of course. Anything that upsets the Independent villages works to your advantage, doesn't it? Even if the story is that the Weroansqua was at the bottom of her granddaughter's murder. The problem is, Hunting Hawk knows that the only way out is to learn who murdered her granddaughter. Once the culprit is identified and punished, she can mend strained relations with the other clans and villages. If she doesn't, the Mamanatowick will be collecting tribute from what's left of the Independent villages by spring planting. The only difference is that his Weroances will be sitting in the Great Houses directing its collection."

"You always have the answers, don't you, old man?"

"Not always. But I tend to find them eventually."

Copper Thunder tugged angrily at his copper necklace. "I *didn't* kill the girl." He made a fist. "But tomorrow you'll be leaving. My warriors will take you home."

Panther chuckled. "Yes, I'm sure they will, so long as my 'home' is at the bottom of the Salt Water Bay. Once out past shore, they could whack me in the head, weight my body with rocks, and pitch me over the side. When they return a couple of days later, who is to doubt that they delivered me safe and sound to my island?"

Copper Thunder narrowed an eye, making the tattoos look especially fierce. "You've pushed me as far as I will be pushed."

"I doubt it." Panther cocked his head. "The mere fact that I'm still upright tells me just the opposite. Of all the people alive, you want to kill me the most. You blame me for your father's death, for your mother's slavery. That I am still breathing indicates a weakness on your part. No, Grass Mat, I don't think the Independent villages need you nearly as much as you need them. Otherwise, why would you stay here?"

"I warn you, old man . . ."

Panther stepped over to inspect the baskets hanging from the wall. Some were woven from splits of cedar, some from supple willow, and others from slender sumac branches. Most contained nuts, dried fruits, and other foodstuffs that would mold inside a sealed leather sack. "You know, I could be mistaken." He turned speculative eyes on Copper Thunder. "You might be smarter than I thought. You have finally come to understand, haven't you?"

"Understand what?"

"That you *can't* build a chieftainship here like the ones you so obviously admired among the Serpent Chiefs. You've figured out that you can't maintain a full-time warrior class, that your warriors have to hunt and fish part time. You can't produce the food surplus to support them. The soil won't grow enough in this hilly land with its narrow floodplains. Like the Independent villages, you *need* allies. Yes, you've whipped the Mamanatowick's warriors, and Stone Frog's Conoy, too, but you understand now that in the end they will wear you down. Like sand rubbed on steatite, over time they'll hollow you out, gut your forces.''

"No one can stand before my warriors!''

"Maybe not, not when they are massed for an attack, but the enemy keep coming back, bleeding you a little nip at a time. It's like killing mosquitoes with a war club. If you could just connect, you could squash them all. But all you can do is flail the humming cloud while they bleed you bit by bit until you're sucked dry.''

Panther shook his head. "My poor little Grass Mat, still a puffed-up boy with dreams of greatness, and no way to make them happen.''

The Great Tayac's throat worked, the veins standing out in his neck. "Get out, Raven!'' He seemed to be choked on the words. "Get out of my sight!''

"As you wish, Grass Mat, But I'd—''

"You'll *never* call me that name again! *You hear me?*''

"Names are transitory things.'' Panther shrugged. "One's as good as another.'' He swung his blanket about his shoulders. "But, as I was saying, I'd take a hard look at Flat Willow. I think he's unreliable. Come, Sun Conch, we should see if that fish is still hot and steaming. Oddly, despite the company here, my appetite seems to have come back.''

When Panther cast a last look over his shoulder, Copper Thunder's face had turned purple, contorted. And then Panther was outside, walking through the veils of snow.

"Elder,'' Sun Conch whispered. "Why do you do these things?''

"What things?''

"Enrage him like that. He was ready to kill you!"

"Sun Conch, he was ready to kill me the moment he knew I had entered the village. It is an old thing between us. The issue is not whether he would kill me, but when. And, as for today, I was perfectly safe."

"Safe?" Sun Conch rushed around to stand before Panther. "He needed but to reach out to break your neck!"

"Oh, but had he done so, everything would have been in ruins for him."

"I don't understand."

"Then you don't know the Weroansqua." He veered around Sun Conch and kept walking. Sun Conch followed. "You don't think she'd leave him alone with me, do you? No, no, my brave young woman. This was a carefully planned event. Copper Thunder told Hunting Hawk he was going to have it out with me, put me in my place as a demonstration of his authority. He hoped I would trip myself, say something that would condemn me as a witch or troublemaker. Grass Mat was never clever at these things, and he's no brighter now that he calls himself Copper Thunder."

Sun Conch opened her mouth, then closed it.

"The Weroansqua handled that particularly well, don't you think?" Panther blinked as the snowflakes caught on his eyelashes.

"She did?"

"Oh, yes. Hunting Hawk is no one's fool. She was there the whole time, hidden behind the mat divider, listening to the entire exchange. That's why Copper Thunder couldn't just kill me. It would look like he was trying to silence me, and that would have strengthened Hunting Hawk's position. She'd use the knowledge like a club against him."

Sun Conch took a deep breath, including a snowflake,

and coughed. "You play dangerous games, Elder."

"Yes, yes, but Sun Conch, I'm too old to live carefully." Panther proceeded on his way. In his imagination, he was already picking at a warmly cooked fish.

Twenty-five

Nine Killer stopped before the doorflap of Yellow Net's longhouse, and called, "It is your cousin, Nine Killer. Might I speak to you?"

"Come, War Chief," Yellow Net called.

Nine Killer ducked through the doorway and stamped the snow from his moccasins. It took a moment for his eyes to adjust to the dim light. Pungent smoke filled his nostrils, along with the smells of cooking corn, boiling walnut milk, and roasting tuckahoe: the root of the arrow arum. To prepare tuckahoe properly, the roots needed a long roasting to leach the acids from the pulpy flesh.

With a warm smile, Yellow Net rose from her seat behind the main fire. "You are welcome to my house, War Chief. What can I do for my cousin today?"

Nine Killer walked across the matting and slicked snow water from his brow. "I had hoped to speak with Quick Fawn. Is your daughter here?"

Yellow Net studied him with suddenly guarded eyes. She started to say something, paused, then called out, "Quick Fawn? Would you come here?"

From beside the warming fire in the rear, Quick Fawn's slender figure rose. A loop of cord hung from her long brown fingers—she had been playing the string game with her younger brothers and sisters. That game occupied most of the children when the weather was bad.

Nine Killer watched the girl approach, her hair swinging with each step. She wore a deerskin apron decorated in patterns of shell beads and knotted on the left hip. A fringed deerskin mantle was fastened over her left shoulder, leaving her budding right breast bare.

Quick Fawn's face was a mask of apprehension. She lowered her dark eyes, and fumbled with the string, as if unsure what to do with it.

In all of his days as War Chief, Nine Killer had never had trouble with the girl. Rather, if anything, she seemed to avoid the behavioral snares that her peers often entangled themselves in.

Nine Killer twitched his lips at Yellow Net, and tilted his head slightly. She read his meaning and left them alone, saying, "Quick Fawn, keep an eye on the food, please."

Nine Killer seated himself on the matting, gesturing Quick Fawn down beside him. She sat cautiously, hands clasped around the string in her lap.

"It's a good snow," Nine Killer told her. "We were lucky to get our catch in before the storm hit. We filled a canoe with fish yesterday. I think your mother got some."

"Yes, Elder. We ate several last night." She sounded subdued.

Nine Killer sighed. "Do you know why I'm here?"

"About Red Knot?"

"Yes, cousin. I need your help." He studied her, but she didn't raise her eyes to look at him.

"You were with Red Knot that night. White Otter told me that she left the two of you alone."

Quick Fawn nodded.

"Cousin, please, tell me what you did that night. What

she told you. I need to hear everything, even if it doesn't seem important. Any little detail might help.''

Quick Fawn hesitated, then said, ''Elder, she's dead. Does it make a difference?''

''I think it does. You've heard the rumors. You know that we almost went to war with Three Myrtle Village. It's a dangerous time for us. If we can determine who killed Red Knot, the clan might avoid making another mistake.''

She nodded reluctantly. ''I understand.''

Nine Killer steepled his fingers thoughtfully. ''I already know that White Otter slipped out that night. Did you? Did Yellow Net know that you were out?''

She sat perfectly still, shoulders slumped.

Nine Killer lowered his voice. ''What you tell me will be between us for the moment. I didn't come here to make trouble for you and your mother. If you did something really bad, we'll work it out between the two of us, all right?''

Quick Fawn sucked a breath and nodded.

Nine Killer laced his fingers together. ''I'll tell you what I know so far. Red Knot planned to run away with High Fox. She was to meet him at Oyster Shell Landing, and from there, they would paddle away. I also know that they had been coupling despite the fact that she was still a girl. This was by her will, wasn't it?''

''Yes, Elder.''

''How long had this been going on?''

''Since the weeding last summer. Remember when Hunting Hawk asked our neighbors to come for a feast? That was when they started.''

He frowned thoughtfully. ''I see. Did Red Knot tell you about this?''

''No, Elder. I . . . I saw them. I was frightened for them. The next day I asked Red Knot about it. She didn't seem to care. She wanted to be with him.'' Quick Fawn frowned then, the lines etching her smooth brow. ''She really loved him, and he loved her. They knew it was wrong, but it was like they couldn't help themselves.''

''I see.''

''Red Knot told me that they were going to be together, that High Fox was going to be great someday, maybe as great as the Mamanatowick . . . and she would be by his side.''

''Everyone has a right to their dreams. It must have come as a shock when the Weroansqua promised her to the Great Tayac.''

''I'd never seen anyone so upset. She told me that she couldn't say anything, that she was Hunting Hawk's granddaughter. She said that nothing would be worse than telling Hunting Hawk and Shell Comb no. She couldn't dishonor her clan by refusing. She was trapped, Elder. It was because everyone expected so much from her. Then, that night, after her celebratory dance, High Fox asked her to run off. She said she'd changed her mind, said that after all, she was only Shell Comb's daughter.''

''What did that mean? Shell Comb's daughter? Of course she is.'' He stared skeptically at the fire, thinking about Red Knot, and how closely she resembled Shell Comb. Like mother, like daughter? Did that mean that Red Knot, had she lived, would have tormented some future War Chief with secret and forbidden desires?

''You asked about Red Knot?'' Quick Fawn asked in a fragile voice.

''Yes. I'm sorry. Go on. What happened that night?'' He inclined his head to listen.

''Red Knot told me to meet her after the dance was over. So I came back with Mother and checked on the others. The rest of the family was asleep. Mother was very tired. I think she was asleep as soon as she lay down. I put wood on the fires and left. Red Knot was waiting for me. She was very excited. I thought she'd be exhausted after all the dancing, and sweats, and ceremonies, but she was bouncing up and down.''

''Where was this?''

''Over on the far side of the House of the Dead. In the shadows where the light from the bonfire wouldn't shine on us.''

''And what happened then?''

''I asked her what she was so excited about. She told me she was running off with High Fox. That she was leaving as soon as she could see to find the trail across the ridge. That she'd meet High Fox at Oyster Shell Landing at dawn.''

''Did you think it was a good idea?''

''No!'' She gave him a horrified look. ''What about Copper Thunder? Her responsibility to the clan to marry him? When I asked, Red Knot spat and shook her hands out, like when you have something sticky and loathsome on them. She said that he was uglier than a puffer fish, and she hated him. That if he crawled on top of her, she'd throw up.''

''That bad?''

Quick Fawn gave him a sidelong look, still unsure of herself. ''I'd rather couple with a serpent, myself. He's enough to make your skin prickle.''

Nine Killer raised a warning eyebrow. ''White Otter said you were arguing when she arrived. Was that what you were arguing about?''

Quick Fawn took a deep breath. ''I told Red Knot that she was crazy, that she and High Fox would never get away with it. That the Weroansqua would order you and the warriors to hunt them down. When it was all over she'd still be Copper Thunder's wife. Instead of going to him in triumph, she would go in disgrace, as a prisoner. Elder, I told her the clan would suffer for her actions, that we'd all pay for her foolishness.''

''Cousin, you are beyond your age in wisdom.'' He rubbed the back of his neck to ease the tension. Such foolishness and disobedience. All this trouble because of a young headstrong woman? How had things gone so wrong in Shell Comb's daughter? Of all the freshly made women in the clan, Red Knot should have understood the profound responsibility that was hers.

Quick Fawn shrugged. "She told me I was a foolish child. She said that I'd never understand the path to greatness. And then she told me something that made no sense."

"And that was?"

Quick Fawn frowned, concentrating as if to get the words right. "She said, 'She can cover her tracks with ashes, if she wants. But this mistake is taking her life into her own hands.'"

"What does that mean?"

Quick Fawn shook her head. "I don't know. I've thought about it. 'She' could be the Weroansqua. Red Knot didn't say 'I am taking my life into my own hands.' That would make you think she might have been talking about herself."

"And the ashes?"

"I don't know. Do you? Did you burn something for the Weroansqua?"

Nine Killer shook his head. "No. I mean, nothing out of the ordinary. We've burned longhouses on raids, but not on special orders."

"Is there some adult ritual I don't know about? Some ceremony where tracks are covered with ashes? Maybe something in the *Huskanaw*?"

"No. Nothing like that." He paused. " 'She can cover her tracks with ashes, if she wants. But this mistake is taking her life into her own hands.' That makes no sense. How can a mistake take her life in her own hands?"

"I told you, Elder, I don't know what she meant, but she sounded very serious about it."

"I believe you, cousin. Then what happened?"

"I asked her one last time, pleaded with her not to run off. I started to tell her about her duty again, and she cut me off."

Quick Fawn stared hollowly at the steaming pots. From the vacant look, she was reliving that night. "She got this hurt look in her eyes, Elder. As if she couldn't believe I would be telling her this. 'I thought you'd be happy for me, Quick Fawn,' she said. Then she shook her head. 'But I guess I've misjudged you just like I've misjudged so many others.' "

Quick Fawn wiped her hand under her nose. "I said I wanted her to be happy, but that there were things we all had to do. That for her, as part of the Weroansqua's family, she had even greater responsibilities than the rest of us."

"That is true," Nine Killer replied. "Everything comes with a price, cousin. Especially authority."

" 'I could tell you about responsibility in the Weroansqua's family,' she said. 'But I won't rob you of your precious illusions.' She laughed then, mocking me. She said, 'You're so pitiful! Go ahead. Be a slave to them for the rest of your life.' That's when White Otter showed up. She didn't even say anything. She must have heard the tone in Red Knot's voice. White Otter just turned around and walked off."

"And then Red Knot left?"

Quick Fawn swallowed hard. "Red Knot said, 'There goes another fool. Marry her to that monster—or marry him yourself, but promise me one thing.' I said I would."

"And what was that?"

"She said, 'Don't tell anyone I've gone. They'll find out soon enough.' " Quick Fawn wrapped her string around her fist, pulling the fiber tight enough to stretch her smooth skin. "I just nodded and turned around to leave. I went halfway back to the longhouse and stopped. I couldn't just let her go. I had to go back and tell her that I'd go to the Weroansqua if I had to. Anything to stop her.''

Nine Killer heard the reservation in her voice. ''Then, why didn't you tell someone she was going? As a clanswoman, you could have come to me.''

''I would have awakened Mother and told her first. She could have taken it to you, or the Weroansqua.'' She looked up, expression anguished. ''Red Knot would hate me for the rest of my life. But I couldn't let her leave, let her disgrace our clan that way. We'd all have to pay. It wasn't right to do that to the Greenstone clan, to her mother, and the Weroansqua.'' Quick Fawn took a breath. ''But then I didn't have to. I thought the man and woman would tell on her instead.''

''Man and woman? What man and woman? Did you see someone else out there?''

Quick Fawn nodded. ''I cut across behind the House of the Dead this time, thinking I'd catch Red Knot on the way to get her things.'' Quick Fawn twisted the loop of string into a knot. ''They didn't hear me coming. They had been in the shadows behind the House of the Dead, just around the curve of the wall from where we'd been standing. I could see them silhouetted against the firelight reflecting on the palisade. They were standing up, arguing in whispers.''

''Could you tell who they were?''

Quick Fawn shook her head. ''They were like shadow figures against the light, and I was too far away. You know how long the House of the Dead is? I had just come around the corner.''

''But you know it was a man and woman?''

Quick Fawn gave him a knowing smile. ''They were naked when they first stood up. They were grabbing for clothes, you know, like people do when they've been surprised, but not caught.''

''Did they say anything?''

"Nothing I could understand. I know they were arguing. I could tell from the hissing sound of the whispers. And then the man grabbed the woman's arm, as if trying to restrain her. She jerked it away and said something really terrible to him. He flinched, and just stood there. I've seen prisoners stand that way when your war parties bring them in. He looked defeated."

Nine Killer narrowed his eyes and pulled at his ear. "Do you think they were close enough to hear you and Red Knot?"

Quick Fawn nodded and gave him a guilty look. "That's why I didn't tell Mother. The woman pulled on her clothing. She kicked at the blankets on the ground. Kicked the way she would if she were angry. Then she gave the man one last look. She had that resolute kind of stance, one foot forward, fists clenched. I guess you'd say defiant. Then she turned and walked purposely away. I thought she was going to the Weroansqua's to tell on Red Knot. If she did, I didn't have to break my promise. Red Knot wouldn't have hated me for the rest of my life for betraying her."

"And the man?"

"He just stood there, his head hanging." Quick Fawn took a deep breath. "I sneaked back the way I'd come. I didn't want anyone to see me. It was almost dawn."

Quick Fawn lowered her head again, staring aimlessly at her hands.

A man and a woman, loving each other behind the House of the Dead? But who? "Quick Fawn, what about their hair? Was the man's head roached like the Great Tayac's, or his warriors'?"

"No, Elder. His hair was like our men wear. It wasn't one of the Great Tayac's warriors."

Nine Killer cocked his head. "What if . . . Quick Fawn, do you think it could have been Flat Willow?"

"Flat Willow?" She gave him a puzzled look.

"Could it have been him?"

She considered the idea, then lifted her hands. "I can't say, Elder. It was dark. All I saw was a naked man's shadow. I didn't see him get dressed, so I couldn't say if he had any distinctive clothing."

Nine Killer watched the steam rising from the cooking pots. Flat Willow was supposed to be on guard that night, and White Otter thought she saw him leave with Copper Thunder. Could Flat Willow have just done his job at the gate? Identified the Great Tayac, escorted him out beyond the palisade, perhaps to relieve himself, and then left his post to meet the woman?

"Elder," Quick Fawn whispered. "It's my fault. If I had told, she'd be alive today."

"Cousin," Nine Killer said gently, "when we are faced with a decision, we do what we think we must. It is only after we have acted that we learn if it was the right choice or not. Maybe if you'd told your mother, Red Knot would be alive today, and married to Copper Thunder. Maybe Flat Willow would have told the Weroansqua about High Fox coupling with her, and I'd have had to kill him. Who knows? We do what we think we must, but all decisions are gambles."

She said nothing, her mouth in a pouting frown.

Nine Killer indicated the steaming pots. "You've helped me, but I think you'd better see to the food or your mother's going to skin you."

Quick Fawn turned her attention to the cooking pots, stirring the stew with a stick so that it wouldn't burn. She checked the steaming tuckahoe, and prodded it to see if it was done.

The man and woman coupling there in the darkness had surely overheard Quick Fawn and Red Knot, but had that led to the girl's murder? The village had been full of visitors who had come to celebrate Red Knot's ascension to womanhood. Sometimes a man and woman came together in such circumstances, coupled, and parted ways.

Quick Fawn kept giving him nervous glances as she added water to one of the cooking pots, then steered another closer to the coals.

"Why did they stay?"

"Elder?"

Nine Killer cocked a quizzical eyebrow. "If a couple were disturbed while they were locked together, you'd think they'd just move to a more secluded spot."

"Or call out and ask us to leave," she said. "That's considered polite."

Yellow Net picked that moment to duck through the doorway, her suspicious gaze on Nine Killer. She stopped short, standing there as if he had intruded too long into her domain.

"I should be going. Thank you for your help, Quick Fawn."

She hesitated, fumbling with one of the pots. "Elder, am I in trouble?"

"Only with yourself, Quick Fawn." He stood. "You are the one who must decide if what you did was right or wrong. What do you think?"

She pursed her lips and nodded. "I know."

Nine Killer smiled down at her. "If you think of anything else, please, come and tell me. It might be very important."

With that he walked to the doorway, and nodded at Yellow Net. She replied with a blank stare, and he stepped out into the snow.

Sitting across from Nine Killer, Panther puffed contentedly on his pipe, his belly full, and the stripped bones of a large rockfish filling his wooden plate.

The fire in Rosebud's longhouse was particularly warm on this frozen winter night. Outside, the sky had cleared and the cold had intensified. In the rear of the longhouse, White Otter laughed with her siblings as they played a gambling game with reeds, alternately betting nutshells, and casting the reeds upon the ground. A total of eighty-one short reeds were tucked into a bundle and tossed on the hard-packed dirt so that they bounced and scattered. The object was to grab as quickly as possible and pluck up either seven or eleven reeds. The player who won added to his cache of nutshells.

Rosebud bent over one of the sleeping benches and fished a hoe from beneath it. She then collected a deer's scapula, some sinew, and a shark's tooth, and walked over and settled herself across from Nine Killer and Panther. She laid out her materials and, with the shark's tooth, began sawing off the old clamshell that had been bound to the bottom of her hoe handle. "Solstice is coming," she said reflectively. "It's time to start fixing up the tools. In three moons, I'll have wished I'd done this now." She pointed to the blunt clamshell; its rounded edge battered and chipped. "This one won't cut air anymore, let alone soil."

Sun Conch entered, a blanket around her shoulders. "Cold out there," she said, puffing as she stepped across the floor and settled next to Panther, holding her hands out to the fire. At sight of the hoe, she said, "Preparing fields is at least three moons away."

"Well, Rosebud isn't one to let things slide to the last moment." Panther watched Rosebud saw at the gritty sinew binding that held her hoe together. He took a puff on his pipe and flipped the fish skeleton to the prowling dogs that waited patiently behind him. Then he placed the wooden plate where they could lick it clean of the last grease.

Nine Killer cast him an appraising look. "This life

seems to fit you, Elder. Your belly isn't the gaunt cave it was when you first came here.''

Panther smiled and took his pipe from his mouth. ''I must admit, War Chief, I've come to like your household. I'd hate to make a habit of it. It might become hard to leave.''

Rosebud gave him an amused glance as she worked. ''Surely we're not as entertaining as sitting around alone on that island of yours. Don't you miss your crows and seagulls?''

Panther sighed, all too aware of the warm glow in his soul. Fellowship was like a drug, it left a man wanting more. ''As contented as I am to stay here and eat your food, I'll be going when we bring this to a conclusion.''

''If Copper Thunder doesn't kill you first,'' Sun Conch remarked. ''Honestly, Elder, you wear my nerves thin sometimes.''

Nine Killer raised his head. ''Copper Thunder threatened to kill you?''

''As I have said before: It is an old thing between us.''

Rosebud severed the last of the bindings, freeing the clamshell from its handle. ''Tell me, you three, what *have* you accomplished? Hmm? Are you any closer to finding Red Knot's murderer? The entire village is abuzz with this rumor and that. It's become bothersome for me to walk across the plaza with all the pestering questions.''

''And what do you tell them, sister?'' Nine Killer asked.

''That they'll hear anything from the Weroansqua, if it's to be heard.'' Rosebud placed the joint end of the scapula against the handle bottom, trying to find the best fit.

''So, what do we know?'' Nine Killer tapped the dottle out of his pipe and pinched freshly chopped leaves from the little bowl beside him. ''High Fox asked Red Knot to leave. They'd been lovers for at least six moons. Red

Knot said she'd meet him at Oyster Shell Landing. She couldn't just pack up and run off; she had to tell Quick Fawn. At the same time, White Otter sees Copper Thunder and Flat Willow in a furtive conversation; then they both step out beyond the palisade. Quick Fawn pleads for Red Knot to stay, but is turned down. The argument is strained enough that White Otter won't even join the conversation, but retreats. Quick Fawn starts home but has second thoughts and tries to head off Red Knot, only to discover a man and woman in the shadows. They've had their lovemaking interrupted by the girls, and they've overheard everything."

Nine Killer lit his pipe with a twig and puffed to set the fire. "We don't know who the man and woman are, but he tries to grab her arm. She jerks it away. They have heated words. She kicks at the blankets still on the ground, gets dressed, and storms off. We don't know what happens to him."

"Meanwhile," Panther said, "Flat Willow is not at the gate. He isn't seen again until midmorning when High Fox comes charging down the trail. Flat Willow then goes on to 'discover' Red Knot's body. Meanwhile, White Otter sees Copper Thunder reenter the palisade in the early morning. Where has he been all that time?

Rosebud added, "And the Weroansqua wasn't present that morning for breakfast. Where was she?"

Panther lifted a shaggy eyebrow. "Where indeed?"

"I just don't see why she would have killed her granddaughter."

"Maybe her mother wanted her dead?"

"Shell Comb?" Nine Killer's face tightened with distaste. "No, I can't believe that. Why would she kill her own daughter? Or, better asked, *how* could she kill her own daughter? Surely not just to marry Copper Thunder."

"You tell me, War Chief. Had Shell Comb wanted to

marry him in the beginning, could she? Is she that driven by a hunger for authority?''

''No, Elder. I mean, she may indeed be a driven woman when it comes to her passions—Okeus knows—but it doesn't make sense. If she wanted him, she could have stepped in at any time and married him. Red Knot would have shouted with relief. I have already thought this through, and there is simply no reason why Shell Comb would kill—or have the girl killed. In the beginning, we might have suspected that she would want to stop the alliance with the upriver villages, but now she's practically offering herself to save it.''

''Shame?'' Panther asked. ''She couldn't stomach the thought of her daughter running out on her people?''

Nine Killer arched an eyebrow. ''Believe me, Shell Comb isn't one to make a great deal about a little sexual indiscretion now and then. If anything, she'd be secretly gleeful that her daughter had the nerve to try it.''

''So I gather,'' Panther said dryly. ''She's quite the adventuress, isn't she?''

Nine Killer dropped his gaze, aware that Rosebud was giving him a hard eye. ''For a mother to kill her daughter takes a great deal of desperation and resolve. No matter what her indiscretions, she had too many ways to either avoid or have Copper Thunder. In the end, she doesn't have a reason. That pot doesn't hold water.''

''And the Weroansqua?'' Panther asked mildly. ''Was she so desperate that she could see no way out?''

''Not that I can determine. Elder, we can't forget Winged Blackbird and his warriors,'' Nine Killer pointed out. ''Did he just happen to show up at that moment?''

Panther shrugged. ''It's too early to tell. Collusion with Copper Thunder? Is that what you're thinking?''

Nine Killer watched blue smoke rise before his nose. ''Am I? Is it a possibility? He said Corn Hunter had sent him with a message to express his displeasure about Red

Knot marrying the Great Tayac. Was that a ruse?''

Panther scratched his ear. "I don't know for sure, but I think not. My guess is that Copper Thunder is desperate for this alliance with the Independent villages. When Red Knot turned up dead, he stayed on, waiting to see what happened, ready to step in and exploit any opportunity that developed. He's clever, but not deep. Rather than manipulate others, he pounces on chance events and turns them to his favor on the spot."

"Then why allow the Weroansqua to send me off on that raid? It almost ended in disaster." Nine Killer stared at the red embers in his pipe.

"Suppose you'd succeeded?" Panther countered. "You didn't expect Stone Cob to betray your plans. Without that, you might very well have succeeded in snatching the boy. Now, as I know your Copper Thunder, I'm willing to bet he'd have pleaded for the boy's life. What better way to cement himself with the Independent villages than as a peacemaker? He cared not a whit for Red Knot once she was dead, but as an aggrieved party, he could demand a settlement, smooth over the friction between Flat Pearl Village and Three Myrtle. Once that was done, and Hunting Hawk was eternally grateful, together they would search the clan for a marriageable woman."

"So he gets Shell Comb instead," Nine Killer groused. "And, thereby, he's a generation closer to control of Flat Pearl Village."

"Oh, to be sure, he's not only allied by marriage, but his status among the villages would almost be equal to the Weroansqua's. After all, he solved a problem that would have meant disaster." Panther chuckled. "I think by now, War Chief, Copper Thunder knows the situation within Flat Pearl Village better than you do. You have a cunning spider in your midst, and he's privy to your innermost secrets."

"And how would he know that?"

"From Flat Willow. Copper Thunder can smell out the weakest wall in the pot, and that's where he's going to start chiseling away. Flat Willow is not only disaffected, but disgruntled on top of it all."

"But wait," Sun Conch interrupted. "Flat Willow wanted Red Knot. He loved her—and hated High Fox for mating with her. Why should he help Copper Thunder with anything? The man was promised the very woman Flat Willow loved!"

"I wouldn't put it past Copper Thunder to have told Flat Willow that he could eventually have her." Panther smiled warily. "Remember, he's been telling the young people that there will be new territory after he drives the Mamanatowick back. If—and I admit it's a big if— Copper Thunder wanted to gain Flat Willow's support, he could have suggested that our young hunter might become a Weroance under the Great Tayac. A High Chief often marries a wife off to a Weroance as a measure of his faith, and to cement an alliance. Sun Conch, you know Flat Willow best, what would he have said to being a Weroance, and having Red Knot? Two birds in one bag?"

Sun Conch grimaced. "He'd have jumped at it! But, would Copper Thunder really have done that? Given him those things? What about the alliance to Greenstone Clan?"

"Oh, not right away." Panther stared dismally at his pipe. The embers had gone cold. "After all, Copper Thunder would want several children out of her first. By then, he would have added at least a second Greenstone wife, and probably one apiece from Star Crab and Bloodroot clans to solidify his hold on the Independent villages."

"If he kept Flat Willow around for that long." Nine Killer shook his head in disgust. "That would depend on how useful he was over the long term, wouldn't it?''

"Indeed it would.''

Nine Killer took a deep breath. ''Well, that kills my idea that Flat Willow might have been the man who overheard Red Knot and Quick Fawn that night.''

Panther used a twig to dig the ash out of his pipe. ''But it does explain what Flat Willow and Copper Thunder were doing after White Otter saw them slip out at night and before their return in the morning. In all the days of feasting and dancing, Copper Thunder would have been watching for a loner, someone who seemed unhappy with his lot in life. Your Great Tayac doesn't miss much. He is an excellent judge of people. My guess is that he would have measured Flat Willow down to the moccasin bottoms—even the desire in his eyes when the hunter was watching Red Knot at the dance.''

"What made you suspect Flat Willow?'' Sun Conch asked suddenly.

Panther lifted a shoulder. ''His attitude when I first talked to him. That, and the fact that he has cut his hair to resemble Copper Thunder's. He's so blinded by the Great Tayac that he can't see himself.'' Panther hesitated. ''And, he knows something, or at least suspects something, very disturbing about Greenstone Clan.'' Panther lifted an eyebrow. ''Anything you'd like to tell me before I discover it on my own?''

Nine Killer frowned, a mystified look in his eyes. ''Nothing beyond the usual family scandals. We're nothing special. Every now and then we have a man beating his wife for a sexual indiscretion. There was one petty thief that the Weroansqua had me execute a while back. We broke his legs and threw him on the bonfire. Last year, old Green Stick started nosing around his oldest daughter and we had to take him out in the forest for a little discussion. Since then, he's behaved himself. We keep a close eye on him to make sure. The *only* thing that could destroy Greenstone Clan would be a charge of incest.'' Nine Killer glanced toward the back of the long-house and the reed game. ''I have a niece who slips out every so often, but I think I've taken care of that.''

Rosebud had bent her head so that her hair spilled around her face, all of her concentration on the length of sinew she used to bind the scapula to the hoe handle.

Sun Conch sat with her eyes downcast, her fingers moving anxiously in her lap.

Despite the honesty reflected in Nine Killer's eyes, Panther sensed the unease among the others. Was there something, or wasn't there? If so, Nine Killer genuinely didn't seem to know.

Or is he finally lying to you? And, if so, why?

Panther sighed. Well, all in good time. ''That still leaves us with a dead Red Knot. Struck down on the ridge trail to Oyster Shell Landing with a double-headed war club.''

''So who does that leave?'' Sun Conch asked, as if relieved by the change of topic. ''We've just scratched Flat Willow from the possibles. Assuming, that is, that you're right about his deal with Copper Thunder. He wouldn't kill the girl, not after Copper Thunder's offer.''

''There's High Fox,'' Nine Killer said stubbornly. ''He still has the means, reason, and opportunity. Maybe Red Knot changed her mind at the last minute. Maybe Quick Fawn's arguments made her feel guilty as she ran up the trail?''

''And maybe,'' Sun Conch said, her spine stiffening, ''Copper Thunder killed her after all.''

''How's that?'' Panther asked. ''We're pretty sure he offered her as bait to Flat Willow.''

''Elder,'' Sun Conch said, ''Copper Thunder was out there, remember? Maybe he saw her leave, followed her, figured out that she was deserting him. You know him, Elder, better than any of us. You saw that rage in his eyes. His alliance with Greenstone was running off to meet some callow youth. His deal with Flat Willow was about to paddle off to who knew where? That was a slap to his pride and manhood. How do you think he'd react?"

Panther stared absently at the fire. "I must be getting old to have missed that. Blood-streaked bats, he'd have followed her to see what she was up to—and once he'd determined what she was about, he'd have gone into a rage. In that state, he'd have killed her without a thought."

"And," Nine Killer reminded, "his war club has that stone ball on the end and a copper spike just below it. It would have left two dents in the girl's skull."

Waterfall

When I was young, I used to sit at the base of a waterfall on the Black Warrior River, just to watch the misty halo gleam. The water had climbed as high as it could, and lingered in sparkling glory.

Like my life, that halo was a place of eternal suspension.

And how I prized that!

Floating above was so much easier, and cleaner. Though the water was in fact blood, I could not see it. Those were not bones grating beneath my feet, but rocks. Not cries I heard, but wind in the trees. I couldn't see anything . . . except myself haloed in glory.

I took great care to sustain that halo, so that I could hide in the blinding brilliance.

I had to witness many Comings of the Leaves—oh, let me see, perhaps five tens and five—before I realized that the Suspended Life was neither.

No matter how I tried, I couldn't stay aloft. That brilliant sparkling halo was cut from nothingness. It blinded me to the fact that I stood nowhere. I had no place to stand. In my entire life, I had never built anything solid or lasting.

If I had only known. Blessed gods, I wish I could have seen myself for what I was.

Empty. Utterly and completely.

I did live suspended. For a few brief Comings of the Leaves.

But when I fell, the sparkling halo became a whirlpool of tiny glinting knives. Spinning and murderously beautiful, it cut me to pieces.

And I'm still falling.

And afraid, terribly afraid, that I lived suspended for so long, there may be no bottom. Not for me.

My sentence may be to fall forever, my soul evaporating as I tumble through the emptiness. Watching things go by. Reaching out. Never able to touch, or hold.

. . . Or close my eyes.

Twenty-six

Hunting Hawk mused on a great many things as she sat before her warming fire. Around her and her family, the slaves collected dishes. The meal that night had been the last of Nine Killer and Many Dogs' catch of fresh fish. A big pot of hominy, now half-empty, still steamed by the side of the fire.

For herself, Hunting Hawk had concentrated on the clams, collected by Yellow Net's family and steamed in a fold of damp cloth. Midwinter's extremely low tides exposed mud banks hidden through the rest of the year. People and gulls scavenged this virgin territory by day, raccoons by night.

Hunting Hawk's old dog lay by her side, allowing her the privilege of scratching her silky ears. The bitch made snuffling sounds through her gray muzzle, and her fat tail thumped the mat; a particularly sensitive spot had fallen under Hunting Hawk's arthritic fingers.

Across the fire, Copper Thunder glared into the coals; the red light emphasized his forked eye tattoos, the spider gorget, and the gaudy copper necklaces. Since his meeting with The Panther, a sullen anger had hung around him like a black mist.

Fascinating, Hunting Hawk told herself. *A most interesting exchange.* So much had come clear. Here, in her village, two old enemies, like circling spiders, were spinning out their final conflict. Somehow, Red Knot's death had become the focal point for both of them.

And for me, Hunting Hawk reminded herself. What had once been a desperate, risk-filled gamble had now grown into something more. Not just for the future of her clan and the Independent villages, but for the entire Eastern Shore of the Salt Water Bay. When that blow landed on Red Knot's head, a flood of events had been unleashed, a torrent cascading down upon them.

Hunting Hawk sucked at her few stubby front teeth. *Okeus, tell me, did I do the right thing?*

She let her gaze travel around the warm room. Shell Comb—perpetual problem that she was—sat to the right of Copper Thunder. With a bone awl, she poked holes into a deerhide apron. As each set of holes punctured the supple leather, she used a stingray spine needle to sew on a tubular blue bead. Cut from quahog clamshell, these were the very valuable beads her people called *peak*. The number of them that Shell Comb now sewed on the apron was worth a clan's ransom.

Yellow Net was directing Quick Fawn as she laid out the bedding for the guests. As Hunting Hawk watched Yellow Net work, she couldn't help but notice the woman's concise action, the way she composed each thought before she implemented it. Young Quick Fawn had inherited that same sense of deliberate competence. Perhaps it was in the blood, passed from mother to daughter. But, then, what had happened between her and Shell Comb? How could Shell Comb have turned out the way she did? In any comparison Hunting Hawk made between her niece and her own daughter, Yellow Net seemed so much more efficient. Yellow Net carried herself with reserve, whereas a wonton abandon had plagued Shell Comb since infancy.

Okeus help us all if I die too quickly and Shell Comb becomes Weroansqua. Hunting Hawk ran aching fingers through the ruff on her dog's neck. She wished her sons had lived. Brown Jaw, her oldest, had had a clever head on his shoulders. He would have made a worthy successor to her, had Stone Frog's Conoy not killed him in a raid. Her second son, Green Clam, had broken his leg in a bad fall. Despite its having been set, evil had entered the leg where the splintered ends protruded through the flesh. Green Clam had lasted almost three moons, the last one punctuated by fevered sweats and chills, his mind wandering in and out of delirium:

Okeus, you have treated me unfairly when it came to my children. Only Shell Comb had lived to follow her, and of Shell Comb's children, only Sea Nettle and Red Knot had survived. Sea Nettle now lived in Duck Creek Village, the farthest west of the Independent villages. Sea Nettle—happily married to the Weroance of Duck Creek—had declared emphatically that she would have nothing to do with her mother or Flat Pearl Village. No communication had passed between them for many Comings of the Leaves.

Of course, information still shuttled back and forth like the very winds. Sea Nettle was nevertheless Greenstone Clan, and she'd borne four children, two of them girls. From the reports, Sea Nettle's offspring were well thought of, responsible, and all potential leaders.

So, should I call Sea Nettle here? See if she would inherit? Hunting Hawk mused distastefully on the question as she watched Shell Comb's eyes straying to Copper Thunder, lingering on his broad shoulders, and the way his muscular thigh jutted to one side.

No! No matter what, I cast the reeds long ago, and I shall bet on what I could grab. Sea Nettle turned her back on me. That was her *decision. I shan't go crawling to her, now.* Curse the girl, anyway. She'd cut the ties with mother, home, and this very Great House. Well, by Okeus, she could live with the consequences!

Her old dog moved uncomfortably, and Hunting Hawk realized she'd knotted her fist in the bitch's hair. In apology, she patted the animal and returned to stroking the soft fur.

She studied Copper Thunder, reading anger in his flashing black eyes. The Panther had unleashed a maelstrom in the Great Tayac's soul, and that brooding fury, in turn, stoked a deep-seated worry in Hunting Hawk.

He's capable of anything. One by one, she considered her options. Were she to order it, Nine Killer would ambush the man and kill him and the handful of warriors left in his retinue. In one fell blow, she'd have solved the problem of Copper Thunder. Next, she could pin Red Knot's murder on the Great Tayac, and fight a sporadic but prolonged war with the upriver villages. To do so would add even more pressure to the alliance than the constant attrition caused by Water Snake and Stone Frog.

The second option was to go ahead and let Copper Thunder kill The Panther. Canny as the old man had been in his manipulation of Copper Thunder, he'd forgotten one important weakness: People thought him a witch. A smart Weroansqua like Hunting Hawk could poison someone's food with mayapple root until they became sick, then reluctantly admit in public that she'd caught the old man casting spells. Mayapple was a tricky poison. She'd have to measure the dosage perfectly. Among the Lenape, a boiled concentrate from the root was the preferred means of suicide. She need not fear repercussions; with a witch, accusation by a Weroansqua was as good as a death order. After they'd executed The Panther, the sick person would slowly recover and she and Copper Thunder would be vindicated.

She ran the fingertips of her other hand along the angle of her jaw. *But, do I want to do that?* In all honesty, she rather liked The Panther. Not for some time had anyone dared to look her in the eye with the same audacity he did. That, for some odd reason, refreshed and entertained her.

At the sound of giggling, Hunting Hawk scowled at Quick Fawn. Yellow Net had turned to the Great House slaves, directing them to see to the hominy pot in the next room. White Otter had entered, back bent under a corn husk basket brimful of shelled corn. Now she and Quick Fawn were giggling nervously next to the room divider and casting uneasy glances at Copper Thunder. What silly grouse young girls were.

Hunting Hawk turned her thoughts back to the problem at hand. Her third option was to marry Shell Comb to Copper Thunder. The Panther had been right—and she'd been a fool not to see it. Unlike Hunting Hawk's desperate gamble, Copper Thunder *needed* this alliance. She'd naturally assumed that he'd been hanging around looking for weakness, but in truth—as The Panther had observed—the Great Tayac was an opportunist looking for a way out of his own dilemma.

Thank The Panther for it, her position had strengthened in relationship to the Great Tayac. If she married Shell Comb to the man, she could bargain for a great deal more from the upriver villages and their indispensable trade route to the interior. Concessions could include territorial access, shared resources, and who knew, perhaps even some token tribute.

White Otter and Quick Fawn were still laughing, but had started shoving each other. The action seemed oddly stiff and forced, as if they were putting on a show. But for who? Her? No, they'd know better than that.

White Otter had picked up a section of matting, cavorting around as if it were dancing, and she mimicking its gyrations. In the process, she tipped over a jar of chestnuts, spilling them along the sleeping bench where Copper Thunder's few possessions were stacked.

"Here!" Hunting Hawk finally snapped. "You two stop that silly foolishness!" She gestured at them to desist. "You clean up that mess, and then pick things up around here. Go on, get to work."

"It's the weather," Shell Comb said absently. "The cold is keeping people inside." Her nimble fingers continued driving the bone awl through the leather, the *peak* now forming a pattern of overlapping chevrons.

To Hunting Hawk's satisfaction, the girls looked duly chastened and scrambled to their duty. White Otter rolled the mat into a tube and laid it aside as she bent down to scoop up the spilled chestnuts. Quick Fawn busied herself by picking up the bowls that Copper Thunder's warriors had left scattered around the longhouse.

Hunting Hawk sighed. "Yes, the cold is terrible this year. I don't think I've ever seen such a gray winter. The solstice celebration is almost upon us. The greening of spring won't come a bit too soon for me."

Copper Thunder made a fist, watching the muscles slide and knot under the smooth skin of his forearm. "The time has come for a choice, Weroansqua. I would have been happy to wait for you to consider all options, but I think the old man has forced us to cast the reeds." He raised his hard black eyes to meet hers. "What are you going to do?"

The muscles tightened in Hunting Hawk's rickety back as she met Copper Thunder's challenge. "I will do nothing, Great Tayac, until I know who killed my granddaughter, and why." She raised a placating hand.

His eyes narrowed. "Am I to think that you believe me to be the killer?"

"No, Great Tayac." *Careful, Hunting Hawk. This must be done with the greatest delicacy.* "Were I convinced that you had killed her, you would already be dead." She smiled slyly. "And, since you're alive, I'd say that speaks for itself."

He laughed, the sound bitter. "Thank you for your confidence and reassurance." He shot a quick glance at

Shell Comb. "I will wait . . . but not for long, Weroans-qua. In the meantime, the old man will continue to work his poison into our bodies and souls."

"We've cleaned up," White Otter called, all the while looking as if she'd been caught stealing food from the elderly.

Did I snap at the girl that harshly? Hunting Hawk took a deep breath. The tension was wearing on them all. "All right. Go now, and thank you." She waved her frail old hand to dismiss the girls. Quick Fawn and White Otter scooped up the rolled mat, carrying it between them as they hurried for the doorway.

Copper Thunder rubbed his hands together, the callused skin rasping as his biceps swelled and rolled. "I warn you now that I will not put up with his accusations. Weroansqua, please, think about what he's doing. He has come here on his own to work his evil. What is his purpose? To find the person who murdered Red Knot? I ask you, why? What interest does he have in a girl he never met? Why would he do this? Answer me that."

"I can't."

"No, you can't. And now, I want you to think about this: Raven was a War Chief for one of the most powerful of the Serpent Chiefs, yet, here he is, a broken-down old man, living on an island in the middle of Salt Water Bay. How does a man like Raven become The Panther? What makes an influential War Chief into a reclusive witch?" Copper Thunder gave her a menacing glare. "Don't you wonder about that? About who he really is?"

Hunting Hawk nodded. "I most definitely wonder. But he never seems to slip, to give any indication."

"Well, consider . . . I remember the night he left White Smoke Rising's service. Raven had just returned from a successful raid. He and his warriors had delivered his captives to White Smoke Rising. They had built a pyramid of severed human heads at the foot of the Serpent

Chief's high mound. Copper plate, shell gorgets, brightly colored feathers, strings of pearls, and man-sized statues of the gods, taken from the plundered temples of Sun City, were placed on the chunkey field in the plaza so that all could come and see the terrible strength, authority, and Power of White Smoke Rising and his warriors.''

"Is there truly such wealth among the Serpent Chiefs?'' Shell Comb asked. She had stopped short to hang on his words.

"That, and more.'' Copper Thunder smiled. "The size of their cities would leave you in awe.''

"Go on with your story,'' Hunting Hawk told Copper Thunder, and scowled at Shell Comb. How like the girl to ask about nutshell when the meat was at issue.

Copper Thunder leaned back, hands clasped around his knees. "Raven had been feasting inside of White Smoke Rising's high temple. Something happened between them. I don't know what they argued about that night, but everyone within the high walls could hear their voices, if not their words. From the tone, the fight between them was bitter.

"I was waiting at the gate in the wall that protected Raven's high house. It stood on a mound on the west end of the city, over the Black Warrior River. From there, I could watch as Raven came stalking across the plaza. He paused there at the pyramid of heads. They were stinking, rotten, covered by a black blanket of flies during the day, wiggling with maggots at night, but Raven let out a growl, and climbed atop them. A most frightening whimpering came from his throat as he tossed them, one by one, like heavy pumpkins to thump on the hard ground.

"I watched in horror as he pitched the last one like a perverted chunkey stone. It rolled peculiarly—a man's head not being really round—and finally wobbled off to one side. Then Raven came on a dead run. I hid in the shadows as he climbed the steps three at a time to the top of his house mound. When he came through the gate, I saw his face in the moonlight. Tears streaked his cheeks in silver threads; his expression was horrible—that of a man in agony.''

Copper Thunder stared thoughtfully into the fire, as if seeing that night again.

''And for that you call him a witch?'' Hunting Hawk asked.

Copper Thunder shivered, as if taken by a sudden chill. ''You should have seen him. If ever a man was possessed of evil spirits, that night Raven was.''

''What did he do next?'' Shell Comb asked, her beading forgotten on her lap.

Copper Thunder shook his head. ''I only know what my mother told me. She was in the house. She didn't talk about it after that but for one thing: She said that she kept him from killing himself.'' Copper Thunder's lips twisted. ''An act for which I shall never forgive her.''

Hunting Hawk sucked at her lips. ''Did he ever say what it was that made him so crazy?''

Copper Thunder shrugged. ''I was a frightened boy, I hid. The next morning, he had gone. Vanished. No one ever saw him again. I thought he was long dead until I walked into the War Chief's longhouse and found him there, alive—and as pustulous as ever.''

''Whoever he is, he wasn't born among the Serpent Chiefs,'' Shell Comb gestured with her bone awl. ''He has no accent.''

''No, he's from here,'' Copper Thunder agreed. ''He and Mother used to talk about the clans, the seasons. He was born here.''

''But, what is his clan?'' Shell Comb had a genuinely puzzled look. ''All he will say is that they consider him dead. That he is clanless. Did he ever mention anything to your mother?''

"If he did, she never said anything to me."

"What happened to your mother?" Hunting Hawk asked.

"The man White Smoke Rising appointed to follow Raven as War Chief finally tired of her. Unlike Raven, when he mounted her, she cried out in pain. He beat her head in with a war club." The jaw muscles in Copper Thunder's head knotted.

Hunting Hawk patted her dog, gestured to one of her slaves, and took the woman's hand to rise to her feet. Hunting Hawk swayed on prickling legs, and sighed. "It's late. I'm going back to find my robes. Great Tayac, I must say, it's been an enlightening evening. I will consider your words, and your advice, most carefully."

With that she turned, and hobbled back behind the mat divider. No sooner had she undressed and settled on her sleeping bench than Copper Thunder bellowed, "Someone has taken my war club! Who? Who has done this thing? When I find him, *I will kill him*!"

Nine Killer entered the House of the Dead with the matting-wrapped bundle under his arm. He nodded to The Panther as he passed the outer fire. With uncharacteristic reverence, he touched the Guardians as he passed down the long corridor to the sanctum. He nodded in response to the question in Green Serpent's eyes, and laid the bundle on one of the sleeping platforms.

"So, that's it?" Green Serpent asked from where he bent over Red Knot's bones.

"That's it." Nine Killer took a deep breath, uneasy at the conspiracy he had entered into.

The Panther entered the sanctum, hands clasped expectantly before him. The eternal fire lit the House of the

Dead with a dancing yellow light, the wood popping as if in protest of what they were about to do.

Panther unrolled the matting, lifting the heavy war club from within. He held it up, staring at the polished hardwood with its intricate carving. "I'd never noticed before. It's crafted in Black Warrior style."

"That means something?" Nine Killer asked as he glanced across at the old priest. Green Serpent was singing a prayer song to himself, gently shaking his rattle to appease the ghosts.

The statue of Okeus, illuminated by the jumping flames, seemed to be grinning at them, his shell eyes gleeful. The god's expression was enough to set Nine Killer's teeth on edge. He jumped at each creak when the building reacted to the wind. The scamper of a mouse behind the matting might have been an angry demon stalking ever closer.

Panther raised the war club in the light, his eyes tracing each of its smooth lines. The copper spike reflected a bloody orange. Just moments before, at the entrance to the House of the Dead, Nine Killer had taken the mat-rolled war club from a half-frantic White Otter before she dashed off to her mother's house and well-earned safety.

Nine Killer shivered, aware of the ancestral ghosts staring down at him from the raised gallery where their smoked bodies lay wrapped. Okeus' eyes had a jaundiced sheen now, one that could sicken the soul.

"This pointed kind of stone on the end"—Panther tapped the sharpened tip—"comes from the mountains above the bend of the Serpent River. This stone is traded all through the central region, portaged over the divide and carried down the Black Warrior River. Some is carried down the Serpent River to the Father Water and clear to the coast."

"And the copper?" Nine Killer asked, almost envious

of the thick spike protruding from the heavy beam of the war club.

"From the far north. Up beyond the head of the Father Water. It comes down the rivers, much better metal than what you have in the mountains here. I've seen sheets of it as long as two men's arms, and almost as wide. I knew a chief one time who wanted to be buried in a copper-lined grave. I don't know if he was or not, but that's the kind of wealth the Serpent Chiefs have."

"Amazing," Nine Killer muttered.

"No, War Chief, just a bunch of people like any others. No better, no worse. Save that wonder for the birth of your next child. Now there, my friend, is something truly miraculous."

Nine Killer ran his fingers down the shaft of the war club. "I'll say this, Copper Thunder did good work when he made this."

Panther chuckled. "Copper Thunder? Make something like this? Don't wager your life on it. No, indeed, War Chief, he *stole* this."

"Stole it?"

"But of course. Just like he stole the spider gorget and all of his accouterments. Okeus alone knows who he found to tattoo his face, but it certainly wasn't done in a nobleman's house atop a mound. No matter who he is today, he was a slave among the Serpent Chiefs. And before that, he was the son of a Trader."

"I don't understand."

"Indeed? War Chief, could a slave become a Wero-ance?"

"Of course not! They'd have to be born into the . . . Ah, I see."

Panther's eyes glinted. "Curious, isn't it? A Weroance can always end up a slave, but never can a slave end up as a Weroance."

"Except for Copper Thunder. He seems to have ended up as a Great Tayac."

"True." Panther grasped the heavy war club, extending it, hefting its weight and balance. "Kwiokos, I believe we are ready for you."

Green Serpent raised his voice in the last of his song, the rattle shish-shishing in time to the droning words. Then he faced Okeus and the ancestors, raised his hands, and bowed.

The Spirits appeased, he slipped his rattle into the rope belt at his waist and crossed to the other side of the fire, where Red Knot's bones lay on the matting. Her skin soaked in a pot to one side, the tanning process now under way.

Green Serpent picked up her skull and brought it over to the platform. "Forgive us, Red Knot, but we must see to this. Help us, Red Knot. We seek the man who did this to you. Give us your help in bringing this killer to the punishment he merits."

After Green Serpent set the skull on the platform, Panther lifted the war club, placing the pointed stone tip in one hole, and trying to align the copper spike with the other indentation.

Nine Killer took a deep breath, and used his fingers to steady the war club against the girl's skull. "Let's turn her the other way." He reached out, grasping the skull. The smooth bone was cold, like stone under his warm fingers. As Panther held the war club, Nine Killer tried to fit Red Knot's skull to the two spikes.

Green Serpent raised a mousy white eyebrow. "I would say that it does not fit."

"So would I," Nine Killer agreed. "The distance between the spikes on Copper Thunder's club is too great."

"Yes, it is. And the indentations don't match the shape of the war head." Panther bent close and squinted at the conical stone point set into the war club. "The club that broke Red Knot's skull had a square head.''

"No copper spike made that second hole," Nine Killer added. "The copper spike on the Great Tayac's war club would have jabbed a slit through the bone. Sort of like driving a thin section of shell through a pumpkin. The blow that hit Red Knot crushed rather than punctured.''

Panther sighed and lowered the war club. From the pouch on his belt, he lifted the fragment of broken wood from the murder site, and carefully inspected the war club. The weapon wasn't missing any such chip. "Alas, another trail dead-ends in a thicket." He stared thoughtfully at Red Knot's skull. It grinned back at him in the firelight. The one odd peglike tooth seemed to gleam in the light.

Nine Killer rubbed the back of his neck. "How I would have liked to have those holes match. I would have taken a great deal of pleasure in demonstrating the fit to Copper Thunder.''

"Don't discount him yet," Panther warned. "All we know is that *if* he did kill her, it wasn't with *this* club. That chip we found might match another war club.''

"But you have to admit, he would have preferred to use his own weapon. After all, he carries this one around like some sort of personal totem.''

Panther grunted as he stared at Red Knot's skull. "The answer is here," he said thoughtfully. "She's showing us something. But . . . what?''

Nine Killer gave the skull a skeptical look. "Elder, it's only a skull on a mat.''

"Indeed, War Chief." Panther's eyes went suddenly vacant and he propped himself on the war club's handle. "I've seen a tooth like that.''

"Elder?" Nine Killer bent down to study Red Knot's teeth. Bloodstains darkened the roots, but the teeth had been polished white where they protruded from the bone.

"A thought, War Chief. That's all. Something I must look into."

"Would you care to—"

"No. Not at this time. I want to . . ."

At that moment, shouts rose outside. Nine Killer straightened, hearing a voice call out: *". . . Stole what?"*

"I think the Great Tayac has discovered the loss of his war club." The Panther's lips curled in a catlike smile. "If you will excuse me, I will return his property to him."

"You, Elder? From what I have heard, he already wants to kill you."

"All the more reason for me to take his war club back to him, don't you think? An attempt to, well, smooth turbulent waters?"

"Oh, yes. Isn't that what brews hurricanes?"

"Only at certain times of year, War Chief." And with that Panther nodded his gratitude to Green Serpent, slung the heavy war club over his bony shoulders, and plodded for the door.

The morning dawned brittlely cold, the sky clear. Pink shaded the east as the winter sun beamed through the bare branches above the ridgetop. His breath rising before his face like a fog, Panther walked out past the palisade to look across the fields.

The blackened stumps of the long-dead trees rose like jagged dark teeth from the choppy surface of the field. Weed stems and occasional dead grass—material too fine to collect for fuel—gave the track-pocked snow a tawny hue in places.

Yesterday had been warm enough to melt the top layer of snow, but in the night it had frozen to a resistant crust.

With each step, Panther's moccasins punched through to the soft snow beneath.

Interspersed throughout the fields stood humpbacked longhouses. Frost glittered on the thatch, and thin twists of blue smoke rose from their smoke holes. It didn't take much imagination to believe that magical whales lay hunched in the snowy waves of the field.

Panther saw his quarry stand up from emptying her night water and resettle her dress. He pulled his blanket tighter around his sunken shoulders and fought the urge to shiver in the morning cold.

"Greetings, Shell Comb," he said amiably as he walked up to her. "I'm surprised to see you up so early after all of last night's excitement."

She gave him a skeptical inspection, one fine eyebrow cocked. "Excitement of your doing, Elder." Her lips quirked. "I'd still like to know how you stole Copper Thunder's war club."

"I'll bet he would, too." Panther shrugged, and lowered himself onto the weatherworn stump. When the people opened a new field, they girdled the trees to kill them, then alternately chopped and burned to clear the land. Since the stumps could not be removed, they simply planted around them until they rotted away.

She smiled then, a sparkle in her eyes. "Tell me, did you do that just to goad him? If so, you were successful. He was stamping around cursing all night long. I think, had he the privacy to do so, he would have killed you on the spot."

Panther mocked surprise. "What? He didn't believe me when I said that I found it in old Green Serpent's firewood pile? I would have sworn it was placed there as an offering to Okeus. What better way to honor the crooked god, than with a nice warm bonfire?"

She crossed her arms, exhaling frosty breath. "He hates you, you know. Eventually, he will kill you."

"He might. I'll make it difficult for him." Panther waved the thought away. "Shell Comb, I'm an old man, and, to be honest, if I survive another five winters, it will be a miracle." He rubbed his knees. "These joints don't have the spring they used to. I think a man can feel his time coming."

"How old are you?"

"Too old. Almost seven tens." He smiled wistfully. "Odd, isn't it? Most of our old men are lucky to see four tens of Comings of the Leaves. But then, we have the one or two odd ones like your mother and me, the ones who seem to go on forever."

"Not everyone lives to be called Elder with the reverence due one of your age."

"No indeed." He stared out at the field, pimpled with the little humps of dirt where corn, beans, and squash had been harvested. The three plants did well together, each sharing the soil with the other, mutually satisfied with each other's company. Why couldn't different tribes of people be so considerate? "And some, like young Red Knot, never even come close."

She nodded, lowering her eyes. "Last night, at the Weroansqua's fire, Copper Thunder raised a good point. Why do you care so much?"

"About Red Knot?" He spread his hands wide. "I have my reasons. Besides, I'm a crotchety old man. Most people consider me to be a terrible witch. Since I can't change the way they think, I'll do things my own way, and for my own reasons."

"You lost a daughter once?"

"No. A . . . a good friend. A lover. Someone denied to me."

"I've never lost a lover." She glanced away. "That is one tragedy I've avoided."

He tucked his elbows tight against the chill. "Then, are you going to marry Copper Thunder?"

She shrugged. "At this point, I don't know. In the beginning, I thought it was a good idea, a way to insure the alliance. Now I'm not so sure."

"What's this? Sense from the senseless Shell Comb?"

"Is that how people think of me?"

"Answer that yourself."

She stared out across the field with dull eyes. "They should indeed, Elder. The problem with avoiding responsibility is that in the end, Okeus catches up with you. No matter what, we all pay for our mistakes."

He nodded. Looking back, through time, he could see her, those large dark eyes staring up into his. He could see his hand reaching out, sliding down her glistening raven hair, then following the contour of her cheek. How smooth her skin had been. The ragged hole in his heart yearned for her as it had yearned through his long life.

At Shell Comb's gentle sigh, he looked up. What an attractive woman she was, her hair still black and full, her skin barely lined. Yes, he could see Red Knot in her, a stunning version of Shell Comb, but younger, the bright promise of life not yet tarnished by age and care.

She noticed his attention, asking, "What look is that in your eyes, Elder? Surely not desire?"

"I'm only old, Shell Comb—not dead. You're a striking woman."

She shifted uncomfortably, smiling at the compliment. "You flatter me, Elder. Given your clever mind, I wonder at your purpose."

"I have no purpose. If a man can't admire a beautiful woman—and perhaps wish a little—he'd be better off lying on the platform with the rest of them in the House of the Dead." He hesitated. "Smile for me, Shell Comb. Look me right in the eyes, and give me the biggest, most wonderful smile you can."

She hunched down on her knees, placed her hands on his shoulders, and eye-to-eye gave him her most radiant smile, flashing her perfect white teeth. After a long moment, she added, "There, is that enough for you?" An eyebrow arched. "Or, do you want more?"

He chuckled. "Of course I want more, but I'm also well aware of what age does to a man. No, no, my dear, my time of lying with a woman is over for good and all time. You see, the problem with age is that your parts wear out. The only thing that particular part is good for now is passing night water."

She patted him on the shoulders and straightened. "By Okeus! You know, Elder, I wish you'd seen a few tens of Comings of the Leaves less. I'll bet you and I would have made quite a match." She paused. "You're not Greenstone Clan, are you?"

"No, not Greenstone. Not now, or ever." He glanced up. "Still thinking about running off and sidestepping all this clan business? As I recall, on that very first day, you looked at me with longing. You could still go, you know. Maybe wait until the solstice celebration is over and leave."

"It's too late for that," she said sadly.

"Ah, yes. I forgot, you didn't like the strangeness among the Susquehannocks." He let the sun warm his face. "How long ago was it that you made that journey north?"

"Since then I've seen the leaves come ten and seven times."

"Are the memories still fresh?"

"Oh, yes." She closed her eyes and smiled. "I can see it as if it were yesterday."

He grinned at her. "What did you think of the White Dog ceremony?"

She made a face. "It was a little ridiculous. Just think, a strong nation like the Andaste have to kill a little white dog, and burn his body to send a message to god? How would you feel if you were Okeus, and people sent you a dog for a messenger? It's . . . well, insulting!''

"And it goes on for days."

She nodded. "Maybe they don't have anything else to do, being locked in their longhouses for days on end with nothing but snow everywhere."

"It's the middle of winter. Up in that country, what do you expect?" He paused. "Well, if you think sending a little white dog is ridiculous, what would you send?"

"A person, of course." Shell Comb shrugged. "Isn't that why our ancestors are so cared for in the House of the Dead? Unlike the Andaste, we can speak for ourselves."

"And the Green Corn ceremony? Is that so different from our own, here?"

"Indeed it is, Elder." She used a finger to emphasize her point. "Those silly Andaste, they do the same dance for each ceremony. Always the Feather Dance. No matter what the ceremony—winter, spring, corn-ripening, harvest, or fall. The same thing over and over. I don't think I was ever so bored as during the *Ah-do'-weh*. Speech after monotonous speech. And the masks! False faces, bushy faces, cavorting around like monsters!" She shook her head. "I think we're a great deal smarter. The Spirits come and live inside our Guardian posts. We don't invite them into our bodies." She glanced at him, suddenly uneasy.

"No, Shell Comb, I'm possessed of no other spirit than my own, and it, I must say, is more than I've ever been able to handle." He smiled up at the bright morning sunlight. "I find it curious that no matter how I protest, people insist on believing that a person *wants* to be a witch. I'd no more make that bargain with Power than cut off my right arm."

She fiddled with the corner of her feather cloak. "If you could go back, do anything differently, what would you do, Elder?"

His brow knotted with thought. "Oh, everything, I suppose. Presuming, that is, that I could go back—knowing what I do now—to counsel myself. That's what you mean, isn't it? For, after all, it was passion and inexperience that led us into our mistakes in the first place." He shrugged. "What about you, Shell Comb?"

A terrible pain lurked behind her dark eyes. "If I could change anything, I would have been born as you, Elder."

"Me?"

"Yes, I'd be you. How much better to have lived your life than my own." And with that, she turned on her heel, walking rapidly toward the palisade gate.

He watched her go, the sunlight dancing on her swaying hips and filtering strains of blue out of her shining black hair.

"Ah, beautiful Shell Comb, I begin to understand. You and I, what a pair. Okeus rides on our shoulders—and laughs, and laughs."

Twenty-seven

Nine Killer crossed his arms and cocked his head. He stood beside Panther at the canoe landing. A chilly breeze was blowing in off the water, and Nine Killer pulled his feather cloak tightly about his shoulders. The old man was like a dog sniffing after a rabbit, and the way he was nosing about now, you'd think he was nipping at the rabbit's very tail.

"You understand what you're to do?" The Panther called after Sun Conch. She pushed her canoe farther into the inlet and stepped into the wobbling craft. The vessel cut a narrow V across the undulating surface. The water had darkened in the winter cold. In summer, it grew murky and green for reasons Nine Killer had never understood.

Sun Conch used her paddle to back water. She called, "I'm to find Stone Cob at Three Myrtle Village, and give him the piece of copper the War Chief gave me." Sun Conch lifted the shining piece of metal, and shot them a smile before she dipped her paddle into the water, turning her canoe toward open water. "He's to bring Black Spike and High Fox here, to Flat Pearl Village."

"And if Black Spike doesn't want to come?" Nine Killer called.

"I tell him that The Panther will come to him—this time, at the head of Flat Pearl's warriors."

"Tell him that we will lay this accusation against High Fox to rest!" Panther shouted, hands cupped around his mouth. Then he waved as Sun Conch drove her slim dugout away from shore.

"Lay the accusation against High Fox to rest?" Nine Killer asked softly, glancing sidelong at Panther.

"Oh, that's not a lie, War Chief." Panther smiled crookedly. "One way or another, we will have the truth of it. Even if the boy ends up thrown onto the bonfire with his arms and legs broken, there will be no doubt about his guilt or innocence."

Nine Killer propped his hands on his waist. "I hope you know what you're doing."

"All in good time, War Chief." Panther huddled in his feather cloak. "I will have brought this to its conclusion before the solstice celebration. The pieces have finally begun to fit. Like a big pot dropped on the ground, it takes a while to place each shard in relation to its neighbor. Then, all of a sudden, there it is, the shape of the vessel before it was dropped."

"But it will never hold water again," Nine Killer reminded.

"Of course not," Panther said sadly. "But, then, once the pot was dropped, we knew that, didn't we, War Chief? The world was sundered when that blow splintered Red Knot's skull. Nothing will ever be the same for the people involved. Especially for the murderer."

"You're talking in riddles, Elder." Nine Killer watched Sun Conch round the bend, her canoe obscured by the tree-covered point that stuck out into the inlet.

"Riddles? Not at all." Panther turned. "Come, let us go to your sister's. She was cooking squash when I asked you to join me here."

They turned, picking their way among the overturned canoes. The day had warmed enough that snow was melting, leaving the landing muddy and slick. Nine Killer's moccasins were soaked through, his feet cold.

"I still don't see why you need Black Spike and High Fox." Nine Killer swallowed hard, his keen mind drawing the only conclusion. "Bat dung and gull droppings! You don't mean . . . ?"

Panther made a face, his rubbery skin reddened from the cold. "The youth lied to me, Nine Killer. I promised I'd have his hide if he did; but for that, I could have gone there, to Three Myrtle. I *need* him here. He's the final piece of the pot, you see. The proof, if you will."

Nine Killer grimaced. "I still have trouble believing he killed Red Knot. With everything we've learned, it's got to be someone else. I'd even believe the Weroansqua did it before I'd believe it was High Fox."

"She might want you to. If what I suspect is true, the Weroansqua is going to be a very unhappy woman."

Nine Killer's gut churned. "Stop hinting around and tell me what you suspect, Elder."

Panther stopped short. "Not yet, War Chief. What I suspect will upset a great many people. I'd like to prove it to myself before I decide how I will act on the knowledge.''

''You're not making sense!''

''But I am.'' Panther's kind smile and wounded eyes belied the worst of Nine Killer's fears.

''Elder, I know everything you know. If it's so clear, why don't I see it?''

''Because, my friend, you are blinded by your own truth.'' Panther resumed his journey toward the palisade. ''People see the world as they were taught to see. You have been taught one way, and when you look another, all you see is the patterns as you expect to see them. Like a man looking into the mist. You expect the world to be the same when the mist lifts. Perhaps, War Chief, I don't want to jerk that mist away. I still might be wrong about what's on the other side.''

''That doesn't reassure me.''

''It wasn't supposed to, War Chief.''

They stepped through the palisade and crossed the plaza. The Guardian posts cast long shadows while the sunlight shone on the carved faces. People had already begun placing offerings at their bases in anticipation of the solstice. Solstice was the second most important ceremony the people had, after the greening of the corn in late summer. This was the time when they demonstrated their thanks to First Man for the year past, and implored him to begin his journey northward to bring warmth and life to the world again.

The House of the Dead looked gray today, the bark siding weathered. Nine Killer could almost feel Red Knot's presence through the walls. He could imagine Okeus sitting there in his dark niche, his eyes malignant in the firelight. A shiver traced up his back.

''If this turns out wrong, Elder, what will it mean for the Independent villages? What am I to prepare myself for?''

Panther fingered his sagging chin, his thoughtful gaze on the ground before them. "The worst."

"War with the Great Tayac?" Nine Killer's glance strayed to where some of the young warriors stood to one side, talking to Flat Willow, eyeing his roached hair.

"Don't forget the Mamanatowick. Water Snake is always coiled in his lair, waiting, ready to strike at a moment's notice. And, even if he ignores a sudden opportunity, Stone Frog and his Conoy warriors are lurking in the north."

"Of them all, I'd rather deal with him. He has a longer way to go, and water to cross."

"Unless the fog rolls in—or he moves on a moonlit night."

"There is always that." Nine Killer pulled at the feather cloak that warmed his shoulders. Old man Mockingbird stood before his daughter's longhouse. "Elder, if you will excuse me, there is a man I must talk to. I will join you in Rosebud's house in a bit."

"Go, War Chief. But, be warned, if that squash is as good as last time, you may not find much remaining."

Nine Killer nodded over his shoulder, striding across the plaza. He reached out to touch the Guardian posts as he passed. They watched him with expressionless wooden eyes, as if judging his soul.

Old man Mockingbird was almost as old as Hunting Hawk, his back bowed with age, and his skin like a walnut husk left too long in the sun. In his younger days, he'd been a noted warrior, but now his eyes had gone dim. His thick knees grated so loudly when he walked that people could hear them. Because of the pain, he rarely walked far.

"Greetings, Elder," Nine Killer said as he approached. The old man tilted his wrinkled head, bending a fleshy ear to hear better. His wispy white hair gleamed in the sunlight. A single bluebird feather pierced the thin knot he continued to wear on the left side of his head.

"Who comes?" The old voice was scratchy.

"Nine Killer, Elder. The War Chief."

"Come to call me to battle, did you?" Mockingbird barked a hoarse laugh. "Let me get my bow. But, you know"—he smiled, exposing toothless gums—"I'll be more dangerous to our warriors than the enemy!" He wiped a gnarly finger under his age-swollen nose.

Nine Killer shared the laugh, and said, "I imagine you'll do just fine, Elder. You'll do damage enough."

"Yes, indeed, War Chief." He extended a withered arm. "So long as they are this close, eh?" He patted his sunken biceps. "They'd have to be. I can't shoot much farther than my toes these days."

"Ah, but you did once." Nine Killer crossed his arms as he smiled at the old man. "It is said that in your youth you could draw a more powerful bow than I. I would have liked to shoot against you in those days—just to learn a little humility when you beat me."

Old man Mockingbird nodded, head wobbling on his stringy neck. "Yes, it would have been good." He licked his thin brown lips. "The only shot I ever missed was in battle with the Mamanatowick. I had a clear shot at old Blue Gill. For all the mischief he caused us, I wish I'd skewered his miserable heart that day."

"Well, we'd have all benefited. His son, Water Snake, isn't much better. Was that before or after the boy was born?"

Mockingbird frowned, his face drawn into a strained pattern of wrinkles. "Can't say. After, I think. But, with the old man dead, maybe the little whelp wouldn't have learned some of the tricks he did, eh?"

"Maybe."

Mockingbird smiled up at the sunlight, his faded old eyes looking into the past. "Those were good days. Yes, good days."

Nine Killer let the old man relive his memories for a moment, then asked, "Elder, I have come with a question for you."

"Yes. If I can help."

"Do you remember the morning after Red Knot's dance? White Otter said you were up early, walking around the plaza."

"Huh? Yes. Walking, you say?"

"Very early. You were one of the first ones about."

"Can't sleep well, these days." He sucked his lips and lifted a shoulder. "Age, you know. An old man doesn't sleep so much. And all that noise, the singing and clapping. I got up. Stepped out so that I could get around before the plaza got filled up with people. I don't see so well, you know. Bump into things. Get in the way. I like it quiet."

"Did you see anything?"

"Eh? I just said, I don't see so well."

"I know, Elder. But that was the morning Red Knot was killed. Maybe you learned something that morning. She would have just left the—"

"Ah! Yes, I remember. I was out looking for my cloak. I'd laid it down the night before and went to find it." He grinned happily. "Sometimes I forget things."

"It doesn't take age for that, Elder."

"Huh? No, no, I suppose not."

"Did you find your cloak?"

"Eh? Oh, no. No, it turned out that my niece brought it in the night before. She gave it to me the . . . Let's see, yes, later that day." He nodded seriously. "I did good by her. She was a handful as a youngster. Got that from her father, I think. Old Half Hand, remember him? Married my sister back, oh, let's see, must have been four tens of Comings of the Leaves ago. He's been dead a long time—and a feisty bear of a man he was. Thought I'd have to take a war club to him to teach him manners.

But that girl he gave my sister, she's a good one. Takes good care of me.''

"Tell me about that morning, Elder."

He rubbed a callused hand on his wrinkled neck. The fingernails were long, cracked, and brown. "I hobbled around. Couldn't find the cloak, but it was cold that morning. Not so bad as recently, but my old knees sure gave me a pain. No, didn't find the cloak, but I found a blanket.''

"A blanket? Who did it belong to?"

"Don't know. Thought someone would come for it."

"Where did you find it?"

"Why, over against the side of the House of the Dead. It was just lying there . . . on the ground. I'd have missed it, but whoever left it there just forgot it . . . and it like to tripped me." He shook his head. "Not so nimble on my feet these days, and it wrapped around my foot. Folks ought to have a care for old men like me. We fall over the silliest things, and these knees, they don't forgive much foolishness.''

"What did you do with the blanket?"

"Eh? Oh, why I put around my shoulders. It was a cold morning, you see, and I didn't have my cloak.''

"Over on the far side of the House of the Dead? What were you doing over there?"

"Why, I thought my cloak might have been there."

"And why there, Elder?"

Mockingbird grinned, his timeworn face almost insolent. "It's dark there, you see. And these knees don't work. And during the dancing, there were all these people for me to fall over and get in their way. Even an old bear like me has to make water time to time, and, I tell the truth, War Chief, when you get old, your water don't come as quick and easy as when you're young. Takes me a while to drain the sack. Since that dark shadow was close, I could feel my way along the wall, and leak in private. An old man like me doesn't want these silly kids talking about how long it takes him to pee."

"I see. So you thought maybe you left your cloak there?"

"Well, it falls off my shoulders sometimes."

Nine Killer thought that perhaps there was something to be said for dying young. "About that blanket, Mockingbird. Do you still have it?"

"Eh? Yes, yes. Someone would come asking about it. Being cold that morning, I put it over my shoulders and brought it home. Better to have it in the house, nice and dry, than leave it out for the dogs to mess on."

"Would you mind if I took a look at it?"

"Think it's yours, do you?"

"No, but—"

"You shouldn't leave a nice blanket like that lying around where an old man might pee on it. That, or the dogs might mess on it. Or, if you leave it lying around, put it someplace where an old man like me won't trip over it."

Nine Killer winced. "I—I will, Elder. Forgive me."

The old man bent down, his body crackling, and ducked into the doorway to the longhouse. Nine Killer could hear his knees grating: bone rubbing on bone.

As Nine Killer waited, he looked across the plaza to the tall House of the Dead, and the far wall that lay in shadow when the bonfire cast its light. A great deal had happened back there during Red Knot's last night.

When Mockingbird finally shuffled out of the doorway, he carried a fine deerskin blanket cradled in his hands. The workmanship was exquisite, *peak* sewn onto the leather in intricate design. When Nine Killer took it, and unfolded it, the image of a buck deer glistened in the firelight. A small piece of copper had been sewn to each corner.

"That is yours?" Mockingbird asked.

Nine Killer took a deep breath. "No, Elder." His heart skipped a beat, and he carefully refolded the soft leather. "But I know who it belongs to. I promise you, I will see that it is returned to its rightful owner."

"Eh? Well, good. And, War Chief, you be sure to tell him not to leave things where an old man like me might fall over them. Get to be my age, well, you fall down, you might not get up!" And he chuckled gleefully.

"Yes, thank you, Elder. You've been a great help."

"Good, good. See you at solstice celebration. Wouldn't want First Man to think we've forgotten him."

"Never that." Nine Killer tucked the folded blanket under his arm and turned toward Rosebud's, but the spring had vanished from his step.

To Panther's surprise, Rosebud was walking toward him, a pack on her back. He stopped short, watching her approach. "I thought you were cooking. Preparing for the solstice doings."

She sighed and came to a stop. "Step back, Panther. Unless, that is, you want your precious male soul endangered by woman's blood."

"Ah, I see. The moon has placed its blessing upon you."

Rosebud studied him. "That's a curious way for a man to phrase it."

Panther grinned. "I have to tell you, once, long ago, I was trapped in a canoe with a woman throughout her moon blessing. I was half-dead, weak, and suffering. Through it all, she nursed me, changed her absorbent and wrung the blood out of it, then used that same cloth to wash my fevered head. If ever a man's soul was endangered, it was mine. My weapons were lying in the bottom of the canoe, and she fed me, often with the stain upon her hands. I was on the mend during the last days of her bleeding, and, upon making land, I met a challenger, and killed him, weakened though I'd been.''

"Maybe your soul is possessed and you really are a witch.''

"And maybe there's not much to this silly superstition of locking our women away.'' He crossed his arms.

"And maybe there is.'' Rosebud glanced around, then smiled and winked conspiratorially. "You don't think it's all that terrible, do you, to have three or four days a month to sit and relax, talk with friends, and catch up on little things like beading? Since you're such a knowing sort, so experienced with life, I'll let you know that at times I sincerely look forward to my moon. In fact, not so long from now, I'll make the change—and I'm not looking forward to that at all. Where will I escape to then?''

Panther laughed. "Rosebud, I promise, your secret will be safe with me. I'll see you in a couple of days.''

"Maybe four,'' she called after him. "Sometimes these things take time, and I'm worn out from feeding that belly of yours.''

He looked back. "But the squash *was* cooked, wasn't it?''

"White Otter is finishing it.'' Rosebud waved, and walked toward the menstrual house.

Panther muttered to himself. *White Otter's cooking! For the next four days!* He'd seen women stand up halfway through a meal and quietly excuse themselves—so rapid could be the onset of their cramps and menstruation. More than once, he'd suspected that women just used the excuse to get away. After all this time, it was nice to have Rosebud confirm it.

A good woman, Rosebud. He locked his hands behind his back, slopping across the mud in the plaza. All in all,

Nine Killer's whole family seemed exceptional.

He was comparing different people he'd met from Greenstone Clan—Nine Killer, Yellow Net, White Otter, and Hunting Hawk's brood—when he approached the doorway to the longhouse.

"Elder?"

He turned at the sharp voice, seeing Hunting Hawk hobbling across from her Great House. Her sassafras walking stick was jabbing fretfully at the mud as she tottered purposefully toward him.

"Greetings, Weroansqua. It's a fine day, isn't it? Just warm enough to melt the snow, but not to dry the ground."

"Indeed, and tonight, with the warm air, the mist is going to roll in from the bay again. By morning, I won't be able to see my hand before my face."

"Better that than a north wind," Panther said. "Those blow in some bad storms."

She was close enough now to glare at him. "There's storms enough, and I'm coming to brew another." She pointed with her stick. "Rosebud in there?"

"No. I just passed her on the way to the Women's House. I doubt we'll see her for another couple of days."

"Uhm. Shell Comb, too." Hunting Hawk rubbed her fleshy nose. "Well, step in. You and I need to talk."

"But this is—"

"*My* longhouse. It belongs to Greenstone Clan," she said. "And, *I* am Greenstone Clan. Come and talk. Some things need to be settled between us, or the War Chief can settle them for me."

He stared down into her hostile eyes, shrugged, and ducked inside. It took a moment for his eyes to adjust, and then he stepped over to the main fire. White Otter looked up, noticed who accompanied him, and beat a hasty retreat to the rear of the longhouse.

"Girl?" Hunting Hawk called. "I want you to go and

find something useful to do besides stealing war clubs.'' She pointed at the terrified White Otter with her stick. ''I won't forget that little antic of yours for a long, long time.''

White Otter stood in abject terror, frozen like a trapped deer, eyes glazed, mouth open. Then she burst into flight, plunging through the doorway.

Panther lent Hunting Hawk a hand as she settled herself before the fire. He grunted as he lowered himself and snaked the hot pot of squash from the coals. ''Don't you dare punish those girls.''

''As I suspected. I thought Quick Fawn was in on it.'' Hunting Hawk gave him a scathing look. ''They're *my* girls. Greenstone Clan, both of them. I'll deal with them as I see fit.''

''Well, whatever you're going to do to them, you do it to me first. I sent them after that war club, so you punish me.'' He met her steely stare with one of his own. ''Did you hear? You take it out of my hide! Not theirs.''

''You can bet I will! And I'll deal with the War Chief, too!'' she growled. ''But, before I slice him into fish bait, you're going to tell me what that was all about. Nobody steals from a guest in *my* house! *Nobody!*''

''It's about Red Knot's skull.'' Panther searched around and found a turtle shell bowl. With it, he scooped out some of the pale yellow squash and blew to cool it. ''Want some?''

''No. But let me remind you, you're here to talk, not eat.''

''I can eat and talk. Besides, if you decide to order the War Chief to beat my head in, I want it done on a full stomach.''

''Let's get back to Red Knot's skull.''

Panther continued to blow to cool the squash. Between breaths, he said, ''She was killed with a double-headed club. Not everyone knows that. Only Green Serpent and the priests, Nine Killer, and now, you. Copper Thunder has a two-headed club. We needed to check it against the holes in your granddaughter's head. It didn't fit.''

Hunting Hawk might have been wood, staring at the fire. No expression crossed her face as she considered this new information. Panther could barely see her breathing.

Panther pronounced his squash palatable, and scooped some from the turtle shell bowl to his mouth.

''Who are you?'' Hunting Hawk asked quietly.

''That depends on who you ask. Most people think I'm a witch. That's an oddity I've still to accustom myself to. To others, I'm a withered old man living a hermit's life out on an—''

''*Who* are you?'' She raised her unforgiving eyes. ''I tolerated you in the beginning because you were a way out of a bad situation—and I'd take any escape I could to keep this alliance together. Now, I'm not sure. Before I leave here, I'm going to know if I made a mistake or not.'' She paused. ''Understand?''

Panther sucked squash from his fingers. ''Weroansqua, you and I have seen life from most of its different sides. Two old warriors like us, we can look each other in the eye and know that each will keep some secrets inviolate. I have mine, you have yours. Some things I will not say. Not because I'm being mysterious, but because I've lived as long as you have, and in doing so I've cursed well earned the right to keep some things to myself.''

She grunted. ''And the rest?''

''Ask.''

''Why did you leave White Smoke Rising?''

Panther stopped in midchew, staring into her black eyes. ''You want the truth?''

''Don't act like a simpleminded fool. Why do you think I'm here?''

''All right, here it is: I was sick to the bottom of my

guts. Sick of leading good men and women out to kill other good men and women. Sick of the success. Sick of the dead bodies rotting in the sun. Sick of them crawling with flies as they swelled up and hissed with gas. Sick of returning to that heartless serpent curled up there on his polished red cedar throne. Sick of knowing that he'd never be satisfied, no matter how many villages I captured and burned, or how many slaves I drove back to kneel before him." He glanced up. "Does that make sense to you?"

"I don't know. What difference did it make to you? They weren't your clan, were they?"

Panther licked a bit of squash from his lips with the tip of his tongue. "Weroansqua, do you know one of the things that makes us human?"

"I know many things. Get to the point."

"I've spent a great deal of time watching animals. For the most part, when they kill, it's done cleanly, efficiently, and without the investment of any more emotion than is necessary to get the job done."

"And weasels?" she countered. "Bobcats? Otters? They enjoy it."

"They do, but the killing of small prey is different for them. They flip it around, bat it here and there. That's play, Hunting Hawk. Play that is done with small inoffensive prey that can't hurt them back." He narrowed his eyes, staring at her. "Humans, however, can always hurt back. Of all creatures, we are the only ones who routinely kill our own kind. Not to eat, or for breeding, but for trophies. The other thing we do, the critical thing for me when I left White Smoke Rising, is rather difficult for most people to grasp."

"And that is?"

"Humans, of all animals, have the ability to imagine themselves in their victims' place."

Her flinty gaze didn't change. "So?"

He shrugged. "So, I started to live too much in their skins. When I dreamed at night, it was to see myself through their eyes. I didn't like the way they looked at me, the way they felt about me. Each child's cry was burned into my soul as I stood over the bloody bodies of their dead parents. There was one little girl, a pretty thing, with all of her life ahead of her . . ." He closed his eyes, squeezing them tight, as if to drive the vision from his soul.

Hunting Hawk waited quietly.

Swallowing hard, he said, "Killing is more than just taking a man's life—it's killing dreams, Weroansqua. Hope, love, ambition, and purpose, all are left to rot with the putrid corpses."

"And that little girl?" Hunting Hawk asked, tone softening.

"Who knows? If she's still alive, she's a slave, her eyes dull with despair, her hair matted with filth. She's never had a chance to love a tall young warrior, never gotten to see his eyes shine for her. If she's borne a child, it was one planted in her by a man who used her as a camp bitch. And the child, if it lived, would only have a life like hers to look forward to."

He poked his finger absently into the squash. "What right had I to do those things, take those things from people? Authority makes us arrogant, Weroansqua. I had been arrogant all of my life."

"So, you left it to find humility on an island in the Salt Water Bay?"

He nodded, then scooped out another handful of squash. "It didn't take all that long to fill my soul with angry ghosts, but I fear it will take forever to lay them to rest."

She picked up a stick to prod the fire. "That doesn't explain why you're here. What difference does it make to you if my granddaughter was murdered? What do you get out of this?''

''The chance to forgive myself for being stupid when I was young.'' He savored a mouthful of squash, letting the sweet flavor run over his tongue. ''In light of the things I've seen and done, it didn't amount to much. Not really. The trouble is, when you are young, and in love, it seems like the end of the world. Sun Conch assured me that High Fox didn't kill Red Knot. I could see the desperation in her eyes, and my curiosity was piqued. One youngster had made a mistake. Maybe I could keep another from making a worse mistake. So, here I am.''

''You came to keep a youngster from making a mistake? I'm supposed to believe that's the truth?''

Panther watched her through half-lidded eyes. ''I've generally found that once you give people the truth, they'd have been happier with a stupendous lie. But, yes, that's the truth. Weroansqua, life usually comes full circle. For days before Sun Conch's arrival, my crows had been telling me that something important was going to happen. To this day, I wonder what would have happened if long ago, in my past, I'd had wise counsel whispered into my youthful ear. How different would my life have been?''

''And instead?''

''I was young, passionate, and unjustly thwarted by my clan. I thought I would show them all, pay them back for the wrongs committed against me. Powered by the arrogance of youth, I ran away, searching for a place where my worth would be recognized.'' He smiled wistfully, voice dropping. ''Fool that I was, I swore that one day I would return at the head of a great band of warriors, and then . . . Oh, yes, things would be different.'' He shook his head at the folly of it. ''In the name of Ohona, what fools we are.''

''Who *are* you?'' Her leathery hands tightened on the

stick. "What is your clan? Which village did you come from?"

He sighed and shook his head. "That, I will keep to myself until death, Weroansqua. That youth died a long time ago. I will not bring him back. If it is so important to you, have Nine Killer crack my skull and see if you can pick it out of my bloody brain with your fingernails, but I suspect that even then, I shall retain my secret."

She watched him with narrowed eyes. "And Red Knot's murder?"

He smiled wistfully. "You shall have the truth of it before the solstice. The answer is coming in Sun Conch's canoe, Weroansqua. The last bit of the puzzle is there."

She closed her eyes then, energy gone. Looking at her, Panther could see the hardship of old age, normally kept at bay by her insatiable will. Now she looked withered and sucked dry by the vicissitudes of life.

In a rasping voice, she said, "And, I suppose I'm not going to like the truth then, either, am I?"

"No," he answered gently. "I suppose not."

Twenty-eight

For two days Panther and Nine Killer waited. True to Hunting Hawk's prediction, the fog rolled in from the bay, obscuring the world. Most of the time, Panther lounged by the fire in Rosebud's house. White Otter fed him, and he warmed his old bones in the heat. Her cooking was surprisingly good.

"What is the Weroansqua going to do to Quick Fawn and me?" White Otter asked nervously.

"Not a thing, child," Panther soothed. "She and I worked it out. She understands now that we took the Great Tayac's club for a reason."

"You were very brave, niece," Nine Killer assured her. "I'm not sure I could have mustered that much courage at your age."

She blushed, smiling.

Nine Killer nodded, then cast a worried glance at the Panther. When the fog lifted, and the weather cleared, either Black Spike and High Fox would arrive, or their plans would lie in ruins.

That same night, as Panther and Nine Killer sat at their fire, Hunting Hawk sent one of her servants out into the night on a most important errand.

Hunting Hawk watched her fire snap and pop, the flickers sending yellow light dancing about the room. The cattail and cordgrass matting had a golden glow. Overhead, and on the storage shelves, the shadows darted about, as if the dark spirits wove and dodged in mock battle.

She shifted to ease her old aching hips. The pain was always worse during the spells of damp cold. This winter it would have been unbearable but for The Panther's willow bark remedy. She had people scouring the countryside for every willow they could find.

She rubbed her face, brooding black thoughts within. From the moment Red Knot had set out on her mad scheme to run off with High Fox, Greenstone Clan had been spiraling out of control like a pelican with a broken wing. Now she could sense the dark waves of disaster in restless motion below her.

How do you save it? The thought rolled over and over, blistering her soul with uncertainty.

In her lifetime, she had seen Greenstone Clan rise to ascendancy among the Independent villages. Now, in the last days before her death, would she see the whole of it come undone like an unfired clay pot in the surf?

She looked up when Copper Thunder appeared in the opening of the room divider. "You sent that girl for me, Weroansqua?"

"I did, Great Tayac. Thank you for coming at such short notice, and so late at night." She indicated the mat across the fire. "Sit."

He did, settling with the lithe strength of a puma, his arms draped around his knees. He studied her with curious black eyes, the firelight playing on his tattoos. He might have been wearing a mask, the way the forked eyes and black stripe hid his expression.

"This is all coming to a head," she told him. "Sometime soon, The Panther tells me, Black Spike will arrive with High Fox. When they do, I might find myself in a most uncomfortable position." She looked up, meeting his excited gaze across the fire. "If things begin to come apart, I may have to depend on you."

"And your War Chief?"

Hunting Hawk shrugged. "I'm not sure of his loyalty to me anymore. But this is not the right moment to replace him. That would take time. His men like him. Too many of them would question my action. And, I'm still feeling the sting of the Three Myrtle raid. If we could only raise half of our force to attack an allied village, how many could I hope to call up for an action within Flat Pearl?"

His intent black eyes reminded her of a snake's when a chipmunk hopped ever closer.

."What do I gain?" he finally asked. "My ten warriors and I can remove Nine Killer, and the few who might stand with him, but I need to know what I'm fighting for. What I'll get from this."

She rubbed her wrinkled palms together, and then studied the parchment-brown skin on the backs of her hands. "You'll get your alliance, Great Tayac. I'll give you Shell Comb . . . and Quick Fawn when she comes of age. Two ties, instead of one. Age, and experience, coupled with youth and fertility. Your eastern borders will be stable, and in the spring we can unite to strike southward into the Mamanatowick's territory. That's what you want, isn't it?"

Copper Thunder's lips curled into a smile. "And, I want the old man, too. I take him back to my village when I leave."

"He is yours." She raised her hand. "But not until I say so. Do you understand me? The one thing I will not tolerate is a mistake. There have been too many of those already."

Copper Thunder inclined his head slightly, the smile of satisfaction spreading. "As you wish, Weroansqua." He paused. "When may I speak with Shell Comb?"

"A couple of days, Great Tayac. For the moment, she's in the Women's House, attending to her phase of the moon. Surely, anything you have to say can wait until after she's through there."

"It can." He stood, his muscles rolling under greased skin. "Thank you for your confidence, Weroansqua. You have relieved my mind. Together, I think we shall be unbeatable."

"Sleep well, Great Tayac."

After he'd left, she returned her gaze to the fire, an emptiness in her soul. In a low voice, she asked, "Did you hear all of that?"

Yellow Net stepped out from behind the mat divider

in the rear of the room. "I did, Weroansqua." Her hands were clenched at her sides. "Did you have to promise him my daughter?"

"Would you rather that I gave you to him? Of course I did. He had to know I was serious about the long term. Shell Comb's womb could dry up at any time. Quick Fawn is healthy, young, and about to blossom."

Yellow Net barely managed to control herself, her face on the verge of disgust.

Hunting Hawk lifted an eyebrow. "Easy, cousin. If this works the way we've planned, the Mamanatowick will fall on the upriver villages like an enraged sow bear. The two of them will tear each other apart and buy us breathing space. That's what we agreed to in the beginning, wasn't it?"

"I've begun to question your plans, Weroansqua."

"Do you question that you will be calling yourself Weroansqua before too much longer? That, in itself, should mollify some of your outrage."

"And Shell Comb? She will not contest?"

"No. I won't make the announcement until after she's left with Copper Thunder. Your position is safe. After Copper Thunder and the Mamanatowick are bleeding each other to death we will cancel Quick Fawn's betrothal to secure her succession."

"How do you know that Shell Comb will accept this?"

"I'll walk over to the Women's House after the first light and explain that she's leaving with Copper Thunder. She'll accept that—especially if I stress that it is best for the clan."

"And if the old man spoils these plans of yours? You don't control him, cousin."

Hunting Hawk smiled grimly. "No, but Copper Thunder will serve our purposes, should we need him."

Yellow Net took a deep breath. "Not all of us have

the same passion for authority that you do."

The flames licked along the oak branch, blackening the wood and checking the surface. "Then you had better develop it, cousin. That's what ruling the clan is all about."

"And the callusing of the heart? Does that come first?"

"Generally, yes. A Weroansqua can't afford to feel, Yellow Net. Kill that part of yourself first, and the rest will come easily."

The morning of the third day, the fog broke, stringers of mist rising through the trees and tracing patterns around the longhouses. The entire village was blanketed in the aroma of food cooking in preparation for the solstice ceremonies.

Black Spike, High Fox, Sun Conch, and two canoes of warriors arrived as the sun crested in the sky. Nine Killer had heard the calls of the lookouts, and hurriedly grabbed up his bow, war club, and quiver before sprinting for the palisade gate.

The long black canoes slipped across the water like a chevron as they angled in for the landing. The Weroance had made excellent time.

When he reached the landing, Nine Killer lowered the head of his war club to the sand and braced himself on the handle. Flying Weir appeared beside him and said, "War Chief? The Weroansqua wishes you to conduct the Weroance to her Great House. There, she will feed him and entertain him as is his due before you and The Panther talk to him."

"Very well. In the meantime, send out two scouts to keep an eye on the approaches to the village. If this turns bad, we don't want Black Spike's people to ambush us from the rear.''

"Yes, War Chief.'' Flying Weir fled to find his scouts.

As the heavy canoes were dragged onto the beach, people gathered around the palisade gate to watch. They stood silently, faces expressionless, as they watched the Weroance walk forward. He was dressed in a fine cloak of painted bunting feathers that shimmered in the weak sunlight. He carried his war club in his right hand, his wounded left arm still treated tenderly.

Behind him High Fox followed with quick nervous steps. Sun Conch walked to one side, her round face like a mask. Black Spike's warriors walked in ranked files, uneasy gazes measuring their reception.

Nine Killer took a deep breath, a queasy feeling in his gut. He stepped forward, raising one hand in the timeless gesture of friendship. "Greetings, great Weroance. Welcome to Flat Pearl Village. The Weroansqua, Hunting Hawk, matron of the Greenstone Clan, asks you to join her for a feast and to share Flat Pearl Village's hospitality and friendship.''

Black Spike walked up to Nine Killer and looked down into his face. A thousand questions seemed to float behind those black eyes.

Nine Killer willed himself to meet them with neutrality. Indeed, The Panther's trap had yet to be sprung, and there was no telling who they would finally catch in it.

"Lead the way, War Chief.'' Black Spike inclined his head. "The Weroance of Three Myrtle Village and his son and warriors accept the Weroansqua's offer of friendship.'' He glanced at the waiting people, gave them an icy smile, and allowed Nine Killer to lead him past the posts of the gateway. Behind him, his warriors walked in close rank, unsure eyes on the Flat Pearl warriors.

Sun Conch caught Nine Killer's eye, an eyebrow lifted inquiringly. He mouthed the words "House of the

Dead,'' and Sun Conch nodded, breaking off for the tall building.

Nine Killer walked casually across the plaza, a fluttering like hummingbirds in his belly. He could sense the tension, stretching like a length of damp cord until water beaded along its taut threads. How much more stress would it take before the fibers were inexorably pulled apart?

Beside the Weroansqua's Great House stood Copper Thunder, his thick arms crossed on his chest, his ten warriors lined up on each side with their shaved heads and high scalplocks. As their eyes met across the distance, Copper Thunder communicated the insolence of victory. But why? What had he won?

"When will this final truth be made known?" Black Spike asked quietly from his place a step to the rear.

"Tonight. After you have been fed and welcomed. We will present the things we have found, and what they mean. You should have time to return home by solstice."

"My son is innocent?"

"Of that, I can't say," Nine Killer replied. "But our discoveries indicate that he didn't kill the girl."

Black Spike exhaled wearily. "Then my relief is complete. Thank you, War Chief."

Do not thank me yet, Weroance. Nine Killer bit his tongue, maintaining his composure. As a good War Chief should, he ducked through the doorway of the Weroansqua's Great House and shouted, "In the presence of Okeus and the Spirits, the Greenstone Clan bids welcome to the Weroance of Three Myrtle Village. The great Weroansqua, Hunting Hawk, asks Black Spike, of the Bloodroot Clan, to enter and share the hospitality of Flat Pearl Village!"

Black Spike ducked through the doorway and strode across the mat floor toward the main fire. On his heels came High Fox and the warriors. At the fire, Yellow Net waited. She wore a finely tanned deerskin mantle draped about her left shoulder, her right breast bare. Firelight shone on her skin, thickly greased and dyed red with puccoon root. Head held high, she ushered the Weroance back through the mat dividers into the rear of the house, where important guests were received.

At the first fire, Black Spike's warriors seated themselves. They watched with wary black eyes, alert to any hint of treachery. No sooner were they seated than Hunting Hawk's slaves carried cups of steaming tea to them, insuring that each warrior was well treated and made aware of his welcome.

Nine Killer followed the reduced entourage past the dividers to the rear chamber. Here, Hunting Hawk was seated on a raised stump, her closest relatives lining the sleeping benches to the side. Leaping flames cast yellow light throughout, occasional sparks rising toward the smoke hole high overhead.

"Greetings, Black Spike of the Bloodroot Clan," Hunting Hawk called. "We welcome Three Myrtle to our village." Like the Weroance, she, too, wore a feather mantle covered in bright-painted bunting feathers. Hers, however, hung down well below her waist. In her silver hair, she wore a polished copper skewer. She had greased her skin, and antimony sparkled like stars to distract from her wrinkles.

"Greetings, Weroansqua. I journeyed to Flat Pearl Village as soon as weather permitted. Your warm reception of myself, my son, and my warriors is most gracious. I am honored by your kind invitation."

"Oh, not my invitation, Weroance. Rather, it came from The Panther and my War Chief, who claim to have made sense of Red Knot's murder." She lifted a hand, cutting the subject short. "But, enough of that for now. You have come far? There is time to talk of death and killing later. Let us eat and drink. Bring the Weroance and his men food!'' She clapped her hands, and the young girls waiting along the walls sprang to comply. In token of his prestige and status, Black Spike would be served by Greenstone clanswomen.

Black Spike seated himself in the place of honor, High Fox, still cowed, dropping to his place beside him. Black Spike frowned, asking, ''And where is Shell Comb? Surely, I would have expected to see her here.''

''The Women's House, Weroance. But, fear not. Once we lay our problem to rest, I'm sure you will be staying long enough to enjoy our hospitality. It won't take her *that* long to finish her duties to First Woman.''

Black Spike nodded and seemed to relax.

The feast began. Freshly roasted deer backstrap, walnut milk, sweetened pumpkin and squash, baked turkey, duck, and quail were laid before Black Spike and High Fox. Black drink in conch shell bowls was handed to them.

Nine Killer caught Hunting Hawk's eye, nodded, and carefully took his leave. He padded silently through the passageway to the front room, checked to see that all was in order with Black Spike's warriors, and ducked out into the afternoon.

A chill had begun to blow down from the north. As he walked toward the House of the Dead, he could see the first traces of haze. The mist would strengthen again into a full fog. By nightfall, they'd be unable to see their hands before their faces.

''Is he feasting?'' Copper Thunder asked from where he still stood beside the doorway. ''Enjoying Flat Pearl Village's hospitality one last time?''

''One last time?'' Nine Killer missed a step and turned. ''I don't understand your meaning, Great Tayac.''

Copper Thunder made an offhand gesture. ''Oh, I don't mean much of anything. After all, it would have been just as simple to send a messenger, don't you think?

A warrior could just as easily say, 'All is forgiven, Weroance. The culprit is discovered, and all is well again. Forgive our silly mistake in believing your son murdered the girl.' Something like that, don't you think? But bringing him here?'' Copper Thunder shook his head. ''I'd smell a trap and stay far away myself . . . but then, from what I've seen, Black Spike isn't that smart, is he?''

Nine Killer knotted his fists to stem an outburst. ''Are you trying to tell me something?''

Copper Thunder stepped forward, dropping his voice below the hearing of his men. ''Oh, I think you know well enough. And, remember: I was out there that morning. I saw him with my own eyes. That's what you and the old man have finally determined through your sniffing around, isn't it?''

Nine Killer tensed, then bid his tight muscles to relax. ''*You* saw him out there? Doing what?''

''Trotting for the trees just before sunup.''

''And what else?''

''He was carrying something. Maybe a war club.''

''Can you identify the club?'' Nine Killer lifted a mocking eyebrow, challenging.

''The same one he's carrying now. It's his, isn't it? Takes it with him wherever he goes.''

''And what were you doing out there, Great Tayac? It was the last of the night. You should have been asleep by then.''

Copper Thunder smiled thinly. ''A man is often sleepless before his wedding night, War Chief. Or have you forgotten that?''

''I've forgotten a great many things. Now, if you'll excuse me, I've some matters to attend to.''

As Nine Killer turned away, Copper Thunder added, ''If you need help subduing him, my men and I are at your call, War Chief.''

A cold shiver crept down Nine Killer's spine. The way

he'd called him "War Chief" had been filled with derision, as if the man knew something he didn't.

He's fishing, that's all. He didn't know about the war club. It's all a ruse. But knowing that made no difference. Something had gone wrong somewhere; Nine Killer just couldn't be sure where, or what, and now all of their lives might depend on it.

When Nine Killer entered the House of the Dead, Panther was seated in the antechamber. On his lap was the blanket Nine Killer had recovered from old man Mockingbird. The carefully tanned hide was smooth, warm over his stiff knees. Beside him a large basket rested.

Sun Conch crouched over the fire, hands extended to the blaze. Her skin was greased, a mantle over her left shoulder, but mud spattered her feet and calves. She looked up, meeting Nine Killer's hard gaze.

"We couldn't leave before the fog cleared," she said. "And I'm not sure that Black Spike would have, had the fog not been so thick. I think he needed to prove that he was still a Weroance, and not even The Panther could just order him around."

"Foolish pride," Panther growled, and ran his fingers over the patterns of *peak*. He folded the blanket and laid it carefully over the contents of the basket. "Are they all eating and drinking?"

"They are," Nine Killer said darkly.

At his tone, Panther looked up. "Yes, War Chief?"

"Elder, something has changed." Nine Killer crossed to the fire and stared thoughtfully down into the flames. "Copper Thunder just volunteered that he'd seen Black Spike outside the palisade the morning of Red Knot's death. He said that the Weroance was carrying his same war club.''

"He might just as well have come right out and said that Black Spike killed the girl." Panther frowned. "But, why now?''

"He's hunting, Elder. Dangling bait to see what rises to take it."

"Oh?"

"Black Spike's war club has a single knob on the end.''

Panther grunted, jerking his head in a nod. "It matters not, War Chief.''

"Oh? Isn't that one of the things we're missing? A war club with two spikes in it?''

"Not anymore.''

"I don't . . .''

Panther grinned. "All in good time, War Chief. It's safe for the time being. When the moment is right, I'll send for it.''

"Send for it? Elder I don't—''

"Now, why do you think Copper Thunder would be hunting for information at this late date?'' Panther cocked his head, staring uneasily at Nine Killer.

"He's acting too cocky. Something about the way he talked to me, almost insolent.''

"That's Copper Thunder at any time.''

"No, this is more. His tone was insulting.''

Panther took a deep breath. The final piece seemed to teeter in his mind, just ready to fall into place. "So many things have been right before my eyes." He glanced at Sun Conch. "Did Stone Cob arrive? Is the old woman with him?''

"He did, Elder. He arrived a short time ago." Sun Conch nodded, then added, "Stone Cob said he would follow your instructions." She hesitated. "Elder, Stone Cob asked if he would be restored to his position of trust after having faithfully performed this mission.''

"Will he, War Chief?" Panther asked, glancing at Nine Killer.

Nine Killer scowled at the fire, his hands plucking at the edge of his breechclout. "Trust him as my second? How can I? He ran off and warned Three Myrtle Village of my raid. I can't overlook that.''

"Everything for the clan?" Panther asked gently. "Isn't that what we're taught? From the first moment we slide from the womb, covered with tissue, wet, and streaked with blood, it's all for the clan. Everything.''

"Are you trying to tell us something, Panther?" Sun Conch gave him a knowing look.

"Only that the clan can get in the way of being human," Panther answered sadly. "And then, sometimes, the innocent must die to protect the guilty.''

"I don't follow you," Nine Killer said uneasily.

"Tonight," Panther replied, "I'm afraid you will, War Chief. Now, more than ever, I will need you to keep your wits about you. I need you to trust me, and, above all, to think before you act. Do you understand? This must be done as delicately as possible." But that didn't lessen the tension and sorrow in Panther's heart. People remained the same capricious creatures they'd always been.

He could feel Okeus' malicious stare from the shadowed sanctuary. As much as Panther hated to admit it, perhaps the old stories were right, and all people were indeed descended from Okeus' loins.

Panther sighed, clapped his hands to his sides, and said, "Now, if you will excuse me, I must go talk to the old woman. The final tracks on this long and convoluted trail lie there.''

"Elder," Nine Killer asked. "Do you need me to go with you?''

"No, War Chief. Stay here with Sun Conch and the priests. You must guard this basket that Green Serpent has put together for us. Let no one look inside it. No one, you hear? Not even the Weroansqua. Without its contents, we are lost.''

Sun Conch chewed on a cold turkey leg. Even with something in her stomach, she felt queasy. The resolution was coming, one way or another. Panther had returned from Stone Cob's clan longhouse but half-a-hand past. He had refused to speak, his brow furrowed. Nine Killer kept glancing at him uneasily as he gnawed on a hard piece of tuckahoe bread. This night could end in disaster for all of them.

Green Serpent stepped out through the dividing mat and looked around, his face tense and his white eyebrows arched. ''I think all is in readiness, Elder. I have instructed Lightning Cat and Streaked Bear to accompany us.''

''Thank you, Kwiokos.'' Panther gave the priest a friendly smile. ''Your help through all of this has been invaluable.''

Green Serpent's eyes softened. ''You are a good man, Panther. And, yes, I believe I see the finger of Ohona on you, tracing your body with Power. May he be with you tonight.'' He rubbed his fleshy nose. ''Now, if you will excuse me, I must attend to offerings for Okeus . . . that he may allow us to proceed without mishap.''

Green Serpent turned, and disappeared down the narrow passageway, headed for the rear. As he went, he reverently touched each of the Guardians.

''A good man,'' Panther noted.

Nine Killer just nodded, jaws working methodically, lost in his own thoughts.

This waiting will drive me insane. Sun Conch tried not

to fidget. Panther gave her an understanding smile.

Quick Fawn appeared just at dusk, leaning in the doorway of the House of the Dead to announce, "Elder? The Weroansqua requests your presence in the Great House. She says to tell you that she expects an end to be brought to this business."

Panther called out, "Kwiokos? It is time."

Green Serpent emerged from the passageway, his head bowed. As he walked, he shook his large gourd rattle, chanting softly under his breath. Lightning Cat and Streaked Bear followed, looking solemn with their skin freshly greased, and feathers in their hair.

Panther indicated the basket, and Nine Killer picked it up, hefting the light weight. Only a portion of the beaded deer design could be seen.

Sun Conch felt a sense of jubilation and despair as they stepped out from the House of the Dead. The plans had been made, the trap set.

As they walked into the dusk, streamers of mist floated past like wraiths. The wooden Guardian post they passed was damp, flecked with tiny beads of water. In the half-light, Sun Conch looked up at the weathered face. She thought it looked menacing, or maybe fearful.

The chill ate through her greased skin and the single deerhide mantle about her shoulders. This was the night when all would come clear. High Fox would be finally and forever freed of suspicion. She had lived for this, dreamed and longed for it.

Her joy was almost enough to overcome the deep-seated worry about what would happen. No matter the conclusion, important people would be angered and disturbed by the revelations they were about to hear.

She shivered as she followed Panther past the Guardian. The sensation of eyes peering at her from the darkness made the middle of her back itch. Warily she glanced about her, searching the mist. Shapes seemed to move in the darkness. Ghosts, or potential enemies?

Ahead of them, the figures of the priests nearly disappeared in fog. Nine Killer's soft steps could be heard behind her. Stealing a glance, she could see the War Chief, his attention on the basket that filled his arms.

Sun Conch hurried, closing the distance to Panther's vulnerable back. Somewhere a child shrieked, and she could hear the steady drip of water from the thatch. Muted voices carried in the thick air, conversations muffled by the Great House walls.

The mist wavered, and in that instant, Sun Conch saw a furtive figure crouched there in the darkness. He was settled on one knee, the left arm extended, the right pulled back to the cheek. The bent curve of the bow might have been an illusion.

Sun Conch cried, "Panther! *No!*" and leaped for the old man. He cried out when the full force of her body struck him and threw him forward.

Sun Conch felt the cold arrow lance through her upper arm, cut a path along her ribs, and lodge beneath her left breast. Staggering, she knocked The Panther to the ground, and covered his old body with her own. The flesh around the arrow shaft tore, and she screamed raggedly, *"Run!"*

"Sun Conch!" Panther cried. "Sun Conch? What's wrong? What—"

"Run!" she shouted. *"He's trying to kill you!"*

From a great distance, she heard Nine Killer shouting orders, and felt Panther wiggle out from beneath her.

Pain filled her world, engulfing her. All Sun Conch could do was curl on her side and hug the hurt into her soul.

Twenty-nine

Nine Killer paced back and forth, smacking his fist into his callused palm. Rage mixed with futility. He glanced down to watch as Panther used a piece of soaked leather to sponge Sun Conch's brow. Green Serpent sang in the background, his rattle shish-shishing in time to the rising and falling chant.

As his warriors scoured the village for the assailant, Nine Killer had carried the whimpering Sun Conch to Rosebud's longhouse. Panther had been dogging his heels, reaching out with trembling fingers to touch the young woman's arm. Lightning Cat had brought the basket, and now it rested across the fire from them, firelight tracing patterns on its side.

White Otter and the other children gathered around to watch with wide eyes. Flying Weir ducked through the doorway, face grim. At Nine Killer's questioning gaze, he slowly shook his head and said, "Nothing, War Chief. We're searching from house to house, but I can't say what we'll discover. People have been coming and going all night."

"Someone must have seen something."

Flying Weir shrugged. "War Chief, the fog is so thick, we could have run right past her attacker. Even the guard at the gate might not have known if a person slipped past."

"Where were Black Spike's men? Were they all in the Great House?"

Flying Weir frowned. "I—I don't know."

"Find out. And the Great Tayac's men, too. Account for each one." Nine Killer took a deep breath. "You'd better include Flat Willow in that list, too."

Flying Weir jerked a quick nod before ducking out into the night again.

Nine Killer exhaled wearily and shook his head. What had they come to that he could be suspicious of his own people? And worse, what would it mean for them if Flat Willow did indeed turn out to be the culprit?

He knelt beside Panther and inspected Sun Conch's wound. The arrow had entered her body from the left, pinning her arm to her side, then slicing deeply under her breast until the point bulged the skin above her breastbone.

Nine Killer winced, and asked, "What do you think?"

"We'll break off the fletching, cut the skin on her chest, and pull it through." Worry filled Panther's moist brown eyes.

"And then?"

Panther shrugged. "The rest is up to the Spirits and, perhaps, the good graces of Ohona." He studied the wound again. "A poultice will only work on the holes. If infection sets in, it will be difficult to drain." He gently pressed down on her breast, feeling with his fingertips. "Ah, that's a bit of luck. The point didn't break any ribs and I can feel the shaft. It's outside of her ribs. Her lung should be safe."

Nine Killer called, "White Otter, bring me your mother's sewing awls. I need a big one, sharp, maybe that one made from the deer's bone."

White Otter whirled and ran for the rear of the house. Within moments she was back, handing him the bone awl. It had been crafted from the long cannon bone, just up from the hooves. The lower joint had been broken off and the shank sharpened into a needle point.

Meanwhile, Panther used a sharpened clamshell to cut a deep notch in the arrow shaft just ahead of the sinew binding that held the split-feather fletching in place. With a quick snap, he broke the shaft. Sun Conch groaned.

"Easy. Easy, Sun Conch," Nine Killer soothed. The girl's face pinched in agony. "This is going to hurt worse than it's hurt so far. We have to pull the arrow."

"Yes," she gasped. "I know." Her throat worked as she swallowed dryly. "I—I'll try to be brave."

Panther smiled down at her. "You're the bravest woman I know."

Her answering smile was weak, strained against the pain.

"Here, let me." Panther took the awl, frowned at the tip, and said, "I've had a little more practice at this."

"Not much, I'd wager." Nine Killer placed his fingers on Sun Conch's skin, pressing down to stretch it over the point.

Panther steadied himself and used the sharp point to dimple the skin. Spinning the awl, he pierced her skin, then used the sharpened clamshell to open the wound. Clotted with blood, the dark stone point could be seen.

"All right." Panther nodded at Nine Killer. "Push."

Nine Killer sought to still the trembling in his muscles. Over the seasons, he'd done this often. One of the terrible realities of war was dealing with wounds. The worst were the ones where an arrow lanced its way through the guts. Even if the arrow could be withdrawn, the wounded person died within days of evil from the punctured intestines. It wasn't a good way to die.

Thinking of that, he reached down and shoved the exposed shaft. As he did, Panther grasped the bloody stone point and pulled it through in one smooth motion. Sun Conch jerked, and clawed the matting with her good hand.

"There," Panther said, and wiped at the sweat beading

on his brow. He discarded the bloody arrow and pressed down firmly on her breast. "War Chief, massage her arm. We need to press as much of this tainted blood as we can from the wound. If we drain it well, the evil can't establish as strong a hold."

"And if we break the big artery?"

"Since the arrow didn't cut it already, I'd say the chances are good that draining won't."

Nine Killer gently squeezed the muscle, watching as clotted red ran out to pool on the matting at Sun Conch's side. He stopped when the blood ran bright and smooth.

"All right, now put pressure on the holes," Panther directed. "Let's see if we can stop the bleeding."

Nine Killer did, watching as the old man worked on the girl. Panther did seem to have a great deal of practice with such things.

Green Serpent stepped up behind Nine Killer and began to shake his rattle, singing his "warding song" to inform any malicious Spirits that Sun Conch was under his protection. His soft chant seemed to ease Sun Conch, for the young woman lay back, breathing deeply. Her eyes were closed, lips slightly parted.

"What next?" Nine Killer asked.

"I'll need nightshade leaves for a salve and cactus pads—fresh if you have any nearby—and smartweed to make a poultice to slow her bleeding."

"We have these things. But the cactus pads are dried, brought from the dunes." Green Serpent gestured to Streaked Bear, and the stocky priest hurried away. In his haste, he almost bowled over Hunting Hawk as she ducked through the doorway on rickety legs.

She hobbled across the floor to stare down at Sun Conch. "What happened?"

Panther looked up from his bloody hands. "She saved me, Weroansqua." He indicated the bloody arrow on the matting. "That was meant for me. Meant to keep me from speaking tonight. Apparently, someone has been driven to desperation yet again.''

Hunting Hawk braced herself on her walking stick and closed her eyes, head bowed. "Then we should hear the truth of this, witch.''

Panther returned his attention to Sun Conch. In a lowered voice, he said, "I am no witch, Weroansqua. Were I, I'd have sent that arrow right back at the person who shot it at me.''

"Whose arrow is it?" Green Serpent asked. "Those markings, does anyone recognize them?''

Nine Killer nodded, hating to say it. "Yes. It belongs to Flat Willow.''

"Then bring him!" Hunting Hawk snapped. "We shall hear of this!''

"My warriors are already searching for him.'' Nine Killer looked up. "But, Weroansqua, if it was he, we might not want to announce it too loudly.'' With a twitch of his lips, he indicated the direction of the Great House.

She read his meaning in an instant, acknowledgment in the slitting of her eyes.

A scuffle, curses, and grunts could be heard outside, and amid growls, Flat Willow was shoved through the doorway to sprawl unceremoniously on the floor matting. Flying Weir and Many Dogs bulled through after him.

Flat Willow, his breechclout half-ripped from his waist, his roached hair flattened and in disarray, barely scrambled to his feet before the two warriors had him by the shoulders, marching him forward. They stopped two paces back, holding him between them.

"What is the *meaning* of this?" Flat Willow squirmed in their arms, his greased skin slipping in their grasp. A lump was rising on the side of his head, already about to swell his eye closed. Flying Weir had been none too gentle.

Hunting Hawk inspected him as she would a side of

meat. Her gaze stopped at his shaved head with the solitary roach so similar to Copper Thunder's.

Nine Killer could read her expression: *Now we will get to the bottom of this.* No one with sense challenged the Weroansqua when she had that look in her eye.

"That arrow." Hunting Hawk jabbed at it with her walking stick. "It is yours?"

Flat Willow stared at the bloody shaft, bewilderment in his eyes. "Mine?"

"The marks on the arrow," Nine Killer said, "are your identifying marks."

Flat Willow blinked and squinted. Nine Killer saw the fear building in his eyes. "Yes. I think they are. But what is it doing here? What's this all about?"

"That arrow was just pulled out of Sun Conch," Hunting Hawk stated flatly. She lifted her head slightly, as if daring him to deny it.

Flat Willow sagged in the warriors' strong grip. He shook his head miserably. "No, Weroansqua, as Okeus is my witness, I didn't do this thing."

"Then how—"

"I *don't* know!" Flat Willow's face went white, and he licked his lips. "I swear, I don't! I left my arrows at my cousin's! I was in the Great House. Keeping an eye on the Three Myrtle men! I did it just like the Great Tayac asked me to! Ask them, any of them who were there!"

"And how did we find you?" Flying Weir shook him like a dog did a snake. "Standing around in front of the Great House!"

"*I just stepped outside with the others!*" His legs had turned limp so that he dangled in their grasp. "Ask them! Ask . . . them . . ."

"I believe him," Nine Killer said. "Most everyone was in the Great House tonight. But, Flat Willow, could anyone say they were with you the whole time? That you couldn't have slipped away for just long enough to retrieve your weapons and ambush us?''

"I . . . Yes, yes, Crab Spine! Ask Crab Spine! He was sitting beside me the whole time.''

Nine Killer's certainty fled. ''He's a good man. A solid warrior, Weroansqua. If Crab Spine says this is so, then Flat Willow didn't do this thing.'' He paused. ''Many Dogs, go and check with Crab Spine.''

Many Dogs regretfully released his hold on Flat Willow and left as Streaked Bear entered with several decorated leather sacks. He stepped around Flat Willow and handed them to The Panther.

Panther quickly sorted through the medicines, finding what he needed. Placing grease in a bowl, he mixed a weak salve of crushed nightshade leaves, saying, ''Sun Conch, I'm rubbing this on your temples. It will ease the pain, make you sleep better.''

"Thank . . . thank you,'' she whispered.

He applied the green paste using a flattened reed. Then he mixed the crushed smartweed with grease, smeared it on the cactus pads, and tied it over her wounds, insuring that the binding wasn't too tight. That finished, he leaned back and sighed wearily.

"Will she be all right?'' Hunting Hawk asked.

Panther shrugged, expression solemn. ''That is for the future, Weroansqua. For now, all I can tell you is that I have done what I can. If it festers, I will attempt to drain it.''

"What about searing the flesh?'' Green Serpent asked.

"Not an arrow wound like this.'' Panther rubbed his callused hands, trying to scrub the dried blood from them. ''Burning seals the wound. Poisons and evil can't escape.''

Many Dogs ducked through the doorway, a grim look on his face. When all eyes turned to him, he said, ''Crab Spine tells me that Flat Willow was indeed sitting beside him at the time when Sun Conch was shot.''

Nine Killer glared at Flat Willow: "Very well, hunter, you can go. But I don't—"

"*Not* yet, War Chief.'' Hunting Hawk looked like her namesake, a predatory bird, its attention centered on its prey. "Flat Willow, you said you were there at the Great Tayac's will? Watching the Three Myrtle men?"

He nodded, enough overcome with relief to forget his caution. "Yes, Weroansqua. He told me to—"

"You are through!" she snapped. "You will gather your things and be gone. You have no place in this village. *I* am Weroansqua here, and you are under *my* authority. Get your louse-ridden body out of my village. Tonight! And, Flat Willow, if any of my warriors see you in my territory again, they are to kill you for the vermin you are.''

"But, Weroansqua, where will I—"

"I don't care! Maybe the Great Tayac will take you in, eh?" She pointed with her sassafras stick. "Now, be gone! Or I'll have your legs and arms broken, and we'll throw you on the fire!"

"Weroansqua, the Great Tayac—"

"Is the reason you're going to live, boy! But for him, you'd be burning and screaming in half a hand's time!"

Flat Willow squared his shoulders, and headed for the doorway, but his knees were shaking as he ducked out.

Nine Killer picked at the blood that had clotted around his fingernails. "I think that is good riddance.''

Hunting Hawk snorted displeasure. "He wasn't that good a hunter anyway.'' She bent her flinty gaze on Nine Killer. "He's not the only one whose loyalty has become suspect.''

Nine Killer felt a chill filter through his bones. He rose to his feet, stepping over to meet her angry stare. "If you are dissatisfied with me, you may dismiss me at any time, Weroansqua.''

Before the old woman could open her mouth, The Panther said, "That's enough. Strained passions can give voice to bitter words that aren't meant, but can't be recalled." He pulled himself painfully to his feet, wincing at the stiffness in his joints. "Come, I think we should all bring this to a close." He glanced down at Sun Conch with a wounded expression. "Assuming I can make it to the Great House this time, we'll have the truth of it."

Nine Killer looked the Weroansqua in the eyes, and she lowered her gaze, growling to herself as she hobbled for the doorway.

Panther folded his arms across his chest as he seated himself on the bench that lined the Weroansqua's inner chamber, the heart of Greenstone Clan. The room was packed, hot and stifling despite the misty chill outside. The big fire crackled and popped, sending sparks toward the rafters with their hanging baskets.

"I suppose this is it," Nine Killer said. He'd been closemouthed since his hot words with Hunting Hawk.

"Indeed, War Chief." Panther steepled his old fingers, aware that he hadn't been able to scrub Sun Conch's blood away. Half of his soul lingered with her.

All this blood, and every drop of it spilled by youngsters.

Next to Nine Killer sat Green Serpent, and then Lightning Cat with his basket. Streaked Bear stood beside the matting at the far end of the room. Flying Weir hovered nervously by the door, his war club in hand.

On the opposite bench, Black Spike sat, head bowed. High Fox was at his side, his eyes half-wild with anxiety. And well they should be. His life might still be forfeit.

Copper Thunder was next, searching each face like a wolf on a blood trail.

Hunting Hawk glared angrily at everyone from her hide-draped stump at the back. To her right, Shell Comb's place remained conspicuously empty, awaiting her return from the Women's House. To her right sat an expressionless Yellow Net. Next to her, Quick Fawn, clearly uneasy, tried to find something to do with her anxious hands, but ended up just twisting the hem of her deerhide mantle.

Beyond the divider, in the main room, people crowded to hear. No wonder an assailant could steal Flat Willow's arrow. Everyone in the village was packed into the Great House, waiting to hear about Red Knot's killing. The building almost shook from the babble of voices. In fact, Panther could feel the walls trembling as bodies brushed against them.

Hunting Hawk glanced this way and that, then raised her sassafras stick, jabbing at the air. "Silence!" she called. "I want silence!"

Nine Killer stood and bellowed, *"The Weroansqua calls for silence!"*

The din faded into a sudden stillness. Nine Killer glanced around, satisfied that order had been restored, and seated himself.

"All right," Hunting Hawk said, tapping the matting at her feet with the sassafras stick. "As you all know, my granddaughter Red Knot was murdered less than ten days ago. At the time, we thought it was High Fox who did it."

She glared at the young warrior, and he swallowed hard, trying to sink back against the wall.

"It may have been ill advised, but we sent our warriors to bring him back." She turned her attention to Black Spike. "If that was a mistake, I apologize to the Wero-ance, and to Three Myrtle Village. But we had been told that High Fox might have been the killer. Sometimes people lose sense when a relative is senselessly murdered.''

''I understand,'' Black Spike said graciously. And he flashed Hunting Hawk a warm and forgiving smile.

Panther craned his head, staring at Black Spike with unabashed interest. Black Spike noticed, and his smile faded.

Hunting Hawk continued, ''It so happened that the man known as The Panther arrived and stopped the fighting, offering instead to determine exactly who killed my granddaughter. Wishing to avoid hostilities with our good friends—and especially with kin—the Weroance and I agreed to let The Panther try. Now we are in this place to hear what he has learned.''

She gave Panther a narrow-eyed look, as if daring him to disappoint her.

Panther rose to his feet and stepped before the fire. The flames threw his shadow on the back wall like a leaping monster. ''Weroansqua, I think that everything will come clear tonight. But first, you must humor me to recite the facts as I know them.''

''I don't allow people much humor, Elder.'' Hunting Hawk gave him a sour squint.

''In this case, I fear you will have to.'' Panther clasped his hands together. ''You see, Red Knot's murder isn't just a simple matter of taking a life. For that, we might depend on war, or vengeance, or even punishment for a crime. No, this is a different matter, for Red Knot wasn't killed as part of a raid, or vendetta. Her death was an act of desperation.'' He gave Hunting Hawk a bitter smile. ''And therein, Weroansqua, lies the crucial difference.''

The room was totally silent, the only sound that of the crackling fire.

''How does a person become this desperate?'' Panther raised an eyebrow. ''Young Red Knot was in love with

High Fox. So much in love that she flouted the rules of her family and clan, freely coupling with the young man.''

Flying Weir started, then glared at High Fox.

Panther studied Hunting Hawk for a moment, curious at her lack of reaction. Not at the accusation—she'd heard it the day Panther had faced Copper Thunder—but at the public statement before witnesses. So, apparently the Weroansqua knew, or at least suspected. "The clan is everything," he quoted. "And Greenstone Clan was in trouble. Copper Thunder had united the upriver villages, controlling the trade. The Mamanatowick had begun to put new pressure on the Independent villages. The balance had been upset.''

Copper Thunder laughed and crossed his arms, a smug look on his face.

"Oh, Grass Mat," Panther chided. "I wouldn't be so sure of myself, were I you." He gave Hunting Hawk a knowing glance. "You thought to have it all your way, didn't you, Weroansqua? Red Knot was becoming a problem, following in her mother's tracks. What better way to rid yourself of a potential embarrassment than by—''

"I *didn't* kill the girl!" Hunting Hawk had fire in her eyes.

With aplomb Panther said, "I didn't say that you did.''

"But you . . .'' Hunting Hawk snapped her mouth shut, glaring.

"I was going to say, what better way to rid yourself of a potential embarrassment, than by marrying her off to Copper Thunder. It was a master stroke. Cunning old fox that you are, you would thus sting the Mamanatowick into action. Copper Thunder scared you, didn't he? Here was a new dynamic leader upsetting the old balance—and right downriver from him lay the Independent villages. But there was a clever way to eliminate that threat, wasn't there?''

''What?'' Hunting Hawk scowled irritably at him.

Panther cast a measuring look at Copper Thunder. ''With a marriage alliance between Greenstone Clan and Copper Thunder, the Mamanatowick would be forced to throw all of his might against the upriver villages. The perceived threat lay there, with the upstart. While the Mamanatowick fought it out with Copper Thunder, the Independent villages would be spared. Anyone's best guess would be that Water Snake would crush Copper Thunder within two Comings of the Leaves. And then, when you faced him, Water Snake's forces would have been weakened, buying you even more time.''

''That makes sense,'' Nine Killer agreed, seeing the logic. ''But killing Red Knot wouldn't serve the Weroansqua's purpose, would it?''

Panther shook his head. ''I don't believe that Hunting Hawk had the girl killed.'' He looked at Copper Thunder, who now frowned uneasily at Hunting Hawk. ''You and the Mamanatowick were being played like fish on a string, Grass Mat. The Weroansqua's real fear was that you might deal with Water Snake—trade with him rather than fight. That realignment of power would have eventually strangled the Independent villages. Hunting Hawk understood from the beginning that you couldn't build a chieftainship like the one you dreamed of. The upriver villages don't have the resources to support it. What worried her was how you would react when you realized that truth.''

Copper Thunder's eyes had narrowed to slits. ''And the trick with Shell Comb? Did you toy with me, Weroansqua?''

Panther answered for Hunting Hawk: ''Red Knot was dead. The Weroansqua's plans were in jeopardy. She would marry anyone to you if it would create an alliance unacceptable to the Mamanatowick.''

Hunting Hawk stiffened, ''I *will not* listen to this any longer! War Chief, seize him!''

''Where were you that morning, Weroansqua?'' Panther asked mildly. ''People said that you were absent all through breakfast. Why? What were you doing during that critical time?''

Nine Killer stood, flexing his hands, as he studied Hunting Hawk. ''I would prefer to hear him out, Weroansqua. I think this is clan business.''

''If you will not, Flying Weir, I want you—''

''No!'' Yellow Net stood, her angry eyes fixed on Hunting Hawk. ''I agree with my cousin, Nine Killer. This must be heard for the sake of Greenstone Clan. We still do not know who killed Red Knot.'' She bent to stare into Hunting Hawk's angry eyes. ''You said you didn't kill her.''

''I didn't!'' Hunting Hawk cried. ''You should know! I was with you that morning.'' She pointed her stick at Copper Thunder. ''Trying to figure out what to do about him!''

''Did you *have* her killed?'' Yellow Net demanded, face distrustful.

''No!'' Hunting Hawk stared aghast at her cousin. ''What do you think I am? A monster?''

Panther placed a gentle hand on Yellow Net's shoulder. ''The Weroansqua didn't kill her granddaughter.''

''You know this?'' Yellow Net demanded.

''I'm fairly sure.'' Panther gave the fuming Hunting Hawk a sidelong glance. ''Had she done so, she would never have sent the War Chief after High Fox. Instead, she would have ordered him to track down Winged Blackbird and then attack White Stake Village. She would have needed someone to take the blame, and Corn Hunter would have been perfect for the purpose.''

Black Spike cocked his head. "Then she really believed High Fox killed the girl?"

Panther nodded. "Red Knot's murder caught Hunting Hawk by complete surprise. She knew that Corn Hunter's warriors hadn't committed the act: the body would have been desecrated. That left the most likely suspect as High Fox. And, forgive me, Weroansqua, but the one thing you will not tolerate is a personal affront, or an insult to your clan's honor."

She gave him a grudging nod.

"Then, who killed the girl?" Nine Killer demanded. His gaze shifted to Copper Thunder.

"I didn't do it!" Copper Thunder raised his hands in defense. "Why would I?"

"Jealousy," Nine Killer countered. "You couldn't stand the thought that she'd run off with a mere boy. Your honor demanded that the slight be paid for in blood."

Copper Thunder gave the War Chief a crooked smile. "I didn't care if she'd coupled with a camp dog. I needed an alliance and a child out of her, nothing more." He tilted his head at the Weroansqua. "Two can play at subterfuge."

"I'm sorry, Grass Mat. Your best spy has been kicked out," Panther added. "Flat Willow was banished this very evening. In fact, I'd say, Great Tayac, that your alliance has just evaporated before your eyes. These people are not the same as you knew among the Serpent Chiefs. They don't have the discipline. They weren't raised to believe, to obey, to be dominated."

"People can change." Copper Thunder propped a fist on his hip.

"Can they?" Panther indicated Yellow Net and Nine Killer. "You just saw two cousins claim this as clan business, in defiance of their ruler. In what circumstance would White Smoke Rising have allowed that kind of challenge to his authority? Even were it his own son who spoke up?''

Copper Thunder's mouth twitched.

"And even more to the point," Panther added, "where are all the warriors you brought with you? Sent home. Why? So they could fish, hunt, and trap. Unlike a Serpent Chief, you can't hold your warriors to one task. The most you can commit to your efforts here is ten."

Panther stepped over to appraise Copper Thunder. "The truth is, you'll ally with whoever asks you. You've tried to build your fighting force, and trained them well, too. You were able to whip Water Snake's warriors and Stone Frog's Conoy, but then your elite force faded away. Your warriors wanted to go hunting, or maybe they worried about the Monacans up beyond the fall line to the west, or the Susquehannocks to the north. You couldn't hold them despite all your tattoos, your stolen spider gorget, and that war club you took from White Smoke Rising's trophy house."

Copper Thunder rose with powerful grace. "I've had enough of you, Raven."

"That's why you were trying to talk warriors into joining your cause." Panther locked his hands behind his back. "You were looking for young men who would make that full-time commitment. Problem was, all you could find were the malcontents like Flat Willow. He, and his kind, are hardly the stuff of a great rank of warriors, are they?"

"I'm warning you." Copper Thunder took a step forward, only to have Nine Killer place himself between them.

"Oh, relax, Great Tayac." Panther waved him back. "As much as I'd like to blame you for killing the girl, you needed that alliance, and when Red Knot was dead, I'll bet you were desperately anxious to see what other opportunity would present itself." Panther paused.

"From your actions tonight, I'd say that the Weroansqua has found something workable."

Hunting Hawk muttered, "My dealings with the Great Tayac are none of your business."

Panther shrugged agreeably. "As you will."

Copper Thunder clenched his fists in frustration. "You're just stirring up trouble, Raven. Are you going to get to the point, or waste the rest of the night?"

Panther gave him a cold smile. "You've always been impatient. Too impatient to learn what kind of family you almost married into? I tell you, you're not going to like the answer. Even less so, since I'm going to be the one giving it to you."

Hunting Hawk hissed, "Old man, if you don't get on with this, I'll see you *burn*!"

Thirty

Nine Killer wished desperately that he'd brought his war club. Copper Thunder's face darkened like a winter storm. If the meeting erupted into violence, Nine Killer could count only on the quick discipline of his warriors to protect the Weroansqua and to restore order.

The tension in the Great House felt like some fierce beast breathing down their backs. Hunting Hawk looked as if she'd swallowed a bitter draught of mayapple root, her undershot jaw stuck out defiantly. Yellow Net had stiffened, face thoughtful. Of them all, only Panther and Green Serpent seemed unconcerned. Were they made of wood, or had old age just blinded them to the danger brewing around them?

Panther rubbed his hands back and forth before him. "The killing of Red Knot had nothing to do with the things we've been discussing here. They simply helped to precipitate the event."

"Then why did you bring all that up? To humiliate us?" Hunting Hawk demanded, waving her stick angrily.

"No, Weroansqua. Actually, I was doing you a favor." He looked at Copper Thunder with evident distaste. "You see, those innocent people with a reason for killing the young woman needed to be cleared of wrongdoing, or questions would dog them for the rest of their lives. I want this closed so that everyone can begin to put their lives back in order."

Black Spike had crossed his arms, looking bored.

The Panther considered his words for a moment, and finally said, "The story begins a long time ago, almost ten-and-seven Comings of the Leaves past. At that time, Shell Comb was married to Monster Bone, Weroance of Three Myrtle Village. Married though she might be, Shell Comb was—"

"Was what?" she asked, stepping into the room. Her hair was damp from the mist, her dark eyes fixed on The Panther. "Did you intend to discuss me, Elder, while I was still in the Women's House?"

"I had no choice," Panther said easily. "The Weroansqua appointed the time . . . apparently without consulting you."

Shell Comb gave her mother a grim smile, and flashed a probing look at Black Spike. She seated herself with a flourish, removed the damp feather cloak from around her shoulders, and shook her long black hair back over her shoulder. She flashed a smile at Nine Killer, enough to make his guts tingle, and then she beamed at Copper Thunder before stretching her hands to the fire.

Nine Killer couldn't help but watch the way her lithe body extended itself toward the fire's warming rays, but he noticed that Black Spike had locked his jaws, the muscles of his cheeks tight. His gaze never left her.

And Nine Killer saw the desperation locked behind the Weroance's strained expression—and knew it for what it was.

"Yes, let's see," Panther resumed. "Ten-and-seven springs ago, Shell Comb traveled north, up the Salt Water Bay. The journey was ostensibly a trading expedition. North she went, passing a year among the Susquehannocks and the Seneca."

"I think you have confused the time we spent there, Elder." Shell Comb smiled coyly at him. "I recall it more like three moons."

Panther's voice softened. "I'm sorry, Shell Comb, but you betrayed yourself the other day. The Andaste White Dog ceremony occurs in midwinter, just after the solstice. The Green Corn ceremony happens in late summer. You saw both of them. How else could you know that the Feather Dance was done at both?"

"I was told," she said coldly.

"No, you needed time to bear the child." Panther crossed his arms. "I assume that Monster Bone would have known the child wasn't his, that it was his brother's. So you and Black Spike left, traveled north to bear the child where your husband wouldn't know. And then, what happened? Couldn't you bear to part with the child?"

"That's ridiculous!" Shell Comb gaped at The Panther.

Nine Killer caught the sudden horror on Black Spike's face—as if his entire world was growing dark. He raised his hands, fumbled with them, and finally placed them on either side of his face.

Panther took a step and shifted his attention to the

sooty roof overhead. "When I was in Three Myrtle Village, the old woman, Moth, tried to—"

"Moth!" Shell Comb cried. "She's crazy! You old fool! You didn't believe a word she said, did you? Monster Bone took her in a raid against the Mamanatowick. She's been hit in the head so many times she doesn't know night from day!"

"But she knew that Monster Bone's longhouse burned from the ground up," Panther replied evenly. "Burned the night *before* you and Black Spike landed on your return from the Susquehannock."

"Longhouses burn!" Black Spike cried. "It happens!"

"It does"—Panther pointed up at the roof—"but the sparks usually catch up by the smoke hole. Monster Bone's house was set on fire so that no one could escape—and in this case it brought you good fortune. Your brother burned to death. You became Weroance, and kept your child. That's why your wife's clan never came to claim the child, isn't it? She never bore High Fox."

"She died in childbirth!" The pitch had climbed in Black Spike's voice. "In the presence of Okeus, I swear it."

"No matter what happened to her, she never returned with you, did she?" Panther goaded. "Dead, left with the Susquehannocks, it matters not. She was out of the way, unable to expose the truth."

Black Spike's eyes had glazed, and he shot a frightened look at Shell Comb.

Shell Comb's eyes seemed to enlarge as she fixed them on The Panther. The corners of her lips jerked, and then with a sudden smile she nodded. "An able concoction, Elder, and I can see how a person could string the facts together like a pattern of beads. But it is a fashion of your own, *not* the way it was."

"Indeed?" Panther looked around at his rapt audience.

High Fox was staring, openmouthed, at Shell Comb. "I think that in a few moments, we will see just how well I can string these beads of fact upon their cord. Then, Shell Comb, we shall see whose neck they will fit."

"Mother!" Shell Comb hissed. "Stop this! Now! The old fool's out of hand!"

"No,'" Hunting Hawk said woodenly. "I think we will hear him out."

Panther turned to face Green Serpent. "If you would be so kind, Elder?"

Green Serpent reached into the basket resting between Lightning Cat's knees and lifted out the skull. Chanting to appease the young woman's ghost, he handed it to Panther. The elder took it in his wrinkled hands, holding it carefully.

"Observe." Panther pointed to the ugly dents in the smooth curvature of bone. "The skull was crushed in two places. From the extent of the damage, Red Knot would have dropped instantly, probably dead before she hit the ground."

Panther met Nine Killer's eyes. "War Chief, would you take the weapon from Green Serpent and demonstrate how the blow was delivered?"

The Kwiokos extracted a long-handled war club from the basket and extended it. Nine Killer swallowed hard and took the slender handle of the polished war club. The smooth wood chilled his hand. As Panther held out the grinning skull, Nine Killer reached out with the war club, aligning the business end with the side of the girl's skull. The two stone heads matched the holes exactly. Even from where he stood, Nine Killer could see the strands of long black hair caught in the settings of the war club. "Elder, that hair. Is it . . . ?"

Panther nodded. "When the club was replaced in the House of the Dead, the killer didn't notice that some of Red Knot's hair was stuck in the club."

"That could be anyone's hair!" Black Spike objected, his voice hoarse. He couldn't seem to pry his gaze from the grisly exhibit.

"But it's not," Panther replied. "The War Chief and I searched most diligently for the weapon, even to the point of stealing Copper Thunder's war club to match it to the wound. Grass Mat, you'll be happy to know it didn't fit."

"Of course not!"

"Where? Where was it?" Nine Killer demanded—and suddenly, he knew. He'd seen it so many times. "By Okeus, taken from the very hand of the god! It's the war club from the altar!"

"The very same," Panther replied sadly. He reached into his belt pouch. "But if there is any doubt, I will now lay it to rest. This piece of wood was chipped out of the stone setting by the impact of the blow. The War Chief, Sun Conch, and I found it the day we inspected the ridge where Red Knot was killed. You will notice, it fits perfectly." Panther pressed the triangular piece into place where the stone and wood were joined.

"So, you have the war club that killed Red Knot," Hunting Hawk said dryly. "Anyone could have entered the temple that night and stolen it."

Panther cradled the skull gently in his arms; it might have been a precious egg. "That is correct, Weroansqua. When I began, I told you, it was the *reason* of Red Knot's death that eluded me. Almost everyone in this room might want the girl dead, but to kill her took a special kind of desperation. Flat Willow was desperate enough, but he would have used his own war club, and besides, he was out plotting with Copper Thunder at the moment Red Knot was killed. High Fox might have wanted her dead, but White Otter and Quick Fawn have told me that Red Knot wished to leave with him. Thus, he had no reason to kill her."

"Wait!" Nine Killer cried. "What about High Fox's necklace? Red Knot had it clasped in her hand."

Panther nodded to Green Serpent, who lifted the necklace from the basket. High Fox gasped at the sight of it, his face working.

"High Fox?" Panther took the necklace and dangled it before the young warrior. "Would you care to explain how this came to be with Red Knot's body?"

High Fox stammered, "I—I put it in her hand, Elder. That morning. When I found her dead . . . bloody. She was so cold. I just couldn't . . ." He looked up, aching. "I *loved* her! Don't you see? I'd have died for her! We were going away to be together—happy for the rest of our lives. And then to find her that way, dead, and covered with blood. I just . . . I took off my necklace, and placed it in her hand. Something . . . don't you see? Something of me for her. So she'd know that I still loved her. That I'd always love her." He dropped his miserable stare to the matting. "For all time . . . forever."

Panther stepped over and used a finger to raise High Fox's face. Tears left shining tracks down his cheeks. "She will know, High Fox. And your necklace will rest with her bones. I promise."

High Fox smiled in relief as The Panther handed the necklace back to Green Serpent; then Panther hesitated, his gaze fixed on the boy's mouth. He whispered, "It all comes clear."

It took a moment for Panther to recover his thoughts. "So, let us go again to that last night of dancing. Place yourselves there. Red Knot and High Fox meet outside the palisade after the dance is over. She tells him how much she detests Copper Thunder. He asks her to run off with him. She agrees. She is to meet him at Oyster Shell Landing at dawn—giving High Fox just enough time to paddle around the point. When she returns and meets Quick Fawn, Quick Fawn tries to talk Red Knot out of

514 • Kathleen O'Neal Gear and W. Michael Gear

doing such a mad thing—and in the process, Red Knot tells Quick Fawn what she is doing. Isn't that right?''

Quick Fawn nodded, head lowered to avoid the hostile glares of her aunt and mother.

"You can't seriously mean one of the girls killed her!" Copper Thunder laughed and slapped his knees with his hands.

"No." Panther took a deep breath. "Just around the corner of the House of the Dead, back in the shadows, a man and woman were coupling. They overheard every word. It upset them so much that they argued after the girls left. So heated was the disagreement that the man forgot his blanket. Old man Mockingbird found it the next morning." Panther nodded to Green Serpent.

The priest lifted the folded blanket from the basket, and opened it to expose the distinctive pattern of *peak* shells. The deer seemed to dance in the firelight.

Black Spike sprang to his feet, face ashen. "You *stole* that!" He whirled, face livid, pointing at Hunting Hawk. "This is *your* doing, you filthy old bitch! Well, I won't have it!"

"Enough!" Copper Thunder roared, leaping to his feet and grasping Black Spike's arms from behind. For a moment, they wrestled, teetering for balance. Black Spike might have had a chance but for his healing arm. Then Copper Thunder's thick muscles corded and literally bent Black Spike back to the bench. High Fox leaped out of the way as the Great Tayac pinned Black Spike in place.

Spittle wetted Black Spike's chin as he struggled against the iron grip.

Panther said softly, "Shell Comb told me that everything was done for the clan. And so it was. All done for the clan." He paused, and added, "Mistakes had to be paid for."

Shell Comb had trouble focusing her eyes, as if seeing

beyond a great distance. Her expression was slack, lips parted, as if in disbelief.

Panther lifted Red Knot's skull, tapping her peglike incisor with a thumb nail. "Anyone who looks will see that Red Knot's tooth is malformed. Exactly like yours, Black Spike. And, I regret to say, exactly like High Fox's. Both of your children have the same malformed tooth, Weroance. They got it from you."

For the briefest instant, Black Spike met Shell Comb's horrified stare, and his love for her lit his eyes, along with pain and resignation. He smiled, as if reassuring her. Then he glanced at his son, started to reach out, as if to touch him.

High Fox gaped, mouth working silently, as he tried to comprehend the information. He shrank back from his father's hand, swallowing hard as the horror began to sink in.

Black Spike pulled his hand back, straightened, and said, "I did it. It is my fault. I killed the girl. That was Shell Comb and me out there, locked together, rutting as we always had. I overheard that conversation. I said I was going to stop them. Shell Comb told me to wait, that she would talk Red Knot out of doing this forbidden thing."

"Is that when you argued?" Panther asked.

"Yes. She pulled away from me." Black Spike seemed to nerve himself, his eyes clearing as he bravely committed himself.

"No!" Shell Comb hissed, fists clenched. She started forward, but Hunting Hawk tapped her on the shoulder with her walking stick. Shell Comb stopped as if struck, watching Black Spike with a glassy-eyed, stunned stare. High Fox was making strangling sounds, as if choking.

"Shell Comb couldn't find the girl," Black Spike insisted. "She was frantic. So, I made up my mind. I went into the House of the Dead, knowing the god would have a weapon. With it, I sneaked out, ran to the ridgetop, and arrived just in time to stop Red Knot." He closed his eyes and tears leaked down his cheeks. "I didn't mean to kill her, but she wouldn't listen. Wouldn't believe me when I told her that High Fox was her brother. She just laughed. And . . . and something let loose inside me and I hit her. I—"

"*Father?*" High Fox clutched at the empty air in front of him, as though reaching for something only he could see. "Red Knot? She's . . . she's . . ."

"Now it makes sense," Panther said dismally. "Reason and desperation—acting together to motivate murder: Both High Fox and Red Knot sprang from Shell Comb's womb, both planted by Black Spike's seed." Panther raised pained eyes. "Weroansqua, High Fox and Red Knot are both *Greenstone Clan*!"

"Incest!" Hunting Hawk hissed. "Incest!"

"No!" High Fox howled, shrinking back, and huddling in on himself. "I *didn't* do that! I *didn't*!"

A rumbling of voices broke out from the other side of the divider and rolled the length of the Great House. Hunting Hawk sat as if riven by lightning. Shell Comb might have been frozen, her glazed eyes locked on the miserable Black Spike.

Nine Killer shook his head, his senses swimming with the import of what he'd just heard. *Incest!* The most horrible of crimes!

"What . . . what do I do with you?" Hunting Hawk asked when her shock finally began to ebb. "You, and your demon-spawned child?"

Black Spike filled his lungs, muscles tense as if in final preparation. He gave Shell Comb a pleading look, then stated calmly, "My son is innocent. He didn't know. I killed your granddaughter, Weroansqua. To save my son, I offer myself in Red Knot's place." He turned, seeing his warriors as they crowded into the doorway. "You men! Back down! I order you! I do this freely! There must be no vengeance from Three Myrtle!''

''No!'' Shell Comb said in a strangled voice. ''What are you doing? Why are you doing this—''

''I *killed* her!'' Black Spike interrupted. ''I accept the responsibility, Shell Comb. I could not allow them to mate, to be married in incest. They *had* to be stopped!''

''Take him!'' Hunting Hawk snapped. ''Build up the fire in the plaza. Break his arms and legs . . . and burn him!''

High Fox dropped his face in his hands, and sobbed. ''I didn't know! He *lied* to me! His own son . . . he lied! It's *not my fault*!''

''I'll decide what to do with you later,'' Hunting Hawk growled at High Fox.

Nine Killer nodded to Flying Weir, who stepped forward. Copper Thunder refused to relinquish his grip on Black Spike, and together, Copper Thunder and Flying Weir rushed the doomed Weroance through the doorway, shaking the frame and rattling the matting. A path opened before them as they made their way down the crowded Great House.

''Wait!'' The Panther's cry was drowned in the chaos.

''My warriors!'' Black Spike screamed. ''Do nothing! Keep the peace! I did this! I will pay!''

Blood and dung! Incest! The very thought of it left him reeling and sick to his stomach. Nine Killer nerved himself as he followed in their wake. He would be the man who broke Black Spike's arms and legs. That responsibility fell on the War Chief.

Duty and clan honor demanded no less from him. If not for justice, he'd do it for Red Knot, for a murdered clanswoman.

''War Chief, wait!'' Panther called from behind him. ''A word please. This isn't—''

''Not *now*, Elder! Please!'' Didn't the old man know

that it was hard enough to do this without other distractions? Nine Killer rudely shoved his memories aside: images of him and Black Spike on the war trail; feasting side by side, joking; the shared hunts; and nights on the bay, a fire in the center of the canoe, and their spears in hand as they gigged fish rising to the firelight.

"How did it go so wrong, Black Spike?" Nine Killer muttered under his breath. His stomach knotted and cramped at the thought. Incest! Loathed by the gods, it had almost stained Greenstone Clan, its corruption leaching into his own family. But to kill? He couldn't make himself believe that Black Spike had murdered the girl. Couldn't he have found another way?

But then, as The Panther has been trying to tell you, people will always surprise you with their darker sides. Black Spike was practically bragging that he'd done the foul deed. How did a man argue with that? And, as the Creation stories told them, people were descended from Okeus. The sickening settled in his soul.

Panther was pulling at his arm from behind. "War Chief, I must tell you—"

"Elder, leave me alone! We'll talk later!" He shook off the old man's hand, and then lost him in the jostling crowd of elbows and shoving bodies as they ducked out into the darkness. Copper Thunder and Flying Weir dragged the struggling Black Spike across the plaza. Around them, the mist swirled as if alive, churning with the very breath of the dark god. The shadowed Guardians watched ominously, their faces obscured by night and fog.

How quickly it happened. People materialized out of the mist, casting logs, branches, and kindling into the blackened ceremonial fire pit.

Nine Killer stood anxiously beside Flying Weir as he and Copper Thunder restrained Black Spike. The Weroance had begun to sag. Someone appeared with a ceramic pot full of glowing coals and cast them upon the heap of wood. More people followed, throwing coals from their fires onto the growing pyramid of wood.

"Okeus, help me," Black Spike whispered as the flames turned the mist into a blazing halo of yellow light.

Flying Weir, too, looked sick, his eyes glassy with distaste at holding such a vile being as Black Spike. His jaw was clamped, as if he was determined to do his duty.

Nine Killer could see Copper Thunder's tattooed face. He was grinning, evil gleaming in his hungry eyes.

Stone Cob stepped up to Nine Killer, handing him his old battered war club. The familiar handle felt wrong for this night's terrible work.

Nine Killer lifted the sturdy weapon with both hands as his grip tightened on the leather-wrapped handle. *I don't want to do this!* But he would have to, as he'd had to in the past. Copper Thunder and Flying Weir would hold Black Spike, or throw him down. Nine Killer would strike, swinging his war club around in an arc. At the impact, he'd feel as well as hear the snap. His own bones would cringe.

Black Spike was my friend . . . my friend . . . Even after the Weroance's confession, some stubborn part of him refused to believe. It vied with the rising horror that curdled his blood. *Incest!* High Fox had lain with Red Knot! Better to pitch the youth onto the fire himself, cleanse the entire ugly thing, here and now. He nerved himself, aware that the fire had caught, a rush of sparks whirling into the murky air.

"War Chief?" Panther called anxiously as he stalked across the plaza. "You must hear me!"

Nine Killer took a deep breath, turning to face the old man. "Make it quick, I've enough . . ."

Shell Comb rushed up, hair tangled, eyes frantic, like

those of a trapped animal. She knocked people aside, and threw herself at Flying Weir, screaming, "No! Don't *do* this thing! It *wasn't* him! Black Spike *didn't* do it!"

As she clawed at Flying Weir, Black Spike twisted his arm loose, balled a fist, and struck Copper Thunder full in the face. The Great Tayac jerked away, and Black Spike pulled free.

Before Nine Killer could react, Black Spike shouted, *"I killed her! I'll pay!"* He took one last look at Shell Comb, and leapt into the center of the roaring fire.

Nine Killer started forward in a involuntary effort to pull the man back. Heat seared his raised arm.

Black Spike shrieked hideously, all that his lungs could manage before he sucked fire into them. He kicked, and then writhed as his hair burst into a brilliant flare. His skin charred, bubbled, and steamed, while greasy black smoke billowed from the flames.

Nine Killer staggered back, and saw Shell Comb, on her hands and knees, crawling toward the inferno. Horror in her wide eyes, she extended one hand, reaching toward the blackened figure.

Nine Killer ducked down under the heat, pulling her back from the fire's draft. She fought for a moment, then went limp in his grip as he pulled her to safety. Streamers of greasy smoke mixed with the wavering yellow light. Nine Killer hugged Shell Comb to his chest. She sobbed like an infant.

As he patted her tenderly, he looked across at The Panther, and asked wearily, "Yes, Elder? What is it?"

Panther's sad face worked, as if he were trying to speak. In the gaudy yellow light, he studied the blackened body that slid down into the coals, then he looked at Nine Killer, and the grieving Shell Comb in his arms.

Shaking his head, he turned, and walked slowly away, his old shoulders bent, the crowd parting to let him pass.

Thirty-one

As the first light of dawn filtered through the gaps in the thatch, Panther sat by the fire in Rosebud's longhouse, arms locked around his knees. Memories of the terrible night kept spinning in his head. Sun Conch lay sleeping on the bench behind him, her breathing labored. Nine Killer sat across from him, head bowed, a great and terrible sadness in his eyes.

White Otter puttered around the fire, attending to the cooking—as if anyone had any appetite.

Panther watched the longhouse fire pop and spark. What he'd uncovered had wounded his soul. "Has anyone seen High Fox this morning?"

Nine Killer rubbed his face wearily. "No. In the excitement last night, he slipped away. Maybe, if we're lucky, he went out and drowned himself. It beats being a pariah."

"He hasn't the courage, War Chief. For the moment, he has to blame everyone but himself." Panther paused. "Why didn't Shell Comb simply marry Black Spike? Why carry on like this and ruin people's lives?"

Nine Killer plucked at frayed bits of matting, some of it still stained by Sun Conch's blood. "The Weroansqua refused her permission. Her marriage to Monster Bone strengthened the alliance. He'd given her a son, White Bone. The boy drowned later. Another son, Grebe, was killed by a lightning strike.''

"What sort of man was Monster Bone?"

"Just the opposite of Black Spike. Blustery. Tough. He and Shell Comb fought like cougars. In the end, I can't say that I'd have blamed her for turning to Black Spike. I think Hunting Hawk always expected too much from Shell Comb. Shell Comb wanted excitement, ceremony, and adventure. Much like Thin Bird, her father. I've heard that Thin Bird was the muscle, and Hunting Hawk was the brain that carried Greenstone Clan to prominence among the Independent villages.''

"Shell Comb never remarried?"

"Oh, she did. For a year here, half a year there, but she always came home divorced. Now, I know why. She wanted to be close to Black Spike. Had she married Copper Thunder, it would have been the same.''

Panther blinked to clear Black Spike's burned body from his mind. His soul felt like old fabric, wrung out and empty of any joy it once might have held.

As if reading his expression, Nine Killer said, "How will High Fox manage? His only mistake was falling in love with the wrong young woman. As it is, he's ruined forever. What woman would marry him? What village will take him? He lay with his sister. He's forever tainted by it.''

"That's why Green Serpent heard Red Knot's ghost sobbing." Panther rubbed his face. "Only in death did she find out what they'd done to her.''

"Why did Black Spike throw himself on the fire like that? How could he do that?" White Otter shook her head in amazement.

Panther whispered, "He was afraid his nerve might fail him at the last.''

"What nerve? He had only to endure." Nine Killer plucked a piece of matting loose, studying it absently.

Panther closed his eyes and took a deep breath. "War Chief, this isn't over. Black Spike anticipated me. He acted before I could finish. You see . . ."

Voices shouted outside, cries of, *"Run!"* and *"It's an attack!"*

Nine Killer jumped to his feet, grabbed his weapons, and dove for the doorway.

Panther grunted as he climbed to his feet and hurried after, cursing his old bones all the way. Outside, dawn had whitened the mist, leaving the longhouses in ghostly relief. Men and women seemed to appear and disappear as they sprinted past.

"Where?" a man called. "Where are they?"

"Beyond the main gate! A big body of warriors!"

Panther kept to the side lest he be bowled over, and hurried into the plaza. An arrow stuck out of the ground, the feathered shaft slanting back to mark the direction from which it had come. Shouts erupted from all sides.

A knot of warriors huddled in the protection of the palisade, peering through the cracks out into the fog. Every now and then, one would loose an arrow at a darting shape beyond.

Nine Killer stood just inside the palisade gate, gesturing with his heavy bow. "I want women and children to check along the palisade! The enemy could be circling, seeking to break through in our rear! Stone Cob, see to it! Leave no area unguarded."

Panther sidled up to the palisade and stared out at the lifting fog. "Who is out there?"

Copper Thunder appeared at a run, flattened himself against the post next to Panther, and glared out at the dawn, the tattoos pulled tight by his angry squint. "Who comes here?" he bellowed. "Name yourselves, you gutless cowards!"

From the curling mist, a voice shouted back, "The warriors of the Mamanatowick, Water Snake! I am Winged Blackbird, and I will have your head before this day is through!"

"Come and take it!" Copper Thunder bellowed back. "We'll see who is shorter come sunset!"

Panther sighed and shook his head. "Perhaps I can stop this."

Copper Thunder gave him a dismissive glance. "You, Raven? This isn't your place! Who do you think is out there? White Smoke Rising?"

Panther ignored him and walked purposefully toward where Nine Killer lined up his warriors. As he passed, an arrow thunked hollowly into the palisade above his head.

"What has happened so far?" Panther demanded.

Nine Killer shot him an irritated look. "Elder, I don't have time for—"

"*What* has happened, War Chief! You will tell, and tell me now . . . or have you forgotten your last battle at Three Myrtle?"

The irritation vanished to be replaced by a wry smile. "Forgive me, Elder. One of our two scouts—the ones I placed last night to guard against an attack by Black Spike's warriors—he warned us just in time. Many warriors are out there. It would seem that Winged Blackbird has come back in force."

"Come with me, War Chief." Panther started for the gap in the palisade.

"What? Are you crazy? This is not Three Myrtle Village. That's Winged Blackbird out there! If you step beyond the palisade, they'll *kill* you!"

"Perhaps, War Chief. But, perhaps—as much as I hate to—I can stop this battle, too." Panther hesitated at the last of the palisades. "Your lungs are better than mine. Find out if Corn Hunter is there."

Nine Killer stepped up behind him and cupped his hands around his mouth, shouting, "Who leads this attack? Is that you, Corn Hunter?"

In a sudden lull, a voice answered. "Corn Hunter is here, but we come in the presence of the Mamanatowick! He is here to personally watch the destruction of Flat Pearl Village!"

A great shout went up from the fields as the Mamanatowick's warriors shouted their determination. Nine Killer winced and leaned back against a palisade post. "From the sound of it, he must have tens of tens of warriors. Never have we faced so many without warning."

"How long can you hold out?"

Nine Killer rubbed his face. "Not long, Elder. If he is here in force, he can probe and prod. Eventually, he will find a weakness. If the fog lifts, and he can fire the longhouses, well, it will only be a matter of time."

Panther chuckled, although sorrow built within him. "Everything for the clan, eh?" He paused. "Very well, War Chief, raise your voice for me again." Panther's stomach ached from an unaccustomed nervousness. "Tell the Mamanatowick . . . tell him that his uncle, Eight Rocks, wishes to speak with him."

Nine Killer stared, expression incredulous. He swallowed hard, and asked, "Who? Who did you say?"

"You heard me. Eight Rocks. Go on, tell him." Panther waved out at the mist.

Nine Killer cupped his mouth, and shouted, "Mamanatowick! Hear me! Your uncle, Eight Rocks, wishes to speak with you!"

A long silence followed. Then a derisive voice called from the mist, "Eight Rocks is long dead! Go suck yourself, you whining worm!"

In the following silence, Panther shouted, "If I'm dead, why isn't my body in your House of the Dead?

Can't answer that, can you? It's because I'm still living in it, you simple dolt!''

"Who speaks?'' A man had stepped forward, a mere shape in the mist, followed by others.

"These days, I am called The Panther!''

"The witch!'' the hiss carried through the gathered attackers.

"Call me witch if you will! But this same man gave Water Snake's mother her very first piece of copper!'' Panther cocked his head, hearing muted conversation springing up from both sides.

"Come forward!'' came the reply. "You will not be harmed if you are telling the truth.''

Panther took two steps before Nine Killer matched his pace. "What are you doing, War Chief? Go back before some glory seeker pins you with an arrow.''

"You're not going out there alone, Elder. Sun Conch isn't here. If something happens, you'll need me to cover your back.''

"But if it goes wrong, you'll be needed to coordinate and lead the defense. One can't very well attend to that duty when he's lying facedown on the ground with his skull split open.''

"Maybe, after last night, I don't have much to live for.''

"Fool! You've got White Otter and the other Greenstone Clan children to see to.'' As Nine Killer matched him, pace for pace, Panther gave in. "All right, then, we'll be fools together.''

"Indeed,'' Nine Killer muttered out of the side of his mouth. "We've actually done fairly well together, haven't we?''

Panther smiled, the first hope glimmering in his breast. "No matter what, War Chief, I want you to know that I value your friendship.''

"And I yours, Elder.''

At that Panther squared his shoulders, walking forth with a renewed sense of pride despite the quivering in his legs. After all the trials in his life, his soul hovered on the verge of dissolution at facing his family. So many Comings of the Leaves had passed. What would they think of the coward who'd run off so ignobly? Could he stand to look them in the eyes?

As they plodded across the bumpy field, warriors materialized from the mist, as if suddenly sprung to life.

Panther's toe caught in a withered vine, and Nine Killer reached out a hand to catch him. That grip, reassuring, steadied more than just Panther's body. Nine Killer smiled as he asked, "Are you all right?"

Panther's mouth had gone dry as old leaves. "Yes. Thank you, War Chief."

A wary warrior approached, squinting through the mist. He wore a stuffed blackbird tied to the right side of his shaved head. "Nine Killer? That's you, all right. No other is shorter than a woman, and twice as dumb."

"Intelligence has never been your strong point, Winged Blackbird. Now, stop jabbering like your namesake and take the elder to the Mamanatowick. He has important things to discuss."

"Like the destruction of Flat Pearl Village, and everyone in it?"

"Mind your tongue, warrior," Panther barked, "or I'll have your head on a stake!"

Winged Blackbird started at the commanding tone, his frown deepening. "This way." Then he hesitated. "Nine Killer, leave your weapons here."

"He'll carry them," Panther said, "just as an escort for an elder of the Sky Fire Clan should. And, if you disobey me once more, I shall have more than your head!"

Winged Blackbird chewed his lip in indecision, frowned, then started off at a rapid clip.

Panther had to rely on Nine Killer's steadying hand as he struggled to walk over the uneven ground. The thick knot of warriors closed in around them, blocking any retreat.

"Still think this was a good idea?" Nine Killer murmured.

"Better than the alternative."

"First incest, and now this! Okeus has condemned us!"

"Gull droppings! This is nothing more than bad timing."

"The fate of my clan hangs in the balance, and I'm stuck with a heretic."

Panther raised an eyebrow. "I could leave?"

Nine Killer smiled in resignation.

The Mamanatowick was seated on a blackened stump, a deerhide shelter propped over him to keep the moisture off. He wore a bobcat hide over his left shoulder, a great copper gorget on his sunken chest. The breechclout sported the design of a bobcat in *peak* and copper beads.

He was an older man, his face deeply lined, and his long hair streaked with silver. Chin propped on his palm, he studied Panther pensively as he and Nine Killer stopped before him.

"Greetings, nephew." Panther nodded politely. "You've done well for yourself. You have your father's look. Your mother would be proud."

"And I'm supposed to believe you are Eight Rocks? The mysterious Eight Rocks who vanished into thin air so long ago? I see only a withered old man. I am to believe that the witch called The Panther is my long-lost uncle?"

"I didn't disappear. I left." Panther crossed his arms. "The reason why is my own."

"Why?"

"I told you, that's my business."

Water Snake glanced at Winged Blackbird. "Go on, attack the village and kill them all. Start with these two."

As Winged Blackbird turned toward them, Panther said, "Wait!" He took a deep breath. "Very well, Water Snake. I left because of a woman." He paused. "Her name was . . . was Warm Fall."

"She was my aunt."

"If you are Blue Gill's son, she is. She was promised to my brother, White Fire."

"You're telling me . . . what?" Water Snake made a distasteful face.

"I'm telling you that she was promised to my brother, and I was in love with her. I'm telling you that I couldn't stand the thought of her going to him. I despised White Fire. He was a pampered monster, even as a child. And Mother promised my precious Warm Fall to *him*!"

Water Snake leaned forward, searching Panther's face as if for a clue to this bizarre twist. "You were firstborn. You were in line to be Mamanatowick. And you turned that down because you were denied a woman? You expect me to believe that?"

"Believe what you will, nephew. I was a very young man, and I loved her with all of my soul. She begged me to run off with her, to take her away, but I had learned my lessons very well. Everything for the clan: duty, honor, responsibility. My body, soul, and heart belonged to Sky Fire Clan. Instead of dishonoring my clan by running off with Warm Fall, the woman promised to my brother, I only dishonored myself. I watched her marry him, watched her take his hand and dance with him—and in that moment I knew I couldn't stay, couldn't live next to her . . . next to him." He shook his head. "I never allowed myself to love another woman."

"Blessed Okeus," Nine Killer whispered.

"Please," Panther said, raising his hand. "If you must bless, do it in the name of Ohona."

Water Snake was thinking, his face grim. "The disappearance of Eight Rocks has been a great mystery. Some things make sense now."

Panther struggled for breath, wondering at the tightness in his chest. "That night was unbearable. I could only imagine him mounting her. I wanted to beat my brain out, but instead, I left the village and headed west. I couldn't stand to dishonor her any further."

"So you've just wandered? Like some ragged Trader?" Water Snake asked. "Why didn't you come home? It sounds like you wasted your life."

"Yes, nephew, I wasted a great deal of it." Panther shrugged. "But come home I did. And, when this is all over, I shall retire to my island and live the rest of my life as I please."

"If you are Eight Rocks, you will come back with me. Back to your clan and family."

"No, nephew. I made my choice a long time ago. But for stopping this attack of yours, I would have died as I have lived: alone and unknown. The only reason I have revealed myself to you is to keep you from destroying Flat Pearl Village. I am an elder of Sky Fire Clan—"

"*The* Elder of Sky Fire Clan. The rest are dead."

"Very well. As the Elder, I want this attack stopped."

Water Snake gestured out toward the village, now just visible in the rising mist. "The usurper who calls himself the Great Tayac is in there! I have waited for this moment. I can crush two problems with one great blow."

Panther drew himself upright. "Before you do, you will strike me dead. Right here."

"Why are you doing this?" Water Snake cried, rising from his seat. "What are these people to you?"

"I have friends here. One is a young woman by the name of Sun Conch. She's not quite a woman yet, but I want her to have that chance—and not as one of your slaves. Another is named White Otter. I would like her to grow up to become a woman like her mother.''

''Because of *your* wishes, I should stop an attack I've dreamed of for ten Comings of the Leaves? All that, for a couple of *girls*?'' Water Snake raised his arms incredulously.

''Given what I've seen in my life, I can't think of a better reason. Make your choice, Mamanatowick: Leave Flat Pearl village, or kill your clan elder.''

Water Snake brooded for a moment. ''There's got to be another way. I could just order my warriors to hold you until—''

''No, Mamanatowick.'' Nine Killer stepped forward. ''Issue that order, and I will kill you. I am Nine Killer, War Chief of Flat Pearl Village. I am the elder's escort. I am here to protect him from his enemies.''

Winged Blackbird immediately nocked an arrow in his bow, but Water Snake waved him back. ''Elder, your escort is a brave man. Worthy of your status and rank. For that service, Nine Killer, I shall spare your life.''

''You will spare more than that,'' Panther growled. ''War Chief, hand me your club. If necessary, I will fight Water Snake for the right to rule the Sky Fire Clan.''

Water Snake's mouth dropped open. ''You would challenge me?''

''It is my right, under clan law.'' Panther took the war club from Nine Killer's hand. ''I could demand a clan meeting to discuss my claim to the mantle of Mamanatowick. I am the firstborn son of White Gull, sired by Stone Sliver.'' Panther smiled maliciously. ''Or you can call off the attack, and I'll forget I ever saw you here.''

Water Snake arched an eyebrow. ''But what of Copper Thunder? Do you think I should just let this upstart go as well? I've been on the trail for six days now. I am missing the solstice ceremonies. I'll not go home empty-handed.''

''No, you'll take me back and we'll discuss your right

to be Mamanatowick. That, or you can carry my body back and explain why you killed your clan elder. That is all I offer you. Decide, here and now.''

''I am *not* happy about this.'' Water Snake glared back and forth between them, weighing his options, and finding none of them palatable.

''No, I suppose not. But, nephew, I know clan law, and my rights, just as well as you do. You *know* who I am, don't you?''

Water Snake swallowed distastefully, torn between the desire to destroy his enemies, and the laws of kinship.

''Perhaps,'' Nine Killer offered, ''you could go home with full bellies? As a member of Greenstone Clan, I offer you the hospitality of my clan.'' He glanced around. ''You have a great many warriors with you; the feast might stretch the Weroansqua's resources, but if there was an understanding, say, that there would be no raiding during the next two Comings of the Leaves, I'd bet that the Independent villages could recover.''

''And, I think I can sweeten the broth.'' Panther handed the war club back to Nine Killer. ''I offer you the return of another of your relatives. Today she is called Moth, but you knew her as Sweet Stick.''

''*Warm Fall's sister?* She was married to White Fire as a second wife.'' Water Snake was turning the implications over in his head. ''The Weroansqua would agree to this?''

Panther said evenly, ''I think she would be happy to entertain and feed you and your warriors. And Moth is slave to a man who owes me a favor. Um, you haven't killed anyone yet, have you?''

''Only one scout out in the forest. The other got away and warned everyone else that we were coming.'' Water Snake tilted his head. ''Perhaps a gift could be given to the dead warrior's clan?''

''It might be arranged,'' Nine Killer agreed.

"But only for two Comings of the Leaves," Water Snake insisted. "And I will deal with the upstart on my own."

"That is between you and him," Panther said amiably. "I think, however, that he, too, might be amenable to some sort of arrangement."

Water Snake smiled crookedly. "It won't last, you know. Eventually, I will have these villages."

"Perhaps," Panther answered, "but for now they do serve a purpose. What you lose in authority, you gain by their ability to buffer Stone Frog's Conoy. A wise Mamanatowick would consider these things."

"You think I'm wise?"

"It's in the blood, nephew."

This was the first night of solstice. Sun Conch lay on her back in Rosebud's longhouse. Pain lanced her body, and fever played with her swimming senses. Her long hair covered her bedding like a shiny black halo, and sweat poured from her skinny body. She had just enough strength to watch the firelit shadows prancing over the walls. The main fire had burned down to a steady flickering blaze. The house was utterly still, but outside, she could hear the singing, the clapping hands, and the dancers panting with exertion at the plaza.

Sun Conch had listened to the talk about Black Spike's death. She had lived in the Weroance's village, and knew him for a good and fair man—despite the way he'd treated her that day in the plaza. What would Three Myrtle Village do without him?

High Fox committed incest with Red Knot!

She closed her eyes at the horror of it, and smoothed her fingers over the soft deerhide that covered her chest.

She had been wanting High Fox for so long, yearning to see him, but she didn't know how she felt now. If he was wise, his shame had sent him scurrying from Flat Pearl Village before the Weroansqua could convene a council meeting to determine the manner of his death. But she wished he'd come to say goodbye, or sent word, some small gesture.

I risked everything for you, High Fox.

She prayed he was on the run. She could imagine him, bravely facing the world, carving out a place for himself in some distant land.

Would he act like The Panther, seeking out an island to deal with his demons? *I could wait, go there, and help him to overcome this terrible tragedy.* She wasn't afraid, not of High Fox. It hadn't been his fault. He hadn't known.

Sun Conch inhaled and started shaking as her body went cold with chills. It hurt to breathe. To take her mind off the pain, she looked up at the baskets and loosely woven sacks that hung from the rafters. She could see the dried stems of beans, and several large squash, as well as a variety of nuts. The longhouse smelled sweetly of the wild rice bread and rosehip tea she'd had for breakfast. A full gourd cup of tea sat near her head, but she had no desire to drink. Or to do anything else. She could barely keep her eyes open.

"Mother?" she murmured, and a sob caught in her throat. "Mother, I miss you."

She had been dreaming that her mother was here, taking care of her, her hands cool, her voice loving. The familiar smells of their home had been comforting: roasting corn and wood smoke, the dried rose petals that her mother mixed with warm water to wash her hair.

A tear traced down the side of her face. Her mother must be wondering about her, probably worrying herself sick. For the first time since she'd left, Sun Conch longed to run home and throw herself on the mercy of her family. If she pleaded long enough, Aunt Threadleaf would forgive her.

Except . . . except she couldn't go home. The Panther had kept his part of the bargain, and for that, she owed him her life.

Sun Conch's eyelids felt as heavy as stone. She fought the sensation, blinking and trying to concentrate on the longhouse door, visible just beyond her feet. For a time, she seemed to float, hovering above the warm hides, gliding toward the ceiling with the fire's smoke.

Then the shadows by the doorway shifted furtively, and Sun Conch saw a hesitant figure straighten and peer anxiously about. Seeing she was alone, he crept forward, shoulders hunched, as if expecting a blow at any minute. For an instant, she thought him but another of the floating illusions brought on by her fever; then he spoke: "Sun Conch?"

"High Fox? I thought you'd gone."

"I—I did. No one was watching, so I slipped out into the fog and hid in the forest. But it's night now, so I came back. I had to see you." He wore a plain tan blanket around his broad shoulders, and looked pale, his eyes sunken into twin black circles, his hair hanging loosely about his shoulders. He knelt beside Sun Conch and reached down to take her limp hand. His skin felt cool, so cool. Sun Conch let herself drown in the sensation.

"The village is full of the Mamanatowick's warriors. And everyone is at the dance. With the blanket over my head, no one would recognize me. I had to see you, to beg you to come with me. Sun Conch, I need you now, more than I ever needed you before." He sniffed and wiped his nose on his sleeve. "I'm so alone! The whole world has betrayed me!"

"You just need to go away, High Fox, like The Panther did. Find a place for yourself where no one knows you."

"Go away? But I didn't know she was my sister! It's not my fault! My father did this to me! That lying, stinking vermin did this on purpose! He ruined me!"

"No, High Fox, please. It's time for you be courageous. You—"

"You're not listening to me! You didn't hear a word that I said!"

"High Fox—"

"I *need* you, Sun Conch. Everyone else has turned their back on me. I'm afraid. Don't you see? Just being here, someone could kill me. They blame me for it!"

"High Fox, you must face—"

"Run off with me, Sun Conch? Please. I beg you!"

She closed her eyes, feeling as if her soul were draining away, being sucked into him the way a leech drew a person's blood.

"Sun Conch? If you don't help me, I . . . I don't know what I'm going to do."

She said nothing, frightened for him. What had The Panther said? That he was a coward, a whiner?

He squeezed her hand tightly. "The Panther's been watching over you like a sow with her first cub. This is the first chance I've had. I came to take you with me. Right now."

"I can't go, High Fox. I'm hurt badly. You must be brave enough to leave alone."

High Fox pressed her palm to his cheek. "But I don't want to leave. I didn't do anything wrong! My father killed Red Knot. This is his fault! I knew he was a murderer at heart. It used to sicken me the way he acted on battle walks. Do you remember the gleam he got in his eyes? He *enjoyed* killing, Sun Conch!"

"No . . . no, High Fox. Don't . . ."

He reached down suddenly and drew something from

beneath his tan blanket. It looked like a bone, split, blackened. "I pulled this from the ashes. I'm going to keep it, to remind me of what he did to me, and to himself!"

He clutched the bone, and a soft mournful sound strained against his closed lips. "I'm tainted forever, Sun Conch, and it's *his* fault. He let me commit incest! You should see it. People won't even look at me! Me! You'd think I was some horrible disease walking past. Someone will kill me, I know it."

Sun Conch struggled to make her thumb work, to press High Fox's cheek. "Look at me."

He lifted his head, and in his eyes, she saw hatred.

For a moment, her heart stood still, then a tingling sensation filtered through her body. "Your father," she said, and tried to get air into her lungs without flinching, "was a . . . a good man, High Fox. Don't . . . hate him."

A sob came to his throat and he placed her hand back on the deerhide, and clutched the bone to his heart. Rocking back and forth, he bawled like a child. "Come with me, Sun Conch! You and I, together, we'll show them. All the people who have ever hurt us! We'll pay them back! That's it. We'll make them suffer until they scream for forgiveness!"

She watched him tiredly, looking for something. Some shred of strength or, perhaps, love for her. She didn't know. She was so weary.

High Fox shifted to sit cross-legged beside her. Wiping his tears on the corner of his tan blanket, he said, "Sun Conch?"

She let out a slow painful breath. Less than a quarter-moon ago, she would have said, *You have me, High Fox. Don't worry, I'll take care of you.* But as he sat there clutching that charred bone in his fist . . .

She said, "Go away, High Fox. Please . . . just go."

"No, you listen, Sun Conch. I'm going to be a dangerous man. Everyone will fear me." He grinned at her, desperation firing his eyes. "If you think they feared The Panther, wait until they see what I do to them! All of them! I'll make them wish they'd never . . ."

The Panther stepped quietly into the longhouse, and draped the curtain back. His gray hair shining in the firelight, he stood and looked at them. "What are you doing here, boy? She needs her rest. Are you bothering her?"

Before High Fox could answer, Sun Conch said, "Yes. Yes . . . Elder. He is."

She let her head fall to the side, and closed her eyes.

"Maybe I ought to call out that you're here, High Fox." Panther's voice held an ominous note. "The Weroansqua's been wondering what happened to you."

She heard High Fox rise, and his swift steps as he ran for the door.

Then Panther knelt and tucked the hides around her, his old hands gentle. "I didn't think he'd dare to come back."

"What will happen to him?"

Panther sighed. "Girl, he's going to be a very miserable young man. No clan will offer him shelter. He'll have to go far away, leave everything and everyone he knows, to outrun his reputation."

"It wasn't his fault."

The Panther snorted. "Wasn't it? He coupled with a girl. He asked her to run off with him when she was promised to another. He isn't even disgusted with himself, is he? He should be sick with loathing for what he did, but he's not. If he lives, he'll convince himself he was right all along. After a couple of years, he'll be bragging to himself about having had Red Knot for those few months."

Had she ever been so tired? "Yes," she whispered. "I know."

"Sleep, Sun Conch. There's nothing here that requires

your attention. Besides, you need to get well so that you can go home."

"The island?"

"No," he said, and brushed her damp hair away from her face. She opened her eyes and saw him smile. "I'll take you home. *Your* home. When we get there, I think I'll have a little discussion with that irritating aunt of yours. I'm releasing you from your vow. As soon as you're healed, you're a free girl again."

"But . . . you need me."

"Yes, I do," he said. "More than you know. But I'll be safe out on my island. It will make me very happy, though, if you came to visit now and then. Maybe bring me some squash."

Sun Conch tried to smile, but her lips barely moved before she was fast asleep.

Thirty-two

The Panther waved at Sweet Stick as she passed through the palisade gate. She rode out into the afternoon sunlight and freedom on that second day of solstice celebration. She was carried on a deerhide stretcher by four husky young warriors. Upon being informed of her return to her people, and the Mamanatowick's offer of immediate transportation home, she hadn't waited an instant.

Flat Pearl Village bustled. The very earth under his feet shook with the shuffling stomp of the solstice dancers as they circled the bonfire to the beat of the pot drum and the shishing rattles of the priests. Over the singing voices, Panther could just hear Green Serpent's high wavering voice as he led the ritual songs that rose to First Man. The words thanked him for the life he'd given in the last year, and asked that tomorrow morning, he begin his journey northward across the sky again.

On a platform, the statue of Okeus had been placed to watch over the festivities, his shell eyes gleaming in the slanting sunlight. He looked even more malevolent than usual, as though seeing into Panther's soul, and sneering at the grim truth hidden there.

Panther shook his head, his gloom heightened by the sight of Nine Killer working his way through the knots of visiting warriors. Those who were not dancing with Flat Pearl Villagers sat about their fires. The War Chief stopped at each, assuring himself that their needs were met, sharing a joke here and there, and moving on.

The men smiled up at him, often reaching up to clasp his hand, or to offer a taste of their food. Was it Panther's imagination, or did the Guardians smile in the bright sunlight? The smell of cooking fires and roasting tuckahoe, hominy, steaming walnut milk carried over the sweeter smell of tobacco shared in friendship.

Finally, the War Chief stepped over to Panther's side. He looked out over the assemblage of warriors and dancers, his hands propped on his hips. He wore his feather cloak over his shoulder, his war club tied onto his breechclout, his quiver over his back, and the famous bow hung unstrung over his shoulder. Not only had he greased his skin and stained it red with puccoon, but he'd used a dusting of antimony to add sparkle.

The War Chief noted Panther's lingering gaze, as he watched the old woman disappear through the gate. "Did High Fox quibble about letting the old woman go?"

"I never bothered to ask. I just freed her. Besides, that little weasel owes me. He lied to me."

"One thing is sure, I'd hate to be the man who crossed

you.'' Nine Killer glanced over at the big bonfire. Every once in a while, through the gyrating dancers and leaping flames, Black Spike's blackened skull appeared down among the coals. Within days, it, too, would be consumed to ash.

Panther leaned against one of the Guardians, feeling the chill closing around him with the cool air. ''I wanted to thank you. I couldn't have asked for a better friend out there. It's something of a new feeling for me.''

Nine Killer unhooked his war club and rested the head between his feet, his alert eyes on the feasting warriors. After all, this was still a hostile force, and a great many injuries were being smoothed over for this one special day's peace. ''You never had a friend? In all of your wanderings?''

''War Chief, people are the same everywhere. I was always an outsider, one who never spoke about his past. No matter where you go, tribes are made from clans, and clans from lineages, and lineages from families. No one has room for a clanless man.'' How long would it take for High Fox to discover that?

''You're no longer clanless, Elder. You're Sky Fire.''

When Panther started to shake his head, Nine Killer added, ''And, if you're not Sky Fire at that particular moment, you're Greenstone. By Ohona, I'll swear to it on my life.''

Panther smiled and clapped the War Chief on his shoulder. ''You're a good man, Nine Killer. I'm happy to share a clan with you.''

''I stopped by the longhouse just a while ago. Rosebud is back. She's keeping an eye on Sun Conch in case High Fox tries to return.''

''I saw her, too.'' Panther felt his good mood drain away. ''Sun Conch is mending, I believe. I'll have to drain the pus again tomorrow, but the fever's breaking.''

He had talked with Rosebud about the Women's

House, and learned the other dark facts. He considered telling the War Chief, then realized that Nine Killer was enjoying himself walking among his old enemies, being pointed out and admired for his courage.

No, keep this to yourself. He smiled. "Did you hear the latest? Copper Thunder and Water Snake were drinking black drink from the same cup. Hunting Hawk was gloating over both of them, acting as if she had authority over the whole world."

"He's still angry with you."

Panther shrugged. "A man doesn't forget an injury. I killed his father, enslaved him and his mother. He has a great deal to hate me for."

"I suppose he does." Nine Killer paused. "But he and Water Snake and I had a little talk earlier. For now, Copper Thunder is willing to let bygones be bygones—especially since you are Sky Fire Clan."

"I'm not Sky Fire, War Chief. I turned my back on them long ago. When I leave here, and return to my island, I shall be clanless again."

"You are Sky Fire! Leave it at that for now, Elder." Nine Killer shook his head. "Honestly, you can be as stubborn as a spring bear on a patch of grass. If Copper Thunder kills you, Water Snake will be obligated to retaliate. After all, you're the clan elder, even if you're way out in the bay on your little island. If you leave him alone, he'll leave you alone. That's a fair trade."

Panther smiled. "I see. I sense your hand in this. Very well, I suppose it is a fair trade."

Nine Killer studied him from the corner of his eye. "And, also in fair trade, I can't seem to remember a single thing you said to the Mamanatowick this morning."

"About Warm Fall?"

"Who?" Nine Killer asked mildly. "Never heard of her."

"Thank you, Nine Killer."

"Yes, well"—he glanced around—"I'm going to keep visiting, just to insure that no one forgets that we're all being friendly while we celebrate solstice together." He paused. "It won't last. Maybe not even for the promised two Comings of the Leaves."

"That can be a long enough time." Panther nodded to himself. "And . . . one never knows."

"Indeed, one never knows." Nine Killer walked on, nodding to warriors here and there.

Panther rearranged his old blanket, patted the Guardian affectionately, and ducked into the House of the Dead. The grimness—ameliorated briefly by Nine Killer's presence—resettled around his heart.

As he passed down the narrow hallway, he touched each of the Guardians. In the god's sanctuary, he found her. She was sitting, looking up at the newest of the mat-covered bundles that rested on the platform over Okeus' empty seat.

Despite the removal of the god, Panther could feel him there in the shadows, watching. Those shell eyes gleamed in the imagination. The war club, with strands of Red Knot's hair still stuck in the stone settings, was gripped menacingly in his right hand. Hollow laughter echoed just beyond human hearing.

"Here you are, in Okeus' place. The two of you are a great deal alike," Panther said quietly. "Each of you is dark and chaotic. A matched pair if I ever saw one."

She never turned, but watched the bundled corpse as if seeing through the wrapping to the girl who had once embodied those carefully cleaned bones.

Panther stepped forward and eased himself down beside her. "Why didn't you stop him? You needed but to speak."

Shell Comb barely shrugged. "I couldn't."

"I'm not very bright about such things, but a man who loved you that much deserved better."

Again, Shell Comb barely shrugged. "He was braver than I was. He was always braver. I was the coward. I was the one who always panicked and did crazy things."

"What happened between you and Monster Bone?"

"An injury."

"Did Black Spike sire all of your children?"

Her mouth worked. "My oldest boy, I think he was Monster Bone's. And Grebe, I'm sure he was. Then Monster Bone was hit during a battle. His penis wouldn't stiffen. It drove him half mad to lie with me at night and nothing would happen. The first time Black Spike planted a child inside me, I tricked Monster Bone into believing he'd actually done it. The child was stillborn. That's when we started fighting all the time. I think . . . well, I drove him to it. I mocked him when I shouldn't have."

"And then you realized you were pregnant with High Fox?"

She gave him the briefest of nods. "So Black Spike took me north. His wife suspected. Insisted on going with us. I used a leather sack to smother her. Not a mark on her. Black Spike thought she'd just died. I don't think he suspected my hand in it. I gave birth to High Fox, but I couldn't give him up and leave him with those horrible people. I couldn't stand the thought that he'd be raised Susquehannock. That someday he might come paddling down the bay at the head of a group of warriors and make war on me, his own mother."

"So you hid your arrival and burned Monster Bone to death in your longhouse?"

She nodded. "He was better off dead. It was the easy way, don't you see? Had I divorced him, people would have learned that his manhood was broken." Her eyes flashed then. "I *did* him a favor!"

Panther sighed wearily. "All that time, Black Spike

covered it up. Or, did he help you set his brother on fire?''

"No. I did that. He couldn't . . . wouldn't.'' She shrugged again. "I was just waiting, you see. As soon as Mother died, I would be Weroansqua and I would marry him. But Mother just lived, and lived, and lived . . .'' Shell Comb knotted a fist. "Sometimes I think she will never die!''

"Even then, you'd never have married him.''

"What do you know?''

"Enough.'' Panther pulled at his chin, sensing that Okeus was grinning evilly at him. "You were never a one-man woman. Black Spike knew that, but as long as you came to him every so often, he could overlook your many faults. Love blinds a man.''

"Love can blind a woman, too.''

Panther looked up at Red Knot's body. "Indeed it can.'' He considered his next words. "When Hunting Hawk dies, you will step aside and name Nine Killer Weroance.''

She started, then stared at him incredulously. "You're crazy, if you think I'm going—''

"You will,'' Panther insisted. "If you don't, I'll ruin you, Shell Comb. I can do it, and you know that I will. I know everything, right down to the reason you were coughing when you stepped out of the House of the Dead that morning. Your throat hurt from running, didn't it?''

She stared at him with that same glassy look of disbelief.

"Shell Comb, I don't mind if Black Spike offered his life in place of yours—I honor him for it—but I will never forgive you for hurting Sun Conch.''

"Sun Conch!''

"You weren't in the Women's House the night before last, were you? Rosebud saw you slip out early, just after sunset. You thought she was asleep. In less than fifteen paces you reached Flat Willow's weapons just inside the door of his cousin's house. You knew he was considered a possible killer, and you just assumed he'd catch all of the blame for my death.''

''You're insane!''

''Maybe, but you'll never be Weroansqua.''

''It will be your word against mine.''

''You will promise me, Shell Comb. Right here. If you assume the mantle, I will hound you to ruin.''

She frowned, as if baffled by his words. ''I *paid* for my mistakes.''

''No, Red Knot and Black Spike paid. High Fox will continue to pay with what little life remains for him. You got away with it, again.'' He shook his head. ''You disgust me.''

She seemed to come back to herself. ''I don't know what you're talking about. Mother will die soon. She can't hold out much longer. When she's up there''—she pointed to the bodies—''I'll be Weroansqua. And then, I'll do as I please. Maybe even have you burned, witch!''

Panther shook his head. ''Look at me. In the eyes. You will name Nine Killer as Weroance. Yellow Net will fight it, but you have the right. You will use that right to name Nine Killer.''

She met his determined gaze. The crazed look lingered there, on the rim of her soul, held back by the barest of restraint. Even as he watched, her soul began to cave in. The reality of what she'd done ate through, and her resolve wilted into nothingness. Her shoulders slumped and she began to cry.

He'd won. But what sort of victory?

Through sobs, she asked, ''What are you going to do?''

''Nothing. Unless I have to.'' Panther stood up, his soul numb and empty. ''What will you do? Your lover is dead. So is your daughter. You don't know it, but your future is just as much a corpse as Red Knot up there.''

"Black Spike did that! He said so!''

"He did, didn't he? I came here to punish you for hurting Sun Conch.'' He stepped back to the passageway. "But I think your punishment is just beginning. The moment you crushed your daughter's skull with that war club, you killed yourself.''

"Even I draw the line at incest! I paid for Monster Bone, for Black Spike's wife! I *paid* for my mistakes!'' She looked down at her right hand, opening and closing the fingers, as if gripping a war club.

"No, as I said, Red Knot, High Fox, and Black Spike paid. You knew that Hunting Hawk couldn't allow them to run off. She'd drag them back, and it would all come out. The murders, the incest between High Fox and Red Knot. You'd be destroyed —and Greenstone Clan with you.''

"I protected the clan!'' Her voice had turned brittle.

"Green Serpent said he saw Red Knot's ghost that morning, but in the dim light he mistook you for her when you were replacing the war club.''

"I set aside my feelings! I did it! I hardened my heart like Mother always said.'' She was shaking now. "For good of the clan, I *am* worthy!''

"Okeus help you now, Shell Comb, you're the one who has to live with it. At night, when the dreams come, and you see your lover and your daughter staring at you, how will you explain it to them? When you hear of High Fox, living in the forest like a hunted animal, what will your soul feel? Each passing moment, you will know that your boy is a loathsome pariah, despised and wretched because of you. And, when he finally kills himself, or is killed by some uneasy warrior, his ghost, too, will come and stare from the shadows of your soul.''

She whispered, "Black Spike? Where is Black Spike? Please? I need to see him.''

"He can't come, Shell Comb. Not ever again."

"Black Spike . . ." she mewed, then collapsed onto the matting, rolling herself into a fetal ball. Sobs racked her, and tears slipped down her soft cheeks in silver threads.

Panther turned, walking slowly up the passageway toward the exit, and the clarity of the cold afternoon light.

Bibliography

Abler, Thomas S., and Elizabeth Tooker
1990 "Seneca." In *Handbook of North American Indians*, Bruce G. Trigger, ed. Washington, D.C.: Smithsonian Institution.

Amos, William H., and Stephen H. Amos
1985 *Atlantic and Gulf Coasts*. Audubon Society Nature Guides. New York: Alfred A. Knopf.

Boyce, Douglas W.
1990 "Iroquoian Tribes of the Virginia-North Carolina Coastal Plain." In *Handbook of North American Indians*, Bruce G. Trigger, ed. Washington, D.C.: Smithsonian Institution.

Coffey, Timothy
1993 *The History and Folklore of North American Wildflowers*. New York: Facts on File.

Custer, Jay F.
1984 *Delaware Prehistoric Archaeology*. Newark, New Jersey: University of Delaware Press.

Custer, J. L.
1989 *Prehistoric Cultures of the Delmarva Peninsula: An Archaeological Study*. Newark, New Jersey: University of Delaware Press.

Dent, Richard J.
1995 *Chesapeake Prehistory: Old Traditions, New Directions*. New York: Plenum Press.

Dogget, Rachel, ed.
1992 *New World of Wonders: European Images of the*

Americas. Seattle: University of Washington Press.

Feest, Christian F.

1990a "Nanticoke and Neighboring Tribes." In *Handbook of North American Indians*, Bruce G. Trigger, ed. Washington, D.C.: Smithsonian Institution.

1990b "North Carolina Algonquians." In *Handbook of North American Indians*, Bruce G. Trigger, ed. Washington, D.C.: Smithsonian Institution.

1990c "Virginia Algonquians." In *Handbook of North American Indians*, Bruce G. Trigger, ed. Washington, D.C.: Smithsonian Institution.

Ferguson, Alice L., and T. Dale Stewart

1984 *An Ossuary Near Piscataway Creek with a Report on the Skeletal Remains*. La Plata, Maryland: Alice Ferguson Foundation; Dick Wiles Printing Co.

Foster, Steven, and James A. Duke

1990 *A Field Guide to Medicinal Plants: Eastern and Central North America*. The Peterson Field Guide Series. Boston: Houghton Mifflin Company.

Goddard, Ives

1978 "Delaware." In *Handbook of North American Indians*. Bruce G. Trigger, ed. Washington, D.C.: Smithsonian Institution.

Harriot, Thomas

1590 *A Briefe and True Report of the New Found Land of Virginia*. Reprint. New York: Dover Publications, 1972.

Hudson, Charles M., ed.

1979 *Black Drink: A Native American Tea*. Athens, Georgia: University of Georgia Press.

Hurley, Linda M.

1990 *Field Guide to the Submerged Aquatic Vegetation of Chesapeake Bay*. Annapolis, Maryland: U.S. Fish and Wildlife Service, Chesapeake Bay Estuary Program.

Israel, Stephen

1985 "Archaeological Investigation of the Bradley Site, 18CV219, Mears Creek, Calvert County, Maryland." *Maryland Archaeology* 21:1, pp. 10–34.

Kent, Barry C.

1989 *Susquehanna's Indians.* Anthropological Series No. 6. Harrisburg: Commonwealth of Pennsylvania, The Pennsylvania Historical and Museum Commission.

Kent, Bretton W.

1994 *Fossil Sharks of the Chesapeake Bay Region.* Columbia, Maryland: Egan Rees & Boyer, Inc.

Kraft, Hebert C.

1986 *The Lenape: Archaeology, History, and Ethnography.* Newark, New Jersey: New Jersey Historical Society.

Kurath, Gertrude P.

1964 *Iroquois Music and Dance: Ceremonial Arts of Two Seneca Longhouses.* Bureau of American Ethnology Bulletin 187. Washington, D.C.: Smithsonian Institution.

Lippson, Alice Jane

1973 *The Chesapeake Bay in Maryland: An Atlas of Natural Resources.* Baltimore, Maryland: Johns Hopkins University Press.

Lippson, Alice Jane, and Robert L. Lippson

1984 *Life in the Chesapeake Bay.* Baltimore, Maryland: Johns Hopkins University Press.

Morgan, Lewis Henry

1851 *League of the Iroquois.* Reprint. New York: Citadel Press, Carol Communications, 1962.

Papenfuse, Edward C., and M. Mercer Neale

1993 *Close Encounters of the First Kind, 1585–1767.* Maryland State Archives: Documents for the Classroom. Publication no. 4198; Maryland State Archives; Baltimore.

Porter, III, Charles W.

1972 *Adventurers to a New World: The Roanoake Colony.* Office of Publications, National Park Service; United States Department of the Interior; Washington, D.C.

Potter, Stephen R.

1993 *Commoners, Tribute, and Chiefs: The Development of Algonquian Culture in the Potomac Valley.* Charlottesville, Virginia: University Press of Virginia.

Rights, Douglas L.

1947 *The American Indian in North Carolina.* Durham, North Carolina: Duke University Press.

Rhode, Fred C., and Rudolf G. Arndt, David G. Lindquist, & James F. Parnell

1994 *Freshwater Fishes of the Carolinas, Virginia, Maryland, & Delaware.* Chapel Hill, North Carolina: University of North Carolina Press.

Roundtree, Helen C.

1989 *The Powhatan Indians of Virginia.* Norman, Oklahoma: University of Oklahoma Press.

1990 *Pocahontas's People: The Powhatan Indians of Virginia Through Four Centuries.* Norman, Oklahoma: University of Oklahoma Press.

1993 *Powhatan Foreign Relations: 1500–1722.* Helen C. Roundtree, ed. Norman, Oklahoma: University of Oklahoma Press.

Schmidt, Martin F.

1993 *Maryland's Geology.* Centreville, Maryland: Tidewater Publishers.

Silberhorn, Gene M.

1982 *Common Plants of the Mid-Atlantic Coast.* Baltimore, Maryland: Johns Hopkins University Press.

Stephenson, Robert L.

1984 *The Prehistoric People of Accokeek Creek.* Accokeek, Maryland: Alice Ferguson Foundation. Dick Wildes Printing Co.

Sutton, Ann, and Myron Sutton

1985 *Easten Forests*. Audubon Society Nature Guides. New York: Alfred A. Knopf.

Tantaquidgeon, Gladys

1972 *Folk Medicine of the Delaware and Related Algonkian Indians*. Harrisburg: Commonwealth of Pennsylvania, The Pennsylvania Historical and Museum Commission.

Williams, Jr., John Page

1993 *Chesapeake Almanac: Following the Bay through the Seasons*. Centreville, Maryland: Tidewater Publishers.